SECRET

KINDLE ALEXANDER

Secret

Trademark Acknowledgements

The author acknowledges the trademarked status and trademark owners of the following trademarks mentioned in this work of fiction:

ABC: American Broadcasting Companies, Inc.
Advil: Wyeth, LLC
Amazon: Amazon Technologies, Inc.
Ambien: Sanofi Societe Anonyme
Armani: Giorgio Armani, SPA
Associated Press: The Associated Press Corporation
Beverly Hillbillies: CBS Broadcasting, Inc.
Bluetooth: Bluetooth Sig, Inc.
Cheshire Cat: Disney Enterprises, Inc.
Clippers: LA Clippers LLC
CNN: Cable News Network, Inc.
Discovery Channel: Discovery Communications, LLC
Dolce and Gabbana: GADO S.r.l.
Duke University: Duke University
Ferrari: Ferrari S.p.A.
Fruit of the Loom: Fruit of the Loom, Inc.
Gatorade: Stokely-Van Camp, Inc.
GQ: Advanced Magazine Publishers, Inc.
Harvard: President and Fellows of Harvard College Charitable Corporation
Heineken: Heineken Brouwerijen B.V.
Hilton: HLT Domestic IP LLC
iPad: Apple, Inc.
Jägermeister: Mast-Jaegermeister SE societas europae
Men in Black: Columbia Pictures Industries, Inc.
NBA: NBA Properties, Inc.
Neiman-Marcus: NM Nevada Trust
One Direction: 1D Media Limited
Science Digest: Science Digest, Inc.
Sperry: SR Holdings, LLC
Southern Methodist University: Southern Methodist University
Texas Instruments: Texas Instruments Incorporated
Uber: Uber Technologies, Inc.
U-Haul: U-Haul International, Inc.
University of Oklahoma: Board of Regents of the University of

Oklahoma
Wolfgang Puck: Wolfgang Puck Licensing LLC
Yahoo!: Yahoo! Inc.

DEDICATION

This is for Bo.
Your friendship and encouragement mean everything.

Perry, you are missed every day.

Kindle, you are forever in our hearts.

CHAPTER.01

A sudden flash of blinding light struck seconds before thunder rumbled so strongly the windows rattled in the seventh floor meeting room of Secret Networks' North Dallas office complex. Dylan Reeves watched as all the attendees' eyes shot up to the overhead fixtures that flickered wildly. The latest round of thunderstorms raged loudly outside, rocking and shaking the building. And from the ferocious sounds coming from outdoors, it seemed spring planned an early arrival this year.

He held his breath for a full second, waiting to see if the electricity would hold this time or if that strike had been the one to finally cut the lights and leave them sitting in the dark. When the power held, Dylan exhaled a sigh of relief. This meeting was critical to the future of his company, and he needed everyone in complete agreement before leaving for the night.

Every piece of information had been examined numerous times, even before this impromptu meeting had been called, but this decision was just too important to leave to chance.

The current silence surrounding the table signified his senior staff's acceptance of the magnitude of the proposals laid out before them. It wasn't every day millions of dollars were thrown on the table for the company Dylan and his team had spent years developing.

"So we're narrowing the offers down to Wilder and Yahoo!?" Rob Jacobs, one of Dylan's two senior executives asked, breaking the silence.

"Those are the best offers so far. I think our game plan should be to check those companies out first. If they aren't serious, we can look at Amazon, they're next in coming close to our asking price," David Masterson, his other senior executive stated.

Dylan responded more slowly. He sat back in his comfortable leather chair, took a long drink from his water bottle and propped his tennis-shoe-covered feet up on the small office table. The file folder he read from rested in his lap as he continued to thumb through the pages, looking for anything he might have missed. After another lengthy moment of silence, he finally agreed, "Yeah, confirm Wilder for this weekend. Let's put Yahoo! off until we see what Wilder has to say. They're the strongest of them all, and they have the technical support policies already in place. If handled right, it should be an easy transition for everyone involved."

Rob jotted down notes as Dylan spoke, but David was the first to respond. "They're big enough to absorb our company, plus I like Southern California. I think I'd do well there."

"Shut-up, dickhead. You'll jinx the whole deal," Rob said, still making notes.

"I'm just sayin' I'd rather live there than Northern California. Out of all of us, I was the one young enough to watch *The Hills* growing up," David added, as if that explained anything. He pushed the folder out of the way and reached toward the center of the table to one of two half-eaten boxes of pizza. "Not to mention, when we move to California, we won't have to deal with this crazy Texas weather." He grabbed a slice of the cold pizza and took a big bite, reclining back in his chair.

Dylan lifted a hand to head off Rob's comeback. He looked down at his watch. It was almost seven in the evening. They'd been in this meeting for hours and needed to wrap it up. He dropped his file folder back on the table and stood, looking around for his cell phone to pull up his schedule for the next day to confirm his memory. "I think we have fittings tomorrow morning at Neiman Marcus. Don't be late."

"I'm taking this pizza with me," David said, gathering all the remaining slices into one box. David was the youngest of the three. A true millennial to the core. Since Rob was older, he'd dramatically rolled his eyes at David's boldness, muttering something about the youth of today. Dylan had heard those same words muttered from Rob to David about a million times since they had started working together.

His assistant, Kim, opened his office door and stuck her head inside the room. She should have been gone hours ago, but she always waited around to make sure he no longer needed her. Actually, most of his staff had the same dedicated attitude. They took care of both him and the company they worked for. In return, Dylan did everything in his power to give back to them. "There's a call for you, Dylan. It's pretty urgent. They couldn't get you on your cell, so they called your backline number."

He started looking in earnest now, patting the outside of his jeans, feeling for the phone. His eyes scanned the table again. He lifted some of the paperwork, but it wasn't there. "Who is it?"

She looked sheepish when she replied, "The Highland Park Police Department. I'll send them to your landline now."

She retreated as soon as the words were out of her mouth. His heart did a little seize in his chest, and he single-mindedly stalked toward the phone on his desk. It rang, and he reached out, quickly grabbing the receiver and lifting it to his ear. "Dylan Reeves."

"This is Officer Bradley with the Highland Park Police Department. Are you the father of Chloe Reeves?" he asked in a deeply Southern voice.

He wasn't certain he hadn't lost years off his life as he answered that question. "Yes, sir, what's this about? Is she hurt?"

"She's fine, sir, but she's been taken into custody. We need you to come down to the police station."

"What's happened?" he asked.

"We'll explain once you arrive."

"Is she okay?" Dylan asked, somewhere in the back of his mind he registered David and Rob were now close by, but he ignored them both.

"Sir, as I stated before, she's fine. Probably a little upset. We'll explain once you arrive." The call abruptly ended, giving him no clue as to what had happened to his daughter. He placed the receiver back on the cradle and shoved his hands inside his jeans pocket, searching for his keys. As he dug them out of his pocket, he spotted his cell phone on his desk and grabbed that too.

"What happened?" David asked.

"No idea. All they would say is that they had Chloe. I've gotta go pick her up."

"I can ride with you," Rob offered.

"Thanks, but no, I'll pick up Teri. Can you close everything down for me?" Dylan was already across his office. Kim stood at his door, holding his jacket out for him. He took it with a quickly mumbled thank you as he headed toward the bank of elevators. He pushed the call button while working his phone. He'd missed six calls from the same local number, which he assumed to be the police station.

The panic inside him started to recede, slowly turning more to anger. What had his daughter gotten herself into? The elevator doors opened as he punched in Teri's number, but he would wait to push send until he made it out of the underground parking garage.

He jogged the distance to his car and drove a little too quickly toward the exit. At the gate, he finally hit send on his phone as the overhead security device registered his car's parking tag and automatically opened. His Bluetooth connected and the phone began to ring as he pulled out onto the Central Expressway service road. Luck was on his side, the thunderstorm had finally subsided. He absolutely didn't have the patience for cautious drivers right now.

"Hey, you, I'm almost packed. You sure you don't want Nanny Laura to come sooner..." Teri's voice filled the silence of his car and Dylan cut her off in mid-sentence.

"Chloe's been arrested." His tone was hard and unyielding.

"What?" Teri asked, confusion clear in her voice.

"Teri, Chloe's been arrested. They say she's unharmed, but dammit, I knew she was too young to be left at that school. She's lost her head." He'd never wanted his oldest daughter to go off so far away from home. The University of Oklahoma was too far to keep a good eye on her. Visions of skipping class and partying all day and night filled his mind, because that was exactly what he'd done his freshman year of college. Hell, those freshman-year all-night parties were the precise reason for Chloe making her appearance in this world.

Thoughts of his daughter and unprotected sex had a serious scowl forming on his face, taking his already bad mood to a boiling point.

"Dylan, stop and just tell me what happened," Teri said, her tone changing to that firm lawyer voice she used when he got this way.

"I don't know, Teri. All they said was that she's safe, and we need to get there. When I asked questions, they ended the call. Get ready. I'll be by to pick you up in less than ten minutes. I'm making the loop around Northwest Highway now," he answered, carefully navigating the still wet roads.

"I need to get Cate and Chad home. Should they ride with us to Norman?"

"Yeah, that's the other thing. She's at the Highland Park police station," Dylan said, increasing the speed of his sports car until he took the Mockingbird exit.

"Why's she in town?" Teri had just asked one of about the hundred questions he had running through his head on a continuous loop.

"I don't know. I was hoping you might." Norman, Oklahoma, to Dallas, Texas, was a three-hour drive. Chloe hadn't come home last weekend because she had mid-terms this week. There was no reason for her to be home today. He held his tongue on the rant raging through his mind. He wanted to declare he'd been absolutely right when he'd disagreed with Chloe's decision to attend OU last fall. She clearly wasn't ready to make adult decisions.

"She didn't say anything to me," Teri said the words he'd been thinking. "You were right. I should've listened."

That was all the encouragement he needed to state his case. "Damn straight, I was right. Now we're picking her up from a police station. Will this be on her permanent record?"

"There's no way to know at this point, but she has testing this week." The panic was back in Teri's voice. "I bet she's scared to death."

"She needs to be scared to death. Being held at the police station can't be good," Dylan replied. "No, she needs to be scared to death of *me*. We didn't give her that car for her to be traveling back and forth between Oklahoma and here at any given moment. I bet a boy's involved."

"Calm down, Dylan. You're gonna make this worse. Where are you?"

"I'm turning on our street."

"I'm heading outside now." He ended the call when he saw Teri jogging down the front steps toward the street. He came to an abrupt stop long enough to let her get inside before he was off again. Neither spoke as the seriousness of the moment settled in, alleviating some of the anger Dylan held on to. Thank god they lived close by. When they arrived at the police station, the parking lot was crowded with cars, something he wasn't entirely certain was the norm for seven thirty on a Monday evening in this affluent community.

"They're busy tonight," Teri stated, worry in her voice as she watched the hustle and bustle through the passenger side window. "Look, it's Holly and Jack. So Allison's involved."

Dylan eyed the couple closely before cutting his gaze across the parking lot to find the closest vacant spot. Holly and Jack were Allison's parents.

"What happened?" Teri called out to the other couple, getting out of the car before he even had the gear in place.

"No idea. We were just told Allison was arrested. We didn't know Chloe was involved." Dylan could hear the frantic edge in Holly's voice. Teri and Holly fell in step together and walked briskly toward the police station's front doors.

"What was Allison doing tonight?" Dylan asked Jack as they walked toward the front doors at a slower pace.

"As far as we knew, she went to bed early to be rested for her mid-terms tomorrow."

"I should've been suspicious," Holly called out over her shoulder. Dylan shoved his hands in his jeans pocket and kept his mouth shut. He'd never been a big fan of Allison's. She was a wild-child to the extreme and Holly and Jack fostered those beliefs in their daughter.

More and more headlights turned into the police station parking lot as they made their way to the building entrance. "Did they arrest the whole town?" Jack asked.

7

"Looks like it," Dylan said, watching the cars line up along the street, waiting to turn into the parking lot. He opened the front door to the police station and allowed the women to step in first. An officer met them just inside the doors.

As a family, tonight was a first. Back in the day, Dylan had chalked up a few arrests for himself but had never been on this end of a jail-house pickup. He hadn't always lived in the best part of town, but even with that consideration in mind, he doubted a uniformed door greeter had become a standard practice at police stations.

"Your children are safe. The judge has come in and is currently speaking with them," a middle-aged officer said over and over again as the front foyer filled with parents.

"What happened?" Teri asked over the hum of chatter, leaning her back against Dylan when they found an unoccupied corner of the lobby. He could feel her tremble and let some of his frustration go as he wrapped an arm around her waist, drawing her farther against him. The one thing he could say after all their years together, she'd been a fantastic mother and an amazing best friend to him.

More people gathered inside the lobby and the officer repeated his clearly pre-rehearsed speech several more times, but never answered Teri's or any other parent's questions. After the incoming flow of people lessened and several minutes passed without any new arrivals, the officer finally offered new information.

"I've been saving this to only say once. I'm Officer McDaniel. Your children were picked up tonight for disorderly conduct. The best we can tell, social media posted messages for the class of 2014 to meet this evening and protest the tearing down of the old Walter Whitley football stadium in the morning. They were protesting on private property and refused to leave." He did that officer thing where he rested his hand on the stock of his weapon and didn't open the floor to questions or discussion.

"As far as we know right now, the school's not going to press charges on the condition Judge Fredrick's speaks with them now and assigns each one of them ten hours of community service. He's giving them a good, stern talking to. If you all can stay put, we'll call your name and release your child to your custody." As the officer spoke, Teri slowly got her spine back up. She stood on her own and cut an accusing glance back to Dylan when the officer mentioned the words social media. He gave an internal sigh as she refocused on the officer in front of them.

He wasn't responsible for all social media. Clearly the kids hadn't utilized his Secret app. If they had, the messages would have been untraceable within minutes of the file opening. No one would have been able to track the messages no matter how hard they tried.

"Sir, I have a question." Teri clearly hadn't picked up the no-questions vibe the guy was putting off. She raised her hand high in the air to draw everyone's attention.

"Yes, ma'am," the officer drawled, his Texas accent thick on the ma'am. *Well crap*, that ma'am and tone he used would grate on Teri's nerves because as far as his wife was concerned, the officer might as well have called her 'little lady.'

"What exactly did the children do that was illegal?" Dylan lowered his head. *Here we go*. Of course, she would go there right now. Just make this whole thing worse by fighting it out right there in the lobby in front of fifty or so other parents. He wanted to get his daughter out of there.

"This is not the time," he pleaded quietly in Teri's ear. She shooed him away with a backward motion of her hand.

"They were on private property and didn't leave when instructed." The officer's dismissive tone and body language made it clear her question didn't warrant a look in her direction.

"Excuse me, Officer McDaniel, but I believe there's some question whether the stadium grounds constitute private property if it's owned by the city-wide public school district," Teri continued, her tone hardening.

"Not now. Do this tomorrow. Let's just go home," Dylan tried again, whispering in Teri's ear.

"Sir, do you have something for all of us to hear?" the irritable officer asked, dodging Teri's question completely, but looking directly at Dylan as if he were the mastermind behind her words. Teri would take that to mean a woman wasn't smart enough to come up with a challenge on her own. When she looked over at him, the arch of her brow told him he'd hit her thoughts dead on. She was ready to blast this guy.

He quickly jumped in.

"No, sir, I've got nothing to say. We've got nothing to say. We just want to collect our daughter and go home." The officer had grown visibly angry. Surely his pit bull, do-good attorney wife would have all this brought to a head in no time, but that needed to wait until morning. He worried that antagonizing the already pissed off officers would end in them keeping the kids overnight. His wife needed to stop.

Just as he'd done over and over through the years, Dylan hooked an arm around Teri's waist and dragged her through the small crowd in the lobby, guiding her out the front doors. He would gladly clamp a hand over her mouth if needed.

"Dylan, they didn't have the right to arrest those children." Teri pushed out of his arms and faced off with him once outside.

"Didn't you hear him? They didn't make an arrest." Dylan tried to make her see reason.

"They can't give a punishment if there's no violation. The kids should have never been taken off that property. Those children's civil rights were violated tonight." Teri was on a roll and in his face, so Dylan lifted up two fingers to close her lips to stop the flow of words he saw coming.

"Which are all things you can deal with tomorrow. Tonight let's get our girl and go home. Focus, Teri. No matter what, Chloe shouldn't have driven all the way back here during mid-term week. Agreed?" Dylan asked, and she glared at him before finally giving him an impatient nod. Dylan slowly lifted his fingers from Teri's lips.

"How about this? Why don't we blame this whole thing on social media and you play a huge part in that blame…" Teri started, but Dylan placed his fingers back over her lips again.

"No. Not tonight. Again something we can discuss after we get our daughter." He didn't care about civil liberties or the impact of social media at the moment. This was about Chloe and getting her away from the police station and home where she belonged, safe and sound. They could deal with the rest later.

Teri actually stomped her foot. She could have easily gotten out from under the slight pressure of his fingers as he held her lips together, but if nothing else, over the last nineteen years of their marriage, they'd become friends as well as each other's sounding board. They respected one another.

When he heard their name called, he lifted a brow, but kept his fingers over her mouth. "I'm walking inside to get our daughter and then coming back outside where you'll be right here. Correct?"

"Go, before I change my mind," Teri said, stepping back as she crossed her arms over her chest. A *last call* came with their name again being yelled out into the masses. Dylan entered the lobby, and there stood Chloe, right beside the officer from before. He saw the apprehension in the officer's scowl, but he ignored that and scanned his daughter to make sure she was in one piece. Besides the worry on her face, she looked okay, perhaps a little tousled, but in good shape.

"I'm Dylan Reeves," he said to the officer, keeping his eyes on Chloe.

"Sir, you need to sign this paperwork saying you aren't contesting any part of this." Dylan quickly scribbled his name on the bottom of the form before Teri heard the rumor of this part of the deal and went nuts. There were so many issues with this night, the first being, technically, their daughter wasn't a minor anymore. They held no responsibility.

"Thank you," Dylan said and took hold of his daughter's arm, pulling her along with him out to meet her mother. Out of all his children, Chloe was most like Teri. He could see the indignation forming on her face as the fear of being picked up by the police started to subside.

"It's so stupid that the cops found out about this. I'm gonna strangle the person who posted this on Facebook," Chloe said the second they got outside and she walked into her mother's arms. Dylan didn't have time to register those words as Allison broke free of her parents. The girls ran to each other, hugging out their frustrations. By the time he and Teri walked the distance to the girls, there were tears and rambling bits of an angry conversation shooting out between them.

"It's just not fair. That stadium has been here since my granddaddy was a boy," Allison exclaimed. For Dylan, that was a solid reason to destroy the old crumbling building. It had safety hazard written all over it.

"I know, and it was the stupid seniors from this year that put that post up on Facebook. We had it perfectly quiet on your dad's network. No one would have known, and we would have been chained in before the wrecking crew got there in the morning!" That sent a whole new round of tears between the girls with Teri turning to glare at him. *Great.*

"Come on, you two. Let's get you home. We can talk in the morning." Holly wrapped an arm around Allison, guiding her toward their car.

"I have to get my car or they'll impound it," Chloe said after a big sniffle.

"Allison, where's your car?" Jack asked.

"I rode with Chloe," Allison answered.

Again, another great moment in this night from hell. Turned out, his daughter had been the instigator between the two of them.

"We'll stop by and get your car, honey, and your dad can drive it home," Teri said, wrapping an arm around Chloe.

"I'm sorry you had to come to the police station. I knew you were packing for your trip, that's why I asked them to call dad," she explained, hugging her mom tight. Dylan and Jack traveled a step or two behind them toward their parked cars.

"Call me about tee times this weekend." Jack pointed toward Dylan as they walked toward their respective parking spaces. Dylan was smart enough to keep his mouth shut as Holly slapped at Jack's arm.

"It's not time to talk golf, Jack. This is serious." Dylan smiled at their exchange and looked up to find Teri and Chloe already waiting by the car. She still looked mighty angry, with it all directed toward him.

He used the key fob to unlock the doors and held a finger up at Teri as they stared at one another over the roof of the car. Chloe's eyebrows rose, and she quietly got inside the backseat and shut the door. "You and I will talk about this later. This is about her right now." Teri kept that angry, focused gaze directed toward him. Her eyes spoke volumes and her stance never changed, but she didn't say anything when they got inside the car.

Dylan started the engine and began to back out. "Where's your car, babe?"

"We left it at McDonald's and walked to the stadium to try and keep it more secret," Chloe said, the tears had slowed as she stared out the backseat window. He braked the car in the middle of backing out of the spot.

"You walked almost a mile down Lovers Lane by yourselves? Chloe, do you have any idea how dangerous that is?" Dylan scolded, placing a hand on Teri's seat as he turned

13

fully back toward his daughter. Or someone that looked a lot like his daughter because no way any child he raised would be this reckless.

"Daddy, I'm sorry!" The tears started again and Teri placed a hand on his thigh.

"Remember, we'll talk this through in the morning. We need to get her car." Teri gave a firm nod, and all of a sudden, he hated his own words being turned back on him. "Besides, all I'm going to say is that reality television and all this access to each other on the internet skews a child's reality."

Of course she got her dig in. Dylan sighed and turned back around in his seat. He backed the car out, got honked at, let the other car pass, and then kept going. Maybe he'd wake up to this being a somewhat funny, but not really, bad dream.

CHAPTER.02

"Whoa there," Dylan called out, stopping Chloe as she sneaked toward the garage.

"Dad, I'm gonna be late for class if I don't leave now." Chloe came to an abrupt stop in the middle of the kitchen. Funny, since she started college, she'd never voluntarily gotten up this early.

Under normal circumstances, he'd already have a run in before breakfast, but since his jailbird daughter wrecked their evening last night, he'd planned for her attempted escape this morning. He'd have tried exactly the same thing at her age.

"Turn around, take a seat. If you could miss class for a stadium, you can miss class for your mom and me to have a word with you." Dylan poured coffee into his travel mug.

"Busted!" Chad, his middle child, laughed, walking into the kitchen and grabbing the breakfast sandwich Dylan had made for him.

"There's a bottle of orange juice in the fridge," Dylan said absently, reaching for the wallet in his back pocket before Chad could utter his next words.

"Ten-four, Dad. Do you have any money?" Chad asked, his head stuck inside the refrigerator.

"What do you need? I have a five and a ten." Dylan thumbed through his cash.

"I'll take the ten," Cate, his youngest shot out before Chad could respond. She came through like a tornado, dropping her heavy backpack to the floor with a loud thump.

"No, I'll take the ten. You take the five," Chad shot back, plucking the ten dollar bill from Dylan's hand.

"Dad, that's not fair. Why does he always get the most money?" Cate whined.

"Because I'm older and wiser," Chad answered for Dylan, never breaking stride as he walked out the back door toward his truck. This had been his new attitude since the beginning of his senior year of high school. "Come on, Cate! We're gonna be late."

"Get your breakfast, honey." Dylan pulled a small plastic bottle of orange juice from the refrigerator and handed it to Cate. She pouted and dragged her backpack on the floor behind her as she came around the center kitchen island.

"No, ma'am! Go change your skirt. No way that skirt falls in dress code," Dylan said once he got a good look at his daughter. There wasn't three full years age difference between his oldest and his youngest, but Cate was still his baby. Cate loved fashion and always pulled this stunt.

"Daddy, it's in dress code. Look." She slid her hands down the sides of the skirt and her fingertips did reach the hem. She'd pulled out the big guns by using the word *Daddy*. Cate was his baby and she worked that role very well.

"Then lift your arms in the air to make sure your T-shirt doesn't show any belly," Dylan fired back. Her clothes were way too short and tight. He didn't like it at all.

"Caty, kiss me before you go." Teri came in the kitchen, completely dressed in full makeup, hair styled, and wearing a trendy Tori Burch design. "I'm going out of town today. You'll have to Skype me tonight. Where's Chad?"

"Mom, Dad thinks my dress is too short, but look, it comes to my fingertips." Teri kissed Cate on the cheek and walked past her toward the backdoor.

"It does come to her fingertips, Dylan."

"It does, Dad," Chloe added as if her declaration would help anything.

"You sit over there and wait your turn," he said to Chloe before turning to Cate. "I'd feel more comfortable if you changed." The skirt looked short even if it wasn't. She'd almost reached his six foot height, and he could see entirely too much of her long legs. He really wanted her to change that skirt.

"But, Dad, this matches my bow and my shoes," Cate reasoned, pointing to her head and sticking out her foot. A honk came from the garage.

"Dylan, she needs to go. They're going to be late," Teri said, coming back inside the kitchen.

"Thanks, Mom. Don't work too hard and try to have some fun!" Cate grabbed the five dollar bill and darted out the door.

"Teri, she needed to change that skirt." He'd lost the fight, but couldn't let this go. They were supposed to be a unit, a team. They were to stick together on all things.

"You treat them like you did when they were little. They're becoming adults," Teri countered as she poured herself a cup of coffee.

"They aren't adults. They're still little," Dylan said, defeated because she was absolutely right.

"No, we aren't, Dad," Chloe added from her seat at the kitchen table.

"Did I tell you to sit over there and be quiet?" he asked, grabbing his travel mug to join her. "You're the prime example of why age has nothing to do with being an adult."

"My car's arriving in fifteen minutes. Can we get on with this?" Teri asked, giving Dylan a very clear we-need-to-move-this-along expression.

"Where are you going this time, Mom?" Chloe asked.

"Chicago, on a business trip." Teri easily deflected the question. She took her coffee and toast to the kitchen table where Chloe and Dylan now sat. "We need to talk about this problem of you driving back here without letting us know."

"We actually need to discuss the whole thing. But first, I want to know who organized this," Dylan asked, pushing a breakfast sandwich in Chloe's direction.

"Dad, the stadium means something to me and you always say we need to be true to ourselves and fight for what we believe in." Probably as close to a confession as he was likely to get. So she *had* been the mastermind behind last night. He'd pretty much come to that conclusion about five thirty this morning. He let it pass that those weren't his words at all, those were her mother's. Conviction and passion were fine, as long as they didn't put any of his children in danger.

Chloe had always been his little go-getter. She was class president, head cheerleader, and in the top ten of her graduating class.

"Honey, your dad's right about his biggest concern. You took too many risks on this one. Leaving school during mid-terms, driving so far on your own without telling us, and organizing something that got so many kids in trouble may not be the most effective way to accomplish your goals." Teri ticked off the points on her fingers as she spoke.

"I know. I do, I just didn't find out about this until yesterday. I thought the school had to publically announce these things? And I didn't want anyone in trouble. I wanted to exercise my civil liberty to protest the stadium coming down. I thought maybe ten kids would show up. All those kids being there wasn't my fault. I made it clear that we had to keep all communication on Dad's network. None of the authorities would have known if they would have followed the rules. Stupid Jake put the announcement on Facebook for the world to see." Chloe sounded disgusted.

Dylan carefully hid his pride in her words.

Teri had lost two cases over the last ten years when the opposing side presented old social media posts from My Space and Facebook casting doubt on the character of the person she represented. She had long since forgotten that was the entire reason Dylan had created the no-paper-trails social media network called Secret. People shouldn't be held responsible in their thirties for some silly post made when they were fifteen. That was just dumb.

Unfortunately, Teri's thoughts on the computer hadn't evolved. She didn't see the value in anything that allowed people to hide behind a screen. "Dylan, this is exactly what I've been saying for years. You take blame in this too. Companies like yours that give these children so much access but don't teach them to be responsible with it are fundamentally at fault," Teri stated, looking straight at Dylan.

"I'm not doing this again with you," Dylan said firmly, though he realized when his creation had turned into a worldwide revolution, and even his children started using the application, it had probably been the beginning of the end of their unified parental front.

Dylan turned toward his daughter. "Chloe, you need to keep us better informed as to what you're doing. We aren't asking you to lose your convictions, just be smarter about them. We've taught you better than what your actions reflected yesterday. We need to be able to trust you will use your very smart brain in the future."

"Yes, sir." Chloe looked apologetically toward him.

"And if there's any chance that what you're doing will result in calls from the police, please reconsider or let us know before you do it," Dylan reasoned. "If you had let me know how serious this was to you, I would have picked you up and stood out there with you."

"So would I. I'm sure there was a motion or injunction we could have filed to help halt this while you gathered the troops. There were much better ways to handle this whole situation," Teri said in alliance with Dylan.

"Did they already tear it down?" Chloe asked, her uncertainty touched his heart.

"The wrecking crews were there at seven this morning." Dylan leaned over and patted her arm. He knew those words were going to cut deep inside his passionate girl.

"Dang it! This is wrong! They shouldn't be allowed to tear down our history like that. Our elected officials don't represent us anymore. They just bully us and shove their agenda down our throats." Dylan would never say a word about how those ideals wouldn't have helped in this situation. Chloe was upset and the tears were back in her eyes. Her pain now becoming his own.

"And that's why you're getting into law, to make those changes to our world." At those words, Chloe launched herself at her mother. Teri held a crying Chloe in her arms, stroking her hair, trying to give her comfort.

Several helpless minutes passed before she came up for air.

"Promise me, Chloe. No more of this. You'll plan better next time, all right?" Dylan patted her head this time, pushing a few napkins on the table toward her. He was never really good with the tears that came from his daughters, but he wanted that point clearly made one more time before she left.

"Yes, sir." Chloe sounded defeated, swiping at her eyes, cleaning her face.

"And we'll all be smarter next time. Use all the resources we have to make the changes, not just break the law," Teri added, nodding at her daughter.

"Yes, ma'am." Chloe blew her nose loudly.

"All right, sweet girl, I went back into town and I got this for you from the stadium." Dylan stood and went to one of the cabinets where he pulled out a small metal sign that said 'Panther Power' with the school's logo-designed paw print in the middle. That got the tears going again. All he could do was look confused at Teri and push more napkins his daughter's way. He hoped some happy tears were mixed in there.

"Thank you, Daddy." Chloe was up, hugging him like he had given her the most special gift a person could receive. "I'm gonna hang this in my dorm room to always remember to fight for what I love."

Dylan shot a look toward Teri, trying to gauge the drama factor of that sentence. Females were so different than males. When he got a little eye-roll from Teri, he nodded. That had to have rated above an eight on the excessive-drama meter. "Okay, go wash your face and dry your eyes before you head back to school."

"Yes, sir. Thank you, Daddy. Bye, Mom, be safe out of town." Chloe closed the door to the bathroom off the kitchen as Dylan sat back down at the kitchen table.

"Did we even get our point across?" Dylan asked.

"She's good. She'll be a great litigator. She diverts the topic so well." Teri took a long drink of coffee while they waited for Chloe to finish.

Chloe came back into the room more composed, and said, "Love you guys. Thank you for coming to get me." She gathered her things, then blew them kisses before heading toward the back door.

"Be safe. Call me," Teri called out.

"Get your breakfast." Dylan pointed to the wrapped sandwich.

"I miss you making my breakfast, Dad." She gave a slight smile, her bottom lip quivering as she stepped back inside to take the breakfast sandwich. With the metal plate tucked close to her heart and a wave, she was gone.

"Mark's gonna be here soon," Teri announced as soon as he heard Chloe's car start in the driveway. She cleaned up her things at the table and drained her coffee cup.

"Go get ready. I've got this." Dylan took her cup and half-eaten piece of toast. He'd barely gotten the breakfast dishes loaded when the back doorbell rang. It was either Mark or Janie, their housekeeper.

Dylan reached for a dish cloth, dried his hands, and went for the door. Teri got there first.

"Hey, babe," she said, and her whole demeanor changed. She had both her suitcases in her hands and a big grin on her face. Dylan was happy Teri had someone in her life that gave her a smile like the one that lit up her face when she looked at Mark.

"I waited a little while to make sure she didn't come back." Mark gave Teri a quick peck on the lips.

"They should all be gone." Dylan stuck out a hand to shake Mark's.

"I sent you an email with our itinerary. I'm going to be on and off the ship. I'll call when I can. The kids and my parents think I'm in Chicago. If you need me, email me, and I'll check every time we dock," Teri said. Mark grabbed her luggage and started for his car parked in the back of their house.

"We need to go, babe." Mark loaded her things, but looked antsy as hell. Reprimanding Chloe this morning hadn't been factored into the already tight schedule.

"Don't worry about anything here. I'll hold down the fort." Dylan chuckled as they got to the car. "Or bail whoever needs it out of jail."

"Who went to jail?" That stopped Mark in his hurried tracks as he stood there looking confused.

"I'll tell you on the way," Teri said.

Mark slammed the trunk closed and rounded to open the passenger door for her. "I talked to Nanny Laura and she's coming Friday and Saturday to stay with the kids. I think I told you that." Teri gave Dylan a quick hug before getting inside. Mark left the shutting of the door to him and hurried to the driver's side.

"Mark gets better and better looking the older he gets," Dylan whispered where only Teri could hear.

"He's not as handsome as you, but he's a good guy," Teri offered, glancing Mark's way as he opened the driver's side door, got inside, and started the car.

"You've got money and credit cards?" Dylan asked.

"Yes. I'm nervous. I've never left you guys for this long."

"We're gonna be fine. Go have fun!" Dylan said, standing again to shut the car door.

"Babe, you're killing me! We're gonna miss the flight," Mark called out.

"Go get him, cougar!" Dylan kept the grin and shut the door, backing away with a wave. She playfully shot him the finger with a big smirk on her face. When he caught Mark's eye, he lifted a hand to him and stood there appreciating the view as the guy turned the car around and drove down their driveway. She'd done well finding him. Mark was about seven years younger than Teri and Dylan's exact opposite. Mark's Italian heritage gave him dark hair, almost black eyes, and an olive complexion. He also clearly spent a lot of time in the gym—the personification of an Italian stallion. Together, he and Teri were a stunning couple. Besides Teri's fair complexion they were equals on every level. And in her heels she was even close to his height.

Dylan forced himself to turn away when he couldn't see the car any longer. He was happy for her. Mark and Teri had been together for a while now. She'd found someone good to be with...and he left that thought right there, not letting himself expand on what their relationship meant to the overall picture of his life. Those decisions were made a long, long time ago when he'd finally come clean to himself and Teri as to who he was as a man. It had been a tough decision to stay married for their children, but they'd decided not to divorce and stick this out together until their kids entered college. It seemed the responsible thing to do all those years ago.

They were friends, best friends, and that said a lot. Dylan had made his bed so to speak. He wouldn't think about all the fabulous sex she was about to have or the days of playing in the sun with that hot Italian stud. Or the fact he'd done nothing to move his life forward in the relationship department, no matter how much Teri encouraged him to get out and test the waters. He wasn't entirely certain how all of this would work out in the future, and he didn't have time to dwell. Right now, he was going back inside the house to finish the dishes and head to work. *Yay him.*

CHAPTER.03

The alarm on his cell phone chirped an irritating tone, pulling Tristan from his work. That ringtone always grated on his nerves. He'd chosen that particular one precisely because it was impossible to ignore. It couldn't already be that late, could it? He scrubbed a hand over his face and looked up at the large metal clock strategically hung above the fireplace in his home office. *Fuck!* Where had the day gone? Tristan shoved away from the desk and stretched his arms above his head, arching his back as he made his way upstairs and padded barefoot across the tiled floors to the kitchen. He rolled his neck, then his shoulders, shrugging off the day's worries. Boy, could he use a good massage right about now.

Absently, he tapped the remote on the wall and listened as the back patio doors slid open. The salty smell of the ocean scented the air. He took the pitcher of mojitos from the refrigerator and poured himself a tall glass, stealing a quick sip before placing the rest back inside. Lime and the faint taste of mint burst across his palate. Perfect. The cocktail had been made for him by his housekeeper, and like always, she nailed the blend of alcohol and mix.

She surprised him regularly with new drink recipes. He never knew what delicacy sat waiting for him each evening in his refrigerator.

Tristan strolled through the quiet house, the cool tile floor comforting against the soles of his feet. He stopped to straighten a Darko Topalski painting on the wall, before stepping into his spacious living room, which had to be his favorite room of the house. The living room was a mishmash of modern and contemporary with a bit of Old World thrown in, simply because the pieces he'd found while traveling Europe suited his taste. The distinct blend of color reached out into the patio and melded into the brilliant orange and dusty pink sky that assuredly announced the approach of evening. Just like with his bedroom, the living room's back wall slid open, making it impossible to distinguish where the room ended and the patio began.

Dusk was his favorite time of day. No matter where he was or what he planned, he took a few minutes to sit outside and watch as the sun slipped behind the dark horizon, ending the day. Sunset was a symbolic moment to Tristan, a time of momentary pause to ground himself and appreciate the beauty of the world around him. Since Laguna Beach in the early spring was a magical place, he let the hues of the sky take his thoughts from accounting forms and acquisition details that seemed to be the focus of most of his life.

Tristan headed for the lounger. He preferred to kick back and lose himself in the captivating moment. The evening air was a bit chilly for the walking shorts and T-shirt he wore, but Maria, his housekeeper, had draped a hoodie over the back of the chair. Tristan smiled when he saw it. The woman was always a step ahead. An unexpected gust of wind caused a smattering of goose bumps to spring up on his arms and a shiver to run down his spine. He set his glass down long enough to pull the welcomed warmth over his head. As he picked up the drink, he also grabbed the remote control, and turned the stereo on. He chose Sublime's upbeat "What I Got" as the song for tonight, only because he knew every single word.

"Hey," Landry Prescott, his chief operating officer, said as he stepped out onto the deck. Maria must have let him in.

"Hey, there's a fresh batch of mojitos in the refrigerator. Grab a glass. They're delicious," Tristan said, lifting his drink. Landry knew the drill. He'd been with Tristan since the beginning. They attended high school together. They'd been buddies. Tristan loved mathematics and was a certified genuine computer geek. Landry was a jock but also one hell of a genius at motivating the troops. While all the other kids in school were focused on dating and the opposite sex, Tristan had hunkered down and developed the first automated web program, linking site after site together on the internet.

It took about two years, with his family leveraging everything they had to invest in Tristan's ideas to help him build an algorithm and sustainable crawler for the masses. By the time he turned sixteen, he had a staff of eight people, one being Landry, and they worked out of the garage of his parents' home. Now, twenty years later, he employed tens of thousands of people across the world and had his hand in about everything electronic-related on the market. He'd launched his newest offering at the beginning of the year. A social media site called WilderNation. He'd officially tossed his hat into the social media scene, and for the first time in his life, something he touched hadn't turned immediately to gold. Actually, performance-wise he hadn't even earned the bronze. Which now had become the number one priority of his entire senior executive staff.

"God, Maria's talented." Landry sighed, taking a seat next to Tristan, with glass in hand.

"Agreed. And something smells awesome coming out of that oven. I'm lucky to have her," he said, picking up the binoculars. Sometimes he could spot the dolphins in the distance. Those were excellent days.

"Traffic was weirdly light today," Landry mentioned casually, taking the binoculars that Tristan held out for him.

"Dead center traveling north." Tristan pointed to the small pod he'd spotted. "Did you read the last reports I sent?"

"Yeah, I was thinking Secret looked pretty good. It's got more members than we do. The guy worked at Texas Instruments for years before he developed the site. It looks the most stable to me. His concept's proprietary. No one has it yet but him," Landry said, his eyes still on the dolphins.

"I like the idea of no paper trail," Tristan added.

"It's got some serious criticism," Landry replied, giving the binoculars back to Tristan.

"They've handled that well and they're right. Bad people will use anything for their gain. I'm coming to see the benefits of that mobile app. I like messages disappearing. It alleviates all sorts of issues. I think the consumer would devour it if we can just get it in enough hands," Tristan mused aloud, before taking a long drink.

"Marketing has some rough ideas about a global initiative and legal has the paperwork ready," Landry said, already draining his glass.

"The owner's coming this week, correct?" Tristan asked.

"Yep, Thursday and Friday. Maybe Friday, Saturday. I can't remember. He's bringing his senior team along."

"I wanna sit in on all those meetings. We need to push this along. I don't want to string this thing out a year," Tristan stated.

"He's not sure he's interested in selling," Landry said, rising.

"What's his personal background?"

"Upper middle class. He's a computer science engineer, wife's an attorney. They have some kids," Landry answered, placing his glass on the patio table. "I've gotta get going. Amy's got something going on tonight."

"Tell her hello." Tristan resisted the urge to give his buddy a hard time about the whirlwind romance he'd had with his assistant. They had broken every company policy Wilder, Inc. had, but they married a few weeks ago and Tristan had been the best man. He wondered if things had turned out differently, how that would have looked in court. Landry was lucky the relationship worked out like it had.

Landry showed himself out as Tristan went in search of whatever heavenly concoction lay within that oven.

Sometime around midnight, Tristan sat back in his office chair, digging his thumb and forefinger into his eyes. He'd spent the better part of the night working on a top secret priority—if only to himself—robotics program. Something he'd gotten in his head a couple of years ago. He'd never shared his ideas with anyone, but had had prototypes built on a very small scale. The tweaking was making him a little crazy. Fine-tuning the motor skills took time.

Tristan just had a knack for these things, and since he'd made his billions being innovative, he'd tried to stay cutting edge by keeping one step ahead of competition. He always reasoned that was why he had an innovations department that employed several hundred people, all working new, creative concepts to keep his computer software company ahead of the game. He lived for the idea of helping people gather the information they needed, ever since the moment he'd realized his web crawler was a viable product all those years ago.

Tristan pushed the office chair across the room as his cell phone vibrated. He generally ignored the device, but since he needed a mental break, he decided to answer, effectively ending a song from Hozier playing from a playlist off his phone.

"Hello." Tristan caught Julian's name flash across the caller ID as he answered.

"What're you doing? You occupied?" Tristan thought he detected a slight slur, but at this time of night, he didn't expect anything less.

"No," he finally said. He began the process of shutting down the extensive computer equipment, which took some time. "I was just downstairs, working."

"Well, I'm at your door. You want some company tonight?" Having a regular booty call sure made life a little easier. There was no chase with Julian and absolutely zero commitment. If he'd been in here with another guy, Julian might have asked to join in on the activities. Julian's uninhibited nature and always-up-for-anything attitude was what he liked best about the guy.

"I'm headed up. You alone?" That was another question he'd learned to ask.

"Yeah, but I could call Stephen if you're up for a threesome," Julian replied.

"Nah, I've gotta be up early." Tristan entered the code to the downstairs door, which he kept locked at all times. Maria was the only one who could get inside and that was to do minimal cleaning.

"All right, I promise I won't keep you up all night. Open the door." Tristan took the phone away from his ear and unlocked the front door remotely while taking the stairs up to the main level. He stepped into the foyer as the door opened. Julian was right up his alley for the night. Tall, dark, lean, and more than willing. "Come in."

"Let's get this party started," Julian purred, walking through the door right into Tristan's personal space. That cocky, I-want-to-fuck-you grin in place. "It's my birthday."

"Happy birthday," Tristan replied, trying to remember if he'd known that piece of information.

"I'm twenty-eight. And all these guys getting married are seriously cramping my prospect list." Julian leaned forward to lick across Tristan's lips. He was a bold one.

"So I'm last choice, huh?" Tristan lifted his brow and gave Julian a smirk before shutting and locking the front door behind him.

"It's more like I try to forget you, but damn, it's hard." Tristan wondered how many times he'd uttered those same words already this week. Julian's lips met his and that was all the encouragement Tristan needed. Clothes were gone and they were in his bedroom in a matter of minutes.

CHAPTER.04

"Dad, we don't need a babysitter anymore. I'm sixteen. Chad's gonna be eighteen in like two weeks. We got this," Cate announced while helping Dylan put the dinner dishes in the sink.

"I can watch Cate," Chad piped in, rinsing the dishes and putting them inside the dishwasher.

"I don't need watching. I'm number one in my class. I'm class president..." Dylan stopped her midsentence so he didn't have to hear all this again.

"It's not like that, guys. This time's different. Your mom's working and can't be interrupted, and they've scheduled my meetings until late every night. Nanny Laura isn't coming to watch you, just field any problems for us," Dylan said, deciding the rest of the salad would never be eaten, and tossed the remainder in the trash.

"When are you gonna be home?" Chad asked, rinsing the salad plate Dylan brought him.

"I'll be home Sunday," he informed them as he ran the soapy rag across the granite countertop.

"You know, Dad, none of our other friends have to do the dinner dishes," Cate said, and Dylan just looked over his shoulder at her.

"Cleaning up after yourself is an important part of being the adult I keep hearing you say you're becoming. I'm preparing you for life."

"But we're rich," she whined.

So much for her maturity.

"We aren't rich—" Dylan started to explain, but was immediately cut off by the child who was supposedly the most solid of all his children.

"But if Wilder buys Secret, then we'll be very rich," Chad added, closing the lid to the dishwasher. "Are you and Mom gonna move?"

"No! I have a better question! Are we getting trust funds?" Cate asked excitedly. Dylan ignored her completely, focusing on Chad's question.

"What? You don't like this house?" Dylan asked, a little confused. They lived in a six bedroom, seven bath home in Highland Park. The kids attended the prestigious Preston Hollow Private School. Every one of them had a brand new car. This, by far, beat the two bedroom home he'd grown up in and the college apartment they'd had when the kids were little. "I think you need a refresher course in the power of appreciation."

"No, Dad, I love this house. I don't want you to move. But I'm going to college in a few months, and Cate's going at mid-semester. You and Mom could get something smaller. That's all I'm saying," Chad said, drying his hands.

"You didn't tell me you decided to graduate early." Dylan turned to Cate who stared at Chad, giving him the stink eye.

"I decided today. My guidance counselor thinks it'll look good on my application, and it's easier to get into Harvard in the spring semester."

"You decided on Harvard? Why haven't you told me?" Everything in the room stopped. Dylan had been such a huge part of all of the children's college planning sessions. They knew this was a big move, and she'd made these decisions without him.

"I just decided today. I was gonna tell you tonight," she said, dropping her rag into the sink and elbowing Chad in the ribs.

"Hey!" Chad grabbed his midsection, which Dylan ignored completely. Usually that would have been grounds for him to intervene, but he stayed focused on the new graduation development.

"So this time next year, all my kids are gonna be off at college?" Dylan stated the obvious, looking between the both of them.

"Don't worry, Daddy, we'll be home all the time," Cate promised, going to Dylan and giving him a hug. Of course they would think this was all about them. That was part of being a kid, and he'd definitely raised his children to believe they were his whole life. Dylan's problem, however, was more that he didn't have a life at all. He was a father of almost-grown children who were doing exactly what they were supposed to do—leave the nest. He was also a business owner in the first stages of a buyout. And he was a gay man buried so deep in the closet he questioned if he would ever find his way out.

He finally forced a smile on his face. "I just needed to catch up. I'm proud all my kids are doing so well." He took the towel and gave a playful whip toward Chad. That caused Cate to laugh. "You two make me proud while I'm out of town. No problems, and pass that on to your jailbird sister."

His antics eased the tension in the room and caused both Chad and Cate to laugh, diverting the attention from him.

He normally ran a casual office. His hundred and fifty or so employees weren't required to have a dress code, as long as they kept their clothing within reason, but today he and his two top executives were professionally outfitted with some of the most stylish and, in Dylan's opinion, expensive clothing on the market.

When the Wilder weekend itinerary had arrived via email and it became apparent no expense had been spared in flying them to California or in the list of activities planned for the three of them, it sent Secret's senior management into a frenzy. They easily speculated that WilderNation wouldn't dare spend that amount of money if they weren't highly interested in the company. In return, someone not as budget-conscious as Dylan allowed Neimans free rein to help them look the part of ultra-successful businessmen.

They boarded a private Wilder jet, and for the first time since he'd signed off on their ridiculously expensive clothing, Dylan appreciated the extravagance. Their makeover had also included grooming. While Dylan had always kept his hair on the shorter side, none of his top staff had been this clean-shaven or put together in all the years he'd known them. Making millions of dollars, as well as putting their best foot forward to their potential new employer, had something to do with this GQ-meets-GeekWorld look they now sported.

"Dude, is this how they travel all the time?" David asked Dylan, looking around the private jet's spacious and plush interior.

"I have no idea," Dylan said, as blown away as the rest of them. And his kids called themselves rich. He sure wished they could see this plane. He pulled his phone out to snap a picture to text each of them.

"I can take your bags," a flight attendant offered from behind them. She was already reaching for Rob's carry-on. Another approached from the other side, taking David's bags. Dylan watched in interest as his top team turned to putty in the pretty young women's hands.

"I can take yours too, sir," one of them said to Dylan. There were three passengers and three flight attendants. Wilder clearly traveled in style. "Please take a seat and fasten your seat belt. We'll serve cocktails and lunch when we get in the air." Once everything was locked into place, they made their way to the galley.

"She was into me," David said, puffing out his chest proudly. He was the youngest of them all at not-quite thirty years old.

"She's paid to be into you," Rob said, selecting the seat closest to the window.

"You don't know that," David said, tilting his head to watch the flight attendant as she worked. Dylan snapped his fingers between the two, like he used to do with Chloe and Cate when they were little.

"Not appropriate behavior. We talked about this," Dylan scolded. "Creepy gawking and coming on to the staff's wrong in just about every company's harassment policy. Not your best foot forward, dickhead."

"But I'm not employed there yet," David announced, clearly proud of his argument with the cocked brow he gave Dylan.

"Nor will you be either is the point he's trying to make, dumbass," Rob chimed as the attendant walked back to them.

"Gentlemen, I'm going to buckle up. Once the captain gives the go-ahead, we'll get you guys taken care of." David's flight attendant leaned across Dylan's chair and smiled down at him. She glanced at the others then spoke. "Good. You all figured out how your seat belts work."

She directed her sweet smile straight at Dylan as she turned away. "Dude, they always fall for you," David whispered when she was several feet away.

"I'm married. She sees the ring. I'm safe." Dylan lifted his left hand and wiggled his fingers to make his point.

"Whatever, man. They all fall for you," Rob murmured, too. The roar of the engine almost drowned out his words as the plane began its taxi down the runway.

"You guys are completely off the mark. Now focus. There are millions of dollars on the table. No more of this thing you two are doing. We're professionals. I spent fifteen thousand dollars to look the part—now act like it." When he got the eye roll from his team, he leaned in as far as he could.

"You promised to give me three days." He eyed both of them, waiting for them to respond.

"All right," David finally relented. "I'll ward off her advances, but you owe me, bro!"

CHAPTER.05

Tristan walked into the front doors of his Irvine, California, corporate offices as he'd done a million times over the last ten years, but this time things were different. From day one, his entire corporate culture had been founded on the concept of being open and friendly. For Tristan, cubicles, closed door offices, and departmentalism sucked his will to live. He tried hard to keep that from happening in any of his companies, but he did recognize the difficulties of those core business philosophies with as many employees as he now had. Regardless, even as large as they'd grown, he still managed to maintain a personal touch with free, open spaces. Yet now as he entered the building, he was met with a reception desk in the middle of the atrium with a mid-size clear wall stretched across the length of the lobby on both sides of the desk.

Instead of a friendly face greeting him, now sat three armed security guards. Regardless of Wilder, Inc. being scrawled across the bottom of the reception desk, he'd done an about-face and walked back outside to make sure he'd entered the right building.

Yep, Wilder, Inc. was displayed proudly at the top of the building so he went back inside. He bypassed the desk and tried to enter through one of the half opened walkways in the clear glass wall.

"Excuse me, sir. That's a restricted area. Only employees are allowed beyond this point." A security guard stopped him. Although Tristan wore a suit coat and tie today, he never required any of his employees to dress business formal. This security guard, standing in front of him with a serious case of the don't-fuck-with-me attitude was dressed in the standard issue *Men in Black* kind of suit and tie. He was burly, big, beefy, and intimidating as hell with his hand on his hip, moving the jacket back enough to expose a gun holstered on the side of his belt.

"I'm an employee here," Tristan answered with a smile. It actually took him a second to realize they had no idea who he was. Since he didn't rest on formality, he shouldn't have been surprised, but surely there was a photo here or there of the founder of the company.

"I need to see your employee badge," the no-nonsense guard said.

"When did we start needing employee badges?" Tristan asked, pulling his phone from inside his suit pocket. He swiped his finger across the screen until he found his notes app. He typed a quick reminder to ask why and when they had implemented that regulation.

"It's been that way since I've been here, sir," the man said a little condescendingly.

"And how long has that been?" Tristan asked, looking at the guy's name badge and typing that into his phone too.

"Sir, you need to show your ID or move on back to the reception area and explain your business here," the guard said, his tone turning hard.

"I don't have an *I. D.*" Tristan pronounced each letter very clearly. He texted Landry to get his ass down there and fix this problem. "I do have a question for you. Is this how all guests are treated when they enter this building?"

"Sir, please step this way." The guard took Tristan by the elbow, and he let the manhandling happen as they guided him to a small office behind the desk, escorted now by two of the guards. "If you'll write your name, job title, and direct supervisor down on this piece of paper, we'll contact someone in that department, but you get only one free pass. Next time comes with a written warning," the guard stated, holding a hand over the weapon at his hip.

Was he freaking for real?

Tristan did what the guard asked. Signed his name, gave the title of president and CEO, and marked himself down as his own direct supervisor. He pushed the paper toward the guy, who reached for it, never looked at the written words, and left the room. "Stay here."

Tristan got up and tried the door, finding he was actually locked inside. The whole experience was so different than anything he'd ever had happen in his business that he scanned the room to see if there was a hidden camera. Surely Ashton Kutcher or whoever was about to pop out and laugh at the ridiculousness of all this.

Two minutes later, Landry and the guard were back through the door.

"I'm sorry, sir. I was just doing my job," the guard apologized the second the door opened. Unmistakable fear was written all over his face and showed in his actions. Probably concerned about losing his job, which seemed reasonable to Tristan given the circumstances, but instead of acknowledging the excuses, he turned to Landry.

"This setup has to go. I don't like this. It should have never been approved." Tristan stepped out of the room, making sure everyone in the area heard him.

"It's because of the proprietary nature of our—" Landry started, but Tristan shook his head.

"There're better ways. We need to review this policy by the end of the day." Tristan walked toward the elevators directly behind the reception desk. "People should be greeted by a friendly face when they walk in. And why don't I have an employee badge? Do you have one?"

"Who would have thought you needed one to step inside your own building. Everyone knows who you are," Landry quipped, pushing the up button to call the elevator.

"Apparently not. What's the status of our guests' arrival? I don't want them coming in to this." Tristan typed another note into his phone as a reminder to go over the front desk policy before he left the office today, and then stepped through the doors as they swished open. Landry looked down at his watch as Tristan hit the administrative floor on the keypad inside the elevator.

"They should be landing right about now. A driver will bring them straight here." Tristan punched the top floor button again as the doors shut, but they didn't move. He punched it again, and then again.

"Hell, are we having maintenance issues, too? This is so not the time for all this bullshit." Tristan pressed the button again.

"No, you need your badge and authorization to get to the top floor," Landry explained, sliding his badge through the card reader and pressing the button. They were off.

"But I don't have a badge and why do we even need badges?" Tristan repeated, doing air quotes over the word badge.

How did he not have access to his own building?

"It's been a while since you've been here. I'm sure it's sitting on your desk."

"I want this all discussed by the end of this day. You need to do whatever needs to be done before they get here to make sure they aren't greeted like I was. I liked the old days when you walked in a place and normal people were sitting behind a desk ready to greet you, without guns being shoved in your face," Tristan stated, walking off the elevator.

"Lookin' good, boss man." That deep voice caught Tristan's attention so he looked over, seeing an intern he'd hired a year ago grinning at him, extending a hand to give Tristan a fist bump as he walked past. He obliged and smiled. This guy needed to be downstairs greeting the people walking into his building. Tristan caught the apparently strict new Landry reaching out to give the intern a fist bump too. The intern looked confused but followed through, not leaving Landry hanging too long.

It was clear his company motivator had turned into a stern businessman. This was turning into a day of many new revelations.

"You should dress up more. You're dashing." Tristan couldn't let Landry's obvious attempt in leading him a different direction slip. "Dashing? Really. That might have worked from the intern, but it's not gonna work for you. We're talking about the whole security thing as soon as these guys leave tonight. Are we ready for them?" he asked. Since he didn't believe in offices, but worked with proprietary information, he required some form of privacy on the administration floors. That came by the way of half walls, windows, and large glass double doors he kept open most of the time. Well, most of the time he was actually there. He found his underground lair was the best at keeping his work private.

"The itinerary's on your desk. We have meetings, tours, and dinner plans every night," Landry supplied.

"Good. I want to speed this along. Their asking price is fair. I don't want to nickel and dime them," Tristan repeated for about the tenth time over the last two days since they'd decided this was the one they wanted. Sometimes with his group of senior executives, he had to say specific words over and over, especially about the money. They watched Wilder's dollars closely, no doubt because they liked their year-end bonuses.

"For me, the deciding factor lies in their current staff. We don't need them. Especially that senior executive team," Landry started. He'd done background reports on them all, going over each one in length with Tristan. Landry hadn't been impressed with any of them. Tristan was fine giving them honorary jobs to get the market share they built so quickly, but nothing substantial or long-term.

"Don't make snap judgments. We'll need them to transition. Actually, you're forgetting—they don't need us as much as we need them. Don't be arrogant. They've beat us in this part of the game. Get our team ready, and for heaven's sake, don't let our guests be greeted like I was downstairs," Tristan cautioned again, digging through the piles of paperwork on his desk. He couldn't have their guests see him struggling to get inside his own building.

"I need a box," Tristan called out loudly. "Somebody bring me a big file box." Landry laughed as he left the office. Tristan took off his suit jacket and rolled up his sleeves. A few moments later, a box landed on the desk in front of him. With a few shoves, he dumped everything that had accumulated on his desk into the box, looking over to someone's assistant. Since he refused to have one himself, he regularly shared with his staff.

"Go through all that. Deal with what should be dealt with. Dump the rest," he directed, handing the guy the heavy box.

"Yes, sir," he replied.

"Lose the sir. Apparently I have an employee badge somewhere in there. Find it and put it directly into my hands. Nowhere else. Got it?"

"Yes, sir... S-sorry," the intern stuttered at Tristan's look of disapproval.

"Does this suit look like I'm trying too hard?" Tristan asked. He quickly rolled his sleeves back down and shrugged on his jacket, puffing out his chest and stretching to his full height.

The guy looked startled and momentarily unsure before he gave a croaked, "No."

"Are you sure?" he questioned, even knowing the kid wouldn't tell him the truth.

"Yes," he reassured, leaving the office. Tristan laughed at the hasty retreat. He needed to spend more time here, not locked up at his house and web-conferencing. The Wilder inner community had suffered with his absence. He needed to be in the office to maintain his vision for how his company and employees were treated. On that dismal thought, he went out to see Landry's new bride.

"Amy, did Landry have you send gift baskets to all their rooms at the hotel?" Tristan asked, walking past the shared administrative assistant of the senior executive team. She'd been originally hired for him, but he took care of about ninety percent of his own needs, so over the years she started working with them all.

"Yes, sir. Looking good, Tristan," she said, looking up from her monitor and giving him a wink.

"It feels off," Tristan said, moving his hands in the air over his clothing.

"Looks professional and hot all at the same time," she said, laughing at his grimace. He wasn't the suit and tie kind of guy. He actually hated wearing these things. But these guys were from Dallas—Southern Bible Belt types—and he figured they wore these formal kinds of church-going clothes.

"Don't say that too loud. Landry will hear you, then I'll have to fistfight him in his fit of jealousy, making for an even worse Human Resource nightmare than marrying your boss," Tristan responded loudly. Landry's doors were open and right beside her desk.

"I do think I might have been harassed..." she said as loudly.

"No. It's only funny when I joke about it," Tristan teased. "You can't after all the legal I had to sit through to make sure all parties were completely covered when you two decided you couldn't live without each other. I'm here for another reason besides how I look. I need the weekend itinerary for our guests."

"Sure. I placed a copy on your desk and sent one in email."

"Good job—very thorough. Can you resend it to my email now?"

"Tristan, you should open email. I assist you and I might have something important to tell you," Amy lectured, working at her computer as she spoke.

"Tell Landry." Tristan palmed his phone, pulling up email, waiting for her to resend the original.

"When Landry handles everything, things like the security fiasco downstairs happen," she whispered never looking up, her fingers clicking on the keyboard.

"I knew it was him. That had Landry Prescott written all over it," Tristan scoffed, but he didn't hide the disapproval in his voice.

Amy looked up at him. "It's your vision, Tristan. No one runs this office like you. We miss you here."

"I hear you. Even thought the same thing just minutes ago, but not a conversation for right now," Tristan said, eyeing her closely. He'd hired her for a reason. Even after the sickeningly sweet love she had for Landry, she was still very loyal to him.

"They're here. Jamison, your favorite security guard down there, just sent them up," Landry announced, sticking his head past his office door. His brow narrowed as he stared at Amy and Tristan huddled close together. "Are you still trying to get her to sign that release? I married her for Christ's sake."

"I've decided I can't live without her, and I'm convincing her I'm the one for her," Tristan teased while he glanced over the itinerary on his phone. Meet and greet, tour, dinner, drinks. He stared down apathetically at the dates, times, and names. This schedule contained nothing more than schmoozing for three full days. He hated this part the most. The elevator ding saved them all from Landry's answer. Tristan went directly to the elevator to meet the men himself.

CHAPTER.06

Everything in the Wilder, Inc. office was overly bright and cheerful with a contemporary, pleasingly ergonomic flair. The company clearly spent an incredible amount of money on its environment to bring the employees a stimulating and creative workspace. Dylan himself had looked into changes such as these for his Dallas office but could never fully justify making such sweeping modifications with his already overtaxed budget. Yet, as far as he was concerned, the facility impressed him before they even started the tour. His employees, the ones that relocated, would do well here.

"The concierge service is cool. Even if we don't do this, I think we should add that service for our staff," Rob stated. More so than David, Rob agreed with Dylan and always pushed to give back to their staff.

"I can't see why we wouldn't take an offer if they give us one this weekend," David added quickly, right before the elevator doors opened. David was Dylan's jump-into-the-frying-pan kind of guy. Between the three of them, they covered all the bases. Dylan was most definitely the study-all-the-angles type. He wouldn't let all his employees down by getting overly excited about a showy exterior. He needed to see the details and inner workings before decisions could be made.

"Shhh," Dylan whispered. From the articles he'd read in Science Digest, he easily spotted Tristan Wilder. Two things struck him at once. First, the president and CEO of the multi-billion dollar empire, Wilder, Inc., was standing there, apparently ready to greet them, and second, he was much better-looking in person than he had been in the magazine article. And he'd been damn fine in print.

Dylan let David and Rob step out first. He kept his eyes on Wilder as the man greeted his senior management team. He couldn't help but notice the wide shoulders and broad chest hidden under a well-fitted designer suit. With short-cropped, blond hair and strong facial features, all complemented by a perfectly chiseled jawline, the man had the whole modern day Nordic god thing going on. Dylan found he couldn't quit staring as the striking man finally turned toward him.

"Hello, welcome to Wilder. I'm Tristan." He gave a warm smile that drew Dylan's eyes to his full lips. During his greeting, Tristan took a step back and motioned them from the elevator area. Tristan was about his height, maybe a little taller and had no problem looking him directly in the eyes. His heart skipped a beat under the weight of the man's stare. His body even reacted enthusiastically to Tristan's proximity.

Tristan's hand was warm against his, and as he squeezed, those unusual and intense steel gray eyes never left his. He wasn't sure exactly how long he'd held that handshake when he noticed the corners of Mr. Wilder's smile curl into a smirk. His mouth was suddenly dry, his palms grew a bit damp, and he withdrew his hand quickly as a tall, dark-haired man rushed around the corner.

Hopefully the owner of Wilder, Inc. hadn't noticed his ogling or sweaty palms.

"I'm sorry I wasn't here," the well-dressed man said, barreling down on them. "I'm Landry," he announced and shook all of their hands. Again, Dylan was last. The distraction drew his eyes away from Tristan, and he acknowledged the man he'd talked to the most during the acquisition inquiry phase.

"You're Dylan Reeves?" he asked after hearing David's then Rob's names.

"I am. You're the COO. It's good to put a face with a voice and an email address," Dylan stated. He tried for a casual smile and purposefully avoided glancing in Tristan's direction.

"It is. We sure are excited about Secret around here," Landry said as a couple more well-dressed men met them in the foyer near the elevator. Thank god he'd spent the money to dress his guys, otherwise they'd have come to Wilder looking like the *Beverly Hillbillies*. "We should take this into the conference room."

Landry guided them through the top floor, introducing them to the rest of the executive staff as they made their way deeper into the offices of Wilder, Inc. Dylan loved the openness and modern feel of the place. Each desk was ergonomically correct and outfitted in a cool futuristic design. Of course, much like his own office, everyone had state of the art computers and monitors.

Dylan stayed toward the back of the group, taking everything in. Landry was at the front, making polite conversation with David and Rob as they threaded their way through the maze of workstations toward the back of the building. Since he'd purposefully kept his eyes off Tristan, he had no idea of the man's position in the throng of people moving in the direction Landry led.

"Your flight was good?" The husky voice came from behind. He'd thought he'd been bringing up the rear alone. He turned his head to see who'd spoken, only to find the man he avoided directly behind him.

"Absolutely. I haven't traveled too much on private planes. It was nice. Thank you." Dylan gave a sincere smile and caught Tristan's return grin before he turned forward again. He registered the way Tristan's eyes lit up when he smiled.

"It's a business perk that didn't take too long to get used to," Tristan chuckled. All of a sudden the designs of the building faded as Tristan's breath tickled the exposed skin above Dylan's collar. All of Dylan's attention centered on Tristan and the thrill of him being close.

"No, I wouldn't imagine it would," Dylan said. They were trailing now behind the crew, most likely his fault, so he picked up the pace. "I like the design of your building. I always imagined something like this for my staff."

"It's costly, but they're our greatest asset. I wouldn't be here without them. I need those creative juices flowing," Tristan replied, placing a hand on Dylan's back as he started to turn the wrong way. Electricity sizzled through his body, and he stepped away from the touch, barely registering the hand extended in front of him.

"This way," Tristan said. The genuine smile was still in place when Dylan looked his way.

"I get it better now that I've been here. You promoted synergy before it became a buzzword," Dylan said, forcing himself to focus on business. He remembered one particular article where Tristan was just starting out and had all these ideas about creating a community that worked together. He'd definitely achieved those goals.

"Thank you for knowing that," Tristan added quietly, patting his shoulder as he stepped around him, walking a few feet ahead of Dylan. The warm puff of breath across his cheek and the light touch when Tristan passed by had goose bumps springing up on his arms. As he watched Tristan in front of him, he realized he'd been so absorbed in thought he'd again missed another turn they'd all made. "The conference room's in here."

Tristan caught a door and stopped Dylan before he walked away. He covered his mistake with a laugh. "It's a distracting place."

"I'm certainly glad you like it." Tristan gestured toward the brightly lit room. "We're meeting in here before we start the tour. It's the only room, besides our individual offices, that's truly private. Anytime you need it, it's yours this weekend," he said. Dylan walked in to see an over-the-top conference room. Of course, it had the standard table-and-chair setup, but off to the side was a seating area with decorative plush chairs, a sofa, and a full sink and bar at their disposal. If the rest of the place looked like this and Wilder did make an offer, his staff would do well here. That eased him more than anything else. It had been one of his chief concerns in this acquisition.

"Perfect. I'd really like to see the rest of the place," Dylan added. As one burden eased the other took on a life of its own. He never had these problems. He had to figure out how to shake off his attraction to the company owner. This was business. Important to his life. Too many lives depended on him being on his A game, and yet, he found it hard to concentrate when the CEO was anywhere near him.

He'd been so absorbed in his own thoughts that it took a minute to see David and Rob were both in brisk conversations with the Wilder staff. It amazed him how well everyone seemed to get along. If anything, he was the odd man out, standing on the outside listening as the Wilder top executives were very much like his own. They spoke the same language, used similar analytical skill to come to certain viewpoints on the industry. They were interested in all the same things. If Dylan hadn't known better, he'd have sworn they'd been friends forever.

He watched a little closer and wondered if this might just be part of the game. He'd never been in negotiations like these. Maybe this was the reel-you-in stage. For some reason that thought helped bring his perspective back. Of course

Wilder, Inc. would know how to work them to get what they wanted.

Several minutes into the meet and greet, Tristan clapped his hands at the front of the room, effectively gathering everyone's attention. "I'm changing our plans. Why don't we start with a quick tour? We can have a more extensive conversation tomorrow as we iron out the details. What do you say?"

Dylan was grateful for the mental mind-check. He needed things to go back to basics. It wasn't just the man that overwhelmed him, but the whole experience. He needed to focus. David and Rob had different agendas. Where they wanted employment, he would never be hired by Wilder nor did he even want that as an option. He just wanted his baby, Secret, in the best possible hands to grow into an international success.

He followed the tour, staying somewhere in the middle of the group, and remained out of the conversations. He was all about the inner workings of the company. The setup and attitude he'd seen on the top floor flowed through to every other floor in the place. That impressed him. Even the mailroom had been designed for optimum performance.

The data center, though, rose to a level he'd never seen or experienced before. The size of a large warehouse, the colorful, complex nerve center of the entire company was filled with an intricate maze of proprietary servers all supporting its daily billion users. Although the company was understandably careful who was allowed beyond this point, Tristan had granted them access to walk through.

Dylan was so impressed he stayed right there in that room, talking frankly and openly with some of the engineers. No one stopped him from asking any question or refused to show him anything he wanted to see. The place was truly state of the art, exceptionally made in every way. He wished he could afford even a portion of a complex like this. He left no detail unanalyzed.

Since he'd taken so long in the data center, the fascinating tour ended about three and a half hours after it began. When he stepped out of the oversized room with Tristan leading the way, they were all waiting for him. The instant conversation and camaraderie of earlier was gone. They were quietly standing there. The windows proved dusk had set in, and he realized he'd probably blown their schedule to hell.

"I'm sorry. I never expected to see your nerve center so closely," Dylan stated.

"We've had someone take your bags to the hotel. They'll be in your rooms when you arrive. I pushed the dinner reservations back by thirty minutes. Should I move them back further?" A woman he'd seen on the top floor stood talking to the group of men. Damn, he had blown the schedule with his uncontrolled curiosity.

"I'm sorry, I shouldn't have taken so much time..." he tried again.

Tristan, who'd stayed relatively quiet, except to answer some of Dylan's more technical questions, jumped in to respond. "Dylan, it was an honor to see someone so interested in our setup. I told you we take great pride in that room. No apology needed. Amy, I think that's a perfect plan. Why don't we head out now? We should get there right on time."

"That sounds good to me," Landry seconded, earning a round of nods from everyone in their party. Dylan went along, following the men outside to the waiting cars. The million or so questions he'd still had were all swallowed. Hopefully another chance would arise to talk more about the inner workings of the center.

The steakhouse was okay, the company pretty good, and the Texans could sure put away the alcohol. If he were assessing the situation at the end of day one, he'd say they were doing a good job at reeling in the final contract. The only concern he had was the company's owner. Dylan's defenses weren't easily penetrated, and he stayed quiet, not offering much insight. Tristan had a feeling there was more to this guy, something he just couldn't quite put his finger on.

Since they'd all seemed to pair up, Tristan got saddled with the quiet Dylan. It wasn't a bad thing, not by any means. He was hot as hell to look at with his auburn hair, wide-set, deep blue eyes, and sexy mouth. A mouth with full fleshy lips that Tristan's eyes kept being drawn to every time the man took a bite of his food. Dylan was also tall and carried himself well. He was smart, funny, and easy to talk to in a one-on-one situation. It seemed as though, at least technically speaking, they were in exactly the same place. When everyone else had become bored out of their minds earlier, Dylan was fully vested into touring his data center, and it was in that moment he knew he liked the guy. The other appealing thing about Dylan was something he prided himself on as well. It didn't matter if you were the lowest technician in the room, Dylan would spend time getting to know the person and the job they performed. He seemed to understand that no piece of the pie was bigger or smaller than the rest. It took everyone to make things happen.

He'd love to spend a few hours talking ideas and concepts. At dinner, they'd done just that. Tristan had thought he'd smoothed some of the reservation out of the guy, gotten him more comfortable. Yet, from the time they'd walked into the nightclub, Dylan had become more reserved than before, if that were even possible.

The after-hours events they planned had them at the high-dollar gentlemen's club. Something Amy had set up for them against Tristan's protests. Apparently her years in the South had paid off. David and Rob were loving the place, having a great time. They'd even migrated closer to the stage with his own team of guys right there with them, but Dylan had stayed back. And contrary to the one drink maximum he'd seemed intent on at dinner, Dylan never allowed his drink to empty, but he also didn't partake in the good time the others were having.

Since he was gay, Tristan hadn't bothered to get too involved in stuffing the G-strings with folded dollar bills, but he loved watching everything going on around him. As the night progressed, he kept going between their reserved six-top in the back of the club where Dylan sat, to the table everyone else occupied up front. Since technically Dylan's signature was the one that was going to be at the bottom of the contract, Tristan felt as if he needed the most wining and dining. On that thought, he straddled the chair opposite Dylan, swiveled around to watch him as he accepted another drink from the waitress.

"Not your scene?" Tristan asked. It just occurred to him that whereas he had loosened his tie and undone his top shirt button, Dylan's suit remained completely in order.

"No, not so much," Dylan responded, taking a good long gulp of his drink.

His eyes were drawn to the movement of Dylan's Adam's apple as he swallowed. Tristan mentally scolded himself for staring and quickly looked away. "I'd have thought this was every guy's good time out. Is it a religious thing? Should we leave?" Tristan questioned, studying the guy closely, trying hard to figure him out. He'd actually been a puzzle since he stepped off that elevator when they first met.

"Nah, it's fine. Everyone's having a great time. I'm good," Dylan answered. He glanced toward the stage, feigning interest. Tristan caught the move and got that the action was designed to derail the conversation, but Tristan wasn't about to let it go.

"Are you religious?" Tristan pressed. Maybe the alcohol still had him questioning Dylan, because clearly the guy didn't want to talk. Tristan took another drink, crunched on some ice, and lifted his near-empty glass toward the waitress assigned to them for the evening.

"Not really," Dylan mumbled.

"You're married, right? Afraid the wife'll get angry?" Tristan questioned. That earned him a half-assed laugh and a scoff that indicated the absurdity of his question. Dylan downed the new glass full of liquor in a couple of swallows. One thing for certain, the guy could hold his alcohol. Tristan had lost count of how much Dylan had drunk that night, but there was no sign of him being under the influence. Religious Bible Belters surely didn't drink that much or give those crazy, inconsequential looks when their wives were mentioned.

"Two more?" the waitress almost yelled over the blare of the music. Tristan nodded for the both of them, and when she was gone, his eyes were back on the perplexing man, staring hard, trying to figure him out. Dylan kept his gaze fixed on the stage. Interesting. Tristan loved puzzles, and Dylan was a big one. He just needed to work the pieces into place before it drove him insane.

"Why aren't you up there enjoying the show?" Dylan asked unexpectedly, his defensive gaze landing on Tristan.

"I'm gay. This isn't my scene at all." Tristan hadn't used those words for shock value since he'd been a teenager, but tonight he wanted a damn reaction out of the guy one way or another. Nothing except data centers seemed to penetrate that carefully laid facade. Dylan's eyes widened and Tristan caught a hint of a blush as he glanced down and started to fidget with the corner of a napkin.

Maybe?

Tristan narrowed his eyes at Dylan's body language and looked down his tense form. The suit pants were of the latest tight-fitting style. Tristan couldn't help but notice Dylan's package, and there was no way the guy was anything but flaccid, even with all these naked women roaming around. "You're gay."

Dylan didn't immediately respond, but his jaw clenched and he didn't bother to even look up at Tristan. He sat there and stared a hole into the table.

"Come on," Tristan said, before he thought better of it. The waitress was back, two glasses in her hands. "Drink this and then this one," he said, shoving both drinks toward Dylan. "I'm telling them we're leaving. I've got a place I think you'll like."

Tristan got off the chair, but kept an eye on Dylan. He hesitated before walking away. Dylan still looked shell-shocked at his declaration. Instinct had him changing his mind. Maybe he shouldn't leave him alone. He palmed his phone while pushing the drink closer to Dylan's hand. He'd text Landry and let him know they were leaving.

"Drink faster," Tristan instructed. They had two cars out front. He was taking one and taking Dylan with him. Finally Dylan did as he'd suggested, and like a seasoned pro, Dylan downed his drink and then Tristan's. The pale color of his skin had him wondering if perhaps those drinks may be coming back up, but so far so good.

"Let's go!"

"Where to?" Dylan asked. He didn't move from his spot at the table. Tristan got the distinct impression Dylan meant more of a *hell no, am I going anywhere with you.*

"Trust me," Tristan replied. He took Dylan's arm as he grabbed his own suit jacket off the chair. "I promise, everyone will have their clothes on."

That seemed to pacify Dylan. He stood, wobbled a bit, but righted himself pretty quickly. "What time is it?" Dylan yelled louder than the music.

"About ten. It's still early." Tristan followed Dylan toward the front. They hit the doors and Tristan looked around for his car. One pulled forward immediately. The driver jumped out, opening the town car door for them. Dylan got in first and scooted across the seat while Tristan followed, telling the driver where to take them. Dylan had moved as far away from him as possible, and he smiled at the gesture. A closeted gay man. How had he not figured that out sooner? Tristan's phone vibrated, and he dug it out of his pocket.

"Did you get my text?" Tristan asked Landry as he answered.

"Yeah. He didn't look like he was having too good a time." Landry must have stepped outside, because as the music faded his voice became clearer.

"Yeah, it's not his scene. I'm gonna take him over to the Executive Club, talk some business," he said, looking Dylan directly in the eyes as he lied to Landry.

"Good. I'll get these guys to the hotel in a couple of hours," Landry said. "Amy did awesome with this one."

"Yeah, she did. I only got one good shot of you in a compromising position. We'll talk about that tomorrow." Tristan chuckled and hung up before Landry could respond.

"I'm not sure I'm in the right frame of mind to talk about business," Dylan said. He'd drunk quite a bit, yet not one of his words came out slurred. It was pretty damn impressive.

"I'm taking you to one of my favorite hangouts. It's discreet, private, and dark. You won't have to worry about anything." Tristan didn't push any further. He looked out the window as the driver drove toward his area of town.

"I think I should just go back to the hotel," Dylan stated flatly, which should have left no room for argument. Tristan wasn't ready to let this go yet, though.

"If you aren't having a good time, we'll leave. No harm, no foul." Tristan refused to say another word. At this point, instinct led him more than anything. Of course he was attracted to the guy. Look at him for Christ's sake, and Tristan had just enough alcohol in him that he did steal a glance, maybe letting his gaze linger a little longer than he should.

Dylan was a hot, sexy man that turned him on, but that didn't mean he'd act on it. No, he wouldn't act at all, but he'd take him someplace a little quieter and maybe a little more appealing to Dylan's eye. He needed to get to know this guy better. At the moment, he wanted Dylan's business more than he wanted his ass. Although, truth be told, he definitely wanted a shot at that tempting ass. Tristan forced his eyes away from the handsome man and prayed he wasn't massively fucking everything up right now.

The flip-flop of his heart made it hard to think. How in the fuck had Tristan figured out what no one else on the planet seemed to be able to? Fear gripped him, but the alcohol truly helped combat his concerns. That was the main reason he'd learned to stay away from drinking. It had a different effect on him than on most people. He didn't get sloppy and slurry, he became completely uninhibited. That was dangerous in situations like this. He'd erroneously thought liquor would help him join in the fun of all those naked women. It hadn't at all.

Dylan watched as they pulled to the front of a high-rise. Nothing about the building gave him any clue what they were really doing, but he had his suspicions.

The alcohol, finding out Tristan was a gay man, and then having that same man call him out had been about all his brain seemed able to process. Never in his thirty-seven years of life had anyone said those words to him. He played the stereotypical hetero husband so well that every person he knew would have sworn the Reeves family stepped out of a Norman Rockwell painting.

Dylan's door opened and he hesitated. His ability to reason made a resurgence, and he couldn't understand why he'd even gotten inside this car. Why hadn't he declared Tristan's words a lie and headed down front to sit with the guys? That would have been the smart thing to do.

Tristan's smooth voice caught his attention as he ducked his head through the open door. "I promise it's discreet. Your secret's safe in here." He hadn't even heard him get out of the car, let alone seen him walk around to Dylan's side. He took a deep breath and steeled his spine. He didn't have to admit to anything. He could deny things starting right now, but at this point, he was holding up traffic and causing a scene.

"Where are we?" he asked weakly. The conviction he just developed hadn't made its way to his voice. There was no way he was going inside a gay bar.

"Chasers. It's a gentleman's dinner club. It's quieter here. A different crowd," Tristan said, extending a hand for Dylan to help get him out of the car.

"I've had a lot to drink. I should probably go back to my hotel," Dylan said lamely, not moving a muscle.

"It's not far. Come have a drink with me, and I'll take you back to your room," Tristan suggested. This time his hand drifted to his arm, gently pulling him from his seat. Dylan stood on the busy street, staring up at the building until Tristan's hand caressed the small of his back. That got him moving. He couldn't let himself be touched. That was too much. Even tipsy, his body stirred and his dick plumped. He moved toward the front doors and decided on water for the rest of the night.

"This way," Tristan said, leading him down a darkened hall to two massive oak doors held open wide. A man dressed in a tuxedo greeted Tristan by name as they entered the dimly lit room.

Funny how he hadn't wanted the guy to touch him, but now that he was here in this place, he didn't want to leave Tristan's side. Staying close, he took in his surroundings. Oversized, black and white prints of men in various stages of undress dominated the charcoal gray walls. A mixture of both large and small tables adorned with black linen cloths and silver table runners filled the room. Expensive crystal fixtures lit the elaborate dining room and bar just enough to give the room an inviting glow. The establishment was completely packed, almost every table occupied. The clientele happened to be all men, no women, and every eye in the place was on him as they entered.

"This way," Tristan said from behind him, and the hand was again at his lower back, guiding him through the room.

A waiter came around the corner wearing low-cut, tight black leather pants, no shirt, but he did have on a bow tie and carried a tray in his hand. He couldn't have been much older than Chad. Dylan stared until Tristan nudged him toward a table in the corner.

"Hey, Tristan, want your usual?" The waiter made his way to their table. Tristan pulled out Dylan's chair before taking the empty one on the opposite side of the small round table.

"That sounds good. Leo meet Dylan."

"Well, hello there, Mr. Dylan, what can I get you?" Leo asked, smiling brightly. The kid was muscular and flexed his biceps. He wasn't sure how to react to the obvious flirting from the waiter. That had Tristan chuckling.

"Water," he stuttered, quickly looking away. The kid was a baby and boldly flirting with him.

"He was drinking a 7 and 7 I believe. Bring him one of those too," Tristan added.

"Got it. Anything else?" Leo asked.

"No, we're fine," Tristan answered.

"Yes, you two sure are," Leo purred, winking at Tristan before leaving the table. Tristan looked around the room, nodding at a couple by the bar, then at another guy dancing on the small dance floor on the other side of the bar. The music was subtle with a seventies feel. Dylan let himself survey his surroundings, but he didn't keep his focus on anyone for too long. As he scanned the room, he noticed almost everyone looked their way. It took a second for him to realize most of the clientele were older and more than one wore a wedding band.

"You come here regularly?" Dylan asked. This actually wasn't that bad of a place. He wouldn't want anyone to know he'd voluntarily come here, but he'd expected something completely different.

"Yes, and you have to have a membership. Very exclusive. No one should know you. What happens here, stays here. Confidentiality's required," Tristan said casually, sitting back and relaxing as he loosened his tie even farther and rolled up his sleeves. "I'm sure quite a few of these men are married to women."

"I noticed the wedding bands, but it's hard to tell nowadays. Do you hide?" Dylan asked, not necessarily ready to give up the panic, but willing to at least listen.

"Not even a little bit, but I get why you do," Tristan said, giving him a wink.

"I haven't admitted to anything." Dylan hoped he didn't sound too defensive as he looked away and back out over the bar.

"No, you haven't," Tristan agreed as their drinks were placed in front of him. "Keep 'em coming, Leo."

"He doesn't say much." Leo inclined his head toward Dylan.

"He will. He's new. We just have to make him feel comfortable." Tristan took a drink.

"Then drink up, the alcohol really helps. Tristan's a good guy. He'll make sure you get home in one piece," Leo urged, grinning down at him. Dylan completely closed up at those words. No way was he commenting on any of this. Leo chuckled and gave Tristan a fist bump before he left.

"He's about the same age as my daughter."

"No, he's not. He's twenty-seven and no way you're old enough to have a daughter that age."

The guy looked much younger. "I'm thirty-seven," Dylan admitted. Tristan lifted his glass.

"See? Honesty's a good thing."

"You're younger than I am." Dylan ignored the last comment.

Tristan smiled as he swallowed. "I am, but not by much. So, tell me, how did you end up with a wife and three children?"

Dylan took a drink of the water, but Tristan pushed the 7 and 7 over to him. "It's really okay. No one will ever know you were here. We're just two work associates having a drink."

Dylan stared at him long and hard before he picked up the drink. "Teri was my girlfriend in college. She was also my best friend, still is. We partied hard together all the time. My college days are a little hazy. Partying, denial, and lots of alcohol have been a part of everything wrong with my life. I decided alcohol gave me something to hide behind. Still does, I guess." He took a long drink.

"What's that mean?" Tristan asked quietly.

"I liked drinking. Perhaps a little too much. You know, it helped me hide all those confusing feelings when I was younger," Dylan answered honestly.

"So, you do or don't drink because you are or aren't an alcoholic?" Tristan asked, clearly confused. Dylan got he wasn't making any sense. He'd never admitted any of this out loud before.

He had at least a dozen or more drinks tonight already. He could see how Tristan had gotten the wrong idea, but his nerves needed a crap load of calming by the time they'd arrived at their earlier venue. Then between the attraction he felt for Tristan and the strip club, his limits had really been pushed. This was exactly why he planned his life so carefully.

"I really don't drink much anymore. I don't think I was an alcoholic, I mean…I didn't have to have a drink. Things were just easier when I did. I never acted drunk so I could hide how much I was actually drinking. I ended up getting my college girlfriend pregnant—three times before I was twenty-one—and I honestly don't remember much about that time in my life. Thanks to this." Dylan held up his 7 and 7 that he was drinking much slower now. "Don't get me wrong, I love my family and I'm thankful for them. I absolutely wouldn't be here talking to Wilder, Inc. about a buyout without them."

"You don't have to hide around me. I'm not going to judge you," Tristan added, clearly trying to keep Dylan talking in order to fill in the holes to this crazy story.

"How did you know about me?"

"I wasn't a hundred percent sure until right now. But the way you avoided my eyes at the strip club when I told you I was gay made me guess," Tristan answered. "I can't promise you enough that your secret's safe with me. Based on what you're saying though, I'm surely not the only one who knows."

"No. My wife knows." Dylan ran his finger down the side of his glass, leaving a trail through the condensation gathered there.

Tristan's head tilted and his eyes narrowed as if he were trying to absorb that little bit of knowledge before he finally spoke. "This gets weirder and weirder."

"Not so much. At least I don't think so. I woke up one day and I had three kids and a wife. Both of us were still in college and I was working my ass off trying to do what I thought I needed to do. We were broke as hell, but making it work. I just couldn't lie to her any longer so we had a heart-to-heart. I told her I was gay. She eventually took it all in stride. She's an amazing woman. We decided to raise the kids together, get our education, and when they grew up, we'd still be young and could go our separate ways, get on with our lives."

"How's that working?" Tristan asked.

"My youngest graduates in nine months. They're all going away to school. Teri's already spreading her wings. She's on a cruise right now with a man she's been serious with for a few years now. I'm just stalling, I guess." Dylan picked up his 7 and 7 and took a long drink. Cate's news that she'd be leaving almost a year earlier than planned and Teri getting serious with Mark made things a little more real for Dylan.

"So you gave up your youth for your kids?" Tristan sounded incredulous.

"It's not like that. They're good kids. I'm lucky to have them. I wouldn't change that part of my life for anything," Dylan reassured him. "Besides, they didn't ask to be born. It wasn't their fault I didn't have the balls to be me. Teri's a good woman; I live with my best friend."

"Okay, I understand that and really have no experience to speak from. Here's another question. You're uncomfortable here, I can tell. You don't want anyone to know…" Tristan's brows lifted and he leaned across the table. "If you haven't told anyone else, who do you fuck?"

Dylan remained silent. What could he say?

"Oh man, no way." Tristan shook his head. He didn't laugh but Dylan could see him hiding the chuckle behind his glass as he drained it quickly. He lifted a hand to get Leo's attention. "Drink up! You deserve to have a good time tonight. It's part of our goal in bringing you guys here from Texas. And we're dancing at least once before we leave."

"No, I can't…"

"The fuck you can't. Leo's right, I'll make sure you get to your room safe. Drink up, have a good time. Besides, I owe this to you. It does my heart good to know you're gay and you trust me enough to tell me. And so you know, every guy in this room wants to know who you are. They're still staring. As for me? Straight guys and deeply closeted guys aren't normally my thing, but you… Yeah, you're sexy as hell. And now I'm glad I pushed, because I get to be here tonight with the hottest man in the room." Tristan flashed that killer smile at him.

Dylan remained quiet. Actually his brain was on overload and just downright fuzzy. Had he heard those words right? Was Tristan flirting with him? Tristan watched him and laughed straight out loud. "I'll remember this quiet thing you do. It makes you mysterious and that's hot as hell, too."

Leo came to the table with two drinks even though Dylan hadn't finished his first one.

"I'm fine," Dylan said, rejecting the second drink.

"Yes, you are, indeed." Tristan winked, keeping his eyes trained on Dylan. He could feel the heat creeping up his cheeks at the compliment. God, he was such a dork. Guys like Tristan Wilder didn't pursue guys like him. He was only being nice, probably because he had come off so fucking pathetic. He should have lied about the sex thing. "Leave the drink, Leo, and keep 'em coming. We're celebrating tonight!"

CHAPTER.07

The dance hadn't been terrible, Tristan thought as he stepped away from the man who was bowed up so tight he could barely execute a proper sway. Last call had come and gone, almost everyone had paired up and left for the night and the few stragglers remaining in the club were well past drunk. It had been the only way he could get Dylan up and onto the dance floor.

"Are you ready to go?" Tristan asked, beginning to regret his decision to bring Dylan here. Who was he to push his lifestyle on anyone, especially someone buried so deeply in the closet? Tristan didn't wait for an answer. Instead, he left the dance floor, walking back to the table as the lights blinked on in the club.

"Closing time," someone called out from behind the bar.

Tristan grabbed his tie, tossing the silk strip carelessly over his shoulder, and scribbled his name on the tab. He did some quick math for a tip, added more than what he should, and looked up. Dylan was a few feet away from him, standing alone in the foyer. The stark white light of the club hid nothing, and he was struck again at what a good-looking man Dylan Reeves truly was. Right now, Dylan had his head bowed, his hands slid deep inside his pockets, and he kicked at something with his foot. The line of that hard tight body was more pronounced, and Tristan wondered how he had missed that before. When they danced, that was when he'd noticed the deep ridges and valleys of his muscular torso and arms. He'd also felt the size of what Dylan had going on in those slacks. It was really the only physical proof he'd gotten all night long that Dylan was into him.

"He's a keeper, man," Leo said from behind Tristan.

"Mmm, I do agree. For someone else though, not me. It's business." Tristan picked up the payment book and handed it to Leo.

"Nah, you need to hear me, dude. He only had eyes for you tonight. Everybody tried to get his attention. He's about you," the waiter replied. Tristan looked back at Dylan who was still kicking at something in the carpet.

"He's got a wife and kids," Tristan found himself saying.

"Yeah and so do half the guys in this place," Leo replied. Tristan looked the waiter in the eyes for several long moments, contemplating what he just heard. Did he miss those signals? Unable to find an answer quickly, he patted the guy on the shoulder and turned to walk toward Dylan.

"You ready?" Tristan asked, stopping in front of Dylan. He placed his hand on Dylan's forearm to test the waters. Dylan moved immediately out from under the touch like he'd done over and over throughout the entire night. Yeah, Leo read him completely wrong.

"It's late. It's been a while since I've been out like this in a bar," Dylan admitted as he walked out the front door.

"Me, too. The hotel's a block or two from here," Tristan added. Dylan stopped and looked down the street, his eyes moving up, looking at something in the distance. Tristan followed his gaze to the tallest high-rise downtown. The building with the bright red H encased in a circle, shooting up from the street and towering in the night sky. He had to admit, from here, the view was quite magnificent.

"Is that where we're staying?" Dylan asked.

"The Hilton, yes," Tristan confirmed.

"I can walk. It'll do me good to clear my head," Dylan said. He wasn't asking, more telling Tristan that he planned to walk the distance. Dylan went to the car, grabbed his suit jacket out of the backseat, and slid it on to his shoulders. "Thank you for tonight."

Tristan got the impression that the response had more to do with those Southern manners he'd heard so much about than truth. Dylan turned away and started walking toward the hotel. "Wait, I'll walk with you. It's not the best part of town."

"I got it. I'll be fine," Dylan called back, now several feet from him. "Goodnight."

"Follow us," Tristan told the driver as he tossed his jacket into the backseat. He had to jog a few steps to catch up. That seemed to surprise the man.

"I'm fine. Really. Get in your car and go," Dylan demanded, his steps faltering.

"I'm not letting you walk alone out here. A walk will be good for me." Tristan dropped his hands in his slacks and walked beside Dylan, matching his stride. "Did you have a good time tonight or did I overstep?" Tristan asked, changing the subject when it looked like Dylan was still going to argue this out. It took the length of an entire block for Dylan to finally answer.

"It scares me a little." Surprised at Dylan's honesty, Tristan gave him a sideways glance.

"How?" he asked. He needed to know exactly where that came from so he could conquer and ease that thought.

"I've kept this secret for so long it's hard to let anyone know," Dylan explained, his eyes on the concrete in front of him with each step he took.

"But you would soon enough. Your kids are growing up. It's time for you to move on," Tristan repeated Dylan's words back to him. Dylan didn't respond to that. "This quiet thing you do's hard to gauge."

"I've always had to keep quiet," Dylan answered, avoiding his eyes.

"You're a good-looking guy. You'll find someone in no time when you finally come out." Tristan bumped Dylan's shoulder.

"It's not about that," Dylan sighed.

"It should be. You've lived your whole life alone—" Tristan started.

"I'm not alone," Dylan cut in.

"Let me finish, you've spent your whole life alone, hiding a main part of who you are. It must be daunting to consider finally revealing yourself. You don't seem like the player type. Once you're out, someone's gonna snatch you up."

Dylan laughed a little as they turned a corner to the hotel walkway. "I'm just an average guy. If I looked like you, I'd totally be a player." Those unguarded words sent panic to Dylan's eyes, and his gaze darted up, colliding with Tristan's. He gave a genuine smile. He'd been told over and over that he was nice on the eyes. He didn't really have a problem getting guys, but something about this man thinking he was handsome made him feel good.

"Thank you for that," Tristan said honestly, his smile still in place. Dylan remained quiet as they walked up the steps to the hotel. A bellboy opened the main doors.

"Where's the reservation desk?" Tristan asked.

"Right over there, sir," the bellhop pointed to an area in front of them. Tristan didn't say anything more as he went to the desk and got Dylan's room key.

"Here you go. Thank you for going with me tonight. I hope I didn't freak you out too much," Tristan apologized as they walked toward the elevators.

"You did, a little. But it's okay. I can get to the room from here. You don't have to walk me up," Dylan said as Tristan punched the call button. An elevator opened, but neither man stepped away. For the second time tonight, they were standing almost chest to chest, staring at each other. Tristan realized then that he hadn't made a mistake by taking Dylan to the club and perhaps the visit fueled the small amount of interest showing in Dylan's eyes.

"I know you can. I'm just finding I like to do these things for you," Tristan answered in all honesty. That drew a hint of color to Dylan's cheeks, but he didn't look away.

"I'm going up now." Dylan hooked a thumb toward the elevator doors that were closing and Tristan reached out to press the up button again. The doors slid immediately open, but neither took their eyes off the other.

"Since we won't speak of this again this weekend, when you do decide to come out, I want to be first on your list of people you visit. Hell, I'll even come to you. I bet you're spectacular in bed." Tristan grinned. He meant those words. But his confession drew nothing but silence from Dylan.

"I'm going," Dylan repeated, and this time, he took a couple of steps backward, throwing out an arm to keep the elevator doors from closing again.

"Goodnight, Dylan," Tristan replied, forcing himself to remain in place. No matter what he thought, Dylan's hesitation wasn't an invitation. He was curious and perhaps relieved that finally someone else knew.

Dylan lifted a hand and stepped inside as the alarm sounded. Tristan was forced to watch as the doors closed, severing that momentary bond he thought he felt. He was proud of himself for not following. His body on the other hand vehemently disagreed. He forced himself to turn around and leave. Those few minutes by the elevator had been intense. He hadn't realized that while he was under Dylan's spell. He slowly made his way across the hotel lobby, thinking about that departing look in Dylan's eyes. It hadn't been an invitation. Right?

That notion had Tristan faltering at the front door. Had he let Dylan slip through his fingers? No. Right? Not knowing what else to do, he walked out the revolving door and down the front steps to his waiting car. He pivoted on his feet, looking up at the high-rise. He wouldn't know if he didn't ask. He went back up the steps and through the turning door, palming his phone to dial Dylan's cell.

"Hello?" there was a question in that sexy voice.

"Let me come up," Tristan blurted suddenly into the phone.

"I don't think that's a good idea," Dylan replied. It wasn't a no, just not a good idea. *Okaay*.

"Then come home with me. I'll get you back to your room in time to change before our meeting tomorrow," Tristan pleaded, and he was met with silence. That had him smiling.

"I won't push you into anything you don't want to do. I just want to spend time with you," Tristan continued.

"Do you have condoms?"

Tristan's head popped up at that question. *Score!* And then his smile faded. "Wait, do you?" If Dylan brought condoms, he wasn't the virgin he claimed to be.

"No, but we can stop. I wanna use them," Dylan replied. Tristan heard the hotel door shut with a loud thump and started toward the bank of elevators.

"I always do. No problem there," he assured Dylan.

"I'm on my way down."

"I'll be waiting at the elevators." Hell yeah, he was having hot Dylan Reeves sex tonight. Damn, that man was sexy. He was amazed at how quickly things were going from good to amazing. Who would have known?

CHAPTER.08

The pounding of his heart overrode the crazy panicked thoughts racing through his head. He pressed the down button on the elevator, and he honestly believed he'd have a heart attack right there waiting for the doors to open. The longer the elevator took, the more he started to panic. This night wasn't in his life plan.

But who would ever know? Thoughts of his very brief make-out session with his college roommate's brother surfaced—he'd never told a soul about that experience. A stolen moment that never really amounted to much, yet taught him without question that he was absolutely a gay man. If he never said a word and was incredibly careful, no one would know about this either.

Dylan groaned and shook his arms to dispel some of the nervous energy coursing through him. He'd promised himself long ago he'd wait until the children were grown to explore what he felt so deeply in his heart. If he went through with this, was he breaking his vow? He was a man who lived by honor. *Rigid to a fault in his convictions...* Those were Teri's words not his. Teri had continually encouraged him to find someone to be with, but he'd always been apprehensive. Yet in just a matter of a few hours, Tristan had him rethinking everything.

The elevator doors opened, and Dylan stood there, frozen in the deserted hallway, not budging until they closed again. His eyes shut and regret filled his heart when he couldn't step on. He'd had fun tonight. He wouldn't admit that before now, but he'd had fun. He'd enjoyed the evening so much he hadn't wanted tonight to end. The single dance they shared had been awkward at first, mainly due to him being so uptight, but he'd tried to relax. Toward the end of the dance, he'd managed to loosen up a little. Not completely, but his anxiety had diminished and he'd been pretty proud of that.

Dylan's hard cock pressed against Tristan while they swayed together on the dance floor. He had no doubt Tristan felt his arousal. And Tristan hadn't been unaffected; he could tell that too with each brush of their hips. But that didn't necessarily mean he was the reason for Tristan's response. There were lots of men there watching the guy closely, but he liked those few grinds he got when they danced.

His phone beeped. *"Did you change your mind?"* Tristan's words appeared on his screen.

Had he changed his mind? He forced himself to push the elevator call button again. Going with Tristan tonight did not mean he had to fuck him. He could put that limit on them when he got downstairs. He had enjoyed Tristan's company, and with all the melancholy he'd been experiencing over the last week, he needed a friend. It was way past time to have companions for himself, just like Teri had suggested.

Decision firmly made, he looked up when the elevator dinged its arrival. Distracted, he took a step forward, unprepared to see Tristan stepping out.

"What do you want, Dylan? What do you feel?" Tristan asked quietly, keeping about a foot of distance between them.

"I'm not sure. What if I'm not ready to take this next step?" Dylan whispered, searching Tristan's face as the elevator doors closed behind him.

"Then we won't. It's as simple as that. You call the shots, but I'd really like to kiss you." Tristan's voice lowered and his gaze dropped to Dylan's lips. "I've wanted to taste your lips all night." Tristan took a single step forward but didn't touch him. That one simple act endeared the man to Dylan. Tristan had kept his word, letting him make the first move. Something occurred to him in that moment; since WilderNation made the reservations, he had to assume he'd been placed on the same floor with Rob and David. He needed to get out of this hallway before one of them caught him.

"I won't push you," Tristian promised.

Dylan nodded and leaned in to press the down arrow again for the third time. The move drew him closer to Tristan who didn't step away. It could have been his imagination, but he swore Tristan bent over and sniffed him when he reached for the button. The awareness had his heart racing even faster. He wasn't sure how to react, so he kept his eyes downcast, finding the dark pattern on the highly polished marble very interesting. He couldn't help the small smile spreading on his lips.

"You smell incredible," Tristan finally said. Dylan stayed quiet, but lifted his eyes to meet Tristan's. They held the gaze until the elevator doors opened. Tristan took his arm and drew him into the empty elevator before he could change his mind.

"I'm glad you decided to come, because I really do want to kiss you," Tristan chuckled, releasing his arm. Tristan stepped to the back and he followed. Could he really do it? He turned his body toward Tristan and lifted his face. No words were spoken. Tristan understood his silence and took Dylan's face between his palms and slowly leaned in for the softest, briefest of kisses. Dylan kept his eyes half open, allowing himself to just be in the moment. His breathing picked up as Tristan's firm lips moved against his. He wanted to deepen the kiss, but Tristan stepped away before the doors opened to the lobby of the hotel.

"You ready, handsome?" Tristan asked, extending a hand, his eyes still focused on Dylan's lips.

Dylan was lost in a haze. He hadn't even known how long he'd stood there before Tristan spoke. He finally turned to the open doors, and with all the emotion rolling through him, he'd assumed every eye in the place would be on him, but no one looked their way.

"I'm parked right out front," Tristan announced, walking stride for stride with Dylan. "The driver can bring you back when you're ready to leave."

"Is he on call all the time?" Dylan asked, going through the front doors. Tristan moved him toward the town car that sat to the right. This time the driver sat inside the car while Tristan got the door for Dylan.

"Pretty much. There are four of them on call twenty-four-seven. I don't drink and drive, so I need rides," Tristan responded, sliding in right next to Dylan. It took a second for him to slide across the backseat. He'd expected Tristan to round the trunk and enter from the other side.

Tristan rewarded him with a deep moan and a "not too far over." He placed a hand on his arm, stopping him in the middle of the seat. "We're headed to my place," Tristan told the driver before closing the partition between the front and backseat. The glass wasn't completely raised before Tristan placed an arm around his shoulders and descended on him. This wasn't the sweet soft kiss from before. Tristan ate at his mouth, his teeth nipping and sliding across his lips, his tongue pressing and probing.

Dylan opened under Tristan's insistence. How long had it been since he kissed anyone with passion? Longer than he could even remember. That thought made him insecure, but Tristan seemed immune to his inner turmoil. Finally he pushed the thoughts from his head and just let himself feel. He gave in to his desire and for the first time in his life, he allowed himself to be swept away by his true needs. Tristan increased the tempo he'd created, turning Dylan's head to delve deeper. Tristan was a pro. Something straight out of a romance novel. Tristan caressed him the whole time, slowly removing his suit jacket and partially unbuttoning his shirt. Dylan concentrated on the kiss until Tristan's palm touched his chest, now only covered in the thin white shirt he'd worn under his button-down. That sensation along with the unrelenting fantastic tongue had him wrenching free, his hand moving to hold Tristan's there against his chest and nipple.

"Damn, you're good at this," Dylan whispered, his hips arched up automatically, seeking Tristan's touch. They weren't exactly lying across the seat, but Dylan was askew with Tristan almost on top of him.

"I haven't even started," Tristan replied. He latched a finger on to Dylan's, keeping their hands together as he slid both of their palms lower. Tristan didn't have to do anything more than graze Dylan's dick through his slacks and his eyes rolled back into his head and his hips pitched forward as a deep moan escaped his lips.

"Fuck, you're gonna be hot tonight," Tristan growled and gripped him, palming him outside his slacks. Dylan pushed at Tristan's hands.

"I'll come," he panted.

"Oh, I plan on it," Tristan chuckled and gripped him a little tighter.

"No, right now. I'll come right now." Dylan panicked and shoved Tristan's hand off him, scooting away. Not that there was a lot of room, they were already stretched across the backseat. He slid to the other side of the car. Tristan followed right behind him. Dylan extended a hand, pushing him back. "It's been too long. Stay over there."

That had Tristan giving him a little bit of a break. He didn't back away. He moved in for another kiss, keeping the contact soft. "I'm so gonna enjoy this tonight."

"And I'm afraid I'll embarrass myself," he said between the small kisses.

"Not possible. We'll take things slow, I promise," Tristan whispered and caressed the side of his face. "We're here."

Dylan looked out the window. The car had come to a stop in front of an over-the-top mansion. His look of shock had Tristan smiling again. "Good. I'm glad you like it. You've kept me shocked and surprised all night long. Turnabout's fair play. Come on, handsome."

Tristan took the front steps up to the house. He held Dylan's hand the entire way. Not for the intimacy of the act, but to keep him right there beside him. Dylan was definitely on the edge of flight mode. He shouldn't have pushed him. He actually shouldn't have gone up the elevator when Dylan took so long, but something about helping this guy discover himself seemed to turn his shit on like nothing else ever had before.

Tristan punched in the security code for the house. The locks were tied into the security system and the front door opened. "After you."

Dylan entered first, looking around the room. Tristan turned on lamps as he walked through the house. When he reached the kitchen, he opened the back of the house and flipped the switch, letting the lights flood the back deck.

"Oh my god," Dylan said from the living room. "Is that the ocean?"

"It is. You can see better during the day. I have a swimming pool out there if you want to take a dip. Hang on,

I'll be right back," Tristan called, going back to his bedroom. He tossed his suit jacket over the rack in his closet and dug out an old pair of jeans and T-shirt. He changed quickly before going into the bathroom and brushing his teeth and running a comb through his sandy blond hair.

He'd not been this excited about a night in a long time, and it surprised him. Taking a closeted gay man's virginity had never been on his bucket list, but he also hadn't ever met anyone like Dylan Reeves. He was gorgeous, no question there, and from the brief grope he got, he knew the man was packing, but he also seemed like an honest-to-goodness good guy. Maybe even one of those salt-of-the-earth types, and he couldn't remember the last time he'd come across someone as intriguing.

On a whim, he stopped by his nightstand, flipping on that light as he grabbed a couple of condoms and a pack of lube from the drawer. This might turn into a deck-side experience. Who knew for sure? Tristan went through the back of his bedroom, laid the condoms on a deck table as he approached Dylan who stood along the deck railing, looking out over the ocean. Tristan did that very same thing all the time. It was the key reason he'd bought this place in the first place.

"Would you like something to drink?" Tristan asked, walking toward him. He saw Dylan had left those few buttons undone on his dress shirt, and now his long sleeves were rolled up almost to the elbow, revealing strong, sexy forearms.

"I'm fine. I've drunk too much tonight already," Dylan said, and Tristan remembered the too much drinking in college story. He strolled over to the rail, and instead of looking out at the ocean, he leaned on the metal bar and watched Dylan.

"You're incredibly handsome. You've never been with a man before?"

"Not sex," Dylan supplied honestly.

"I'm honored you want me to be your first," Tristan said, his voice deep with the reality of how true those words really were.

"You don't have to say things like that," Dylan started, but Tristan stopped him, making his move. He pulled Dylan between his parted legs and gathered him in his arms.

"You'll learn soon enough that I always speak the truth. Sometimes you'll like me for it, sometimes you won't," Tristan admitted, unbuttoning another three buttons of Dylan's shirt before he pulled at the ends tucked tightly in his slacks. "I felt an amazingly hard body under your clothes when we danced. I'd like to see for myself."

Dylan released the remaining buttons, and Tristan was able to smooth his palms up Dylan's chest, across his shoulders, and help slide the dress shirt down his arms until the material fell to the floor. A smile touched his lips as he looked over this very surprising man.

"Nice, but this has got to go." Tristan plucked at the white undershirt that clung suggestively to Dylan's body. "Lift your arms." He gathered the thin cloth in his fists, lifted it over Dylan's head, then dropped it on the ground next to the dress shirt.

"That's more like it," Tristan said as he slid his palms appreciatively up Dylan's slim waist, lightly skimming over his ribs, before stopping on the man's firm pectoral muscles. "Do you swim?"

"I run," Dylan said, looking down at Tristan's hands on his chest. Tristan could feel Dylan's dick swelling against his with each movement he made.

"And lift a little?" Tristan urged Dylan's hips forward until they were nestled tightly together. Tristan was already hard. Had been since they'd slow-danced earlier in the evening. He wanted Dylan to feel exactly how badly he wanted him.

"Not as much as you," Dylan said, running a palm across Tristan's bicep. Goose bumps sprang up on his arm, and Dylan must have felt them, because he immediately stopped. "Are you cold?"

"No, not at all," Tristan said with a laugh. "I'm turned the fuck on, but not cold." That had Dylan's eyes locked on his. Surprisingly Dylan lifted his hands, tangling his fingers in the sides of Tristan's hair, and initiated a kiss. Tristan opened for him, wrapping his arms tighter around Dylan, bringing him closer against his chest.

There were no awkward moments, no testing the waters, almost as if they'd done this before. Dylan slid his tongue in perfect rhythm with Tristan as he slowly began to fuck his mouth. Any concern he had that Dylan might not be as into this vanished. Tristan ran his hands up and down Dylan's back then grabbed each ass cheek and ground forward, matching the kiss with the movement from his hips. Dylan's mouth went slack as he threw his head back and moaned. Tristan latched on to his neck, working his way to his ear.

"I can't wait to make you come. How many times can I make you come in a night?" Tristan breathed against Dylan's ear. Dylan trembled in his arms as he spoke the words. "One...two...?"

"More," he said so quietly Tristan almost hadn't heard him. He began unbuckling and unbuttoning Dylan's pants as he kissed a trail down his chest. He took care with each nipple as Dylan's hands cupped the back of his head and pushed him lower.

It didn't take much to get Dylan's slacks to drop to the deck. Tristan smiled at the standard Fruit of the Loom tighty-whities he wore. Evidently Dylan was a briefs guy. "Change places with me." Tristan bent over and pulled off Dylan's loafers, then helped him out of his slacks before pressing Dylan against the rail.

"You say when you've had enough." Tristan looked up at Dylan as he slid his hand along the waistband and slowly started to lower Dylan's tented briefs. Tristan dropped to his knees in front of Dylan and mouthed that wet spot on those tighty-whities before slowly pulling them down and out of his way. When that perfect cock sprang free, Tristan abandoned the task and immediately reached for the jutting length.

"You're a big boy, Mr. Reeves." Tristan grinned and gave a long slow tug on the cock in his hand, sliding from tip to base and back again. Tristan slid his thumb around the slit, briefly dipping his nail into the small opening. Dylan squirmed and hissed a needy breath, his eyes glazed over as he gripped the rail behind him.

Tristan licked his lips and reached for Dylan's sac; he tugged and pressed, rolling the soft tender skin in his palm, fondling his balls. "Shit, Tristan." The desperation he heard in Dylan's voice let him know that he was close to coming. He obviously hadn't lied when he said it had been a while. So Tristan firmed his grip, fisting Dylan even tighter.

"Hold it for me, Dylan, as long as you can." Tristan kissed Dylan's weeping head then opened his mouth wide, sliding Dylan all the way in. The grip on his hair tightened to painful degrees. Tristan continued to work Dylan's balls, tenderly manipulating them in his hand. He slid Dylan slowly out of his mouth, flattening his tongue against the underside before curling around the tip and sucking lightly. This time he took him all, opening his throat, loosening his jaw. Pre-come coated his tongue and Dylan's essence dominated his senses. Unintelligible words came from the space above him as Dylan tried to push away. Tristan grabbed on to his ass, digging his fingers deep into that firm flesh, and kept him buried in his mouth, sucking and working his tongue in rhythm along Dylan's length.

"I'm coming," Dylan shouted and tried again to move away from him. Tristan held tight and swallowed deeper, urging him to let go. He moaned around Dylan's cock as the salty release filled his mouth and coated his tongue. Tonight, he craved anything and everything this man was willing to give him. Dylan's knees buckled when he began to lick him clean.

Tristan ran his tongue along the shaft before he reached out to steady him and stood, only after finishing his task. Tristan drew Dylan to him, holding him close as the man panted against his shoulder. Minutes passed, neither said a word, only their heavy breathing occupied the space around them. Running a soothing hand up and down his back, Tristan pressed his lips to the pulsing vein in his neck. Dylan's hold slowly tightened around him. The steady heartbeat under his lips started to even out, along with his breathing.

"I tried to pull away," Dylan whispered into his T-shirt.

"I didn't want you to," Tristan replied. Dylan was silent for several long seconds.

"That might have been the best of my life," Dylan confided sweetly, turning his head where his warm breath skimmed along Tristan's neck and jawline. He liked that feeling and held him tighter if that were even possible. "Do you always swallow?"

"Not always, but I wanted to with you," Tristan answered quietly, watching the waves roll across the water. He couldn't remember ever doing this before. Standing fully clothed, content to just hold a man, being totally in the moment with him, while staring out into the ocean. He ran a hand up Dylan's spine into his hair. "What did you think? Was it different or the same?"

"Different. Most definitely different," Dylan responded, then lifted his head. "It was amazing and I... It's just been a long time." Dylan's voice dropped. Tristan could tell the nerves were back.

"You don't have to explain anything. I get it. I wouldn't have lasted that long if I'd gone without as long as you." Tristan kissed the top of Dylan's head.

"You still have your clothes on," Dylan pointed out.

"You could take them off me." Tristan grinned.

"You'd have to loosen your hold." Dylan chuckled and leaned back, giving him a lazy, sated smile. Damn, he loved that he'd put that smile there.

"I don't think I'm willing to let you go, Mr. Reeves. You feel good against me." Dylan grinned at the words and rested his forehead back on Tristan's shoulder. Tristan held him there, running his fingers through his silky hair. Dylan casually slid his hands under the hem of his T-shirt and tugged it over his head, carelessly tossing the shirt aside. Their chests were bare and the cool night air blew across his heated skin. Dylan was bolder now and palmed his ass, pulling him closer. From the feel of things, he'd already begun to stir back to life. "So do you want to do the honors or should I?"

"Do you normally bottom?" Dylan asked after a moment's pause. The look on his face said he'd not been sure.

"Tonight's different." Tristan softly kissed those perfect lips.

Dylan's pupils were huge as he looked him straight in the eyes, need and longing reflected back at him. Damn, this man was pushing his way so far inside his heart. He could see the struggle he was going to have when the time came for him to let go. Leo had been right—Dylan Reeves was definitely a keeper.

"Out here on the deck or in the house?" Tristan finally asked.

"I'd feel more comfortable inside," Dylan answered honestly.

"Then let's go." Tristan took Dylan's hand and pulled him toward the bedroom.

CHAPTER.09

Dylan lay wrapped in the security of Tristan's arms. The scent, the touch, the feel of the other man enveloped him and brought something foreign to the surface of his soul. Dylan had never felt more alive than in this moment. Wanting a connection like this for so long and then being tempted with everything he'd ever dreamed of scared him, but at the same time excited him beyond words.

"Do you watch porn?" Tristan questioned, his breath swirling in little puffs across Dylan's lips. He fumbled with the buttons on Tristan's jeans.

"I don't watch it on a regular basis," Dylan answered. Damn, he couldn't get his hands on Tristan fast enough. He shoved against the material separating him from Tristan's warmth.

"Why?" Tristan helped by pushing his pants down his legs and stepping out of them in the middle of the floor. Tristan guided him toward the bed.

"It's something I can't have, so watching's almost like a punishment."

Tristan's expression softened. "You can have anything you want, Dylan. I'm more than happy to explore each and every one of your fantasies." Tristan took his mouth in a blistering kiss. He opened under the assault, moaning as Tristan's tongue slid against his. He tasted himself mixed with the alcohol he and Tristan had drunk earlier, and damn, it was a heady mix. Just the thought of what Tristan had done to him had him craving more. He took the initiative and deepened the kiss, searching and probing the farthest reaches of Tristan's mouth.

Tristan was completely naked as he broke from the heated kiss and strolled to the bedside table on the other side of the bed. Dylan couldn't tear his gaze from the tempting sight in front of him. His body vibrated from the adrenaline coursing through his veins and the promise of something he had wanted for so long completely within his grasp. Tristan dug around in the top drawer. Both men watched one another, then a suggestive grin slid across Tristan's face as he pulled several packets and a bottle of lube from the drawer.

"In my haste to get you in my bed, I left the other ones outside on the deck table." Tristan shut the drawer and crawled onto the bed, watching him the whole time.

"You're too far away from me." Tristan crooked his finger and motioned for him to come closer. The fire in Tristan's gaze had Dylan's body heating to the point of boiling. "You're so beautiful, you have no idea how much I want you." Dylan's first reaction at hearing those words was to cover his erection, hide his need. He'd hidden his needs for so long that giving in to them now somehow seemed wrong. He was so fucking messed up in his head. It amazed him Tristan would even give him this time. No, he wouldn't spend another second on this mental bullshit. Besides, how could giving in to his desires be wrong and yet feel so right at the same time?

"Don't close up on me now," Tristan said, crawling closer.

"This just seems so…" He didn't know how to put his thoughts into words. He would have used the word surreal but it seemed too clichéd at the moment. The passion he found in Tristan's eyes chased the doubt from his thoughts and made this experience so much more than his first fuck. Tristan was making this moment special and right, everything he'd dreamed of.

"Being here with you just makes everything so real."

Tristan sat up on his knees and held out his hand. It took a moment, but Dylan joined him on the bed. Tristan took Dylan's hand and poured the lube directly on his fingers. He turned around and placed the bottle close by, then spread his ass cheek to the side as he balanced on his knees.

"This is real and I'm all yours. Touch me," Tristan growled.

Dylan could hardly wrap his mind around all the emotions coursing through him at the moment, but this was exactly what he'd always wanted. The man's ass was pure perfection. He ran the tip of his trembling finger around Tristan's rim, making sure there was plenty of lube before he pressed into Tristan's ass. The warmth and tightness that greeted him constricted his balls, kicking up the beat of his heart. Dylan took his time, massaging the rim, exploring the contour and texture of that taut ring of muscle before he slid his slick hand along the crevice of Tristan's ass and then back down again. He watched the muscles in Tristan's back flex as he gently eased his finger past the rim, until his digit was completely inside the snug, warm confines of Tristan's body.

Tristan stayed silent, except for quiet moans of encouragement. He lifted his knee as he lowered his head, and his fingers gripped the duvet. Dylan wasn't entirely certain of everything to do to get a man ready for such a breach, so he winged it, doing a combination of massaging the rim and moving his finger slowly in and out. He'd had sex before, many times, but nothing prepared him for his feelings and emotions at his first sexual experience with a man.

He could feel Tristan loosening, the ring of muscle relaxing with his continued touch. He had the deep desire to use his tongue where his thumb worked. His mouth watered at the thought of licking at the tempting flesh, but he held off and added another digit, better stretching and working Tristan's hot channel. He'd honestly never seen anything so beautiful as his fingers disappearing in and pulling out of Tristan's body. The slight moans and small movement of Tristan's hips encouraged him to keep going. He couldn't believe how easy it was to be with this man. He should be nervous, but he couldn't find it within himself to dredge up that now foreign emotion.

He pressed in and pulled out, over and over. Need and lust like none he'd ever known slammed into him the longer he watched this show in front of him. His cock ached with anticipation. He couldn't ever remember needing to be buried in someone as much as he needed to feel this man's warmth surrounding him.

"That's it, baby, fuck me with your fingers." Tristan groaned and pressed his ass back harder against Dylan's hand.

Dylan searched out that knot with the tip of his finger. He wasn't as experienced as Tristan but he knew all about the prostate. Tristan moaned again and shoved back harder against his hand. He'd finally found what he was looking for and curled his fingers, making sure he massaged that gland every time he entered Tristan's body. God, he wanted nothing more than to give Tristan pleasure. Yes, this was technically his first time with a man, but he'd had his own fingers up his ass plenty and knew exactly how good it could feel. He twisted his fingers and Tristan bucked.

"Give me more, Dylan... Need to feel you stretching my ass," Tristan begged. Dylan's cock leaked pre-come freely now as his balls drew up tightly against his body. He could come from just watching Tristan's ass take his fingers.

With Tristan's encouragement, Dylan slammed his fingers in and out of Tristan a few more times before withdrawing them completely. He couldn't wait any longer or he'd truly come on himself from just the pleasure of giving Tristan what he wanted. He made quick work with the condom, gripped his own dick, and drizzled lube over the latex. With his hand Dylan spread the slick liquid and lined up with Tristan's entrance. This was it, the moment he'd waited for, the moment he'd denied himself for so long. He circled the rim of Tristan's ass with his tip, gasping as the head of his cock slipped past the tight ring of muscle and into the other man's searing heat.

The tightness drew the breath from his lungs as he carefully pushed in deeper. He was slowly drowning in Tristan, losing himself to this man inch by glorious inch.

"Fuck…" Tristan exhaled as Dylan seated himself deep inside his ass. Dylan froze at Tristan's gasp. He didn't want to hurt him. He held himself back even though his body strummed with energy and a need to pound into Tristan.

"This feels so good. I want to hammer into you so badly." He slid his hand up Tristan's hip and along the small of his back. The feel of hard muscles under his palm seemed so right, but also completely foreign.

"Yes, move… Fuck me!" Tristan's voice quivered. "Dylan, please…"

Dylan pulled back slowly and thrust forward, sinking deeper and deeper into all of Tristan's welcoming warmth. Tristan clenched around him, driving all coherent thoughts away.

"Touch me," Tristan commanded, working his hips with the rhythm he created. Dylan reached around and gripped Tristan's cock in his palm. He began to stroke the hard length in perfect time to his pounding thrusts.

"I wanna stay deep inside you. You feel so right." He picked up the pace, reared back, and slammed into Tristan over and over again. The ache in his balls grew with every thrust. His knees weakened as he hammered into that tight channel.

"I can't last…so tight." Dylan canted his hips forward, changing the angle. Tristan's ass clenched and fluttered around him as he aimed for his gland. He wanted to drive Tristan crazy with need.

"Yes, harder," Tristan half moaned, half gasped. He reached down, covering Dylan's hand on his cock and made him stroke hard and fast. "Make me come, Dylan."

He tightened his grip on Tristan's hip, holding him in place with one hand as he began to pound wildly into this handsome, magnificent man's body and continued to work Tristan's rigid cock with his other. Dylan kept thrusting until his own legs threatened to collapse and his heart drummed painfully in his chest. His orgasm built and his balls churned as the familiar heat swelled in the lowest regions of his spine. Dylan drove himself mindlessly in and out of Tristan's ass, the sweat rolling down his temple as the sounds of flesh meeting flesh filled the room. He didn't want this to end, he'd never felt as whole or complete as he did in this very moment.

"Fuck, I'm gonna come," Tristan shouted as Dylan felt the other man's hot release cover his hand. That was all it took for Dylan's orgasm to steal his sight and take his breath. He gave in and rode out the intense pleasure, not wanting the moment to ever end as Tristan's ass milked every last ounce of seed from his body.

CHAPTER.10

The nagging chirp of his alarm woke Dylan from a pleasant dream, causing him to groan at the unwelcome interruption. He kept his eyes closed and reached out to mute the offending sound. Confusion assailed him when his hand brushed against warm human flesh. *What the hell?* His alarm always sat on the left side of his bed, on his nightstand. Still groggy from the sleep-induced hangover, Dylan stretched his arm out for the second time, determined to silence the irritating tone. His hand bumped into an unmistakable, lightly furred chest, and his eyes fluttered open. The sight of a gorgeous, smiling Tristan lying on the other side of the bed, dangling his phone between two fingers, had him all but forgetting the annoying alarm. Tristan silenced the noise and placed the cell back on the bed.

"Umm...sorry about that. What time is it?" Dylan mumbled, hoping he didn't sound like an idiot. His cheeks heated and his body stirred as memories of last night flooded his brain. He really didn't know how to act in this situation.

"Five thirty. We could go back to sleep. We aren't meeting until ten," Tristan replied, that sexy smile still lighting his eyes.

"I set my alarm early. I wanted to run this morning." Dylan turned over onto his back and scrubbed a hand over his face, staring up at the ceiling. He was pretty damn tired. They'd only gone to bed a few hours ago.

"Are you getting up? I can drive you," Tristan offered, scooting closer to him, draping both an arm and a leg over Dylan's body. He drew the covers up around them and laid his head on the other half of Dylan's pillow.

"Nah, you don't have to, unless you want to. It's early. I really think your idea's a much better option." He lifted an arm to wrap around the one Tristan had across his chest. "Do I need to set my alarm again?"

"No, mine's set for eight thirty. Is that enough time?" Tristan asked.

"I hope." A large yawn escaped his lips as his eyes closed.

Tristan nudged him "Turn over. I want to spoon. I like the way you fit against me. And while you're at it, give me a little bit more of your pillow." Tristan chuckled and pulled him closer. Dylan pressed back against Tristan's warmth and fell back to sleep instantly.

"You could wear something of mine," Tristan offered from his closet.

"I need to get back before the guys go down for breakfast." Dylan looked up at the clock. He sat on the end of the bed, completely naked, a pained looked on his face. "I bet they're already down there. I should have gotten up earlier."

Tristan grabbed the Advil he kept in his bathroom and a glass of water, taking them over to Dylan. He watched as the man quickly swallowed them down. Of course he had a hangover. He had made it clear he hadn't drunk much since he sobered up and at least came out to himself. That had sounded like those were during the college years. "They know you run, right. Take some of my athletic shorts and a T-shirt."

Dylan appeared to consider that plan. Well, at least he hadn't gotten the immediate *no* he'd gotten with every one of his other ideas on how to get them to the meeting this morning.

"I can drive you to the hotel," Tristan suggested as he headed back to his closet where he pulled out an old pair of Lakers athletic shorts, then put them back. That screamed California, not Texas. He chose a solid black pair and Nerd Herd T-shirt sent to him when the show *Chuck* was so popular.

"I'll take a cab. I can't risk anyone seeing me coming back this morning after we left together last night."

"It'll take forever for a cab to get here. Just tell them I ran with you this morning," Tristan offered, handing over the clothes.

"Then why would we have your car?" Dylan questioned as he pulled the clothes on.

"We went and got coffee," Tristan answered nonchalantly on his way to the bathroom. "I have a toothbrush and your hair needs to be brushed. Oh wait, I have a ball cap you can use."

"I don't run with a ball cap. David knows that," Dylan replied, bypassing Tristan. For the first time that morning, he noticed Dylan wasn't really looking at him. He'd blamed the attitude on the lingering effects of the alcohol, but now he wasn't so certain. Did he have regrets?

Oh no… No regrets. Last night had been perfect for both of them. The last thing he wanted was Dylan to wish last night away. Tristan moved from the doorway of the bathroom to give Dylan some privacy. Digging through his dresser, he chose what he hoped looked like running clothes. He definitely never ran. Sure, he lifted and worked the elliptical more hours than he could count, but that running thing had never been a draw for him.

He dressed quietly, watching the door. He absolutely didn't want Dylan pulling away from him. He'd loved last night. For him, he'd never expected to feel the emotion he had. He loved holding Dylan in his arms out on the deck, his body trembling, completely sensitive to his touch and breath. And then afterward... Damn, that was incredible.

All of this was so far outside of his personal comfort zone. He never fell for one-night stands. What was wrong with him? He didn't fantasize about the men he slept with, and he sure didn't use the word incredible to describe his trysts. So why should this guy be any different?

That seemed like the million dollar question. But he certainly couldn't deny his night with Dylan had been unlike any other in his past. And he didn't seem to be running from the connection, pretending they never happened.

As he slid on his tennis shoes, he sat on the end of the bed, smiling at the fact that he wasn't sore. He rarely bottomed, yet his ass wasn't protesting this morning. Dylan had been tender while methodically opening him both carefully and gently until he slowly picked up the pace and fucked him senseless. By the time they'd finished last night, he'd come twice and turned into a listless lump of sated human flesh. It took time for him to coordinate his brain with a normal body function like lifting a hand to wipe the sweat from his brow. The teacher had absolutely become the student where Dylan Reeves was concerned. And he'd hoped for a repeat tonight.

"What about my clothes?"

"I can have them delivered to your room today," he offered, handing Dylan a pair of running shoes. "You're about my size."

"You're more bulky," Dylan retorted, dropping each shoe and working his feet inside.

"You can't tell that in the shirt," Tristan grabbed his wallet, cell, and keys. "My garage's downstairs."

"You have a downstairs? I don't remember that from last night," Dylan said, walking out of the back of the room to the deck where he'd left his clothes.

"My clothes are gone," Dylan announced rather loudly.

"They're in here. Maria's here. She's efficient like that." Tristan walked into the kitchen, and as suspected, Dylan's clothes were nicely folded on the edge of the kitchen table.

"Someone's here?" Dylan asked, completely panicked, staying out on the patio. That deflated Tristan a little more.

"She's my housekeeper. She's discreet. No one will know, I promise. What do you need out of these?" Dylan looked around and slowly walked to the kitchen. Tristan wondered what he would have done if Maria had walked out with him in the house. She was good at staying hidden. She rarely let herself be seen when he had company.

Dylan dug through his clothes until he found his wallet. Tristan shut the back walls to his house, closing everything up, and held a side door open in the kitchen. Dylan followed him down the steps toward his garage, still looking around for Maria as the lights came on.

"Oh my god," Dylan exclaimed. That was the first time in several minutes Dylan had dropped his guard. He had to admit the brand new Ferrari parked inside was pretty magnificent, enough so that it apparently made Dylan forget all about Maria. The mood of earlier dissolved as he did a full circle around the vehicle. "This is my dream car."

That had Tristan laughing. "It's mine too. This is my second one. I just got this a few weeks ago. Wanna drive?"

Dylan looked up, startled. "No! I mean absolutely, but no. Of course not. What if something happened?"

"Nothing's going to happen and it's completely insured." Tristan dangled the keys from his fingers.

"No, if anyone sees me, they won't understand why I'm driving your car," Dylan replied. Tristan nodded, masking his features. As much as this whole morning had taken its toll on his emotional state, Tristan could understand how much Dylan's life must suck living under that much concealment and fear of being found out. He used the key fob to unlock the car and opened the garage door.

"Then cancel on the group dinner tonight and come back over here," Tristan said, starting the car. The engine roared to life, and the fascination was back on Dylan's face as he put the car in reverse and backed out. He and Dylan connected on so many levels. Data centers, miles of servers, car coolness factors and their engines. Then there was sex... "You can take her for a spin along the coast. I know a perfect drive to watch the sunset."

Tristan tried for casual with that comment. It had actually surprised him when he suggested they get together tonight after watching Dylan bow up tight thinking Maria might see him. As far as they were both concerned, last night should have been a onetime deal. Taking a car ride along the ocean sounded very much like a date, not a casual opportunity to give his baby a spin. Damn, he'd messed that up and looked over to gauge Dylan's response. The shell-shocked look had returned.

"I don't think that's a good idea," Dylan said softly. Tristan let that sit between them. He'd known those words were coming. For whatever reason, he loved last night and truly wanted to see Dylan again. But he could tell by the way Dylan acted that the man wasn't ready to give up his life of hiding.

"Hey, one night doesn't make you an expert and you should see what they have planned for you guys tonight. I already bailed. Poker with topless serving girls... Not my thing at all." Tristan pretended to shiver. "Your guys loved last night so much they changed things up. I got the update this morning."

"Y'all didn't have to go to all this trouble. We didn't need all that. Just a meeting with what you plan to offer would have been fine. That is, if you even intend to make an offer," Dylan said, staring out the side window.

"These things are always a wine and dine kind of deal. Wilder wants Secret. We want you to want to sell it to us over our competitors. We know you won't really think that just because we can supply topless waitresses, we'll take any better care of the baby you started from the ground floor," Tristan stated matter-of-factly and laughed a little. Dylan gave a deep sigh.

"I'm still not sure it's a good idea. Last night was risky. I never do things like that."

"You're a million miles away from home. Besides, there's more I could teach you," Tristan said. Coming to a stop light, he looked over at Dylan and waggled his eyebrows.

"I'm not ready to bottom," Dylan mumbled softly, doubt clear in his voice.

"What about adding a third?" Tristan asked, pulling that out of thin air. Surprised by his own words, he immediately wanted to take them back. What was he thinking? Had he just pushed too far to get Dylan back to his house?

"What? Do you know people like that?" Dylan asked incredulously, quickly covering his surprise.

"Of course I do. Are you doubting my hookup skills?" Tristan chuckled and that had Dylan smiling.

"No, not at all. I'm doubting mine more than likely." Dylan scrubbed a hand over his face and ran his fingers through his hair before finally looking over at Tristan, perhaps more cautious than anything. Dylan hadn't come right out and said no, but he hadn't said yes either. He got the impression Dylan was more inquisitive than not, and curiosity was something he could work with.

"Look, we can take a drive. If you're interested in the other, I'll have him on standby," Tristan said, pulling onto the street where the hotel was located.

"Guys just wait for you on standby?" Dylan asked disbelievingly.

"This one will. I'll pull up on the side of the building and you can get out, jog around if you want. I'll see you later," Tristan said, wishing he'd kissed Dylan before they left the house, but at the time, the guy was too spooked. Dylan got out, back in panic mode, never even saying goodbye.

Tristan watched for a moment and lifted a hand, knowing it wouldn't be returned. He drove away, wishing the guy who had made love to him so tenderly last night would have been the same guy he woke up to this morning.

Instead of dwelling, he called his buddy Julian, explained the situation, and had him on standby for tonight. He made another call to ask Maria to pack him a dinner to-go. He mentally took inventory of the alcohol he had in the house. He could completely see why Dylan had stopped drinking since he had planned to hide his life away. He wasn't a sloppy drunk. Hell, you couldn't even tell he'd been drinking, but he was up for anything with liquor in his system. If Dylan wanted to drink tonight, there would be something available for him.

As for Tristan, he wasn't done with Dylan Reeves by a long shot. Dylan just needed to get on board with his plan.

Dylan hightailed it up the stairs, bypassing the elevators, hoping to avoid David and Rob. Once he got inside the room, he'd tell them to go on without him. In stealth mode, he stuck his head out the stairwell door and looked around. The hall was empty. He jogged the few steps to his door. He couldn't believe he hadn't flat out told Tristan no. He'd always been curious about threesomes, even fantasizing about the act, but was it something he could actually go through with? As he pulled the card key from his wallet, David walked out of a room almost directly across the hall from his. Rob followed behind, catching him going inside his room. *Dammit!*

"Hey, man, it's time to leave. The driver's here." David waved a hand at him and his clothes.

"Y'all go on without me. I'll catch a cab there. I got caught up in the run and lost track of time." His lie was so stupid he just kept his back to the guys, walked inside his room, intent on letting the door shut in their faces. Unfortunately, Rob was quicker and stuck a foot inside his door before it closed.

"What happened to you last night?" Rob asked, pushing his way inside. It wasn't unreasonable that he'd walked inside Dylan's room uninvited. Thankfully, these were mini-suites. He busted a quick move, going into the bedroom section and ripping the bedspread off the bed, trying to make the mattress look like he'd slept there.

"Nothing, man. That whole scene wasn't for me. I came back to the room and caught up on messages," Dylan lied again, that one more plausible while avoiding eye contact with either of them. He went to the closet, where his suitcase hadn't been moved since he got there. He tried to cover that by keeping the closet door partially closed as he pulled out his toiletries bag.

"I figured Teri would have kicked your ass if she knew you were there," David said, clearly giving him a hard time.

"Nah, she wouldn't care. We're just here for serious business," Dylan started and couldn't even finish the thought after everything he'd done last night with the key negotiator of the contracts. *Fuck!* How had *that* just occurred to him?

"Did you talk to him last night? They're pretty much saying they want us." Dylan hadn't talked to Tristan about any of this except to find out the schedule change for the night.

"It's gonna come down to numbers and whether they're willing to take the whole staff or not. You guys know I don't want anyone without a job," Dylan replied, repeating the same thing he'd said before.

"It's a given, man. Stop worrying. They're trying too hard to show us a good time," Rob said. "You didn't open your gift basket?" Dylan looked up and saw the overflowing basket sitting over in the corner. He hadn't even seen the thing and decided to ignore that question.

"I gotta dress. I'll grab a cab and meet you guys at the office. Text me and tell me where to go." Dylan stood in the doorway of the restroom, pulling the T-shirt over his head and tossing it toward the closet before starting the water. He shut the door in their faces when that hadn't been enough to get them going. He dropped his underwear as he heard the main door to the room close and stepped under the spray.

He felt reasonably comfortable that he dodged them well enough. They hadn't appeared to pick up on his lies. Hell, he detested lying. And then he laughed at that thought. Except his whole life was a damn lie. Dylan reached for the hotel shampoo, opting not to step out onto the cold floor and dig through his bag soaking wet.

He scrubbed his hair and then his entire body, washing away any traces of the man he'd spent the night with. He hated washing Tristan's scent off him.

"You didn't do anything wrong last night," he said out loud to himself, but his inner thoughts were far louder. He was disappointed in his actions. The alcohol had lowered his resistance, and he had given in to years of carefully hidden desires. He'd promised himself he wouldn't act on these needs until his children were grown and gone. When they were babies, he thought eighteen made him an adult, so he had eighteen years to wait before he could explore his inner self.

Chloe had proved that wrong not even a week ago. Besides, when he was eighteen, he'd been a binge drinker, living on his parents' hard-earned dime, and had enough unprotected sex to have three children back to back.

If he'd been as mature as he thought he'd been, he would have never brought his babies into the world when he had no job, no education, no life whatsoever except partying and envisioning a great big, perfectly cut cock every time he fucked a woman.

Last night had been a selfish, weak moment. He had promised himself, Teri, and his children he would wait and give them the foundation they deserved. After all, they hadn't asked to be brought into this world. But he wanted what Tristan offered him tonight more than he was willing to admit, more than he'd ever wanted anything in his life. He scrubbed his soapy hands over his face.

"It was just sex, Dylan. Teri has it all the time and no one knows." He tried to reason with himself. He leaned back into the warm stream and rinsed the suds off his face. That was a good point, but his negative inner self wasn't on board yet. She did manage to have an outside life. She balanced being an incredible mom, an attorney, and had a discreet long-term relationship. She had encouraged him to do the same thing. Why hadn't he considered that before?

Because he promised himself he'd wait. Finding out their mom had an affair was easier to deal with than finding out their father was gay and the whole life he'd created for them was a sham. Dylan reached for a towel and dried himself off before laying it neatly on the tile floor.

He cracked open the bathroom door and wiped a hand towel across the mirror. He pulled out his shaving gear and went about his normal grooming routine. When it came to his hair, he usually let it air dry. He changed that up today. He pulled out the gel and used the hairdryer to flip the front off his forehead and lay the short sides just right. After closer inspection, he plucked at his eyebrows. He'd told himself he did all this to feel confident in their negotiations today.

After a solid thirty minutes, he left the bathroom and headed to the closet. He dressed quickly. He chose his power suit—a pinstripe ensemble that the saleswoman swore he looked the best in. After years and years of wearing jeans and polos to work, he had to stand in front of the mirror to tie the knot correctly. The sound of a knock threw him off.

He opened the door to find a delivery driver standing in the hallway, a small bouquet of flowers in his hands. "I'm looking for a Dylan Reeves."

"That's me," he said, confused as the guy handed him the bouquet and a sealed note. Dylan took both, placing the flowers on a side table.

"Hang on. I'll get you a tip," Dylan said, going in search of his wallet.

"It's okay. The tip was covered," the delivery driver said, and he was gone. Dylan went back to the flowers. They were a pretty pavé-style mix. He opened the card, wondering if they were from Teri, but he saw a man's penmanship scrawled across the notecard.

I couldn't have enjoyed last night more. You're amazing. I've never enjoyed bottoming so well. You inspired me to send these. Let's take that ride along the coast tonight. No pressure, just bail on dinner with them this evening.

No signature.

Dylan read the note twice before tearing the card into little small pieces and flushing them down the toilet after deciding the note's destruction would be more permanent than a trash can, from which it could be pieced back together. He rolled his eyes at his own actions. Who in their right mind would even consider doing that? But he still completely disposed of the incriminating content.

He decided he'd give the flowers to the front desk. He finished dressing. Tucked his wallet in his back pocket and his phone into the front breast pocket and smoothed his hand down the front of his trousers. With one last look in the mirror, he adjusted a stray hair back in place and went for the flowers.

He'd never been given flowers before, and now he got why women liked them so much. He put them down, but then decided to go ahead and give them away. It didn't look like he'd be spending too much time in this room and someone needed to enjoy them. He took his phone out, took pictures of them from every angle, then left the room with the flowers in hand.

The concierge's face lit up when Dylan handed over the bouquet downstairs. He asked for a cab and had one in seconds. He had to remember the use of a floral arrangement in the future. This one bouquet had secured his night with Tristan and gotten him a cab meant for someone else. They were magical things.

CHAPTER.11

In the conference room, Tristan watched as Dylan and the guys sat through hours of the Wilder executive team's presentation as to why they should be given the right to buy Secret Networks, Inc. Tristan stayed quiet for most of the meeting and also during the proposal Wilder had put together with the specifics for acquiring Dylan's company.

Tristan understood body language; he'd used it to his advantage in many negotiations. Secret's executive team put out all the right signs they were interested. Of course there were a few sticking points, but those weren't anything that couldn't be ironed out in the long run.

What Dylan and his guys didn't seem to understand was that they weren't playing the buyout game correctly. They'd come in too low with their asking price. Honestly, Tristan would have assumed they'd have asked for about double what they did and probably would have gotten close through negotiations. He'd been clear to Landry he wanted to pay what they asked, but like what appeared to be the new normal with Wilder, Inc., Landry had gone around him. His COO had come into the meeting with a note waiting on top of Tristan's presentation folder explaining Landry's newly developed game plan to undercut the deal.

Since he'd been substantially late, he hadn't had time to change the course of the meeting.

He didn't know Dylan well, but he had learned he would never sign over Secret with Landry's bottom-line condition. Landry was against Secret's all-or-nothing employee stance. Specifically with David and Rob. Under Landry's current transition plan, they really had no place for the two executives sitting across the table from them. Actually, Landry only wanted about fifteen percent of Secret's current staff.

Over the years, Tristan had trusted Landry's decision-making ability. He'd never steered them wrong on anything other than their social media site. That situation was a lot like this one. Landry had something in his head that didn't balance with what the consumer actually wanted.

Wilder's current social media division was a one hundred percent loss. No matter how much money they pumped into WilderNation, it still ranked at the bottom of the barrel in user access. Secret had accomplished what no other network on the planet had—undocumented social access that had a quarter of a million new users signing up every day. Tristan wanted that technology, and his gut told him Landry could blow the whole deal.

After a few more minutes of staring at Dylan, who hadn't looked his way since he entered the room, Tristan cleared his throat, stopping the flow of the presentation. "Can you all give me a few minutes alone with Mr. Reeves?"

He could feel every eye turned his way. Dylan was slower to respond. He'd been reading from the contract and lifted his head, business clearly on his mind. But the minute their gazes met, Tristan got why Dylan had avoided eye contact. His gaze held a mixture of both heat and need. Sparks flew between the two of them and Tristan smiled.

"You heard him," Landry said and began shooing everyone out. As the last person left, Landry came to the center of the table, standing between the two of them. He clearly thought Tristan's request hadn't included him.

"Landry, I need a private discussion with Mr. Reeves," Tristan said, rising from his seat at the end of the table. Landry came immediately to him, standing in front of him, blocking Dylan from seeing or hearing anything he said.

"I don't think that's a good idea," Landry whispered so quietly Tristan barely heard him. "We almost have them, I can see it."

Tristan cut his eyes over to Landry's and motioned with his head for him to move along out the door with everyone else. Landry's brow furrowed and he started to shake his head. Tristan stared at him with intense attitude until he finally left the room. Tristan had no doubt he'd stand right outside that door. There wasn't too much of Wilder, Inc. that Landry wasn't included in, and he certainly wouldn't like being put out of a meeting he'd orchestrated. Tristan moved to a chair directly beside Dylan who hadn't uttered a single word since his request for privacy.

"You look nice today," Tristan said quietly, smiling as Dylan's cheeks grew red.

"Is that why you made everyone leave?"

"No, of course not. I could have just told you later, but that whole look's perfect on you. The hair's hot. Pinstripes fit your frame remarkably well. You look taller, more intimidating. Great look for negotiations or the cover of GQ. You could do both." Tristan scooted closer. "Did you get my flowers?" he asked even quieter.

"I did. Thank you, but that was a risky move," Dylan said, clearly ignoring the compliment.

"I wrote and sealed the card myself. What did you do with the flowers?" Tristan leaned forward, then moved in a little more, smelling Dylan's cologne. That had Dylan pushing back in his chair.

"I gave them to the concierge that helped me this morning," Dylan answered and then backtracked. "I didn't think I'd be in my room very much and didn't want them to go to waste."

"I figured you'd do something like that. It's why I picked those colors. So that means you're coming with me tonight?" Tristan asked, his eyes still focused directly on Dylan's.

"We'll see how things go today. I'm not sure about all this. You lowballed me and I was just reading about the staffing…" Dylan started, but Tristan lifted a hand to Dylan's lips to stop his words. He let his fingers linger as he spoke.

"I don't want to talk business yet. I honestly was only informed of the changes to personnel when I walked in today. From this point forward, you and I will decide how this sale goes, no one else, but before we do, I want to put personal before business because they are two separate entities between us. Will you please go with me tonight? I need to cancel some things if you're not coming," Tristan added at Dylan's skeptical look.

"Are you still thinking about adding someone else?" Dylan asked, but his look never changed.

"I'm flexible, but I've made that arrangement." Tristan nodded, sitting back in the seat.

"All right. I'll go, but I don't want to be pushed into anything. If I just watch, everyone needs to be good with that," Dylan advised, stating his terms clearly so there was no confusion.

"Fair enough, but it's only a threesome when three people participate." Tristan laughed.

"We'll see. I'm way outside my comfort zone with all this. Will he come from that club last night? He won't ever say a word that I was there, right?" Dylan asked. He had that panicked edge again.

"I swear your secret's safe. I give you my word," Tristan soothed. Leaning forward, he lowered his voice. "But you're a pro at sex. My ass isn't even a little bit sore today. You were perfect." Tristan winked, smiling at those red cheeks and lust-filled, hooded eyes that replaced the worry.

"Now, on to business. I haven't discussed this with my team, but I've been watching Secret for a while now. What's it going to take for me to get your company?" Tristan asked, and eased back in his seat, waiting for the answer.

"I like some of the details you've outlined, but the money isn't right and my biggest concern lies with my staff. They've been very good to me," Dylan stated.

"Yes, they have. My team doesn't think we need them." Tristan could see that might not have been the best thing to say. Dylan got his back up right there, immediately dropping walls between them. "Wait a second. I don't see it like that. I've never had multiple facilities in the same country. I like to keep my company together if that makes sense. I'm certainly not saying it's the right way of things, but it has been my way. But we've failed where you've succeeded," Tristan explained, getting more comfortable in his chair.

"Here's what I would like to propose to you. I'll pay twenty percent above your asking price, in full. I want your staff, but understand I'm not agreeing to keep every single one of them for the long-term. I run a lean ship, but for the next year, every single employee of your company will stay employed. If you agree, I've decided to continue to run Secret from your Dallas location. My people here need to get a taste of what it takes to run a successful social media network. Your people can help us gain that knowledge."

Dylan looked surprised. He'd totally blown the proposal out of the water. It was confirmed when Dylan closed the folder and pushed the file away.

"I purchased the high-rise where we run our operations," Dylan stated absently, staring down at the table.

"We'll rent the space from you or I'll buy it. Whatever you want."

"David has a firm knowledge of the inner workings of my company." Dylan was still in that thoughtful mode, contemplating the offer. "He'd make a good leader for that division of Wilder."

"I can see that. He's my Landry." Tristan chuckled, hooking a thumb at the frosted-glass door. He could see the shape of a man standing right outside the door. "He's gotta be crazy pissed off from being excluded from this conversation."

Dylan closed his eyes and pressed his thumbs against his temples, trying to catch up with everything being tossed his way. Wilder's first offer had come in low with most of his staff being terminated. Now he stood to make twenty percent more on the sale of Secret than he'd planned, money up front and in full, while keeping every one of his staff employed in Dallas. No relocation of anyone. Granted, he didn't run in these circles, but what in the hell just happened?

The technology was his exclusive project. He'd developed the software by himself. If he went through with this, he would be giving away his concept, but that was inevitable. He reminded himself he didn't have the resources to grow the company more than what they already had. Secret needed deeper pockets to handle the load of subscribers and to go international.

"I'll give a tentative agreement. I want my legal team involved before a final acceptance," Dylan said as he looked over at Tristan.

"Of course," Tristan said, as if that were a given. "But I wasn't done. I also want you running the division."

"I'm sorry, what?" Dylan asked. He'd been thinking over the possibilities of the buyout and was afraid he hadn't heard him right.

"You'll head the social media division of my company. I want to carve that piece out, let you oversee the development. You've created innovative processes in this market, you aren't afraid to take a risk, and you listen to what the people want. I'm lacking that in my organization. I'm finding out that we're still in the same mindset we were ten years ago—we think we tell the consumer what they want. I've got my own work cut out for me around here."

"I appreciate the offer, but I've been my own boss for far too long. I'm not sure I could play well with the likes of that senior team you have hovering out there." Dylan answered off the cuff but was completely serious. He and Landry would butt heads at every turn. He had no interest in fighting to keep moving them forward or getting in a cock-and-bull fight over the politics in corporate America.

"You'll report to me. You'll be given a budget, but you're used to that, and have carte blanche after that. I want Secret to remain the brand name, we'll have Secret envelop WilderNation—you'll run it all—"

Dylan cut him off. "I'm not sure it's wise to work for you." Actually since he'd sat there with an intense hard-on while talking something as boring as acquisitions, he knew without a doubt working for Tristan wouldn't be a good idea.

"Like I said earlier. There's the personal side and the business side. Neither has anything to do with the other," Tristan replied neutrally.

"But somehow they always seem to find a way," Dylan interjected. They had last night, he'd agreed to tonight, but after that, there would never be anything more between them. If Tristan was coming in and out of his home town, how would he manage all this emotion evoked every single time he looked at the guy?

"We could outline a legal document—that's what my HR team would like, but that would mean more people knowing and you don't want that. We're both professionals. I can keep the two separated. I believe you can too."

"After I leave here this weekend, there won't be another time we're together," Dylan stated very reasonably as though it were something he'd already considered.

"Then problem solved," Tristan remarked. He had no intention of following Dylan's line of thinking, but he'd hold that bit to himself for now.

Silence ensued while they stared at one another. For Tristan, he had a hard time keeping his mind focused on the buyout. Dylan was a seriously attractive guy. He carried himself in such a way that just turned Tristan on, and he did it on a level that had him wanting more. He couldn't ever remember having to deal with confusing feelings like these before. Hell, even yesterday, when he met the guy, he'd grown half erect in front of the damn elevators, and at that point, he'd been fairly certain Dylan was a married straight man.

"I don't want to be held to a long-term contract. I need an out if things don't go well," Dylan commented.

"All right, as long as you give me enough time to replace you, but I assure you, you will have open access to whatever you need to get this division up and running. Nothing will get in your way." Tristan nodded toward the door where they could see the silhouette of the still-hovering Landry.

"And what if I can't move all this forward?" Dylan questioned.

"Then we'll mutually part ways, but I don't see that happening."

"And you're comfortable working together after this weekend ends?" Dylan asked, his face flushing after the question.

"Of course I am." Tristan resisted the urge to laugh and make it very clear they weren't over after this weekend by any stretch of the imagination.

"All right. It'll be good for the kids to have their home base continue. Dallas is ripe for technology. The staff won't have to relocate." Dylan ticked off all the positives.

"And you get the capital you need to take your company to the next level," Tristan added.

"It'll be your company," Dylan corrected.

"Ours then. I intend for the stock options to be substantial. Give you incentive. I'm sorry I didn't make that clear on the front end." Tristan extended his hand for a quick shake, sealing the tentative deal. "Now, do we bring them back in and tell them together or would you like the conference room to let your staff know? We can take ours to legal now, begin the paperwork."

"Probably privately," Dylan said, the handshake continued as they stood there staring at one another.

"Off the record, I'm glad you took the deal. I need people like you on my team."

"Thank you. I've been very impressed with what you've built. It's an honor to be here," Dylan added sincerely.

"I'm going to let go now and open the door. Might want to fix that." Tristan looked down at the other man's crotch with a satisfied grin, calling attention to the tenting in his slacks. Dylan looked down, ripped his hand free, and immediately adjusted himself.

"I'm sorry. I can't help myself when I'm around you." Dylan blushed; his words were uncensored and that was a rare moment with this man.

"No, don't apologize. I rather enjoy it. You can't tell now anyway." Tristan went through the motions of tucking himself in to help alleviate Dylan's embarrassment. After a second, he called out, "Landry, bring everyone back in. We're ready."

CHAPTER.12

Dylan did a quick change, opting for jeans and a light blue polo. He packed a small overnight bag for his running gear just in case he stayed at Tristan's place through the night. He had one last morning to run Crystal Cove, and he wanted to make that happen before he left tomorrow afternoon.

He still had twenty-five minutes before the car was scheduled to pick him up. Nervous energy made him antsy. He looked around for something to do. His laptop was open, email checked, but he wasn't interested in doing what needed to be done or replying to any of those unanswered messages. Instead he went in search of his phone and decided to check in with his family. If he remembered correctly, Teri and Mark were off the boat and staying in Houston for the night.

He plopped down in one of the recliners and dialed Teri. She answered on the third ring, "Hey, you. Having a good time?"

"It's all right. What about you? You having a good time?" he asked.

"It's been good. I'm glad I got away." He could hear the happiness in her voice.

"Sorry I haven't called before now," Dylan offered up.

"That's okay. I figured it was either intense or fun…"

"It's actually been both," Dylan said with a chuckle. Teri felt like home to him. She calmed him. He hoped this never changed between them.

"Okay, that sounds weird. What's up?" Teri asked.

"We got more than full asking price. The staff stays intact. The stock options are more than what I wanted. The base stays in Dallas and they want me to take over the whole WilderNation media division."

"Babe! That's great! I'm so proud of you! Oh, I wish I was there to help celebrate!" Teri sounded truly happy.

"It's a little surprising."

"Wait, it's just registering. Did you agree to work for them?" Teri asked. He could hear the confusion in her voice.

"I did," he said and laughed. He'd always assumed he'd be moved out of the company once the deal was finalized.

"Are you sure that's a good idea? You don't like to have your hands tied or take orders well," she replied thoughtfully. Teri's typical direct nature had him laughing a little bit too.

"I made sure I have a solid out, and they want me to keep the building like we have, but now I'll have deeper pockets to push things forward. And I have you, my legal division. You'll make sure all that's there for us." Dylan still couldn't believe the turn of events.

"Well, you're good at building things from the ground up. So you're happy?" she asked.

"We'll see when the contracts come if it's all there, but right now, I call it a success," Dylan declared, lifting his hand to give no one a high five. "How are the kids?"

"Everyone's good. Chad's working like crazy on gathering a part for some robotic thing for the science fair.

He's determined his senior year is the year to take home the top prize. Cate's fine. She's forgetting she's got at least eight months before she graduates. She's applied at Harvard and Duke, but her real concern's planning her dorm room and looking at meal plans," Teri said, quickly filling him in.

"Of course she is." Dylan laughed. That was her mother in her, planning everything out about a million times before the event actually happened. "How's jailbird?"

"You know she hates that," Teri said.

"I know. I've been texting her that every day. She's refusing to answer now."

"Well, she's becoming our little activist. Her newest concern's equality. There's a march in Tulsa in a couple of weeks. She's going, but she asked first. I thought that was a step in the right direction. We might have to get her out of jail in Tulsa," Teri said, laughing.

"Equality, huh?" Dylan asked.

"I thought you'd like that," Teri responded. Dylan remained silent, thinking that piece of information over. "Did I lose you?"

"No, I'm here. I'm just proud of them. They're good kids. Somehow we managed to raise good kids," he said thoughtfully, wondering how they accomplished such a feat. They had both been a little bit of a train wreck in the beginning.

"I agree. We're lucky," Teri confirmed.

"I gotta go. I've got to be downstairs in a little while," Dylan said, looking at his watch.

"Have a good time. You know celebrating wouldn't kill you."

"I have been. It's been a good trip," Dylan said quietly.

"Oh, I like the sound of that. You'll have to fill me in when you get home," Teri stated.

"We'll see about that. I need to go."

"Bye," Teri said and hung up. Dylan was slower to lower the phone. So many people would consider them dysfunctional, but they weren't at all. Teri was his best friend, and he'd done well by having her in his life. They were fine. The kids were good. They were doing well as a family.

The alarm on his phone beeped, jolting him out of his thoughts. He had five minutes to get downstairs. He quickly went through the room, closing his computer and disturbing the bed before he grabbed his bag and the still unopened gift basket he planned to leave for the staff and headed downstairs.

"Walk about a block to your right. Meet me out front of the Sheraton. I'm parked at the end of the circular drive." Tristan sent Dylan a text when he saw him walk through the front doors of the Hilton. He watched as Dylan promptly turned to the left and then picked up the phone to call.

"Your other right," he said with a chuckle when Dylan answered. "You look good in jeans. Those sunglasses fit your face perfectly."

Dylan turned around, then glanced up and down the street. Tristan knew the moment he spotted the Ferrari. "I thought a driver was taking me to your place?"

"We finished early today. It seemed like a waste of time to wait to have someone bring you to my place." Tristan watched Dylan walking toward him. He was such a nice-looking guy. Tristan's body physically reacted every time he saw him. "You're hot."

"That makes me uncomfortable," Dylan said, staring at Tristan.

"Sexual harassment in the workplace doesn't begin until you're officially employed," Tristan shot back. That had Dylan laughing.

"Noted." Dylan gave him a genuine smile through the window.

"What's in the bag?" Tristan asked.

"My running gear and your clothes from this morning. I didn't wash them," he said, disappearing around the back of the car. The passenger door opened and Tristan ended the call.

"My mom always told me it was rude to bring clothes back dirty," Tristan joked, cheekily. He liked teasing Dylan. He actually liked bringing a smile to the guy's face. He seemed too serious all the time, but when he let his guard down and eased up some, he was spectacular company.

He shifted into gear, driving forward into the heavy downtown Irvine traffic. "I learned those same lessons, and I considered washing them, but I didn't wanna pay the twenty-five dollars to have the hotel clean them," Dylan said, putting his bag in the very small space behind the seats before buckling himself up.

"Cheapskate! Which is technically good for me since you'll be in charge of our bottom-line," Tristan said, waggling his eyebrows. "You're more relaxed tonight."

"Maybe because I know we're alone. The guys have been gone for a while. I got a text from David. Your guys took them out fishing before the big poker night," Dylan replied.

"That's right. I forgot that. I hope Landry's playing nice." Tristan hadn't meant to say the last part out loud.

"He bailed on the fishing trip and the poker night. He doesn't like being on the outside of things, does he?" Dylan asked.

"No, not at all. We've been friends since junior high school. I should have run the changes past him, but I hadn't formulated my plan until we all sat together and I got a really good look at what you built and what he planned to offer. He went against my wishes completely. I shouldn't be telling you all this." Tristan took the on ramp and merged onto the highway.

"Landry didn't want David or Rob, did he?"

"No specifics please. I don't wanna cause anymore tension before we even start." Tristan looked apologetically at Dylan, who nodded.

"WilderNation's been under him?" Dylan asked.

"Yes. It's the only other time he went against my directive and look how things turned out. We'll transition them out from under him. There'll be crossover, but he's basically a good guy. He'll work with you in time. I promise." Tristan actually hoped Landry would come around. He'd been pretty pissed off today in the legal department. They'd had a heated exchange, one his legal team felt compelled to document.

"Where are we going?" Dylan asked, watching as he weaved easily through the crowded lanes of traffic.

"I thought I'd take us down the Pacific Coast Highway. It's beautiful there. I grew up in the desert of California. As soon as I hit it big, I moved out here and haven't left. No other part of the world's quite as appealing." Tristan moved steadily down the highway even though the traffic was terrible. "You'll see what I'm talking about."

"It's completely different than the Dallas-Fort Worth area," Dylan replied, watching the scenery as they drove. "Everything feels a little freer here."

"I bet. In every possible way. I met your governor once. How did he keep getting elected?" Tristan asked, focusing on the road.

"He's the tip of the iceberg. I gotta get my kids out of there. I'm working on it. None of them are going to college in state." Dylan looked over at him seriously.

"Sounds like you're doing that, then." Children were foreign ground for him. He didn't really even know people that had kids and certainly none of them were as dedicated as

Dylan and his wife were at raising them. Remembering Dylan had a wife added another layer of complication to them. He'd never been in any sort of relationship with a man who had a wife. How could she not complicate this more than it already was? Instead of letting that become another obstacle, Tristan immediately pushed those thoughts out of his mind. If he continued thinking that way, he'd say something, and Dylan always grew more serious and withdrew inside himself when they talked about his life.

"I packed a dinner. I know a good spot that overlooks the ocean. I hope you're okay with that."

Dylan just looked at him.

"What? Okay, I didn't pack it. Maria did, but I get kudos for the thought." Tristan kept his gaze going back and forth between the road and Dylan.

"What? You don't like eating outside?" Tristan asked when Dylan just kept staring at him. He had no idea what that look meant.

"No, it's fine. I prefer to be outside," Dylan admitted, his focus still trained on him. Tristan kept his confusion to himself. He didn't question Dylan's look or silence as he pulled to the side of the road.

"Wanna drive?" he asked once he'd stopped safely on the shoulder. He shoved the gear shift into neutral and set the emergency brake as he looked out the side window and opened the door.

"Really?" Dylan's whole expression changed. He'd have to get better at reading this man.

"I thought that's why we were doing this, so you could drive her." Tristan was already halfway out of the car.

"No, I mean, yeah, I'm good driving!" Dylan said, hopping out of the car, meeting Tristan halfway. "Anything I need to know?"

"Can you drive a standard?" Tristan asked, just to make sure.

"No, but I'll figure it out." Dylan started to move around him toward the driver's side of the car. Tristan stepped back in front of him, stopping him with both hands on his chest. It was already taking quite a bit to let someone else drive his baby, but to grind the gears... That might be asking too much.

"Maybe we should teach you to drive a standard on another car," Tristan said carefully.

"I'm kidding. I've got a standard. Get in the passenger seat. Stop worrying!" Dylan motioned for Tristan to get moving while giving him his real smile. Tristan stood staring. Dylan had played a joke on him, and it would be so easy to lean in and kiss him right now. He wouldn't do that though. He didn't want to freak him out, because he liked this teasing, laughing Dylan.

"You aren't funny." Tristan jokingly pointed a finger at Dylan's smug-looking face. "I lost a few years off my life trying to figure out how to tell you no." Tristan moved away, denying himself the kiss as he walked around to the passenger side. Dylan was already inside, adjusting the seat and caressing the steering wheel.

"It's not your first time?" Tristan asked, watching as Dylan easily aligned everything for his driving comfort.

"Officially it's my first time to actually drive a Ferrari, but I went to look at them a few weeks ago. I wanted it to be the car I was buying if I sold the company. I decided it's just not a practical purchase with the kids still being home," Dylan said, putting the stick in gear and slowly easing them into traffic. There was not one bit of grinding. Tristan's worry eased, and he sat back and adjusted his seat belt.

"Straight down this highway?"

"Yep, just keep going. We got about a twenty minute drive." Tristan angled his body to keep watch over Dylan. The ocean view was nice, but the driver was so much more impressive. He'd just keep his eyes right there.

"Turn right up here," Tristan directed. Dusk came on strong, painting the ocean's backdrop with a beautiful hue of colors. Dylan slowed and turned off the highway onto a small unpaved road.

"Just pull up as far as you can. It's not designed for cars like this," Tristan said, pointing Dylan over to the left. He carefully pulled the car in that direction, stopping after hitting a good rut.

"Sorry," he glanced over at Tristan.

"Unavoidable. We'll have to walk down there a bit. It looks like no one's here. It's still a little cold. I brought you a jacket," Tristan said, getting out of the car and pulling a small cooler from the inside along with a blanket and two jackets. Dylan walked around to meet him, taking some of the load. He'd been reasonably comfortable, yet, now that the car wasn't between them, his nerves grew much like his attraction had with every mile driven.

Tristan was easy to be around—accommodating and accepting, even polite. That was not the way he had expected the founder and global phenom of the world's first true search engine to be. Definitely not the one he'd read about conducting the business of Wilder, Inc. If Dylan thought about it, most of the industry thought of Tristan as a jerk, a ruthless dick, but Dylan hadn't seen any sign of that at all. Actually, that was more Landry than Tristan in Dylan's opinion.

"Lead the way." He followed as Tristan maneuvered down the small trail on the side of the cliff. It was getting darker outside, but he could still see the beauty surrounding him. The landscape was nothing like Texas. In California, the jagged, rocky cliffs dropped off into churning water. The sound of waves crashing against the rocky outcroppings in the distance somehow made this a perfect spot, almost surreal. The salty smell of the ocean drifted on a chilly breeze. He pulled the jacket tighter against his body and fought off a shiver.

"Julian's supposed to meet us at my place at eight thirty. That gives us about an hour and a half here," Tristan said, snaking around the brush and sandy rocks until they came to a small clearing right underneath the car. He laid out the blanket and put the cooler down, opening the lid. Tristan handed him a Heineken. "You drink beer, right?"

"Yeah," he answered. There was really nothing he didn't drink. He'd vowed to let last night be the only night he fell off the proverbial wagon, but with the possibility of a threesome looming in his near future, he twisted off the cap and took a long drink. "You should drive home."

"No problem. I figured you'd need some liquid courage." Tristan chuckled, dropping down to the blanket and toeing off his tennis shoes. He rolled up his pants legs and looked up at Dylan. "It's cold this time of year, but you can't come here and not put your feet in the water."

Dylan sat, draining the bottle while Tristan laughed at him. "I told you, you call the shots tonight. As far as you want to go. You don't need to be so worried."

"I'm just really not ready to…you know," he said quietly, taking off his Sperrys. He tucked his socks inside and rolled up his pants legs. Tristan was already standing, waiting on him.

"No one's gonna push you. I promise. It's hot though—feels incredible. If you do it like you did last night, it's more pleasurable than you can imagine. You were perfect," Tristan said, extending a hand to help him up.

"I see myself as more of a top." Dylan liked to control his world. He liked to be the one doing the work, moving things forward. He just saw himself as a top in all things.

"I did too, and I usually take the lead, but honestly, now I like sex both ways, all ways really." Tristan winked as Dylan got to his feet. He reached out to link their hands together, holding on tight when Dylan tried to pull away. "Moonlight walks on the beach need to be done holding hands. It's a law here in California."

"You keep pushing at me, don't you?" Dylan asked. He didn't let go of Tristan's tight grip, but he didn't walk forward either. Tristan tugged at his arm.

"I'm not pushing. I'm just showing you what you're missing and what's waiting for you when you come out," Tristan said, finally using enough force to get him moving.

"I don't know if I can ever really come out," Dylan admitted.

"Sure, you will. It's too lonely a life otherwise," Tristan replied, walking them to the water. "Besides, someone like you is gonna be picked up real quick."

"I'm not so sure about that," Dylan said, laughing at the absurdity of that thought.

"I am. You're hot, easy to be around, and about to be loaded." Tristan waggled his eyebrows until they hit the edge of the surf. "Shit, the water's cold."

"You said that before." Dylan shivered as the cold water washed over his feet.

"Too bad it's not summer, we could play in the ocean," Tristan said, kicking his feet around, probably trying to build some warmth. Dylan just stayed at the edge of the water. Tristan never released his hand.

"You surf?" Dylan asked. Tristan looked up and must have noticed Dylan wasn't in the water with him, because he tugged him in a step. "We could just walk on the sand and say we did this."

"Sometimes, just a little bit. I can manage to stay up most of the time," Tristan said, ignoring the walk-in-the-sand suggestion. He seemed determined they were doing this. The more they walked, the more the chill of the water subsided.

"I go to the competitions though. Those are badass. You'll have to come with me sometime." He hadn't let go of Dylan's hand and walked them a little farther in, letting the water cover their ankles.

"You don't have a boyfriend?" Why had he just now thought to ask that question? He realized right then, the whole time they'd been together, every thought had been about him, he never considered Tristan in any of this.

"No. I haven't had a lot of long-term relationships. I've worked ungodly hours most of my life. I just never had time," Tristan explained.

"I get that." He'd worked hard to get where he was, too. If he hadn't had Teri by his side, who knows how his life would have turned out. She had pushed him to go for his dreams and stood by his side each step of the way. "And you don't pick up closeted gay men and school them regularly?"

"Most definitely not," Tristan said and then cut his eyes over to Dylan. "No offense, but the virgin closet guy usually comes with too much drama."

"No offense taken. I can see that." He kicked at the water some, staying quiet a little longer. "Why me, then? I've been nothing but drama."

"I've been asking myself that question. Last night, the goal was to show you guys a good time. I wanted your business. I took you to the dinner club because I didn't think you were really serious about being so hidden. Again, no offense, but I don't know anyone that's sacrificed as much as you have for his family. After I spent time with you, I realized besides being attracted to you, I liked being around you. I mean, I really like everything about you. I wanted to be your first. It's silly, but you always remember your first. I still do after all these years. I wanted you to remember me." Dylan didn't respond. Instead, he just looked down, kicking at the water. He liked some of what he heard. It made him feel good that Tristan was attracted to him. He'd never really known how he fared in other men's minds. Besides, Tristan turned him on like he'd never experienced before. No, Tristan hadn't used those words on him, but it would have sucked for that to be completely one-sided.

"I think what has Landry the most pissed off is that I planned something completely different in my offer to you. You managed to change all that, and he doesn't get it. I don't change my mind very often, yet I'm standing in the cold surf with a closeted man who was able to get me to buy his company for twenty percent more than he asked. You're pretty remarkable." They slowed their pace. Tristan now looked down at the water as though thinking through what he'd just admitted.

"I'm with Landry. I don't get it either, but you have to know I wasn't gonna sell if you didn't secure my people." They were stopped now, letting the water lap around their ankles. Dylan turned to Tristan as he spoke. He was dead serious. He didn't understand anything that had happened in the last twenty-four hours.

"I figured that out. It doesn't take much to see that you live by an honor code. It's real old school. I think it's also why you're so successful. You're genuine. We've lost that in Wilder, if we ever even had it," Tristan said, changing their course, pulling him back toward their blanket on the beach by their still clasped hands. The moonlight guided their path.

"Honor doesn't mean always doing the right thing. I just try to do the right thing," Dylan said, thinking over Tristan's words.

"That's a good point, and I can agree with that. So we have even farther to go as a civilization to reach honor and ethics. That's great. Humanity has no hope. Want another beer?" Tristan asked, finally releasing his hand and dropping down on the blanket. "Here's a towel, your feet have to be freezing."

"Sure," he said, reaching for the towel. His feet were cold, so he covered them more than dried them, trying to build a little warmth. Tristan handed him a beer before digging through the contents of the basket to set out a few things. There was some sort of candle. Tristan lit the wick and set it in the sand before pulling out a few more containers.

"I'm not sure I thought this through very well. We could go to dinner somewhere." Tristan paused, searching for a place to set the food.

"I'm good. I'm not very hungry. What's in there?" Dylan asked, taking a container and lifting the lid. "This is a pasta vegetable dish."

"Oh, that's Maria's specialty. I have fruit. And some cold cuts, cheeses, and some sort of dessert." Tristan lifted the lid and ran a finger across the top to taste the dish. "It's some kind of pudding and whipped cream concoction, I think."

Tristan put all that out and reached for the silverware. "Are you good with eating from the containers? I have plates if you'd rather have those."

"This is fine." He speared a piece of melon and ate it down. "The fruit tastes so fresh here," he said, wiping at his chin.

"I guess it's probably pretty fresh. Taste the pasta salad." Tristan held a spoonful for him to eat. He hesitated. It was dark, and feeding someone seemed intimate, but he opened and Tristan's aim was good. He took the bite. "She uses sweetened milk and vinegar. It's my favorite."

"It's very good." Dylan swallowed the food. Tristan handed him the bowl as he went for the cold cuts.

"You aren't going to drink?" Dylan asked, taking a swig.

"I've got precious cargo to get back," Tristan said, dropping a couple of cheese cubes in his mouth.

"So how does it work tonight?" Dylan questioned, taking another big bite of the pasta.

"What do you mean?" Tristan asked, leaning in, taking Dylan's next bite. "Mmmm." The smile the man gave went straight to his dick.

"I don't know. Just how does it work?" Dylan asked.

"Well, I haven't done anything like this myself in a while, but it's all about the pleasure. It's also amazing visual stimulation. You'll like Julian. He's a male model. You'll set the pace for you. And you know, I'm up for just about anything," Tristan said, opening a water bottle and drinking several gulps. "Here, try the cheese."

Tristan placed a cube of cheese in his mouth and his fingers lingered. It took a second for Dylan to get the hint, and then he licked his way around them, sucking the digits before Tristan pulled them free. Dear god, was he seriously this lame that he couldn't automatically pick up on little flirtatious hints?

As he rolled his eyes at his own inexperience, Tristan moved in, closing the distance between them and pressed soft lips against his. That startled Dylan more than the fingers in his mouth. Tristan held his head in place as he traced the seam of his lips with his tongue, licking and nipping sensuously at his mouth until he opened, allowing Tristan to deepen the kiss.

Tristan moved forward with only the food separating their bodies. Tristan's strong hand slid around Dylan's neck, angling his head as he drove his tongue deeper. The sound of the crashing waves in the distance were almost as loud as the pounding of his heart.

Tristan had intended the kiss to be small and encouraging. Yet one taste of those lips that had haunted him all day had Tristan delving deeper, fully exploring Dylan's mouth, sampling and tasting, finding he needed more. Dylan kissed him like he had the right to be there. God, this guy turned him on. Knowing this wasn't the right place or time, Tristan couldn't help but bend in farther, pushing Dylan backward. Screw the food between them. He lowered them to the blanket, only breaking from the kiss long enough to better position himself. His hand skirted along Dylan's rib cage and across his firm belly as he reached lower, wanting to feel the evidence of Dylan's arousal. He rubbed Dylan's jean-covered length wantonly, moaning into his mouth as the kiss turned frantic.

Dylan Reeves had effectively worked his way under his skin and was heading full steam ahead to capturing his heart. He would be with this man, anytime, anywhere. Dylan opened completely for him, becoming pliant with his touch, turning him on that much more. Tristan shoved a knee between Dylan's thighs and settled between them, moving himself until he was grinding against Dylan's hard arousal.

"I want you." Tristan broke from the kiss and glanced down at the man who was slowly consuming him. Dylan's eyes were half-closed, his lips pink and swollen from the sensual assault. Dylan turned his head, baring his neck. What a glorious sight.

"God, you're fucking sexy," Tristan growled as he latched on to Dylan's neck, sucking the warm skin between his teeth. He was careful not to leave a mark where anyone might see. Tristan pushed up on his forearm and quickly worked at freeing himself. He hovered close to Dylan's ear as he began to work the buttons of Dylan's jeans. He licked around the shell of his ear before thrusting his tongue inside. The response was immediate and exactly what Tristan wanted. Dylan grabbed his hair, holding his head firmly in place as he wrapped both of his long legs around him.

The move was awkward and Dylan had such a tight hold, Tristan had to force himself slightly up so he could grab both of their cocks in one hand. Dylan bucked at the contact.

"It feels good," Dylan gasped, encasing Tristan tightly in his arms. The move was endearing and sweet but not the best position to help jack them off. He pushed up as far as Dylan would allow and began stroking them in earnest. He was close, just being near this man did all sorts of things to him, and that combined with the intimacy of this act, had him already walking the edge. He couldn't hold back his impending release. He tightened his grip, pumping his fist faster and watched his lover's beautiful face as he uttered the words, "Come for me."

Dylan barely had time to lift his shirt before his body arched and his orgasm claimed him, painting his chest and stomach with splatters of thick cream. The moment was so hot Tristan had no choice but to follow suit. His balls churned hotly and the warmth of Dylan's cock moving against his spread along every nerve ending in his body. He was so caught up he couldn't even shout as he marked Dylan's stomach with his seed. He continued to stroke them both till the last sensitive shudder faded.

Damn, that hadn't been planned, but shit... Tristan had a hard time balancing, and he finally gathered enough strength to shove back and rest on his ankles. He looked up at the stars, still trying to catch his breath. *Fuck!* That was amazing.

"I'm a mess," Dylan whispered, his breathing still unsteady. The roughness in his voice made Tristan grin.

"Hang on." Tristan looked over at the food, which was everywhere. He'd scattered every container all over the blanket while laying Dylan back. He dug in the basket and found the water bottles before dousing a napkin. "It's gonna be cold."

Tristan quickly ran the wet cloth across Dylan's stomach and got an immediate reaction. The cold water caused him to quiver and his muscles to ripple. And that still half plump cock, quickly deflated.

"We made a mess." This time Dylan's eyes were on the blanket covered with food.

"I should've let you eat more." Tristan finished cleaning Dylan, before he started working to right some of the spilled dishes. "I don't think we can save it, but I can order in."

CHAPTER.13

Dylan sat up, pushing himself back into his underwear. He zipped up then tucked his shirt back into his jeans while Tristan worked at cleaning the mess on their blanket. He should be helping, but the impact of having such a intimate sexual experience performed in such a public place came crashing down on him.

Tristan did these kinds of things to him. Made him forget himself. He pushed him until he didn't know which way was up or down. Until he gave in and did the exact opposite of what he should have done. No other person on this planet held that much control over him. How did this man do that?

"You okay?" Tristan asked, standing. The food seemingly forgotten.

"I don't know how you do this to me." Dylan tried to explain, and a grin spread across Tristan's face.

"That's something I've been asking myself since I laid eyes on you. Here, carry the basket. It's getting late. At this point, Julian will be there before we arrive." Dylan took the basket Tristan handed him, realizing he hadn't gotten an answer. Tristan scooped up the blanket from the four sides, allowing all the contents to fall to the middle. Without another word, he trailed along behind Tristan, making his way back up the path. Tristan carried the blanket extended away from his body.

When they got to the parking area, Tristan walked to a trashcan and placed the entire blanket inside the big metal container. "I love my car too much. I don't want that to spill. Terrible, huh?" Tristan asked, clicking the key fob. He carefully inspected the basket before allowing it inside. "Wanna drive?"

Dylan shook his head and started for the passenger side. Tristan reached out and stopped him, pulling him closer. "Are you nervous?"

"A little," he admitted. He was still more stuck on the fact he planned to do any of this to begin with. Tristan pulled him against his body, but he pushed back, stepping away. He held his hands in front of him, stopping Tristan from coming any closer. He'd just kissed and fucked Tristan's fist, all in the open on a public beach. Anyone could have seen them. Tristan had the ability to destroy his boundaries.

"It's not wrong. What we're doing, I mean," Tristan said, but he took a step back and then another, and something crossed his face that Dylan couldn't read.

"What we do behind closed doors is one thing, but I shouldn't have let that happen down there," Dylan said. Tristan made his way to the driver's side and opened the door, but didn't get in. He just looked at him over the roof of the car.

"Funny. What I'll remember about that moment is that I was so turned on by you I lost sight of everything just to touch you." Tristan lowered himself into his seat behind the wheel and shut the door. Dylan was left standing there, speechless. Was that a line? Surely to god it was. He opened the door and got inside as Tristan started the car.

"How many times have you used that line before?" Dylan asked.

"Never. You're gonna learn I say what I feel. I'm not the player you think I am. I haven't had to be." Tristan stared at him a moment, and he could see the hurt there...and maybe uncertainty. Tristan shifted the car to reverse and backed them out.

"I'm sorry. It's all me, not you," Dylan apologized, rubbing his sweaty palms along his thighs. "I shouldn't have said that."

Tristan stayed silent as he drove. It was dark, but Dylan thought he saw a small tic in his jaw.

"Really. I'm sorry," he offered. "I just don't understand what I'm doing. This isn't me. I don't do these things and then you look my way and I just lose it. It's me, not you. I shouldn't take it out on you."

"Look, I've enjoyed getting to know you. That's a surprise to me too. At first you were the awkward closeted guy, but that's all changed. I don't know why, but I'm not playing you," Tristan explained, sliding the gear shift into fifth. "I shouldn't have jacked you off out on the beach. Yes, I crossed lines, but I'm crossing every line there is already—I'm trying to buy your company. A smart move would have been to leave you in that closet. I have a lot to lose by hooking up with you, whether you realize it or not."

Dylan let that thought sit there between them. Tristan was right. He hadn't considered Tristan's side of this, and he scrubbed a hand down over his face. "I never considered the possibility I'd be going to work for you. This can't go on past this weekend."

"I haven't asked for a long-term commitment," Tristan said, grinning at Dylan. Now, he felt silly. Tristan reached over and bumped his shoulder. "I'm not trying to make this any more than what it is. When you finally come out, I see a long line of men wanting some of this." Tristan reached down and grabbed Dylan's crotch.

"We'll never speak of tonight again?" Dylan asked, ignoring Tristan's hand on his groin.

"Of course not. That breaks the guy code," Tristan replied and withdrew his hand. He was happy again, lighthearted. It seemed like that was Tristan's preferred disposition.

"Good. I'm really nervous."

"You should be, but it's fine. There's nothing wrong with threesomes as long as everyone knows the score." Tristan winked at him. He'd always wanted to be more adventurous. He wasn't a prude by any means, but things like this just never happened to him.

He picked at a hangnail on his thumb and couldn't meet Tristan's gaze, didn't want him to see the insecurity hidden there.

"You'll see."

"Do I need a safe word?" That had just occurred to him. He needed to know the rules of the game. He was trying to prepare himself so he didn't appear so naïve when the time arrived. He could play any game if he understood the rules.

"What? No! We aren't tying you up and whipping you, unless you want that." Tristan's brow lifted as he tried to hide his chuckle.

"No, I don't think I'm into that." He actually definitely knew he wouldn't be into that.

"I think the word *no* is sufficient for tonight." Tristan smiled and took Dylan's hand back in his, placing a simple kiss on his knuckles. "I want you to like this. Tonight's all about pleasure, everyone's pleasure."

Tristan pulled the car into his driveway and opened the garage door about ten minutes later than they'd planned to arrive. There was a jaguar parked in the driveway, where a figure leaned against the car, arms and ankles crossed. When the headlights flashed across him, the tall, athletically built man looked up, tapping his watch, and all Dylan could think was the man was beautiful. The insecurity building inside grew by leaps and bounds.

"He's a good guy." Tristan slid the gear in first and turned off the car.

"I'm not sure I'm a threesome kind of guy," Dylan said quietly into the dark.

"It can be fun, I promise. But we'll go slow. Remember, no is the safe word."

"You're making fun of me," Dylan said, looking over at Tristan as he opened his door.

"Only a little, come on." Tristan winked before opening the door. He watched Julian walk through the garage and into the back of the house. Clearly he'd made this walk before.

"Get me all excited and then keep me waiting," Julian called out. He stood casually in the doorway, the kitchen light shining down on him almost as if it had been put there to accentuate his good looks. And he was everything Dylan had thought he would be. The guy was extraordinarily attractive. A clean, polished sort of man that looked like he walked off the cover of a Dolce and Gabbana advertisement. "He's pretty sexy in the suburban hot soccer dad kind of way." Julian winked.

"Julian meet Dylan. Dylan, Julian." Tristan introduced them, sliding past Julian. "Give him a break. He's new to all of this."

"A virgin, how sweet and yummy." Julian leered at Dylan, touching his arm, feeling the muscle underneath. The guy started to slide his hand along Dylan's arm to his chest.

"I'm betting he's probably gonna give it more than one try after tonight," Julian purred, squeezing Dylan's ass as he passed by. Funny, he hadn't ever realized he didn't like to be randomly touched and moved out from the hold.

Again, the thoughts resurfaced that three was probably too many for him. He didn't see this turning out well at all. Forcing his mind to change focus, he decided he should consider tonight a rite of passage. Something he needed to experience to know for sure, so he followed Tristan through the house, walking a little faster to keep from being molested by Julian who trailed behind him.

Tristan turned on lamps as he went straight to the wet bar.

"We'll just have to wait and see. He's got rules. Here," Tristan said, pouring Dylan a double shot of Jäger.

"Liquid courage. I remember those days," Julian chuckled. The guy knew his way around enough to open the back windows. "I'll have a shot."

Tristan poured Julian one and refilled Dylan's. "Remember, you can stop at any time."

"But why would he?" Julian sing-songed, pulling his lightweight sweater over his head, tossing it aside. He wasn't bulked up like Tristan, but every muscle in his chest was defined, so was his stomach. Dylan drank the next shot and looked between Julian and Tristan. They were both extraordinary male specimens, and it occurred to him that he was definitely the odd man out in this room. He set down the shot glass for another.

"Is it a requirement to look like you guys to live on Laguna Beach?" Dylan asked, downing the next shot.

"I'm from the Valley, hon." Like that explained anything to Dylan. Julian kept shedding his clothes, making this his own little strip show right there in the middle of Tristan's living room.

"I probably need another one." Dylan kept his eyes on Julian, waiting for the liquor to kick in. With enough alcohol and as good-looking as the guy was, Dylan began to see how this evening might possibly play out all right.

"Are you sure?" Tristan asked. Some of the shots were doubles and they hadn't eaten much dinner, but fuck, he was still so nervous.

"Yeah," Dylan said, handing Tristan the glass. He watched as the slacks came off, exposing a half aroused but well-hung cock.

"Will I do?" Julian asked Dylan, stepping closer. Tristan handed him the glass, and he drank the shot down in one gulp. Julian came forward and removed the glass from his hand, discarding it on the bar. He never took his eyes from Dylan.

Finally, he could feel the effects of the alcohol beginning to settle in.

"Let me guess. I'm pretty good at this. You have a wife, a couple of kids, and you've lived in the South your whole closet-filled life," Julian stated matter-of-factly, tugging Dylan's shirttail from his jeans and lifting the material over his head.

"Did you tell him that?" Dylan turned to Tristan. He thought his words might have been slightly slurred.

"Not even your name before I introduced you in the garage." Tristan grinned, lifting a hand to give his oath. He had a cocktail glass in his hand, drinking something clear with limes. Dylan reached out and took the glass from him, taking a large gulp. It was gin. He handed the glass back to Tristan as he felt his belt buckle being loosened.

"I've just seen it all. It comes with the job," Julian said, fumbling with his blue jeans' button and zipper. "He doesn't know how hot he is, does he?" Julian asked, looking over his shoulder at Tristan.

"No idea," Tristan smirked, drinking from the refresher he'd made.

"What's your job?" Dylan asked, slightly confused. The welcomed numbness made his thoughts a little harder to assimilate.

"Model, escort, you name it," Julian said and slid his hands inside Dylan's pants. His palms were cold and any nerve he built faded as he sucked in his breath.

"Slow it down, J," Tristan said, stepping closer to Dylan. "He needs time. Come sit down. Take it slow with him."

"I've only got a couple of hours. I'm meeting someone," Julian quietly replied.

"That's okay," Tristan assured.

"Are you paying him to be here?" Dylan asked. The alcohol had officially gone to his head, slowing his thoughts. He required Tristan to guide him the few steps to the living room. That ocean view became the backdrop as he sat down in the center of the sofa with Tristan beside him.

"No, it's more of an understanding kind of deal." Julian chuckled and sat down on the other side of him.

"You still have your clothes on." Dylan nodded toward Tristan.

"They'll be off soon enough. Let Julian kiss you." Tristan's voice was deep and smooth as he turned toward him. Dylan moved his head and Tristan's lips were so close he reached out for a kiss. He knew right then the alcohol had done what it always did and allowed him to override his inhibitions and run free. He might actually be able to pull this off.

Tristan kissed him, keeping the moment light. "Can you kiss Julian now?" Tristan whispered against his lips. All he had to do was turn his head and Julian was there. Dylan had the initial shock of new lips on his. The kiss was awkward, but soft and firm all at the same time. Julian persisted, deepening the kiss quickly. Too quickly. When Julian shoved his skilled tongue down Dylan's throat, the image of Tristan, sitting beside him, watching him with this other guy flooded his brain and everything changed.

Tristan took a long drink of the gin, placing the glass on the coffee table in front of him. He watched with interest as Julian's usually clever moves remained unnoticed by Dylan. He'd thought the two of them would have been about the hottest thing he'd ever seen, but instead, he didn't like this idea at all, hated anyone else putting the moves on Dylan but him. He slid his hands down Dylan's shoulders then pressed his chest against the heat of Dylan's broad back and kissed his neck.

The kiss between Julian and Dylan couldn't have lasted more than a minute. He could tell the alcohol was loosening Dylan up, but when Dylan tore free and looked over at him, his whole entire world stopped. He wanted to be the only one kissing Dylan's lips and touching his body. Was he jealous of Julian? No, not him. He wasn't the jealous type or at least he'd never been before. He lifted a hand, brushed his palm down the side of Dylan's face and leaned in, replacing Julian's lips with his own. He opened immediately, kissing Dylan with all the possession he'd just experienced. Dylan turned in his arms, wrapped himself around Tristan, and he did the same. This sexy man began to gently make love to Tristan's mouth with lips, tongue, and teeth.

He had no idea how long they stayed wrapped around each other or how long the kiss lasted, he just knew every part of him wanted every part of Dylan. It wasn't until Dylan jerked and his body pitched forward that he was torn from the trance. Tristan looked down to see Julian swallowing Dylan whole. Dylan had reacted quickly, apparently wanting nothing to do with the act.

Dylan had to be more than buzzed. Four doubles of Jäger slammed back-to-back had to have him good and drunk about now. Dylan kept hold of Tristan. His upper body still wrapped around him as he tried to buck Julian away. Julian was just doing what he did best and didn't seem to understand or pick up on the fact he wasn't wanted until Dylan's knee connected with his jaw in an attempt to get away.

"Fuck, man, I was just trying to make you feel good," Julian mumbled, rubbing his jaw.

"Sorry," Dylan apologized. He was back on Tristan, tugging his shirt over his head as he straddled Tristan's lap. Dylan's mouth descended on his, kissing him again. It took several seconds for Tristan to break free, only to have Dylan latch on to his neck, sucking hard. That was most definitely going to leave a mark.

"Babe, what about J? Do you want him here?" Tristan asked, stroking Dylan's hair.

"I can't," Dylan whispered against his skin. "Only you."

"We'll do whatever you want. Tonight's about you." That earned him another plunge of Dylan's tongue in his mouth as Dylan ground his dick roughly against his belly. Tristan smiled into the kiss as he placed his hands on Dylan, stopping the roll of his hips. He didn't want to take chances with all the grinding going on, just in case he could manage an orgasm under the alcohol haze. He wanted to be the one to coax the orgasm from Dylan's body.

"Thanks for coming over, but I don't think this is gonna happen tonight, J," Tristan said, drawing Dylan back to his neck. He had to concentrate on keeping his brain functioning as Dylan assaulted his ear.

"Like, you want me to leave?" Julian asked, clearly confused.

"Yes, I'm sorry. I was wrong about what I thought he needed. Please lower the garage door on your way out. I'll call you tomorrow," Tristan managed before Dylan was back to kissing him like his life depended on their intimacy. Julian didn't say anything as he gathered his clothing and left. He knew the guy had already made plans for later anyway, so he didn't feel too bad for sending him away. Several seconds passed after he heard the garage door close, and his body was headed to the point of no return with the way Dylan rubbed against him.

"The bedroom. I want you in my bed."

"Are you mad?" Dylan whispered, leaning back enough to look into Tristan's eyes. The passion fled, and he witnessed the insecurity slipping back in.

"No, not at all. Honestly, I didn't like him touching you. It made me feel things I'm not used to feeling," Tristan confessed, maybe his own insecurity forced the quiet words out.

"It didn't feel right. We didn't fit," Dylan replied, leaning back in to kiss his lips again.

"*We* fit," Tristan admitted in a moment of sincerity. He leaned forward and lightly kissed Dylan's lips. "You and I fit. I want you tonight, and I want you to trust me."

The honesty of this moment didn't escape him, and he wasn't sure he'd ever before in his life experienced an intimacy as endearing and sweet. He lifted his palms to Dylan's face and they stared at one another. Several long seconds passed between them before Dylan nodded.

"Good. I want you in me like last night, and hell, I want to bury myself in you, too," Tristan groaned, running his hands up then down Dylan's waist. He wanted the two of them in his bedroom, but loved having this naked man pressed against him. "You know this weekend isn't going to be enough. We fit too well together."

Tristan knew it was safe to say those words. While Dylan should technically be too drunk to even notice, it caused him to put some distance between them. Tristan wasn't going to let that happen. He closed his arms tightly around him again, drawing him back to the kiss. Dylan opened for him, quickly turning the kiss into a frenzy of promised pleasure and sizzling need with both teeth and tongues clashing. He couldn't lift

Dylan off him, so he turned and positioned them across the sofa.

"Should have been my mouth on you, not his," Tristan rumbled, not able to let go of the fact that he had been the one to suggest the threesome in the first place. Grabbing Dylan's cock, he started pumping the thick length as he trailed kisses down his chest. He toed off his shoes and kept stroking Dylan from tip to base, loving the sounds Dylan made at his touch. Tristan sucked and nipped the skin under Dylan's belly button then buried his nose in Dylan's neatly trimmed groin, inhaling deeply. He loved the smell of a man, but Dylan's scent made him dizzy with need. The need to know him, protect him, the need to taste him. He slid his hands up Dylan's thighs and toyed with his balls. When his lips closed around Dylan's cock, he thought he'd be bucked off the sofa.

"Jesus, I love your mouth," Dylan gasped when Tristan swallowed him whole. At that, he lifted his eyes and saw Dylan's head propped up on a couch cushion, watching him, his gaze darkened with desire. He licked around the swollen head, keeping eye contact, then deep-throated him on the next try. That was all it took for Dylan to thread his fingers through Tristan's hair and begin to move. His hips rolled, creating a rhythm all his own. Tristan let him. He concentrated on breathing as Dylan fucked his mouth. Dylan's hips arched forward over and over, strong fingers gripped tightly in his hair.

"Oh, fuck!" Dylan's thrusts became erratic. A burst of pre-come hit his tongue, and he sucked the cock deeper. He used one hand to squeeze the base of Dylan's dick hard, to keep him from coming, the other tugged at Dylan's sac as he pressed his tongue into the small weeping slit, slowing him down but teasing him to madness.

"Aghh, please…" Dylan begged.

Tristan released the hold he had on the base of Dylan's cock, opened his jaw, and took him to the back of his throat. He moaned at every thrust of Dylan's hips.

Dylan murmured some indecipherable language and plunged in one last time, then tried to quickly pull out. Tristan sank his fingers into Dylan's hips and held him in place. Dylan's cry filled the room and Tristan swallowed around the pulsing dick as salty release filled his mouth.

"Mmm, that was…amazing." Tristan ran his tongue up the underside of Dylan's cock, cleaning him before he slid up Dylan's body. He lowered his mouth, but hesitated. The intense look in Dylan's eyes didn't prepare him for when Dylan rose to lick the last of his come off Tristan's lips in a move so damn sexy Tristan's ass clenched and his cock began to leak.

"I'm in trouble…" Dylan mumbled, closing his eyes, his breathing returning to normal.

"That you are. I think we both are. Come to bed with me." From the first time he'd laid eyes on Dylan, he thought the man might be trouble. Now that he'd had a taste, he was positive he was already in too deep.

CHAPTER.14

The blow job had completely relaxed him, but also sobered him up. He'd been completely turned on. Now, his body hummed, so warm and tranquil. He remembered parts of the evening, some things were hazy, but he couldn't forget the feel of Tristan's mouth on him. Other parts he'd just as soon forget. What had he been thinking? There had been another man with them on the couch. His eyes popped open and he looked around the room, but Julian was nowhere to be found. He let out a breath as relief hit him hard.

Apparently he was a vanilla kind of guy after all. He wanted his sex one-on-one, even with alcohol involved.

"Come to bed," Tristan said, leaning over him again. There was a smile there in Tristan's eyes too, and Tristan softly palmed his face before leaning in to kiss his lips.

"He's gone for good?" Dylan asked, feeling confused. He reached up, holding Tristan right there by the back of the neck. His fingers slid through the short ends of Tristan's hair.

"Sent him packing before we got started, but you were too busy mauling me to notice." Tristan laughed, probably at

Dylan's visible relief when his shoulders relaxed, and kissed him lightly.

"Thank you," he said, smiling back. "Will Julian be mad at you?"

"No, it's not like that, we have an arrangement. We both know the deal. Come on. Let's go to bed," Tristan said, pulling Dylan up.

"So this thing between you and Julian isn't serious?" he asked as he reluctantly stood. His head swam and his knees were weak, but that was more orgasm-related than alcohol-induced.

"Not even a little." Tristan left him standing beside the couch and ducked behind the bar to grab a water bottle.

"I need some of that," Dylan said, shoving his fingers through his hair as he walked toward the bar on unsteady feet. Tristan took another long swallow before handing the half empty bottle to Dylan. He drank the water down.

"Want another shot?" Tristan asked.

"No. I know you don't believe it, but I don't actually drink," Dylan said, taking a step back as Tristan rounded the corner.

"That's pretty unbelievable. You didn't wince at the Jäger." Tristan hooked an arm around Dylan's waist, drawing them together so Tristan's hard-on pressed against his stomach.

"You didn't come?" he asked, reaching lower, running his palm against Tristan's arousal.

"No, but I'm getting mine. You promised when I sent Julian away." That set Dylan's stomach roiling. Uncertainty filled him. He'd been clear he wasn't ready. "Stop the worrying. If you don't want it, just say the word, but you said you'd trust me, remember?"

"I did." Dylan bit his lip.

"You're a grown-ass man, but when I see you bite your lip like that, words like adorable pop into my head," Tristan teased.

"I'm not adorable." The attempt at levity worked though, and his body settled down at the prospect of the unknown.

"You know, you kind of are," Tristan said with a wink. His hands slipped to Dylan's waist, pushing him back a few steps.

"That Julian was adorable," he said, watching Tristan closely as he let him guide him backward.

"You liked him? I would have never guessed that by the way you drop-kicked him in the jaw." That had Tristan laughing.

"I did not," Dylan said, stopping their progression. Tristan's chest collided with his.

"Wait—I got the impression you didn't want him here." Tristan's tone changed, his demeanor did too as they stood face-to-face.

"I don't want him. But I can see why you'd like him. He's a good-looking guy," Dylan admitted, and that smoothed Tristan's facial features. He started pushing Dylan back through the house again.

"I found I didn't want him here either. I think I just encouraged it to get you back here tonight." Tristan led them through the kitchen, not letting Dylan turn around or slow down. "Are you hungry? Once I get you in that bed, it's gonna be a good long while before I let you out." Tristan kept him pressed snuggly against his chest, steering him through the house.

"I'm good," Dylan said, and Tristan turned him, guiding him into the bedroom. It was an abrupt move, and he stumbled a bit, but Tristan righted him with a laugh, pulling him back up against his broad chest.

"Keep the buzz a little while longer," Tristan whispered in his ear.

"I'm not sure I even have…" He turned his head to tell Tristan he wasn't as buzzed as he had been. Tristan didn't give him time to finish his sentence. He grasped his face in between his palms and kissed him passionately. Seconds later, he found himself against the bed.

"Trust me, remember?" Tristan soothed. He kept Dylan in his arms, but reached down to fold the covers back before lowering him to the mattress. "Center of the bed."

Tristan went to his bathroom for the massage oils and a towel. When he returned, Dylan was just where he'd instructed, lying there, arms behind his head and a knee bent so his foot rested flat on the mattress. That flaccid cock plumping as Dylan watched him move closer. He stumbled on his feet at the sight awaiting him and realized he liked Dylan in his bed. He wanted more nights just like this. In a matter of about an hour, Tristan had jealousy coursing through him and now wanting the guy to regularly inhabit his life. How in the world did this resistant and stubborn man manage to evoke such emotion from him?

"Julian doesn't have anything on you," Tristan said honestly, averting his eyes, trying to hide all the emotions strumming through him.

"Yeah, right," Dylan barked, laughing out loud as Tristan placed the oils and towels on the nightstand and opened the drawer. Dylan's genuine smile took his breath. He abandoned the task at the nightstand and climbed on the bed, his eyes on that smile. He couldn't even remember what he'd said to cause such a reaction. The true, broad grin changed Dylan's already alluring face into something magical.

"What's so funny?" Tristan asked as he settled beside Dylan, drawing him into his arms.

"Julian's young and hot, and I'm an old man."

"You aren't that old. How old are you? Hold up. I know this answer. You're like thirty-eight, thirty-nine?" Tristan knew Dylan's age, but liked the smile and wanted to keep it going by teasing him.

"Don't make me older than I am. I'm thirty-seven. How old are you?" Dylan playfully frowned at him.

"Well, I'm much younger than you. So you caught yourself a younger man. I guess that makes you my sugar-daddy," Tristan said, laughing at Dylan's laugh. He'd never loosened up this much. He was always serious. What had happened to cause this? Did he dare hope that Dylan was getting comfortable around him?

"Much younger, huh?" Dylan eyed him closely.

"Absolutely." Tristan nodded, running a palm down Dylan's chest, then back up again. He let his fingers linger over those smiling lips. "I'm a very young thirty-six."

That had Dylan laughing out loud. "Yeah, a mere babe in the woods. I think I'm a bad influence."

"I agree and I really like this side of you." Tristan leaned in to lightly kiss Dylan's lips.

"I'm comfortable," he muttered, lying back on the bed. His eyes never left Tristan's and the smile remained in place.

"I hoped that was it! I'll have to remember this." Tristan bent in again, and Dylan met him halfway, his mouth open.

"Turn over. Let me give you a massage," Tristan said against his skin, before the kiss could go too far. "I want to make you feel good, but you have to trust me."

Dylan didn't respond at first and his face slowly morphed back into that serious guy he'd been earlier.

"Trust me?" Tristan asked, reaching for the oil. "Massage oil, see? I'm an expert." He helped Dylan roll over, pushing at his shoulder. "I can't wait to get my hands on you."

Dylan turned, but kept his head leaned back, watching Tristan's every move.

"Relax." Tristan straddled the back of Dylan's thighs. "It's gonna be a little cold," he said, drizzling the oil directly over Dylan's back.

"No shit! You could have at least warmed it in your hand." Dylan whined.

"Stop moving and lie down," he said as he slid his hands through the oil. "I'm romancing you."

That had Dylan lifting his head and looking back over his shoulder. "I'm a sure bet. Besides, romancing me would have been warming that up."

"We'll see. Turn around. Put your head down. You're ruining the moment." Tristan chuckled, slapping his hand on Dylan's raised shoulder. Dylan laid his head back down and his body eased. Tristan took time working Dylan's muscles, slowly but completely relaxing him. He worked from top to bottom on Dylan's back, sliding his hands across his ass, ignoring his own aching cock as he caressed Dylan's skin. God, it would be so easy to just give himself a quick tug. It wouldn't take much, but he refused. He had his goal in sight.

When he heard the soft snores, he smiled and began to knead the firm round globes of Dylan's ass, sliding his hands toward the center crevice. He reached out for the lubricant and condoms, dripping some on his fingers before he decided to switch up his strategy. He parted Dylan's ass cheeks and bent in, sliding his tongue along the rim. That stirred the sleeping man. When he pressed his tongue inside Dylan's ass, the deep moan that came from above let him know he was doing something right.

The sweet musky taste of Dylan burst across his palate. All of a sudden he was a starving man, greedily trying to satisfy his own hunger. He lapped and teased at Dylan's entrance, wanting to please him. Minutes passed before he replaced his tongue with the tip of his finger and trailed soft kisses across Dylan's ass.

"It feels good, doesn't it?" Tristan whispered softly while drawing circles around Dylan's hole with his finger. He slowly pushed a digit inside, easily finding the gland that had Dylan moaning again and pressing back against his hand as if he wanted more. Tristan withdrew his finger and reached for the lube, then sat back on his heels.

"Why'd you stop?" Dylan mumbled sleepily into the pillow.

"I'm not stopping, just taking in the sight of you. You're a beautiful man, Dylan."

He admired every curve of Dylan's body, from the thick muscles straining on his back to the dimples just above his flawless butt. He poured a good amount of lube on his fingers and slid his hand between Dylan's ass cheeks. Something between a growl and a moan rumbled from Dylan as his fingers slipped inside and gently worked him open. Painstakingly slow, he loosened him even more with every twist of his wrist and curl of his fingers.

"I can't take much more," Dylan said and slid his hand under his body. His hips arched off the bed.

"I want to show you everything you've been missing." Tristan repositioned himself and ground his erection against Dylan. After a quick feel across the sheets to locate the packet, he carefully tore it open and then slid the condom down his length before settling on the bed beside Dylan.

"Wait," Tristan breathed. Dylan had begun stroking himself, not heeding his request. He batted Dylan's hand away and rolled him to his side, facing away from him. He nudged Dylan's leg up, bending at the knee and guided him forward. He tucked his forearm under Dylan's neck and propped himself up on his elbow, turning his head as he slightly lifted to kiss Dylan's neck and shoulder.

"Do you want me?" he asked and pushed two fingers inside Dylan before adding a third, making sure he was slick and open, completely ready for him.

"Yes, but go slow...and touch me." Dylan nodded his head and moved his hand back to his rigid cock. Tristan stopped him again.

"I'll do that," Tristan whispered, brushing Dylan's hand aside.

Tristan slid his throbbing cock up and down Dylan's crevice, then positioned his head at the entrance. The need to claim this man nearly overwhelmed him. He took a deep breath to calm himself and slowly pressed the tip of his cock against Dylan, feeling it slip past the tight ring of muscle and into his snug channel. Dylan tensed in his arms, even the air in his lungs seemed to freeze at the initial breach.

"Are you okay?" he panted, lowering his head to judge Dylan's reaction.

"Yes, it's just... I don't know... Move. It feels better." It wasn't that he didn't want to move. It was just that if he did, their time together might not be as long as he'd anticipated. God, Dylan felt amazing, all that tight heat consuming him, drawing him deeper.

"Yeah, don't move. Give me a sec." Tristan gasped.

"I wanna move," Dylan breathed, kissing his arm. Tristan gritted his teeth and held Dylan tighter. He ducked his head against Dylan's shoulder and bit down as he gently pulled out and slowly pressed in again.

"Shit, that's starting to feel incredible," Dylan whispered, awe in his voice.

"I know," Tristan agreed and tried the move again. Part of his body wanted him to hold still, the feeling too intense. The other part of him wanted release so badly, his need to move almost consumed him. Neither was his goal at the moment, so he slid his hand over Dylan's hip and grabbed his cock. He stroked slowly as he forced himself to continue with deliberate controlled movements.

"I need more," Dylan murmured into the pillow and moved his hips back against Tristan.

"Not this time. Take it slow," he forced out and kissed Dylan's shoulder, then ran his nose along his neck and ear. "You're incredible." He sighed.

Dylan fucked back against him, then slowly rolled to his stomach. Tristan never quit thrusting into Dylan's body. He was on top now with Dylan spread out on the bed below him. Tristan anchored his knees in the mattress as Dylan gradually rose, lifting his ass.

"That feels amazing. Now, fuck me like you mean it." Dylan reared back, forcing his ass hard into Tristan. Dylan's hands were splayed out in front of him as he gripped the sheets between his fingers, making a fist. His back muscles tensed and flexed as he dropped his head between his shoulders. "Harder... I need it harder."

"Feels so good." Tristan reached for the lube and clicked open the top, dripping more slick on his cock as he slid out of Dylan's body. He dropped the lube back on the bed and slammed into Dylan, withdrew and rammed forward again. Unintelligible words flowed from Dylan. He canted his hips and aimed for his gland.

"Right there. So... Holy hell, yess!" Dylan's words were drawn out, and his Texas drawl made Tristan's dick grow even harder.

"Fuck," he breathed, gripping Dylan's hips, driving himself forward. Dylan met him thrust for thrust. "Jack yourself for me."

"Aghh, fuck me, harder..."

Dylan's rhythm built and Tristan pistoned his hips to try to keep up. He hadn't heard Dylan's comment, couldn't make out what he was saying with his face tucked into the pillow.

But he knew when Dylan's hand went to his dick and began stroking. Shit, the thought of Dylan jacking himself caused his hips to falter. He was close, and the way that ass gripped him, Dylan wasn't too far off either. He looked down at his lover and smoothed his hand along the outline of his ass.

"Beautiful." His balls churned as he slid the heel of his palm up the length of Dylan's spine and into his hair. He tightened his fingers in Dylan's hair and pulled his head back, plunging himself mindlessly into the sweet, scorching tightness. He screwed his eyes shut and allowed Dylan to claim a piece of his heart. This man completely undid him. Dylan had turned out to be so much more than he'd bargained for.

"Come for me, Dylan," Tristan cried out and thrust into him one last time. Heat swirled in his spine, coursing swiftly through his veins, and his balls drew up.

"Yes!" Dylan's ass clamped down on his cock, his orgasm crashing over Tristan in mind-numbing waves of pleasure. His dick jerked, filling the condom with seed as he came hard in Dylan's clenching ass.

Tristan fell forward, his weight resting on Dylan just as his knees gave way. A groan and one last shudder was all the protest his body could manage when his cock softened and slipped out of Dylan's heat. They were both breathless and gasping for air when he rolled them to their sides.

"It's in my hand," Dylan finally managed to get out as he greedily sucked in air. He held his hand out, trying to keep his palm off the bed as he fell back on Tristan. Every nerve ending in his body was on high alert, his heart threatened to break through his rib cage, his breathing sounded more like wheezing, and he'd loved every single minute. Seconds later, minutes, or maybe even hours—he didn't know, he'd lost all sense of time—Tristan finally made a noise and started moving under him.

"Hmmm, what did you just say?"

"It's in my hand." He was careful how he held his hand, but his hold was becoming harder to maintain when all he wanted to do was sleep.

"What does that mean?" Tristan stopped moving from underneath him.

"My load. I shot it in my hand."

"What?" Dylan had no idea what he'd said that was so confusing. Instead of resaying the words, he waited for Tristan to figure things out for himself. Enough time passed and Tristan finally responded.

"Seriously? You caught it?" Tristan chuckled.

Tristan gently pulled out from underneath him, reached for the towel, and cleaned his hand. Dylan just lay there, spread across the bed, his eyes closed. He felt Tristan moving around him as he slowly centered back into himself.

What an incredible experience. He wouldn't ever be the same again and that thought gripped his heart. How could he ever go back to the way things had been? Now that he'd had a taste, he wanted more. He craved the closeness and caring they had just shared. And he wanted it all with this very man.

Dammit to hell, he was so screwed.

Warm lips brushed across his, and he cracked his eyelids open.

"I didn't manage to close the top and the lube leaked all over the sheets, now the room smells like sex on a beach," Tristan laughed, holding the bottle in his hand.

"I don't think I can move," Dylan mumbled, keeping his eyes on the handsome man.

"Was it too much?" Tristan asked, worry now showing on his face.

"No. Yes. I don't know," Dylan said, closing his eyes. Since their sex had been life-altering and everything he wanted was bent over him right now, yeah, he guessed it had been too much.

"You need a hot bath. It'll help in the morning. I'll change the sheets," Tristan said, his voice trailing off as he walked away. Dylan heard the bathwater filling the tub, but he didn't move, he just lay there. He actually didn't want this moment to end. There had been no horrendous pain, at least not like he'd built up in his mind. What Tristan had done to him was definitely something he wanted more of in the future.

The assumption he was a top seemed laughable now. He'd do that every day if possible. He never would have thought he'd have done anything like this. It must have been the Jäger. Dylan judged his drunkenness on a scale of one to ten and came up with nothing. He didn't feel drunk and that made him smile. These were true, sober feelings after all.

"Come, you can smile like that in the bath," Tristan called out from the bathroom door. He heard water splashing so he rolled over and forced himself to sit up on the side of the bed. Tristan had used enough of that tropical-smelling massage oil on him that he left his body's imprint on the sheet. Tristan had taken time with him tonight. He'd made this moment special and perfect. Something to embrace. Dylan ignored the fear of those thoughts and walked to the bathroom.

He needed to put this entire night in its place. The memories of Tristan and the care he took would stay with him forever. No matter how things turned out for him, he'd always have this evening to fall back on.

"I'm too oily. Let me shower first." Dylan bypassed Tristan who was already lying back in the oversized tub.

"No, come here. Let me wash you," Tristan said, extending a hand. "Come on…the oils are all natural anyway.

I'll wash you in here." Dylan got a good look at the marble bathtub that Tristan lay stretched out in.

"Damn, I haven't ever seen anything like that." Dylan went for the tub. He stepped inside and turned to face Tristan. Not understanding where Tristan wanted him, he tried to sit at the opposite end of the tub, but Tristan stopped him.

"Sit here." Tristan guided Dylan back between his thighs. "Lie against my chest. Let me hold you." Dylan turned around and scooted back into position. "How are you feeling?" Tristan asked, sounding concerned when he'd settled back against him.

"I'm good. Honestly, tonight's been amazing. You were incredible."

"Incredible, huh?" Tristan laughed then poured scrub onto a rag and began to wash him.

"Yeah, I could get used to all of this," Dylan joked.

"I'm afraid I can too," Tristan mumbled softly from behind him, placing a simple kiss close to Dylan's ear.

Dylan hadn't missed the strange tone of Tristan's voice. He cocked his head, turning back to get a better look. "Why afraid?"

"I don't know. There's something different about you, Dylan. Something I can't put my finger on, but I feel differently when I'm with you. It doesn't make a lot of sense when I say it out loud." Tristan sighed and gave him a small smile. "I know you have a family and you're very set in your plans where they're concerned and I respect that. I'm just afraid of being left wanting more with you."

Dylan didn't know how to respond. He'd turned back around so Tristan couldn't see his face. Tristan's words had taken him off guard and made his heart rate speed up. He'd had those very same thoughts lying in bed.

Maybe this was just some after-sex babble and he should take it as such. His precious plans for his future were actually nonexistent at this point. In a few months, all his children would be off to college, starting their lives and Teri would be living hers and he would be alone—that was the reality that he hadn't said aloud. He'd spent so much time focusing on his family and hiding behind them, he hadn't thought about himself, hadn't made plans for the rest of his life. Somehow, Tristan had managed to bring all that to the forefront.

Would there be moments like this over and over as he met different men? He knew that answer. Nothing would ever be this good again. He might be inexperienced, but he wasn't dumb. The way he clicked with Tristan, the consideration he gave, didn't just happen.

"Hey, you," Tristan nudged him. "You got quiet all of a sudden. I hope I haven't said anything to upset you." Tristan scooped the warm water over his chest.

"You didn't. I'm just tired's all." He looked down at the hand against his chest, then at the bath rug, then around the bathroom. Special for him, a day in the life for Tristan. He was way in over his head and needed to keep perspective.

"Thank you for tonight, Dylan." Tristan ran the rag over his shoulders then kissed the back of his neck. "Since the water's getting cold, you're tired, and it's late, let's get out. I want to snuggle you in bed," Tristan said and tugged him up, so he could get out.

CHAPTER.15

What couldn't have been more than a few hours later, Dylan's alarm went off, rousing him from a sound sleep. He reached to silence the phone; whatever made him set his alarm couldn't have been more important than his need for sleep. Unable to locate the object making the offending noise, he forced open his tired eyes and was met by Tristan's confused stare.

"Why the alarm today?" Tristan asked and pulled Dylan closer to him, snuggling back down to sleep.

Dylan lay there several seconds, right on the edge of sleep, loving the feeling of a hard warm body pressed against him. Three minutes later, as he had scheduled, the alarm went off again. "Why does that damn thing keep going off every time we're together? Power it off."

"I planned to go running this morning," Dylan grumbled, pulling away from Tristan. It was now or never since he was leaving California today.

"What time is it?" Tristan asked as he looked at his alarm clock on his side of the bed. "It's five o'clock in the morning."

Dylan rolled to the side of the bed. He sat there a minute, assessing his body parts.

"Where are you going jogging?" Tristan asked as the lamp came on flooding the dark room with light. That had him blinking like crazy, forgetting any aches in his body.

"Man, that light's bright." He ground his fist into his eyes and rubbed. "I've always wanted to run Crystal Cove. I wanted to be there by six." He forced himself up off the bed and stretched out his body.

"You should have told me that. I wouldn't have kept you up so late. Are you sore?" Tristan asked, propping himself up against the headboard. He had bedhead to the extreme. Dylan guessed he probably did too. They'd gone to bed right after the bath.

"I told you about the trail at Crystal Cove when I got in the car yesterday, and I'm not too sore. I can feel my ass, I know it's there, but it's not enough to stop me from running this morning," he said, looking over his shoulder. The covers were all messed up around Tristan's hips, but just on one side of the bed. They'd slept close together last night, apparently all night. "My stuff's in your car. Is your housekeeper here today?" he asked, walking to the bathroom.

"No, not yet. I have an extra toothbrush in the drawer to the right," Tristan called out. Dylan went for a towel. His slacks were somewhere in the house, and he was going to need them. He came back out, his hair brushed down, teeth clean, and a towel draped around his waist. Tristan was gone from the room. Dylan headed to the living room for his slacks when a nude Tristan came jogging across the kitchen floor, Dylan's bag in his hand.

"I would have gotten them." Dylan smiled and took the offering.

"So jogging like running?" Tristan asked, following along behind as Dylan walked toward the bathroom.

"Yes, like running. I need to call a ride." Dylan spun back around to the nightstand to retrieve his phone.

"I'll drive you. Maybe I can run with you. Are the other guys going?" That completely threw Dylan off as he pulled up the Uber app on his phone.

"Do you run? I mean, you clearly work out, but I didn't think you were a runner. I thought you were more into weight training," Dylan surmised, looking at Tristan's body. Hell, he'd take any opportunity to look at that hot body. Tristan came toward him.

"I run all the time. If the guys are going, I can just drop you off, but if not, I can go," Tristan offered, wrapping Dylan in his arms and pressing his lips against his neck.

"Okay. If you want, I'd like the company. I've wanted to run this trail for a while. I saw it on the Discovery Channel." Dylan reached up, threading his fingers in Tristan's hair. Tristan kissed him before he pulled away. They needed to dress quickly and get moving if they were going to make it there by six. They could run the trail and still give him a couple of hours to get back to the hotel and change before the flight home.

"It's seventeen miles through the hills, but three of those are on the beach. I'm too tired to manage them all, but I'll give it my best shot," Dylan added excitedly before disappearing into the bathroom with his bag. He used a side dressing room to give Tristan his own space to dress.

Clearly Dylan was a serious runner, not the occasional jogger Tristan had originally thought. His body looked like a runner's, lean and tall, and damn, he looked good in those running shorts. Tristan had dressed and come along because of the fucking night they'd shared last night. He certainly hadn't anticipated the trail would be seventeen miles... The most he'd ever run was a few miles on the treadmill. Certainly nothing more than five and that had to have been a few years ago. What was he thinking?

"I don't want to hold you back," Tristan said, pulling his Ferrari into a parking space. They were close to on time, only a little past six in the morning. Dylan was already out the passenger side door, money in hand to pay for parking.

"God, it's beautiful out here," Dylan exclaimed as he came back to the car, spreading his arms out toward the ocean. "This is exactly why I wanted to come here."

"I don't want to hold you back," Tristan repeated, but Dylan was off, heading to an area where other runners were already warming up. The experienced stretching he saw left no doubt Dylan could run the entire seventeen miles without a problem. He really needed a way out of this before he embarrassed himself. "I'll hold you back."

"You said you run all the time. You'll do fine. You can set the pace." Dylan lifted one leg close to his chest, then the other, before dropping down to stretch his legs out another way. Tristan wondered how Dylan felt about walking as a pace, but instead of asking, he followed Dylan's lead, mimicking his movements. The guy was on a natural high. It had to be the fresh air, because he hadn't slept for more than a few hours after drinking more in a ten minute period than Tristan had ever seen anyone drink before, and that was less than twelve hours ago.

He said a prayer as they set off.

Seven miles in and Tristan had seen Dylan's frustration, though he'd tried to hide it, for the last three miles, but at least Tristan was trying and still standing somewhat upright. Tristan was huffing hard, dripping with sweat, and dragging. But he never complained, never said anything, not one word, and it wasn't only because his breath wouldn't allow talking. He wanted to impress Dylan with his stamina; he just needed to find it first. Thank fuck, Dylan dropped his speed to a slower-paced jog. He could handle that. Maybe.

"I think I'm done. Unless you want to keep going," Dylan offered, not a hint of fatigue in his voice. Tristan thanked God right there.

"Nah, let's keep going," Tristan huffed, slowly passing by as Dylan started walking. He turned and started jogging backward, showing off for his handsome running partner.

"I'm done," Dylan replied, smiling at him. He had to look like a hot mess, but he kept on jogging backward in place, as though he knew what he was doing. What was the saying? 'Fake it till you make it.' His shirt was soaking wet, and he struggled to breathe and talk at the same time. Dylan probably knew he was grandstanding for his benefit.

After a minute of Dylan's patient smile, he stopped his little act and doubled over, trying to catch his breath. "Thank God...I was hoping you were serious about stopping. I don't feel so good." He dropped to the ground, rolling to his back.

"You should walk it out. You'll cramp up if you don't," Dylan warned.

"I can't cramp any more than I already am," Tristan panted, gulping air, trying to stop the world from spinning above him. Dylan laughed, shaking out his legs.

"Come on, seriously, you'll cramp," Dylan said, extending a hand for Tristan. "We can cut back somewhere here, I think. I read something about that."

"I have people on standby." Tristan looked up at Dylan's hand but completely ignored the gesture, choosing to remain on the ground, still breathing painfully hard. Dylan watched him closely, probably doing a bit of a how-serious-is-this assessment before lifting his brow and grinning down at him. After a second of staring at that handsome face, Tristan dug in his shorts pocket and lifted his phone to his ear. "Come get us."

"What did you just do?" Dylan shook his head and began walking around again, before bending over to stretch out his back.

"About mile three, I feared a heart attack. I put them on notice. They'll be here soon." He grinned up at Dylan's confused look, but still just lay there.

"So that's what you were doing with your phone?" Dylan asked.

"Give me a break. I was dying. Who does this on a regular basis?" Tristan gasped, draping an arm over his eyes. The whir of a golf cart raced toward them, and Tristan turned his head to the side to watch as his rescuer arrived.

"Mr. Wilder?" A guy jumped off and rushed to his side. He had an EMT badge on his sleeve.

"Yeah," Tristan replied lazily, not moving at all.

"Do you need a gurney, sir?" the guy asked, walkie-talkie in hand.

"No, I don't need a fucking gurney." It took a second for Tristan to hoist himself up. The sounds he made must have been what had Dylan laughing. It took several more seconds for him to get himself to his feet. The driver kept trying to help, and Tristan pushed him off, proud when he stayed on his feet under his own power. The EMT handed him a bottle of water, toweling his flushed face with a wet cloth.

"Don't you have water all ready?" Dylan asked.

"I drank that the first two miles." Tristan downed the contents of the water bottle quickly, knowing his stomach would hurt soon, but thirst overrode that concern.

"I would've given you mine," Dylan said, sliding inside the golf cart beside him. Tristan rolled his eyes as they were whisked away. He was in so much pain, he didn't even get to enjoy Dylan's happy mood.

"Now you offer me your water."

"I should have brought my clothes and gone from Crystal Cove to the hotel," Dylan said as he pulled Tristan's sports car into the driveway of his house. He reached up and pushed the remote to open the garage door. "But then someone still would have had to drive you home, probably in an ambulance."

"Har, har. You're never gonna let me live that down, are you?" Tristan had his head back on the headrest, but rolled his face to the left to look at Dylan.

"That was an accidental slip of a joke. That shouldn't happen too many more times," Dylan chuckled, putting the Ferrari in first gear before shutting it down. "You don't need to be driving dehydrated."

"I'm not dehydrated. I'm good now. I'm just not a runner. I work out every day, it's just different out there," Tristan countered.

"You should stay in today, let yourself even out. All that sweating and overexertion, you have to be dehydrated," Dylan advised, getting out of the car.

"I'm fine," Tristan argued and followed along behind Dylan. He had kept an eye on Tristan, and he did seem fine. Dylan entered the back door, thinking of another joke and suddenly came to an abrupt stop as unease gripped his entire body. A little, dark-haired woman stood in the pantry, looking his way.

"Mr. Tristan not home," she said in a thick Hispanic accent.

"He's with me," Tristan called out, stepping in the house from behind him. Tristan gently touched his back. That touch catapulted the fear of being seen by someone else even higher. Being in Tristan's home, having the small laughs and slight touches meant intimacy and that rooted Dylan in his spot unable to move a muscle. Tristan hadn't seemed to catch on and slid an arm around him as he moved to the side, trying to get fully inside the house. Dylan turned quickly toward Tristan and pointed at the woman, then pointed to himself, panic had to be clear on his face. If that attempt at sign language didn't get his point across, surely the fear in his eyes would make him respond. Instead he got nothing but a confused look from Tristan who was reaching for him yet again in front of the woman.

"They call. Gatorade on the counter," the small-framed Spanish woman said. Dylan bolted, and he could hear Tristan follow him instead of going for the Gatorade. That was exactly the opposite of what he wanted. Dylan made a beeline to the living room. He needed to get his clothes and get out of this house.

Fuck! His clothes were gone again! He scanned the living room, then went for the kitchen. He didn't see them on the counter or the table like before.

"What's wrong?" Tristan asked from directly behind him.

"Where are my clothes?" Dylan faced off with Tristan, becoming angry now. Tristan was steps behind him, the concern clear on his face, and that was something Dylan didn't want to see. He took off for Tristan's bedroom. His clothes were folded at the end of a freshly made bed. Everything had been cleaned and put away in Tristan's room as well as the bathroom.

Dylan went straight to his clothes, his wallet and his phone had been placed on top. Not inside the pockets, but on top. That meant she knew who he was.

"What's happened?" Tristan asked, coming up behind him, touching him again. Dylan ignored him completely, grabbed his things, and palmed his phone to search for his Uber app.

"She saw me. She knows who I am. She cleaned up our mess," Dylan finally said, thumbing through all the different applications until he found the one he wanted.

"Maria has never said a word about anything she sees in here. I'm not sure she even reads English," Tristan said, turning Dylan toward him.

"I've got to go. There's a driver a few minutes from here." Dylan ducked around Tristan who stuck out an arm, stopping him in his tracks. That was where the years of weightlifting came in handy.

"She doesn't care. She won't say anything." He jerked out of Tristan's hold, stepping several feet away, and finally got the space he needed.

"I'll drive you to the hotel." Tristan's voice turned hard.

"I don't want people to see me like this," Dylan stated on his way out of the room. He did manage a "yet" as he headed toward the front door.

Seconds later, Tristan was behind him, clamping a hand over the hard oak door Dylan was beginning to open.

"You held my hand on the beach. You let me jack you off on that same beach. Julian saw you," Tristan hissed in his ear. *Fuck*! Dylan hadn't even considered those things as real threats. The beach had been dark and they'd been completely alone. Julian was paid to be discreet. But he had been out for people to see them together. His insecure gaze darted up, meeting Tristan's intense stare. This whole thing panicked him more than ever. Julian especially.

"I shouldn't have done this," he whispered. A range of emotions played across Tristan's handsome face, until resignation was the only thing Dylan saw.

"I promised you were and are safe. I wouldn't have put you in that kind of situation. I won't ever put you in that type of situation," Tristan vowed.

"I can't do this again. Not yet. I've risked too much already," Dylan said softly, but with conviction. The anger was gone. Desolation and the voice of reason took its place. He had solid reasons to stay hidden—three of them.

"You haven't risked anything," Tristan declared. His eyes went to the small glass panels of the door and he got a funny look on his face. Tristan grabbed Dylan's wallet from on top of the clothes he carried and was out the door before Dylan could react.

"Hey," Dylan yelled and took off after him. Tristan dodged the grab Dylan made toward his wallet.

"Better be careful. Someone might see you out here with me," Tristan called out, running from the house. He opened Dylan's wallet, dug through the cash, and handed the driver money. The driver pulled away from the curb, and Tristan ran past him, dropping the wallet back on top of Dylan's slacks still held in his arms, ignoring him as he re-entered the house.

"I'm driving you to the hotel," Tristan stated, his voice coming from somewhere in the living room. Dylan stopped in his tracks and stood there, completely torn. He could tell from the strain in Tristan's voice he'd unintentionally hurt him and that was the last thing he wanted.

He was such a dumbass for even allowing this to get started. He went back around the corner to Tristan's bedroom to try to explain before he brought the driver back. Okay, his actions might have been a little over the top earlier. He would admit he had freaked when he'd unexpectedly seen Maria standing in the kitchen and the fact that Tristan had been right about the night before. He'd been out for the world to see them together. He shouldn't have let any of this happen from the very beginning. None of this was Tristan's fault; it was all him.

Tristan stalked toward him with a new shirt on, sunglasses, and a ball cap pulled down low. His car keys and cell phone in one hand. He walked right past Dylan to the kitchen.

"Maria, can you go into my bedroom for five minutes?"

"Okay?" she said, sounding a bit confused.

"No, go the back way. Just five minutes and I'll be gone. When you hear me leave, come back out," Tristan said. Dylan dropped his head in his hand; a deep sigh resonated in his chest.

"You won't be seen," Tristan called out as he stepped out of the house, the door to the garage slamming shut in his wake. Dylan let the frustration go at Tristan's little show of drama and dominance. Instead of commenting, he opened the door to find Tristan already inside the Ferrari, the engine roaring to life.

"The windows are too dark to see inside."

The driver's side door closed before he stepped fully into the garage. Dread coiled deep inside the pit of Dylan's stomach. He'd been clear with Tristan from the beginning. He wasn't trying to insult the guy; he just had a different life path.

Dylan slammed the passenger side door a little too hard after sliding into the soft leather seat. Tristan ignored him. The car was already in gear, and they were backing out of the garage before he could even fasten the seat belt.

Tristan hadn't been this pissed off in a while. He thought he'd broken through Dylan's barriers last night. They both agreed they fit well together—even declared it. They had fun together, and he envisioned they'd keep this going whenever Dylan came back to California for work. He really liked Dylan and wanted to get to know him better. That had been a huge side benefit in hiring the guy to work for him. Now, with just his housekeeper's presence in his home, all the walls were back in place. He could feel them solidly shut, like the guy he'd talked to the first night in the strip club.

"When you get home and you have time to think this through, don't blame this weekend on the alcohol," Tristan started. Yes, he was hurt and maybe he was being petty, but he needed to say it.

"This weekend was a fluke. I don't drink at all anymore," Dylan protested. Tristan looked over at him. Dylan's tone was hard, and he refused to look his way, turning toward the passenger side window instead.

"You were into last night and when we were on the beach. You didn't have more than a beer the whole time we were there," Tristan defended.

"My problem with alcohol isn't a drunken deal. It helps me forget who I am. I lose my inhibitions and myself. I shouldn't have drunk anything," Dylan answered, a little softer now.

"So, what you're saying is… I'm a drunk fuck? That's a little insulting," Tristan shot back. Not that it was that insulting. He'd know Dylan's guard had been down, but he'd thought or maybe hoped things had changed with all the time they'd spent together. He hated admitting to feeling a little bit hurt, but the dull ache in his heart wouldn't stop begging him to make this right. He took a corner a little too sharply, hoping to throw Dylan off, but he remained tight-lipped, his body tense, with his fist bunched up in the clothing he held. Dylan refused to look at him and kept his head cocked to the right, staring out the window.

They didn't say another word.

Tristan considered pulling right up front to the hotel and making Dylan either talk to him or get out of the car right there, but he resisted that urge as he pulled past the circle drive and turned the corner. He went for the garage, taking a ticket, and going all the way to the bottom floor. He pulled into a parking space in a far back corner, away from any other cars.

"No one should see you down here." Tristan shifted the gear into neutral. Dylan was already opening the door, a foot outside of the car as if he couldn't get away fast enough.

Damn, he couldn't let him leave, not like this. Not after the weekend they had shared.

"Hang on." Dylan didn't stop, didn't acknowledge him, but he hadn't figured he would. He reached out, grabbing Dylan's wrist and held on even as he tried to shake him off. "Hang on, please!"

"What?" Dylan slid back in the seat and glared at him as he closed the car door, so much turmoil reflected in the depths of his beautiful blue eyes. Tristan wasn't sure what he wanted, but that look was exactly the way he felt at this very moment. Dylan sucked in a breath, and Tristan reached for him with his other hand, sliding it around to the back of Dylan's head. The air in the small confines of his car charged with electricity. He descended and Dylan met him halfway, mouth opening for him.

Tristan prayed his kiss conveyed all the heat, passion, and desire he'd felt over the last few days. Dylan reached up to him, running his fingers through Tristan's hair, and in that moment, for Tristan, this turned into a new beginnings kiss. He never intended to let Dylan go. That possession fueled the kiss as several minutes passed, leaving Dylan sprawled across the seat. The angle of Tristan's body had the steering wheel digging into his hip and the console limiting his breath, but he didn't let go of the hold he had on Dylan who held him just as tightly.

He kissed Dylan until he couldn't breathe and moved to his neck, inhaling his scent. "I need to go," Dylan whispered, his sweet breath lingering on Tristan's face.

"I don't want you to," Tristan confessed, trying now to look Dylan in the eyes. "I'm sorry I got mad."

"It's okay. I shouldn't have let this…" Tristan stopped the words. He'd heard those enough; he didn't need to hear them anymore.

"I don't want this to be the last time I see you." He kissed him again. The lustful haze that glazed Dylan's eyes had Tristan smiling. He loved the fact that his kiss did that to this overly reasonable man. "Just go. I'll be in touch," Tristan promised as he pulled back. Dylan closed his eyes, and Tristan couldn't resist the desire to kiss each of his eyelids. Dylan swallowed hard then opened them. Sadness shone from their cerulean blue depths.

"I can't do this again," Dylan said firmly, but he didn't try to leave the embrace. His actions were in direct contrast to his words, and that allowed hope to fill Tristan's heart again. Finally, something other than his own determination that they would meet again.

"You've made that clear," Tristan whispered softly, lightly kissing his lips. Dylan kissed him again on his own.

"I'm glad you were my first," Dylan said, that sadness in his eyes reached his voice this time. Tristan didn't know what to do to banish the look. If he said there was no way he planned to let them end here, panic would return, so he kept those words to himself.

"Me, too. You're sexy as hell, Mr. Reeves." Tristan forced a smile, reluctantly letting Dylan rise.

"Thank you for all this," Dylan replied, gathering his things.

"I'll have the contracts to you quickly. I have legal working on them now," Tristan added, unable to keep himself from looking at Dylan's full lips one last time. These were lips he longed to take again and again. It was unfathomable how in such a short amount of time this man had worked his way in and completely captured his heart.

"All right," Dylan said. Tristan watched the way he squared his shoulders and set his resolve. That was probably the difference between an inebriated Dylan and a sober one. He made himself do what he considered the right thing, at all cost. And that just might be the sexiest thing about the man.

Dylan reached for the door again and Tristan let him go this time. Dylan stepped out and turned around. He ducked his head to give him one last look. Neither said anything, they just stared at one another. Words weren't needed now. Tristan saw everything he felt reflected in Dylan's eyes. Dylan gave a nod and shut the door. He didn't look back as he jogged to the bank of elevators leading up into the hotel.

Tristan stayed there, watching as Dylan entered the elevator. From where he sat, he could see Dylan turn back, look his way, and lift a hand in his direction. No way could Dylan see him, but Tristan lifted his hand and waved. Dylan looked sad. He'd give him a few days, maybe a week, but Dylan would call…he was sure of it. You could only hide for so long, especially after you got a taste of what you wanted.

"Maybe he'll find someone to fuck at home," Tristan mumbled out loud, surprising himself, but he pushed aside that thought and the jealousy those words caused. What they shared was more than a drunken fuck. At least he hoped he meant more than that to Dylan. Dylan would call. If he didn't, Tristan would call him. He just really wanted Dylan to want him enough to make the next move. He needed that to happen.

CHAPTER.16

Tristan went through the house, ignoring the silly feelings of aloneness. Dylan had visited his home for barely more than twenty-four hours. He hadn't had time to put his mark on anything or truly even belong in his space. Yet he'd done a tremendous job at making Tristan wish those things had happened.

Something caught Tristan's eyes. The pool guy was outside. He lifted a hand in greeting as regret and sadness coiled tight in his belly. He'd wanted to make love to Dylan in that pool. How had he let that opportunity slip through his fingers?

That thought had him rolling his eyes. He wasn't sure he did the whole lovesick thing very well. Yes, he was truly sad Dylan had left, but he'd see him again soon. He needed to move on to other things. He went for his cell phone, and with a couple of quick swipes, he pulled up the weekend itinerary again. They were leaving sometime this afternoon, he couldn't remember the exact time. Maybe he could get a quick call in before he boarded the flight. He started to dial, but ended the call and pivoted on his heels. No, he wanted Dylan to make the next move and that was going to take a few days. The guy had the patience of Job.

Instead of making any phone calls, he headed for the bathroom. He'd sweated so much this morning he was sure he was down thirty pounds. He figured he could use a good scrub and then a gallon of water.

Besides all that, he definitely had more than enough work to occupy his mind. Tristan flipped on the shower and waited the second for the hot water to flow. He shook his head when he realized he was actually looking forward to going through his paperwork to keep himself from calling Dylan. And that proved how bad he had it for Mr. Reeves. On a deep sigh, he dropped his shorts and tugged his T-shirt over his head. So be it, paperwork on a Sunday afternoon would be a great distraction. Tristan stepped in the shower and refused to look over at the bathtub he'd shared with Dylan last night.

Three hours later and the great paperwork plan to save his sanity had completely failed. Tristan had accomplished more mundane operational company tasks in the last few hours than he had in the last month, so go him on that one, but Dylan stayed front and present in his mind with every stroke of the keyboard.

Funny how he kept thinking in terms of stroking.

Landry sent him a dozen or so messages through email and text, wanting to have a word with him. Their last meeting hadn't ended well. That usually meant they both needed time before they met again. Against his better judgment, he decided to make that phone call today. He kicked back in his office chair and palmed his phone. Landry answered on the second ring.

"Hey, did they get off?" Tristan asked. Probably not the best starter, but it was the most urgent thought on his mind.

"Yeah, about an hour ago. I need a few minutes to talk to you." Landry sounded tense, so the cooling off probably hadn't had time to kick in. They shouldn't have this conversation now, but Tristan was primed for a fight.

"Can it wait until the morning when I come in? I'm catching up on emails and going over this contract with Secret," Tristan said, trying for reason and to buy himself time. Putting the huge issue of moving an entire division away from the chief operating officer's responsibilities due to poor performance aside, Landry knew him too well. Childhood best friends tended to pick up on simple things like who each other was attracted to. If Landry went there, Tristan would never be able to convince him his actions were purely company-focused, and in those decisions, Tristan only had WilderNation's best interest at heart.

"You're coming to the office in the morning?" Landry questioned, clearly surprised.

"Yeah, I figured I would," he answered.

"If you had a problem with me, you should have told me directly. Not made me look like an ass in front of the entire company," Landry started right in.

"Whoa there, you're barking up the wrong tree," Tristan cut in, trying to stop the rant he knew his friend was headed toward. "It's only the social media division and that isn't much of what we do. Actually it's nothing to the overall picture, except a huge loss that I'd really like to at least make an attempt to break even on."

"It's an operations function of Wilder, Inc.," Landry shot back.

"Reeves doesn't want a long-term deal. We have him for transition, maybe a few years total. He can get us up and going," Tristan replied.

"I call bullshit. If that were the case, you wouldn't have gone around me. Are you fucking him? 'Cause if you are, then don't tie my hands. Let me in there. I can figure out what they're doing right, what we can't seem to understand, and roll it out properly to fit our corporate values." Those words were almost yelled at him.

There was silence from Tristan. He didn't plan to change anything he'd set in place. Landry had been with him from his youth. He didn't want to cause them issues, but he'd seen the problems with his own eyes during the tour of his company. They were becoming stagnant. Honestly, not just on WilderNation's level, but as a whole. Landry hadn't allowed them to move forward. He'd become a serious stuffed-shirt micromanager. Tristan completely blamed himself for all of this. He'd let things go. Let Landry run the show without watching him close enough because they were still making money. Now he saw he needed some one-on-one time with the guy to remind him of the innovative headway they had always made and how they got to where they were as a company. The advertising cash cow of their search engine wouldn't hold them forever.

"You are fucking him! I swear, Tristan, this is fucking business." Landry's tone turned hard. That attitude was just what Tristan needed to stop softening the blow and to finally put things straight between them.

"Prescott, you're letting this happen and you're going to learn from this company and this man. They're doing it right. We aren't. And you're too damn fucking hardheaded to do anything but go in there and dominate until you tear that company down. That's why they're under me now."

"So it's my fault we've slowed down?" Landry shot back with a very distinct defensive-as-hell tone in his voice.

"It's all of our faults. Every member of the executive team is to blame, but you're over all the operations for the entire company. It doesn't take rocket science to know where the problem lies. We can fucking fix our issues or become obsolete." Tristan laid the facts out there. He shouldn't have made this call. He shouldn't have talked to Landry yet.

"We aren't becoming obsolete. We might have bitten off more than we can chew," Landry stated, so completely not a visionary's viewpoint as far as Tristan was concerned.

"If that's the case, after everything is said and done, I'll be spending millions to figure that out, so you better hope I'm right and you're wrong," Tristan countered, and Landry didn't say anything.

"I want in on this," Landry finally said.

"I'm not leaving you out. I just want to see if we can recoup what we've lost. WilderNation's going to Secret," Tristan explained, dropping his latest bombshell decision. It had been Landry that stuck his last name on everything they owned. Maybe the fix was as simple as a new face.

"Another thing you decided without discussing it with anyone. I don't think that's it, you're barking up the wrong tree. It's a market share and first to draw in the baby boomers issue. You need to hear me on that," Landry argued. He'd used those words over and over for the last few years, but technology was a younger person's advantage. That was where they failed in this division. Landry kept targeting the wrong audience no matter what market research kept saying.

"Are you really fucking him?" Landry asked.

"I don't want to discuss him like that," Tristan bristled at the thought. The need to protect Dylan was stronger than admitting the truth to his best friend.

"Since when?" Landry probed.

"Since now. Did they get off okay? Were there any problems?" Tristan asked.

"Why do you care? Of course everything went fine," Landry said.

"Then job well done. I'll meet with the team tomorrow. Pull them together for me about mid-morning," Tristan instructed.

"I'm not your secretary," Landry huffed.

"Then tell your wife for me or put her on the damn phone so I can tell her myself," Tristan shot back.

"I want in on this, Tristan. When you're done with him, he'll bail on us. He's too smart not to have a clause giving him an out. When that time comes, I'll need to pick up the pieces. Those guys he has working for him can't hold the company together. Trust me on that," Landry said firmly, but quietly.

"It's not like that," Tristan tried to explain, but hell, maybe Landry was right. If he pushed too hard, Dylan would be gone, and he'd be stuck with a division himself.

"Don't leave me out. I'm gonna keep pushing on this one. Fifty million with the hundred we've already lost is too much," Landry pointed out.

"We're handling this strategically and very carefully. I don't want him to bolt, but I want his success. I'm not going to jeopardize our company or our reputation." Tristan wanted to be done with this conversation.

"If he's contractually bound, he'll be forced to achieve our goals," Landry commented.

"He's already made it clear, he wants that out clause. If he doesn't get it, he'll continue shopping around."

"Then payments should keep—" Landry started.

"See? You bully your way in. We aren't doing that with this. I've said that for the last six months—before we even decided who to go after." Done with this conversation, Tristan swiveled in his chair, estimating the time. Did it take three or four hours to fly back to Dallas? He couldn't remember. What were the chances Dylan would call him when he got home? *Zero.* That was the true answer and he even mentally called himself an ass for thinking of the possibility.

"Hey, you still there?" Landry's voice broke his train of thought. Shit, he'd thought he hung up on Landry after that last statement.

"Yeah, what else?" Tristan asked.

"Nothing, I guess. Look, this is ultimately your decision, but I'm going to try and change your mind. Think about what I said."

"Since that's all you've said this entire conversation, it's impossible not to think about what you said. Now return the favor. I'll see you tomorrow." Tristan did disconnect the call that time. He opened email and shot off a quick message to meet with legal first thing in the morning. Maybe he could have this contract to Dylan by Tuesday. It would be pushing things, but that seemed his nature all of a sudden.

CHAPTER.17

"Two days and you have a revised, firm contract? That's impressive, Dylan, even for you," Teri said as she sat across from Dylan in his north Dallas office. She flipped through the pages Dylan printed for her. She somehow managed to make the formal business suit she wore look sexy as she crossed her legs, bouncing her foot while she scanned the document.

"It's not a big surprise. You could tell he wanted the company," Dylan replied. Just like every other time she'd brought up Wilder, he dodged the questions with simple answers, but would generally begin to fidget, which he tried to rein in by linking his hands together on top of his desk. She knew him too well, knew the signs of his distress, and would begin to question him even more to figure out the root of his unease. Since he didn't want to talk about things, and his heart was pretty much crushed in his chest, he needed her to stop any inquisition she was considering and do the job Secret paid her to do—review the contract and make sure they were protected.

After a moment of her ignoring him, he felt safe enough to turn toward his computer and pull up his email. He needed to be sure nothing important had come through while they'd had lunch out together today. As he went through several messages, he didn't pay her any attention when she stood, contract in hand, and walked across his office to shut the door.

His sole focus of the day was avoiding the email he'd gotten this morning when his heart teetered in his chest at just seeing Tristan's name appear in his inbox. As much as he'd tried to avoid any thought of the man because it hurt too badly to think of Tristan, he'd almost taken a nosedive when he walked off a curb as he raced to open the email on his phone while coming into the office this morning.

He told himself he wasn't disappointed the email was one hundred percent business-related. There wasn't even a hint to the weekend they'd shared together and Dylan also told himself that was the way he wanted things. He'd actually demanded that of Tristan before he left.

The deep longing in his heart kept getting in the way. He looked down at the time on the computer. Two full days had passed since he'd kissed Tristan goodbye and he hadn't heard one single word from the guy.

The fear of his future had taken on a whole new meaning. He'd fallen in love with his first gay sexual experience. Who did that besides sixteen-year-old boys? Certainly not a middle-aged man with three children. He tucked his head in his hands and rubbed his palm across his face. It took a moment, but he finally managed to school himself. His voice of reason sang a new chorus. He was emotionally attached to Tristan because he had sex for the first time in years. Nothing more. When he forced himself to think like that, all this emotion coursing through him usually settled down and gave him a couple of hours' peace. Once he had sex with another man, his feelings for Tristan would level out.

On stable ground again, Dylan looked back at the professionally crafted email and his heart plunged to his feet.

Surely that response to seeing Tristan's name would go away in time. It just sucked to not be wanted, when he wanted so badly. "No," he said aloud to himself. *This is for the better.* Guys like Tristan wouldn't wait for a closeted man's little girl to graduate and move on to college.

"Spill," Teri said from behind him. She leaned against his desk. Her suit jacket gone. Her arms crossed over her chest. She'd obviously been there awhile and he'd completely forgotten she was even in the office.

"What are you talking about?" Dylan asked, exiting out of his email.

"You've been funky since you got home. You're snappy. No one wants to talk to you because they'll get their heads bitten off, and you're more moody than I've ever seen you. Definitely not a man who just made millions of dollars," Teri pointed out.

He looked down at his hands. His palms were sweaty, his heart raced, and he felt like he wanted to cry. He'd never experienced this kind of emotional turmoil before in his life. He loved Teri, but that had been gradual. She was the mother of his children. As for the kids, he'd just looked at them and knew love. But Tristan was different. Did he really, truly fall in love with him in a forty-eight hour window?

Absolutely.

No! *No!* Lust. He lusted after Tristan. It was lack of sex and all that crap he kept telling himself.

"You met someone," she exclaimed, a huge smile growing on her face. "I wondered if you got laid, but you're not acting like a man that got any after your self-imposed, very long dry spell. But you did and you like him, don't you?"

"It's not like that," Dylan started, because the truth was way too confusing, even to him.

"Oh no, you're doing that thing you do—denying yourself everything because of your perceived mistakes. You ruined it, didn't you?" Her tone was hard and Dylan looked up to see her smile gone.

"You know, this is really not the time for you to point out everything you think's wrong with my life. I met someone, but I ended it." Dylan started to rise, but she pushed him back in his seat, placing both arms on his chair.

"Love's hard to find, and when you do, you don't throw it away. I've got Mark. I love him, Dylan. I'll marry him when we're divorced. He gets what we're doing, he's willing to wait, and no one—not even you—knows all the time I spend with him," she said, looking him straight in the eyes. "It's because I'm not stupid enough to throw away my chance at that kind of love."

"I can't be gone every time you come home," he argued.

"Yes, you can. Our kids are grown," she said louder than he thought she'd intended. That had her pushing away from him. She paced in front of him, watching him closely with each step she took. "You're such a frustrating man sometimes! Now, who is it? Do I know him?"

"It doesn't matter. I'm not pursuing this. It was one weekend out of his life. He's not pursuing me. It's over. I had sex this weekend for the first time in a long time. It meant more to me because it's been so long," Dylan reasoned.

"So you both agreed on just sex?" she asked.

"Yes," Dylan replied with a firm nod because that was the absolute truth.

"But it meant more to you?" Teri questioned, bringing her pacing to a stop in front of him.

"No...yes. You know. Maybe. I don't know." Dylan stalled. "He's not from our world. He didn't really get what we're doing here." Dylan motioned a hand between the two of them.

"No one gets it. I'm not sure I get it anymore," Teri added.

"I didn't know things had gotten that far between you and Mark," Dylan responded to Teri's confession.

"I didn't want to worry you. I'll stay until Cate's settled like we agreed. But I'm telling you, it's good to have someone to love. I've lived with my best friend, now I'll live with a man I have passion for," Teri admitted, still watching him closely. "I want that for you, too. I worry about you after we're all gone."

"Don't worry about me. I'll get my groove on." Dylan forced a laugh, trying for funny, but it felt lame. Teri looked sad now and he knew how he looked. Completely pathetic. He hadn't slept or eaten since he'd been home.

"Call him," she suggested, nodding her head toward the phone. Dylan shook his head no.

"I told him I wouldn't. He doesn't want me like that anyway."

"Then it's his loss," she said, pulling away. "Look for someone else now."

"I've got this merger to get through." He turned away from her, back to his computer. "When do you think you can get back to me on the contract?"

"Possibly tonight or tomorrow with the changes marked. Dylan, why does my heart tell me that you need to call him?" she questioned.

"I have no idea. Probably because you worry too much. If you can get it back to me tonight, I'll get you whatever changes we need and shoot it back to you right away. You can send them back to him and his legal department for me. It would make the whole thing faster if you facilitated these exchanges," Dylan asserted, then he was back to his computer. No idea what he planned to do there, but he opened the internet, the Wilder search engine came up.

Damn.

"Then it *was* him," Teri said from behind him. Shit, he must have said that out loud. "Is it safe for you to go to work for him?" she asked quietly.

"I'm fine, Teri. I'm done talking about this. You have work to do," he said, nodding her toward the door in the nicest possible way.

"Okay, but my gut says to call him. I'll have something back tonight." She gathered her things and was out the door without any more of her inquisition. Thank god! Talking about Tristan made things more real, and honestly, he understood Teri's concern. He was incredibly worried about the prospect of seeing Tristan again.

CHAPTER.18

Close to midnight, Teri sat in bed, her iPad in her hand. Dylan was finally sleeping, something he hadn't done since he'd gotten home on Sunday. Under great duress and her threatening to divorce him right then, he finally caved and took something she'd gotten from their doctor to help him sleep. He took the pill and crashed within twenty minutes. He'd been sound asleep ever since.

The lights were turned down low, only the lamp on her side of the bed was lit. She generally took this time to talk to Mark, but not tonight. The concern she had for Dylan took up all the space in her mind, because every single day he deteriorated a little further and that worried the hell out of her.

After talking through the latest round of contractual changes with Dylan this evening, she sat for hours with the new changes in hand. From the very first day Dylan had finally confessed to her about his weekend tryst, up until this point, every counter she made, they got with no argument. Wilder, Inc. agreed to every one of her requests within minutes of her emails. Dylan's stock options had increased, his performance expectations lowered, and he had a firm 'out' clause, with no time limit for his future employment. Wilder, Inc.'s plans were actually incredibly good for Dylan. He must have gone there and impressed the hell out of them, because he got every negotiating point he'd wanted, with nothing taken away in the process. That never happened.

Teri had even found an added stipulation she wasn't sure Dylan had seen. There was an extra five million dollar incentive by signing the contract within a fourteen day period and entering into the execution phase within thirty days. Again, Teri had never seen anything like this contract before.

Yet she still stalled on finalizing the deal.

No matter how good this might be for Secret Networks, Dylan was tanking before her eyes. He wasn't eating right, he hadn't run since he got home, and the kids were keeping their distance, which had never happened since he'd stopped drinking. She couldn't let this continue. So in return she found contractual fault when there wasn't any.

The problem with her current plan was every condition she fought, they gave in right away. That made no sense. Did guilt or emotion drive Wilder, Inc., because this certainly didn't feel like business as usual.

On nothing more than instinct, Teri pulled up her email, did a quick reply only to Tristan, not his legal rep, and typed out a hurried message. Her gut said Tristan Wilder wanted Dylan, not just Secret Networks. This time she refused to talk herself out of the action because Dylan kept insisting that was how women handled things, reading more into a situation than what was truly there. She made her message short, sweet, and to the point.

I'll look over these latest changes and get back with you next week.

Definitely not the message she wanted to send. She wanted to point out all of her husband's attributes. Actually what she really wanted to say was… *What the hell is wrong with you*, but her message started a conversation nonetheless.

God, this is a killer, Tristan thought to himself. He took a long swig of the gin and tonic he'd just poured. It was Friday night, or perhaps a better way to mark the date, this was day five of not hearing a word from Dylan.

They had clearly connected—that last kiss was the most intense of his life. Dylan had to have experienced the draw between them. The way he clung to him, so reluctant to let him go. That kiss meant something. It was a game changer. *Right?*

Wrong. Tristan wouldn't have gotten through the first forty-eight hours without having called him had Dylan not pushed him off on his wife, ending all communication between them. A monumentally symbolic gesture. Hell, he'd hounded his legal department, paid overtime to get that contract completed in order to send Dylan an email before he broke down and called the guy only to get a very clear message from Teri Reeves that she would handle their negotiations in Dylan's place.

His phone vibrated for the fourth or fifth time in a row. Julian wasn't taking a hint. Tristan palmed the cell, sent a text to Julian blowing him off, and looked up when his computer dinged. The email was from Teri Reeves. Tristan frowned and looked down at the time on his computer.

It had to be midnight in Dallas. He stared at the screen. He couldn't stand seeing another cc'd exchange from his legal department to Dylan's legal team. He'd given in to every one of their demands, but much like driving past a train wreck, he couldn't help but look because it was currently the only connection he had to Dylan.

He opened the message from the person who got to sleep next to Dylan every single night. True resentment began to form.

Frustrated, he knew he had to stop this. Business wasn't personal, yet that was all this was for him. He scanned the one line message. *Another week?* Everything drove him to urgently push this contract through, because, at its end, he'd get to spend time with Dylan, if even in a strictly business setting.

Lord, what did that say about him? Dylan wasn't a fifty million dollar piece of ass like Landry referred to him. Pain sliced across his heart. He took another drink before he responded.

I'm afraid I'll need things tied up early next week, Tristan typed back. He noticed this message was just between the two of them. That was a first. Maybe a mistake? And then another email came through.

He's a good man. One of the best. That was all the message said. Eight little words. What did they mean? Weary of having this exchange on both a professional and personal level, Tristan paused before he typed a simple sentence back.

I'm very aware. Did those words reveal too much? He hit send and waited, staring at the screen.

Are you a good man? Teri sent back. Did she know? Did Dylan tell her anything about their time together, or him? If he had, wouldn't she already know that answer? Unless Dylan hadn't thought of him as a good man. Shit, he'd nearly died of a heart attack on that trail; didn't that say something to Dylan about the kind of man he was?

I'm not as good a man as him. I'm not sure anyone I've ever known can compete on his level. What's this about? Tristan typed and hit send before he had time to rethink this whole exchange.

Do you use Secret? Teri emailed back, and Tristan smiled. There would be no history if they used Dylan's social media site.

Of course. I'm logging in now. What's your screen name? he asked.

MondayBlues. I'm logging in now, Teri sent in reply. Tristan searched her name and friended her. He heard his email ding again and switched over. Teri had sent another email. *Are you TalkNerdyToMe?*

Yep, he responded and switched back over, waiting for her to accept his request. When she did, her profile opened to a background picture of their family together. Tristan was mesmerized by the genuine smile Dylan wore as he laughed with all three of their children at some sort of theme park. He did a quick *save as* on the photo. Secret had technology disabling even screen shots of their site except on the profile pages. He then looked at each of the children, then at Teri. The boy looked most like Dylan, tall with rich auburn hair, a strong jawline, and full lips just like his father's. The daughters were darker like their mom. He looked closely at Teri. She was beautiful. Tall, with a porcelain complexion, long black hair, and delicate features. In the picture Teri was smiling with the kids, probably at something Dylan had done.

Tristan hit the other photos as the chat box opened. The concepts of the site were incredible. Things were so basic and the apps were phenomenal. He wanted his hands on that emoji application—what a remarkable concept. He smiled when he saw Dylan's picture had an emoji graphic surrounding his head announcing Secret's newest game. He saved that picture too.

"*Hi,*" Teri chatted.

"*Hi. You have me curious.*" Tristan replied back, still completely unwilling to out Dylan. He hadn't had enough history to truly know Dylan and Teri's relationship.

Kindle Alexander

"You have me a bit frustrated," Teri replied. And that had Tristan furrowing his brow.

"Why is that?" he finally replied back.

"You shouldn't have played with him like that." Teri's words appeared on the screen.

"How did I play with him?" Tristan asked.

"Please stop. I know what happened. He's too good a man to be played," she replied. Okay, Dylan's wife was a spitfire.

"I can assure you, I didn't play him at all. I'm following his rules, not mine," he responded. Then there was a delay.

"What are his rules? And why aren't they yours?" she asked. Now, he delayed. These were two very intimate questions. Dylan's rules were simpler.

"You and the children. The code of ethics he follows. They have no place for me."

"I see. Dylan's a nester and monogamous by nature. What are your rules?" Teri questioned and Tristan let out a groan. He looked at the ceiling before responding. It was only a small break, but he needed the time to think.

"That's a much harder question. They seem to be changing," he answered honestly.

"How so?" she asked. The attorney in her wouldn't stop asking until she had what she wanted. He'd figured that much out over the emails he'd seen between her and legal this week. The problem was that these questions were too personal. He was pursuing a man who didn't want to be pursued. Logically, he got that Dylan needed to make the next move since he was the one with barriers between them. Illogically, he was spending money he didn't really need to toss away just to stay close to Dylan. How did he say that?

"It's not a hard question," she responded when he didn't answer.

"I disagree, it's incredibly hard," Tristan replied, giving nothing away.

"*Then let's try this before I shelve this contract and hold everything up.*"

"*Why would you do that?*"

"*I'll answer that question in a minute. Do you have feelings for Dylan?*" she asked, straight to the point.

"*Yes,*" he answered. He felt the truth was the easiest way to answer her.

"*I couldn't imagine you would see him as a passing fling. No one can be that shallow, and if you were, he wouldn't have been interested.*" He agreed with her words even though they came with quite an impact.

"*I'm not sure how to respond to that. I know many people that are shallow. I hope I'm not one of them,*" Tristan replied.

"*Why haven't you called him?*"

"*I left my door open to him. He needs to make the next move,*" Tristan typed.

"*So you do play games?*" she fired instantly back.

"*Not at all. He's freaked, skittish, and very clear there can't be more between us.*" There, Tristan bared the root of their problem.

"*I see. So it's him. I suspected that could be the case. He took the blame. I just needed to know for sure.*"

"*I'm doing what I can. He was adamant he's got too much to lose—per him. I did try to make him see I was willing to be discreet, but he spooks easy.*"

"*In nine months our youngest will graduate and go off to college. I've told him this week that I'm out as soon as she's settled. How do you feel about that?*" Teri's straightforward words blinked at him on the screen. This whole *family first* thing they had going on was beyond belief to him. He'd never met two people who'd sacrificed as much as Teri and Dylan to do the right thing.

None of the pictures he'd seen showed anything but a happy, healthy, successful family.

"*Again, I don't know how to respond to you. I guess I'm a bit selfish. Nine months doesn't seem that long. I'm hopeful for me. Perhaps concerned for Dylan, he'll be completely alone if something doesn't change.*"

"*It's the reason I finally messaged you tonight.*"

"*How is he?*" Tristan had to know.

"*Not too good. He's not eating or sleeping. He's edgy,*" she described.

"*Then we're doing about the same,*" Tristan replied.

"*What are you going to do about this?*" Teri asked. Damn, that woman got right to the point.

"*Where is he right now?*" Why hadn't that occurred to Tristan earlier?

"*He took something. He's sleeping right beside me,*" Teri replied.

"*Can I see him?*" Tristan asked. His palms turned sweaty as he waited for Teri's answer.

"*How?*" she asked.

"*Turn on your webcam. Secret makes it simple. Click the button on the bottom. The one that looks like a camera.*" Tristan turned his on and waited.

"*I don't want to wake him. He hasn't slept all week.*"

"*I know the feeling. I'll sleep better if I see him,*" he confessed. "*Lower your volume before you accept the final directive. Leave chat up,*" Tristan said. After a minute more, Teri appeared on his screen. He smiled and lifted a hand to wave at her. She began to type.

"*Ignore the dark circles and my unruly hair.*"

"*You're beautiful,*" he typed and her smile deepened.

"Well, all I can say is, I can see why Dylan finally broke. He's done well with you." She typed and that had him smiling. *"Do I just put the pad to his face?"*

"Yes, but minimize me, so if he wakes, he doesn't freak," Tristan responded. Teri looked to her left and came back.

"I should fix his hair. He's been sleeping hard." Her words almost had him laughing. He didn't care. He just wanted to see Dylan. God, did he want to see the guy. The thought of getting a look had his heart pounding in his chest.

"He's perfect like he is," Tristan said, ready for her to move this along. She lifted the pad and kept her face positioned so she could make sure her angle was right. When she realized he had the perfect shot, she moved out of the way. Tristan had a sleeping Dylan on his screen. He took a picture of the screen with his phone just to have the shot as he continued to stare.

Dylan's full lips were slightly parted and he had the most peaceful look on his face. He hoped he was dreaming of him. Tristan's body grew hard. He ignored what was going on in his pants. He'd take care of that later with the picture he'd taken. Dylan stirred, probably the light in his face. Teri jerked the pad away, placed it back on her lap, and he heard Dylan's deep sleep-filled voice.

"You should go to sleep soon," Dylan mumbled. Tristan heard the bed and assumed Dylan had turned away. He typed quickly.

"Thank you. I needed that." Tristan was still grinning from the small glimpse he'd gotten.

"You need to call him. He won't call you. I've tried to get him to. He's too worried about us, and he thinks you don't want someone like him," Teri said.

"That's funny, because he's all I want. I planned to call him if he hadn't called me soon. I wanted to give him time to get right with things. I also planned on coming to Dallas soon. Check out the place, sign the contracts in person. Put

myself in front of Dylan," Tristan typed, and as Teri read, she shook her head.

"*Keep things separate. He won't jeopardize Secret's staff for anything. You could always come here and just have a date night with him.*" Tristan read her words and frowned at the screen.

"*Trust me,*" she said. He realized she was watching his reactions through the webcam and he looked up to see her smiling.

"*Okay, so I'll call him and ask him out for next weekend,*" Tristan responded.

"*Good, and I'll send you the contract in the morning. I was stalling. He's my best friend—he always will be. I need him taken care of. He's too honorable and loyal for today's world. I'm always watching out for him.*"

"*I can see that from just the short time I've known him. Thank you for reaching out. You made me nervous. I didn't want to give anything away. Seems he keeps his secrets wrapped up tightly.*"

"*I'll send all my contact information to you. Maybe we can meet when you're in town next weekend. A quick something. We'll need to double-team him I think,*" Teri proposed.

"*That would be great. I'll overnight my signed contract. If we can work it out before I get there, then I can keep everything separate. Don't kill me if I have to combine the contract with the date though. This gives me hope. After our last few minutes together, I didn't expect him to hold out so long. We got along really well,*" Tristan responded honestly.

"*I'm happy. Thank you for letting me pry.*"

"*Thank you for prying.*" Tristan smiled.

"*Good night then.*"

"*Good night.*" Tristan lifted a hand and Teri returned the smile before the video went dead. Just like Secret promised,

Tristan watched as the screen slowly ate up the message until there was no trace of it left.

Feeling a little better about things, Tristan quickly selected Dylan's photo as his background picture on his phone. He and Teri had met and she seemed to approve of him. That had to be a milestone, even if Dylan wasn't aware of the exchange. At least he had someone on the inside to have his back.

After seeing Dylan, his body ached. He needed to jack off. He grabbed his phone and left his home office. Tomorrow, he'd plan a trip to Dallas. He couldn't really remember much about Dallas, except the incredible summer and the terrible politics. None of that mattered. He said a quick prayer. Something he rarely did.

Please let him accept my invitation.

CHAPTER.19

Four days since Tristan had his heart-to-heart with Teri, he found himself talking to her every single day. She secretly kept him posted on Dylan, on his mood, how he acted, and anything she could get out of him about the two of them. She also sent him several pictures through email and text messaging. They were photos of a young Dylan and some through the years. One of him cooking dinner in their kitchen with two of their children helping in the process. Dylan never knew she'd taken that shot.

The contracts had been finalized, signatures being obtained. Everything moved forward as planned, all except this one little hitch, Dylan still hadn't spoken to him in nine long days.

Planning his timing, Tristan paced the outside deck. Teri said Dylan always ended his day in his office, tying up the loose ends. They'd made a plan for him to call about five o'clock that afternoon, Dallas time. He'd thought about what to say over and over again. Practiced different scenarios, but in his heart, he knew Dylan needed to keep the personal side personal and the business side business, like Teri suggested. Tristan just had to learn to keep all those areas straight too.

Biting the bullet, he blocked his number and dialed Dylan's direct dial extension. On the third ring, Tristan's heart plummeted, on the fourth ring it soared.

"Dylan Reeves." His voice sounded professional and maybe somewhat distracted. Whatever the tone, Tristan's dick took notice.

"Hey, Dylan, it's Tristan," he said casually, staring out into the ocean. He watched the waves break in the surf as he listened for the man on the other end of the line.

"Did I lose you?" he asked after what he suspected was a full minute's lag.

"No, I'm here," Dylan answered and cleared his throat. "I thought Teri got everything to you this afternoon."

"She did. This isn't a work-related call." Tristan paused, waiting for Dylan to respond. Nothing again. He took a deep breath, hoping to calm his own butterflies in his stomach.

"Did I lose you this time?" Tristan asked again.

"No," Dylan said, his voice softer now.

"I waited until we got all the business settled between us. I want to come there and take you out," Tristan blurted out nervously. Like an *idiot!* That was real smooth…he didn't want to scare Dylan off, and he prayed he hadn't overstepped that boundary.

"I thought we'd schedule an introduction-slash-celebration deal for the staff. Not just surprise them with you and your team showing up unannounced," Dylan replied.

"No, that's mixing business and personal. I want to come to Dallas this weekend and take you out on a date. I miss you," Tristan tried to explain again. That confession had Dylan completely silent. Tristan held the line, waiting. He had an arsenal of comebacks and excuses prepared for however Dylan decided to decline his invitation.

"I don't think that's wise," Dylan cleared his voice again.

"Just a date, nothing else," Tristan shot back. He'd already decided, this wasn't just about sex. He liked Dylan, liked him a lot, and wanted to spend time with him.

"No sex?" Dylan asked very quietly.

"Right," he assured, immediately regretful. They were absolutely more than sex, but he'd been without for nine long days already. "Absolutely. Just the two of us hanging out."

Dylan stared down at the desk phone like the thing had grown three legs. His brain had a hard time catching up. He blamed his slowness on the deep rich baritone of Tristan's voice. Something he'd dreamed about for the last several nights. One of the hazards of taking sleeping medicine at night.

"You don't want to have sex with me? You just want to go out?" Dylan asked again in his usual very direct way. "I'm confused. That's all we did was have sex."

A deep sigh filled the phone. "We did more than just have sex. Of course I want to make love to you, but not this time. We need to start things over—you know, from the beginning."

"You know I can't go out with you. Certainly not around here," Dylan responded, sitting back in his chair, letting the familiar creak of the springs lull him as he rocked the nervous energy from his body.

"Then I'll get a place. We can have dinner in my room," Tristan offered up quickly. The man had definitely prepared for any excuse Dylan made.

"With no sex in your hotel room? And this isn't business?" Dylan asked. Then what the hell was it?

"Correct. I'm thinking Friday night now," Tristan stated.

"Dinner in your hotel room, no sex, and no business, on Friday?" Dylan asked, again disbelieving.

"Yes," Tristan answered.

"I should say no." Dylan wanted to answer yes, but his logical and moral compasses made the decision hard for him. He missed this man too much. He hurt on a level he had never experienced before in his life and the pain never subsided. His heart never stopped hurting no matter what he did.

"But you're not going to, are you?" Tristan questioned.

"No, I'm not going to." Dylan finally gave in. "Mainly because I can't figure this out." The conversation they were having now and what it meant, the depth of his desire for this man he'd known for all of a few days…none of it made sense.

"I'll take what I can get. Now, until then, you can put me out of my misery and text me from time to time? Every email I've sent you includes my personal cell phone number," Tristan pointed out.

Dylan stayed silent again. Personal stays personal, business stays business, and a date with no sex. Okay that was different than anything they had done before. Could Tristan be trying to move them in the direction of friendship? Better question, did Dylan even have it in him to go there with the guy? Probably not. He already knew he wanted more. He couldn't hide his feelings well enough to pull off friendship.

Yet, if they could manage to be friends, then the next few years wouldn't completely suck as he worked for Wilder and figured his life out.

"All right," he finally said, not having any idea what he'd say in a text to Tristan.

"That didn't sound convincing. What's your cell phone number?" Tristan asked.

Dylan started to rattle off the digits and stopped. "You have my number. You've called me." Before he even finished, his cell phone beeped. There was a text with a California area code.

"I think I heard your phone. That's probably from me."

"You just said 'Hey, it's Tristan.' Not a lot to work with to start a friendly conversation," Dylan responded into the phone, trying for some humor.

"We have to start somewhere," he said, laughing a little. "I'm glad this worked. I've missed you. You're good company." On a deep sigh, Dylan closed his eyes and forced himself to treat Tristan like he would any of his buddies.

"Thank you for understanding everything," Dylan said. They didn't have much in common. Maybe Tristan golfed— he'd never thought to ask that question. So they were going to be friends. All right, he'd play along. Worship from afar and figure his shit out when the time came.

"Of course, no problem. I'll message you details as I know them. I'll see you Friday," Tristan said.

"Thanks for calling," Dylan offered, not sure how to end the call.

"Thanks for answering. We'll talk more later. Goodbye."

"Bye," he said, hanging up the phone.

Friends. Okay. He could try friendship. He already knew how to long from afar. Ambien had become his friend where that was concerned. Maybe seeing Tristan in this capacity was better than not seeing him at all, because he knew how bad that prospect sucked firsthand.

CHAPTER.20

"You look good," Teri said, leaning against the doorframe between their bedroom and bathroom. Dylan stood at the sink wearing nothing but his boxers while shaving. He moved his eyes from the swipe of the razor and looked over at Teri then focused his gaze back on the blade sliding across his face. Once done, he rinsed and answered.

"Are you making fun of me?" Dylan asked, bringing the blade back to his cheek for another swipe.

"Not at all. Your hair's perfect. The tan looks great. I saw the clothes on the bed. You're gonna impress," Teri exclaimed, grinning big. "It's been a while since I've seen you this way."

"The best I can hope for is passable. You should see him," Dylan mumbled, rinsing the blade again.

"You're gonna hold your own, trust me. Is there any chance you'll be seen?" she asked. Over the years, Teri had been a professional at being seen out without being noticed. Dylan not so much. He'd be too skittish. He was just never

204

any good at lying. It was why he stayed quiet so much of the time.

"We're having dinner in his room. No big deal. It's not like that anymore." Dylan bent over the sink and ran water over his face to wipe away the remnants of the lather.

"I'm glad you're doing this," Teri piped in. Dylan checked his face, made sure he got everything off, and dried himself before he scooted past her in the doorway.

"I don't know. It's been a hard couple of weeks. I don't want to put the kids through all my moods again." Dylan pulled his slacks on.

"I think they're sturdier than you give them credit for," Teri countered.

"Not now, it's not fair. This should be the time of their lives. Their only focus should be graduating and starting college. Not that their father's gay and can't keep his emotional shit together," he repeated. This time out loud, the other million or so times had been a running chorus through his head.

"That's not the way we raised our children. We're a family and stick together no matter what," Teri started, but Dylan stopped her as he carefully pulled the polo over his head, trying not to mess up the nice cut his hairdresser had given him.

"We've had this talk. When did you become such a fan of Tristan's?" Dylan asked, tucking his shirt inside his khakis before fastening them. The belt was last. He pushed the leather through the loops as he walked across the bedroom to the dresser mirror. He ran his fingers through his hair, smoothing out the ends, satisfied with what he saw.

When he realized Teri hadn't answered, he looked back over his shoulder. She stood there, staring intently at him. She was fighting something; she had the look. He knew her too well.

"What's wrong?"

"You look good, I promise," she said, snapping out of whatever held her thoughts. She walked over to him without giving him any clue. "What about cologne? I think the Armani Code Ultimate I got you for Christmas last year." She fingered through the different scents until she found the dark bottle. "It's unusual."

He didn't question the selection—she always knew better about these things—and gave himself a couple of sprays. He grabbed his wallet, dropping it in his back pocket, and then his keys and money clip—those went to his front pocket.

"Perfect. Are you wearing a jacket?"

"I thought my bomber," he replied.

"Good. I like that one the best on you. You'll look like a classic movie star," she said dreamily as he grabbed the jacket from his closet. Once done he went to stand in front of her for better inspection. She grinned at him, fixing his collar under the jacket.

"He's not gonna know what hit him," Teri stated confidently, her smile growing broader.

"We decided we're gonna be friends. I keep telling you that."

"Take his picture if you can tonight. Damn, I wanna see him when he opens that door." Teri winked at him.

"You're good for the ego, even if you do lie," he chuckled and watched another round of something he couldn't explain cross over her face. "You all right?"

"I'm fine, why?"

"You're being weird." He shook his head at her continued silence. "I need to get going. I'm gonna be late."

"Have fun," Teri exclaimed before opening their bedroom door.

"I'll be home early," he responded, walking down their hall. The kids' rooms were on the other side of the house. A catwalk separated the two areas.

"I hope not," she whispered, taking the back staircase down to the first floor. Dylan rolled his eyes at her. "Stay for the weekend if you can."

Cate entered from the side garage door as he was headed out. "Dad, you look handsome!"

"Thanks, baby," he leaned in for her kiss.

"Mom, you shouldn't let him go out like this. Miranda's dad left her mom for a twenty-year-old. They said it's a mid-life crisis," Cate stated-matter-of-factly.

"Wait a second. Miranda's dad's like fifty. I'm only thirty-seven. I'm not old enough for a mid-life crisis. You give me a compliment, then insult me by saying I'm old?" Dylan teased, walking out into the garage. That got Cate laughing. "Sheesh!"

"It's all downhill from here!" Teri called out. "Have fun. See you later."

"Where's he going?" Cate asked Teri as the garage door closed. He'd escaped that question. He'd have to remember to ask what she said.

Tristan had paced the small suite for the last hour, waiting on Dylan to arrive. His bright idea of a date stressed him the hell out. Besides the fact he'd spent more money on this date than he had on his last trip to Jamaica, now he had to wait for Dylan to arrive.

Tristan looked around the living room. He'd had several matching hollyhock bouquets added to the suite. Dylan had stopped their run at Crystal Cove to touch the delicate blooms lining the path. The fact he remembered had to mean something with all the huffing and puffing he'd been doing. From his estimation, the sheer amount of sweat pouring from his body should have made it impossible to even note Dylan's actions, but it hadn't. Tristan had been sucking in much needed air while watching Dylan carefully take a step or two into the wildflowers, bending ever so slightly to breathe them in.

Not only had he remembered, but that had been the moment Dylan cemented into his heart.

Since calling Dylan on Tuesday, he had texted with him several times. It took some time, but he finally understood that Dylan truly believed that starting over meant building a friendship, not a relationship. Dylan came off totally awkward in his messages, which was something they had never been before. Tristan hated that and the distance Dylan put between them. They fit so well together from the beginning. At least to him, they were fluid from the very first kiss.

Maybe he was bored with life and that was why he was doing all this. Nah, that wasn't it at all. Dylan was a keeper. He just had to find the way to keep him.

Tristan did another sweep of the room to make sure nothing faded under the late start. He had candles lit, lamp shades glowing, soft music playing, and several bottles of grossly expensive wine chilling. He had a waitstaff on standby with a five-course meal prepared by Wolfgang Puck waiting on one single man to arrive. He'd even gone out and bought new clothing for the occasion.

All of a sudden, Tristan felt incredibly ridiculous for all this preparation. Dylan didn't require any of this. He was a normal guy, but dammit, he wanted to romance him into a relationship.

A soft knock sounded from the doorway. Tristan debated right then. Did he have time to change any of this? No, not really. If that was Dylan, he was committed to the evening as he'd painstakingly planned. Damn.

On the second knock, Tristan went for the door, checking his appearance in a side mirror as he passed by.

"Hi," he said, opening the door, plastering a smile on his face. Dylan stood outside the door, his hands in the pockets of his khakis, looking hot as hell. Tristan needed the reassurance of this moment. He knew right then he'd made all these decisions for the right reasons. "Come in."

"Traffic was terrible. I'm sorry I'm late," Dylan apologized as he stepped inside.

"You weren't late at all. It's whenever you could get here. You look different," Tristan said, looking Dylan over, trying to pinpoint what had changed about him. He didn't think Dylan could be a better-looking guy, but something he'd done heightened that.

"You dressed up," Dylan replied. That hadn't answered Tristan's question, but it had him looking down at his clothing. Then over at Dylan's.

"I wanted to dress like I would if you had let me take you out. Is it too much?"

There was silence as Dylan stared at him. It took a minute before he came back with a, "No, you look great. I just dressed like we were having dinner in your room." Dylan looked down at his clothes. Tristan thought Dylan may have clued in right at that moment that this was more than friends for Tristan. They both became nervous, and for some reason, that helped calm Tristan.

"You look great. Incredible actually. Let me have your jacket. I'll hang it up," Tristan said, helping Dylan from his coat. "I have a pretty loaded bar. What would you like to drink?"

Tristan hung the jacket on a coatrack and placed a hand on Dylan's lower back. He hoped his Southern manners kept him by the door until he was invited in, not the panic that coursed through his eyes.

"I swore I wasn't drinking tonight, but one or two should be fine. What are you having?" Dylan asked, walking inside the room until Tristan left him and went to the bar.

"I poured a glass of wine right before you got here, but we can switch to something non-alcoholic," Tristan replied, looking around for anything in the bar that was suitable to drink.

"No, the wine's fine," Dylan said, coming to stand close to the bar. "I'll have a glass of whatever you're having."

"You smell incredible," Tristan mumbled softly as he poured. That earned him silence and he smiled down at the glass. He missed these little shy moments with Dylan. They were the first things he'd noticed about the guy and the most impactful on his heart. "I had planned to sit and talk for a little while, but dinner's ready now. Do you want to eat or wait a bit?"

"I'm easy. Whatever's good." Dylan took his wineglass.

"Let's eat. The chef's a bit of a diva. The waitstaff's been in here about a half dozen times. It'll get rid of them sooner." Tristan reached for the phone on the end table. He picked up the receiver and dialed a number, simply saying, "We're ready," before he hung up. "Come this way."

Dylan stood there, nervous as hell, questioning why he had even agreed to come. He'd known not to do this when Tristan asked. Friends? *What?* Friends didn't gently caress your back as they led you into a room. Friends didn't dress in expensive suits and invite you to have dinner in their room with wine and waiters.

No matter how much pain he'd endured, Dylan could see no reason to extend their perfect weekend together. It would only cause more heartache for both of them, him especially, in the end. Tristan was perfect in every way. Blond, tall, with those damn broad, muscular shoulders that seemed larger in that perfectly cut suit jacket—his complete dream man.

He couldn't let himself go back down that path. The last two weeks had been hell. He had responsibilities and an amazing family to worry over. He didn't have time for games. Certainly not games that were now so close to home.

He resisted the urge to run his fingers over his face, but he did drain his wineglass in a couple of swallows. And seriously, what happened to his no alcohol whatsoever plan? Tristan and alcohol never worked out well for him.

Now, as the minutes ticked by, it seemed his new game plan hinged on staying quiet and out of the way. Not a good one to help initiate or further any conversation, but since he had no idea what to say and felt completely in over his head, it seemed the best option.

He trailed after Tristan, following a step or two behind. Only then did he notice the romantic ambiance of the room. Candles flickered, soft music played in the background, and flower bouquets were everywhere. Almost the same bouquet was artfully arranged in several different locations around the room. He stopped following and took a closer look at one of them. They were hollyhock bouquets in different colors, placed around the living room and dining room. The centerpiece in the middle of the table was an intricate design of smaller cut hollyhocks with deep red roses tucked carefully together, set between the two place settings.

"Is this a coincidence?" Dylan asked without hesitation, looking straight at Tristan. It was hard to gauge the expression. Uncertainty crossed Tristan's face which made no sense.

"A coincidence?" Tristan asked. The question sounded like a dodge, so that meant something in the answer. Dylan stood there and looked straight at him. This said too much. Dylan remembered clearly running along that trail. He'd slowed down on purpose. As toned and muscular as Tristan was, he was definitely not a runner. Dylan came to his first stop in a field of wildflowers. He'd bought Teri flowers over the years and knew these were rare, but to have them growing on the side of a cliff gave him the perfect excuse to slow down, give Tristan the break he needed without drawing attention to why he'd stopped.

"These aren't easy to find around here." Dylan plucked a bloom and walked toward the table where Tristan stood.

"I didn't have a problem getting them," Tristan replied in an even clearer dodge. Everything changed in that moment. This whole thing, from the wine to the flowers to the expensive clothing, had Dylan looking at Tristan in a new light for the first time since they'd met. He'd gone to a tremendous amount of trouble to put this dinner together. This was pure romance, just for him. The playing field changed right then.

"Thank you for remembering." Dylan placed the stem at the top of the place setting where Tristan had set his empty glass.

"Sir, would you like some more wine?"

Dylan turned to see a young man standing there. Black slacks, a white button-down, black tie, and a black apron. Dylan hadn't even noticed him enter the room. After a second or two of both Tristan and the waiter staring at him, he realized the waiter must have been talking to him.

"I'm sorry?"

"Wine. Would you like more?" the waiter asked, pointing to the empty glass in his hand.

He should stop now, switch to water, especially after that last revelation, but instead, he extended his hand to the waiter. "Yeah, thanks."

"How about you, sir?" The waiter turned to Tristan.

"Please," Tristan said, picking up his almost empty glass from the table.

"Here, take a seat," Tristan said, pulling out the chair in front of him. It was a sweet move, just like everything else in the room tonight, and Dylan took the seat with Tristan helping to push him up to the table. Dylan dropped the napkin in his lap as Tristan placed a hand on the table and bent in close, his breath caressing his skin as he spoke softly.

"I noticed your appreciation of the flowers when we ran. When I planned our date night, I wanted you to see I paid attention. It seems silly now. I don't date a lot. I had to go way back to my dates with girls in high school and there weren't many of those. I'm sorry if it makes you uncomfortable," Tristan whispered quietly behind him, leaning in close to his ear. Dylan kept his head slightly bent, listening to every word Tristan had to say. Heat ran through his body in response to Tristan's words.

The confession helped him see that they were both nervous. Who would have thought Tristan would ever want him?

"It's not silly at all," Dylan replied.

"Then look at me," Tristan said in his ear. Dylan lifted his head, but Tristan stayed in his personal space. They were mere inches apart.

"It's special," Dylan whispered at the uncertainty he was met with.

"Can I kiss you?" Tristan asked, leaning in, not waiting for permission. He kept the kiss small, lingering for a minute longer before taking his seat. Dylan was left slightly devastated, all his conscious thought vanished at the press of Tristan's lips. His wineglass was placed in front of him. He might have uttered a thank you, but couldn't be certain. Dylan lifted the glass and took another long gulp, needing the liquid courage from the alcohol. Something, anything, to take the edge off the intensity of the last few minutes.

Tristan hadn't imagined the thrill he'd get from the quiver of Dylan's lips. He'd stayed there a little longer than planned just to feel it again. He inhaled Dylan's scent mixed with spicy cologne. He loved that smell. Dylan's silence and hesitancy since he'd walked inside the room had made his own nervousness heighten. When Dylan stopped at the flowers and then looked up at him, he'd thought for sure that look meant he'd made way more out of their time together than Dylan had.

Thankfully the waiter gave him the second or two to compose himself. Honesty was such a good policy. One he lived his life on. He'd confessed and Dylan seemed to be flattered by his admission. Which technically was exactly what he wanted to happen.

"You've got an incredible restaurant here in this town. Wolfgang prepared our meals himself," Tristan said, dropping his napkin in his lap. Dylan looked blankly at him and that caused him to smile. He reached out and took Dylan's hand, linking their fingers together on top of the table. These were the things that Dylan did so well. He allowed Tristan the simple pleasure of holding his hand or giving a slight caress. They touched his heart in a way that nothing else ever had before.

"I planned our menu. I hope you're good with the selections," Tristan said again, leaning in and lifting Dylan's fingers to his lips for a soft kiss. "I kept it healthy. I saw how you ate in California."

"Thank you," Dylan replied. There was that look again. That stunned look. Dylan was such a strong, well-constructed man, but he clearly wasn't used to people looking out for him. Tristan filed that little piece of information in the back of his mind. If this continued between them, he could see that he needed to spend the time making Dylan feel as special as he could and somehow Tristan knew he was up for the task.

CHAPTER.21

The dinner went off without a hitch, everything turning out as he had meticulously planned. Dylan raved about the delicious food as dishes were removed and, per the pre-discussed arrangements, the waitstaff left the bottle of wine close to Tristan. They remained scarce throughout the meal and scooted out the door when they were done serving the last course. The dessert was left in a covered dish inside the refrigerator. After a while and with only two glasses of wine under his belt, Dylan started to relax and open up.

"Would you like dessert?" Tristan smiled.

"No, I'm stuffed. Maybe later," Dylan said, placing his napkin on the table.

"So, how are your children?" Tristan asked, touching on a subject they'd only talked a little bit about, but in his rehearsal of topics of discussion for tonight, Dylan's children were top on the list. They were incredibly important to Dylan so Tristan needed to get to know them.

"Good, I think. I haven't seen them much. I've been a little out of sorts. I think everyone's keeping their distance,"

Dylan said, nodding at his statement. He lifted his wineglass, taking a small drink this time.

"They're good kids?" Tristan questioned, moving away from the moodiness Teri said and Dylan hinted he'd been experiencing. That conversation would close Dylan up and he didn't want that. Tristan reached over with the bottle of wine, topping off Dylan's wineglass. He figured Dylan would be conscious of drinking and driving. He seemed like that kind of guy, so if he drank a little too much, he'd need to stay longer to sober up. That could possibly lead to make-out time.

"So far they've been great. They're expensive. I think I told you, Chad's going to Duke in the fall. Cate's planning on Harvard. Chloe's at the University of Oklahoma, but she's recently talked about moving to a northern school, something a little more progressive."

"Chloe's the oldest?" Tristan asked, taking a drink of his wine. He'd only let go of Dylan's hand long enough to allow them to eat. He'd resumed the hand-holding the minute they were through. Dylan hadn't resisted and was finally participating in the finger play he'd started.

"She's a freshman at OU," Dylan responded. "We had them back to back."

"And they have no idea? Teri's the only one besides me that knows about you?" Tristan asked and Dylan nodded.

"What're your plans after they leave?" For the first time in a couple of hours, Dylan grew completely quiet. Tristan watched the almost visible withdrawal. "No, don't close up. The subject's none of my business. Got it. I'd just like to get to know you better. I can stick with the other parts of your life."

"It's not that. I just don't really know what'll happen. I see Teri getting a little antsy. When we decided to do things this way, we were young with babies. Thirty-seven seemed so old. It's not as old as we thought," Dylan said and Tristan smiled. He understood.

"We aren't that far off from each other." Tristan laughed at the crazy look Dylan gave him. "We aren't. I've spent the last twenty years building Wilder. The market was nonexistent when I started. You're the one that's helped me see that maybe there's more to life than the newest technology that's consumed me."

"How did I do that?" Dylan asked, clearly not believing him. Tristan paused. He pushed back a little in his chair and reached for his wine, drinking the glass down. Dylan kept an expectant gaze on him.

"Too many ways to say. The biggest ones are the honor and integrity you live by every day. No one does that. Stop shaking your head. No one does that, Dylan," Tristan said.

"I'm small beans in your life," Dylan started, but Tristan leaned in, placing a finger over his lips.

"Stop. You're the only person in my life that doesn't want anything from me," Tristan said, watching those lips, wishing his were covering them and not his hand.

"Have you forgotten how I met you?" Dylan asked with Tristan's hand still on his lips. Tristan laughed at that one.

"I believe my team found your company, and if I remember correctly, I'm paying you far less than your company's actually worth. That doesn't mean you should raise the price," Tristan added with a smile. "I'm interested in you, more than I've been in anyone before."

Dylan remained quiet and Tristan let the statement stand there between them.

"I don't understand why," Dylan finally responded.

"You smell incredible."

"That's the dinner you just served us," Dylan said, the smile was back. That smile was rare and stirred him to a full hard-on.

He'd done a poor job at keeping distance between them. He knew what he felt for Dylan, and those feelings were solid.

Holding back wouldn't change them in the end. Tristan leaned forward, watching Dylan intently as he pulled him closer. Dylan didn't deny him, although uncertainty loomed in his eyes. After a moment's pause, he bent in to Dylan's neck. "Fuck it. I'm the one that's gonna be hurt in this deal anyway."

Tristan took a deep breath, drawing Dylan's scent inside him. He ran his nose along the skin of Dylan's neck, loving the little shiver he got in return. "The way you smell... I love it."

"What does that mean—you getting hurt?" Dylan asked without any acknowledgment to his last comment. Tristan lifted a hand to Dylan's neck, holding him in place when it looked like he might pull away. He made a mistake and glanced down at those lips, so perfect and full. Dylan had amazing lips.

"Kiss me, Dylan." Tristan slid his tongue across Dylan's lips, tentatively testing his reaction. This was his chance. He had to know. Did Dylan share his feelings? Dylan opened and Tristan delved in, his tongue searching Dylan's sweet taste. He wrapped his hands around Dylan's lower biceps and stood, drawing him up against his body. This was what he'd been waiting for all night. And no matter how many different ways he'd told himself he wouldn't push Dylan tonight, there would be no way to stop him unless Dylan put a halt to it himself.

Between the wine and Dylan's incredible company, Tristan's body was hard and ready. He couldn't remember having to show this much restraint ever. Okay, maybe not ever...because he had been just this way with this man before. The time and distance of the last couple of weeks felt like the longest drought of his life.

"Wait, Tristan. Why would you be hurt?" Dylan pulled slightly away to ask the question.

Only under the need to kiss Dylan again did Tristan give in and quickly answer, "I'm very into you."

Dylan widened his eyes at the declaration and stared back at him. He still hadn't caught on. The buyout, the trip, everything he'd done for a simple dinner... "And you're buried deep, with a strong life plan that you've been living for years that doesn't include me. There's no way this will end well for me, but not taking the few moments you're willing to give me seems like a far worse fate. So kiss me, Dylan. Please. And call your family, stay with me tonight. We'll deal with tomorrow later."

Tristan turned his head and captured Dylan's mouth with his own. Dylan met him halfway and wrapped him tightly in his arms. If actions spoke louder than words, then the possessive hold and the intensity of Dylan's kiss proved he liked everything Tristan had just confessed.

Damn, he swore being in Dylan's arms felt like home.

Dylan found himself pushed backward, and Tristan never broke from the kiss. Something solid hit the back of his legs and stopped his feet from moving, but his upper body kept going. In order to stop from falling, Dylan had to take his hands from Tristan to balance himself, something he really didn't want to do. Tristan held on tight, holding most of his weight, completely in control of this moment as he lowered Dylan back on an oversized leather sofa and climbed on top of him.

Tristan was relentless as he devoured him, positioning Dylan's head, driving his tongue deeper, making love to him with his mouth. The soft sensual strokes of Tristan's tongue were mind-blowing. He'd missed Tristan, missed his taste and missed the intimacy they shared. Tristan slid a knee between his thighs to separate them. Dylan scooted lower on the couch, spreading his legs, giving Tristan better access to grind against him.

Dylan pulled at Tristan's shirt, tugging the material free from his slacks. He craved skin on skin with a need unlike anything he'd ever known. The moment his palms touched the warm, bare skin of Tristan's back, he lost it. A strangled moan pierced the silence of the hotel room. He'd only known it was his own voice because Tristan was busy whispering naughty promises against his ear. He hadn't planned on any of this, hadn't thought he'd need Tristan's touch so desperately. He'd been very wrong.

Tristan reached low inside his slacks and palmed his dick. He circled Dylan's tip with a thumb. His strokes were long and slow, tight and fast, and the sensations became too much. Dylan bucked himself against Tristan's palm as he worked his belt free and his slacks undone. He shoved his underwear down and tore free of the kiss as he arched his back, lost in the pleasure Tristan gave him. "It feels too good," he hissed.

"Don't come, not yet," Tristan said and squeezed the base of his dick, removing any hope of relief from his pending orgasm. Dylan exhaled and tipped his face up, his eyes burning into Tristan's.

"But I need to," he objected, threading his fingers into Tristan's hair. "It won't be my only one, you know it. You're all I can think about."

"I'm happy to hear that, but I'm greedy and I want this one in my mouth," Tristan said, sliding off the couch between his parted thighs until his knees hit the floor. Dylan groaned as Tristan removed his shoes and socks then righted him into a sitting position. Dylan helped, tugging his shirt over his head and tossing it aside as he lifted his hips and let Tristan rid him of his underwear and slacks.

Tristan slid his palms up Dylan's thighs and took him in hand. He was lost. All defenses were gone when the warm, wet heat of Tristan's mouth engulfed him. *Fuck!* Tristan swallowed him to the root, the tip of his cock hitting the back of Tristan's throat. He gripped Tristan's head, guiding him down, and lifted his hips up at the same time, wanting more. He was careful not to thrust too hard; he didn't want to gag Tristan...but damn, it felt amazing.

Tristan's head bobbed up and down on him, the friction his mouth created had him bucking up off the couch. Tristan moaned and played with his sac, knowing exactly what he was doing. Dylan realized at that moment he'd never tasted Tristan, only tasted himself on Tristan's lips. He pulled back and held Tristan's head in place, trying to stop him.

"Tristan," he forced out and tried to move away.

Tristan pulled off his dick with an audible pop and looked up at him. "Are you okay?"

"More than, but I want to give you...I've never..." Dylan stopped the flow of words, hoping Tristan understood.

"Are you asking if you can suck my dick, Mr. Reeves?" Tristan's brow lifted and a wicked glint flashed in his eyes. He licked his lips suggestively, wrapped a hand around Dylan's cock, and stroked him slowly.

Dylan swallowed hard. "I want to suck you, but I don't know if I can make you feel as good as you make me feel. I haven't...you know...sucked anyone before." His own embarrassment had him stumbling for the right words. He wasn't sure how to even start, all he knew was he wanted to please Tristan.

"Right now, if you were to blow on my dick, I'd come," Tristan laughed. "Seriously, that's the hottest and sweetest thing anyone's ever said to me. I have an idea." Tristan quit stroking him and stood to rid himself of his clothing before taking Dylan's hand and leading him to the suite's bedroom. Dylan watched in curiosity as Tristan moved to the other side of the room, grabbed the lube and condoms from his suitcase, and gave him that devilish smile.

"Let's just say, I hoped there might be a small chance of you fucking me and I wanted to be prepared." Tristan gave him a wink and moved to the bed. Dylan remained in the doorway as Tristan positioned himself in the middle of the bed and started shamelessly stroking his cock. What incredible visual stimulation. Fuck, he could watch that man fondling himself all day long. Dylan's mouth watered as he thought over what he was about to do. He was nervous about pleasing Tristan, but excited too.

"Aren't you going to join me?" Tristan's voice pulled him back down to earth.

Dylan nodded and made his way to the bed. He didn't stand at the bedside long because Tristan reached up with his free hand and tugged Dylan down beside him. Tristan ran his fingers around the head of his own prick, gathering the wetness from the tip, and brought his fingers to Dylan's lips.

"Taste me, Dylan." Tristan's steel gray eyes bore into him and that deep voice vibrated through his body, making his dick twitch in response.

Dylan licked the moisture from Tristan's fingers then sucked them into his mouth. Tristan's taste wasn't much different than his own, sweeter perhaps.

"God, that's so fucking hot," Tristan growled, removing his fingers, then took his mouth in a kiss. Dylan melted against Tristan. Had he really believed there was any chance in hell he could have resisted Tristan tonight? The kiss grew deeper. Tongues, lips, and teeth met in a frenzy of heated moans. Their hands roamed and stroked one another. Dylan ground his dick against Tristan's hard length, searching for relief.

"In my mouth," Dylan panted, breaking from the kiss. He grabbed Tristan's cock, stroking him as he kissed along his jaw and down his chest and stomach. Tristan groaned.

"Wait, turn around, crawl on top of me and put your knees on either side of my shoulders."

He watched Tristan move down farther on the bed, then did exactly what Tristan suggested and straddled his face. He was on his knees, legs spread on either side of Tristan's head.

Tristan slapped his butt and guided him into position, nuzzling his balls in the process. At first, he felt a little self-conscious, but the things Tristan kept doing with his mouth and fingers overrode the embarrassment.

Strong, sure fingers caressed him and stroked him. "You're in control; take it as slow as you want. I'm so going to enjoy this." Tristan propped himself up. He lifted his head and parted Dylan's ass cheeks and then began to lick around his rim with his warm and moist and very persistent tongue.

"Oh, fuck that feels amazing." Dylan sat back and let Tristan do what he wanted, because it felt so damn incredible. For a split second, he'd almost forgotten his mission at hand.

Dylan gathered his wits after a minute or two of enjoying Tristan's wicked tongue and fingers. He bent, leaning all the way forward, and grabbed Tristan's dick in his hand, giving him a few solid strokes. Tristan was hard as hell and it was all for him. His dick jerked at the thought. He lowered himself to his forearm, admiring Tristan's nice, thick cut cock as it got closer.

Dylan stuck his tongue out for a taste and lapped at the moisture building at the tip. Tristan's essence burst across his mouth. He tasted of salt and Tristan. There was no doubt he could become addicted. The smell of him, like citrus and sweet summer rain. The feel of him, hard steel wrapped in soft velvet, pressed against his tongue. Dylan teased the head of Tristan's cock with his lips, then took in as much of him as he could without triggering his gag reflex.

Dylan had a hard time concentrating with Tristan mouthing at his balls. He slid his lips over Tristan and heard him groan. Dylan bobbed his head careful not to take him too deep. He curled his tongue around Tristan's cock. He liked it when Tristan did that to him, so surely Tristan would like it too.

"You're perfect, Dylan," Tristan said breathlessly and started to stroke him. Dylan sucked him to the rhythm set by Tristan's fist. He was getting braver, taking him deeper each time, trying to imitate all the things Tristan had done to him. Sliding up and down, swirling his tongue around Tristan's tip, while using his hand to stroke his shaft.

"Oh, fuck, yes!" Tristan gasped. "Feels so good."

Dylan sucked harder, alternating between hollowing his cheeks and working his tongue into the tiny slit at the tip of his dick. Tristan stopped stroking and used his arms to push Dylan's knees back so he could slide down lower. He stretched out as Tristan swallowed his dick and toyed with his balls. He fucked into Tristan's welcoming mouth, sucking the man with every thrust of his own hips. The mind-blowing sensation was new and thrilling all at the same time.

After a few hard thrusts, Tristan rolled them to their sides. Dylan mimicked Tristan's technique, enjoying the needy sounds Tristan made with every flick and lick of his tongue. The heat built, tingling in his spine, and he thrust faster and harder into his lover's mouth. Tristan's fingers pressed the area behind his balls and his mouth swallowed him deeper.

Dylan pulled back a moment to hiss, "I can't hold back," before resuming his exploration of Tristan's cock. The pressure built. He couldn't stop. Tristan's mouth drove him completely insane. Damn, he loved that mouth, loved the sounds Tristan made, the smell of Tristan's musk, and the feel of his tongue sliding over him. Everything combined was too much for him to take. His body trembled uncontrollably and he cried out around Tristan's dick as his orgasm burst free. Every muscle seized, paralyzing him as he gave up his load deep down Tristan's throat. Tristan eagerly swallowed every drop, then jerked his mouth off him.

"I'm gonna come," Tristan panted and tried to roll away.

Dylan gripped him harder and sucked him deeper. Tristan froze, his dick jerked hard, and hot come filled Dylan's mouth. He swallowed. He hadn't known if swallowing was something he could do, but he loved every last drop. He kept sucking Tristan as the last of the shudders of orgasm racked his lover's body.

They lay there as their bodies spiraled back to earth. Heavy breathing filled the silence of the room. Dylan floated on an after-sex high, his body sated and still thrumming from his release.

"Damn, that was amazing." Tristan's voice broke through the silence.

Dylan drew back to look at Tristan. He had a big grin on his face, his smile so wide it reminded Dylan of the Cheshire cat.

"I'm not finished with you yet." Tristan sucked him back in, the warm, moist tightness engulfing him made his toes curl. Tristan licked him, making little mewing sounds as he cleaned him with his tongue. Dylan couldn't get his body under control, his hips thrust reflexively. He pressed his lips to Tristan's hip bone and stroked Tristan, licking around his dick like a lollipop. He was already hard again and so was Tristan.

"I want to fuck you," Dylan blurted out. He hadn't meant to sound so crass, but damn, all of his blood had been drained from his brain.

"Thought you'd never ask." Tristan kissed the tip of his dick and scooted away, reaching for the lube and condoms. Tristan turned, moving to his hands and knees.

"This how you want me?" Tristan wiggled his ass and chuckled.

"Yeah, pretty much…" Dylan slid off the bed and stretched his legs. Tristan was insatiable, and he was horny as hell—seemed Tristan brought out the best in him.

Dylan stood at the edge of the bed and pulled Tristan's hips back toward him. He smoothed his hand over the firm globes in front of him. Damn, Tristan had the most perfect ass he'd ever seen. Tristan spread his legs as Dylan slid his hand in between his ass cheeks and teased his hole with a finger. Tristan turned, looking at Dylan over his shoulder.

"I've been dreaming about this since you left California…" Tristan's voice was husky with need.

Tristan scooted the lube in his direction. Dylan slicked his fingers, then added more lube directly to the rim before he pushed a finger in Tristan's tight ass. He watched as it easily slid inside. Tristan pressed back against him so he added another and kept on until he had three fingers working him open. He curled his fingers inside Tristan and found the gland.

"Oh god, just fuck me, Dylan." Tristan dropped his head between his shoulder blades and rocked back.

When he removed his fingers, Tristan let out a loud moan and reared back against him.

"No! Keep going," Tristan panted. Dylan took himself in hand, hurriedly rolled a condom in place, and positioned himself at Tristan's entrance. Dylan pushed against the ring of muscle and felt his tip slip inside. With a long steady shove, he buried himself deep in Tristan's ass, causing them both to groan at the sensation. Tristan pushed back against him again, tight heat surrounded him, drawing him deeper inside. He stopped moving, giving Tristan's body time to adjust.

"Don't stop. Fuck me, please," Tristan commanded. Dylan grabbed Tristan's hips and plunged deep, pulling almost completely out before slamming back inside. He picked up the rhythm and fucked Tristan hard and fast. Their harsh breathing and muffled groans grew louder.

When he nailed his lover's prostate, Tristan moaned. "There, fucking right there…" Tristan's head snapped back and his body trembled. Dylan's hips continue to move of their own accord.

Fire raced through Dylan's blood, straight to his cock. His hips pistoned in and out of Tristan's body, making sure he nailed Tristan's spot with every thrust. Even though he'd already come, he wouldn't last, not with the way Tristan's ass gripped him. This man had him so strung out, Tristan was like a drug. Alluring and hard to resist. He was weak against Tristan's temptation.

"Fuck!" Tristan whimpered as Dylan took hold of his rigid length and began stroking in time with his thrusts. Sounds of flesh slapping against flesh while his groin hit Tristan's ass drove his lover to rock back into him, over and over.

Tristan screamed his name, his ass clenching and contracting around him. He worked Tristan's cock with his hand, twisting and stroking as he pounded into him from behind. He screwed his eyes shut, his balls churned, tightening against his body as liquid fire rushed through his veins.

Tristan pressed his face into the pillow and ground his ass back against him, mumbling incoherently. Dylan held Tristan in place, exactly where he wanted him and thrust into him one more time.

"Aghh… Holy hell!" His body shook uncontrollably as his release crashed into him. His balls emptied in powerful spurts. Pleasure overwhelmed him, drowning him in a torrent of sensation. His legs gave way, and he collapsed against Tristan.

Dylan managed to hold the condom in place and withdrew his softening dick from Tristan's ass. Tristan groaned and rolled to his side, his chest still heaving as he sucked in air. Dylan rolled with him, then knotted the condom and dropped it in the wastebasket beside the bed. Strong arms embraced him as Tristan drew him close. He turned in his lover's arms and gazed into his eyes. He couldn't miss the smile on Tristan's face.

"You just rocked my world. I don't think I've been so close to having a heart attack in my entire life," Tristan said and kissed him. Tristan pulled back from the kiss and grinned at him. "Well, except for that time you made me go running with you."

CHAPTER.22

Hours later Dylan lay back against Tristan in the oversized bathtub, letting the warm water relax his overworked and exhausted body. Tristan sat behind him, his arms wrapped tightly around him, and his skilled hands massaged anywhere they could touch. Tristan's half erect cock was perfectly positioned at the crease of his ass.

"I've kept you busy. Do you need to call home?" Tristan asked.

"I got a text from Teri. She already took care of things for me. She told the kids I was gone for the night." Dylan rested his head against Tristan's shoulder, his eyes closed, and he fought against the sleep his body seemed to want.

"Where did she say you were?" Tristan questioned. With his palm, he pushed the warm water up over Dylan's chest. He also did that breathing thing, caressing his neck as he spoke right against his ear. The two sensations always collided, and like every other time, his cock plumped at the sensual assault coursing through him.

"They're older teenagers. They don't really care unless it directly affects them," Dylan said, smiling and glancing back up at Tristan.

"Good. So you don't have to lie. You don't seem to like lying," Tristan said, smiling back at him.

"Except my whole life's a lie."

"Not really. You're taking care of your responsibilities. Someday it'll be different."

"I hope so," Dylan replied and went back to just enjoying their time together. His eyes closed as he snuggled back against Tristan. Blissfully content in listening to the cadence of Tristan's breathing.

"Me too," Tristan said softly. Dylan thought about the kiss they'd shared after dinner. He couldn't remember if the waitstaff had left the hotel room or not. Dylan hadn't considered them as he dropped to the sofa and let Tristan suck him. Nor had Dylan considered them while Tristan rimmed him and he gave Tristan a blow job. He'd even fucked Tristan into the mattress not minutes later, right there on the big king bed with the bedroom door wide open.

God, it was such a turn-on to be wanted.

"Why do you look a little different?" Tristan asked. "You're a hot guy, but something's different."

"I changed things up a little bit. Actually my hair person did."

"Does she know about me?"

"No, he's been chomping at the bit to make me over for years," Dylan said, his eyes still closed.

"He?" Tristan sounded surprised.

"Yeah." Dylan hadn't missed the tone in Tristan's voice and glanced over his shoulder questioningly.

"I like being the only *he* in your life." Tristan nudged him, then bit at his shoulder.

"You are. He doesn't know. No one but you and Teri know. I told you that."

"So what did he do?" Tristan asked.

"Added some very small pieces of color to my hair and did a subtle spray tan."

"Ahhh, yes, now I can see that. You looked stunning when you walked in, made my mouth water. Did you do all that for me?" That drew silence and Tristan chuckled.

"I bought new clothes for you and spent over a thousand dollars on flowers. I also added blond to my hair, too, and was waxed professionally downstairs just in case you changed your mind," Tristan confessed.

"Really?" Dylan gave another glance over his shoulder.

"Yeah," Tristan chuckled. "I hoped you wanted me as much as I want you."

One of Tristan's hands slid to his ass, while the other moved to his cock. At the same moment a finger began to massage his rim, Tristan's grip tightened around his cock and stroked up. His dick grew painfully hard at the sensation.

"I've been looking forward to this night and I didn't even think we were having sex. I planned on just spending time with you, but I can't keep my hands to myself," Tristan said and kissed the back of his neck sending chills down his spine.

"I thought I could come here and just talk about whatever interested you, too. I made up my mind nothing would happen. But right now I need you to make love to me, Tristan." Dylan lifted an arm, snaking his hand through the back of Tristan's hair, pulling him closer as he turned slightly in his arms.

Tristan angled Dylan's head and kissed him. Dylan continued to turn in his arms. Coming up on his knees, he straddled Tristan's thighs. "You have to help me. I don't know what I'm doing, but I want this."

He didn't say anything, but kissed him soft and oh so fucking sweet. The kiss never got heated or frenzied, just a lazy licking and sampling of Dylan's mouth. Tristan let his tongue slip between Dylan's lips, tasting him. He would never get enough of this man. Dylan was one of a kind and until this moment he hadn't realized exactly how hard he'd tumbled.

"You're perfect. Do what feels right to you," Tristan said, using the slick suds to stroke Dylan's dick. Dylan lifted up on his knees, and sat on the side of the tub. Tristan bent in, licking circles around his soapy dick. Dylan held his head and pressed a thumb into the corner of his mouth, watching intently while he sucked on Dylan's thumb and dick at the same time.

"Damn, you're hot, Tristan," Dylan moaned.

He kept his eyes on Dylan, never breaking their hold and sucked Dylan down to the root, swallowing around him. Dylan thrust his hips forward, causing water to splash from the tub. He loosened his jaw and let Dylan slowly fuck his mouth. Dylan moved his hands to his head and pushed him back.

"You have to stop or I'm gonna come right here and I don't want to, not yet."

Dylan lowered, resting his full weight on him. In this position, their dicks rubbed together in the water. Tristan took them both in hand and started to stroke.

"You'll be coming again tonight. I promise." He lifted his head and grazed Dylan's lips with his. The kiss deepened and his grip tightened on both of them.

Dylan's mouth slid over his collarbone as he whispered the sweet words, "I want you…need you inside me."

"Not here. I want you in my bed." He needed a condom. He broke free and stood, knowing if he didn't break this contact, they'd never make it to the bed. He stepped from the tub and took Dylan's hand, helping him out. He reached for a towel and tenderly dried him off, then himself before he led him to the bedroom. The candles had burned down, but their scent remained and the messed up bed looked warm and inviting. He laid Dylan back on the rumpled comforter and crawled over him, kissing and caressing any part of him he could reach.

He kissed then sucked the soft skin below Dylan's ear and mouthed his way down his neck, marking him with tiny love bites. He ran his tongue across Dylan's collarbone, tasting the coconut body wash on his skin. Tristan circled Dylan's nipples with his tongue then nipped and licked at the tightening buds, earning a deep moan from that move. He wrapped a fist around Dylan's length giving him long, slow strokes. Dylan arched into his fist when he pressed his thumb over the slit, then rubbed back and forth spreading the come across his bulbous head.

"I need you," Dylan said.

Tristan sat up and reached for the table by the bed. Dylan's thighs fell to the side, his body open and on display for him. The sight had Tristan's cock leaking. He took the lube from the nightstand where they had left it earlier and laid the bottle beside them on the bed.

He pushed Dylan's legs back, exposing his hole, and settled himself against his lover's ass. After he drizzled lube on his fingers, he pressed one inside Dylan, making sure he was good and slick before he started working him.

Dylan let out a long groan as he teased his rim, sliding his finger in and out of Dylan's ass. Adding a second, he started scissoring them, dragging them against the gland. Dylan writhed against his hand.

"Please, Tristan, you're making me crazy. Make love to me," Dylan pleaded. Tristan eased his fingers out and reached down beside him, picked up the condom and rolled it on.

"Let me roll over," Dylan said and made an attempt to turn to his stomach.

"No, I want to see your face when I make love to you, because that's what I'm doing Dylan. I'm making love to you."

He kept his eyes locked with Dylan's as he lined himself up and pressed the tip of his cock against his lover's entrance. He pushed forward, sinking into that tight heat an inch at a time. He pushed in slow and pulled out even slower. Dylan's blue eyes remained on his, and he couldn't help but get lost in their depths.

"So tight and so hot. You're killing me," he groaned, loving the way Dylan's body squeezed him perfectly. He pressed his mouth to Dylan's full lips, still swollen from his kiss. Dylan opened for him, and he pushed his tongue inside, searching for Dylan's. Their tongues brushed and tangled as he probed and explored Dylan's mouth.

Tristan set a solid, unhurried pace as he made love to Dylan. Dylan's legs lifted and wrapped around his waist. He pushed one leg back and rolled his hips into Dylan. The feeling was amazing and Tristan couldn't help but smile when Dylan moaned into his mouth. Tristan moved slowly inside Dylan, needing to draw out their pleasure. He shifted to the side and held Dylan's calf, pushing it back against his chest.

"Yes, yes, yes," Dylan chanted when he changed the angle of his thrust, driving into that spot over and over again with every snap of his hips.

Tristan sped up, burying himself in Dylan with strong, deep, lingering thrusts. Heat built at the base of Tristan's spine and engulfed his body in warmth. He was close. This moment with Dylan was so tender, so right. He never wanted it to end.

"Yes, Tristan…" Dylan gasped, his body tensed and his ass clamped down on Tristan. Hot come splattered on Dylan's chest and stomach as Tristan continued to thrust into him. The sweet smell of Dylan's release surrounded him. Tristan couldn't thrust deep enough, wanting to crawl deeper into this man. He was soaring. His own orgasm surged through his body and filled the condom in Dylan's ass.

He bent his head and pressed his lips to Dylan's. Softly, tenderly their mouths worked together. Tristan was still riding out the most intense orgasm of his life. This was something he'd never done or felt before. He was truly making love to Dylan.

They held each other, kissing deeply, hungrily, eating at each other's mouth as their bodies moved slowly together. Tristan softened and slipped out. He remained on Dylan's chest where he'd collapsed. The come cooled on their skin as they lay there softly caressing one another, still coming down off their high. No words were uttered. They didn't need to be. Tristan knew at that moment, at least for him, there was no going back, everything changed.

Tristan didn't know how much time had passed or how long they had lain there. He could spend all night wrapped in Dylan's arms like this. After he had cleaned them, they ended up curled around each other, neither wanting to let the other go. He was so out of his element, yet it felt like the most natural thing on the planet. Tristan nuzzled into Dylan's hair and kissed the top of his head. He pulled Dylan tighter against him. Dylan reached over to make sure they were completely covered before settling back, pressed head to toe against Tristan. A few minutes passed before Tristan whispered into the dark.

"Baby, are you asleep?"

"Close," Dylan murmured. His voice gravelly and thick, proving he'd been sleeping.

"I need to tell you something. I haven't ever said anything like this before, but you need to know so I can sleep." Tristan lifted his head a little, talking quietly into Dylan's ear, trying to keep his heart from racing out of his chest.

"Okay." A solid yawn formed on the word.

"I'll wait for you, however long it takes. I don't care. I'll wait. I'm in love with you," Tristan whispered those last few words softly into his hair. Dylan stilled in Tristan's arms, lying there a moment.

"Did I hear that correctly?" he asked.

"If you heard me tell you that I love you, then yes, you did," Tristan repeated, this time with his head on the pillow, waiting for a response. Dylan turned and Tristan tightened his hold on instinct, for fear he'd bolt. Dylan wedged his way around to where they now were face-to-face. He pressed himself firmly against Tristan's body, snuggling in as he draped an arm and leg around him and nestled his face into the crook of his neck. Dylan placed a simple kiss on Tristan's neck, and in that moment, he'd never remembered feeling that content in his entire life. Everything made exactly right by Dylan's response.

"Thank you for understanding. I love you." Dylan spoke softly, saying those words like they were the most natural thing in the world for him before he went straight to sleep.

So much for earth-shattering moments with possible storming off-and-leaving-in-the-middle-of-the-night confessions. He gently played with Dylan's hair and then ran a hand down his neck, listening to the light snores being made against his neck and ear. He had never slept with anyone curled so completely around him, yet he found he never wanted Dylan to leave this spot. Dylan was made to lie with him exactly like this. Something told him he'd found his other half and he needed to hang on at all cost. Tristan dragged Dylan in closer, if that were even possible, and closed his eyes, relishing the moment before drifting off, sleeping better than he had in weeks.

CHAPTER.23

"I should go." Dylan sat curled up next to Tristan on the sofa in the living room area of the hotel suite he'd rented for the weekend. Dylan apparently loved sports, and they were watching an NBA playoff game. The statement had Tristan reaching over to wrap Dylan tighter in his arms, not wanting him to leave.

The weekend hadn't only been about sex, although he loved that part. They'd stayed inside the hotel suite and gotten to know one another on a level Tristan had never known with anyone else. The more they talked, the more Tristan's heart connected. He found that Dylan was what he seemed to be from the very beginning: a good man who was funny as hell. The overly serious, scared guy still made himself known, but those times were fading as he grew more secure. Tristan found himself regularly assuring him through word and action that he would absolutely be there for the long haul, following all of Dylan's rules. Dylan opened up to him on a level he never expected to see.

They were fluid and natural with one another, like they had been from the first moment.

"I don't want you to go." Tristan leaned in, running his nose through Dylan's disheveled hair. By talking him into staying through the late-night playoff game, he'd hoped he might be able to get another night out of the guy. Then Dylan could leave from the hotel in the morning. If he left now, Tristan would be stuck in this room alone until tomorrow.

"I need to. It's late and I need to pull my life back together. You messed me up the last few weeks. I'm behind. I gotta get caught up and get myself running right again," Dylan said and snuggled against him.

"Tell me about a day in the life of Dylan Reeves." Tristan grabbed the remote, turning the volume down on the television.

"A day in the life, huh?" He looked back over his shoulder, confused.

"Yeah, from the time you wake up until the time you go to bed." Tristan nodded encouragingly, trying to eat up more time.

"Okay, well, I get up every morning about five thirty. I usually begin my day running," Dylan said and Tristan stopped him.

"You run every day?" That might be the craziest thing he'd ever heard anyone say, especially after their run together in California.

"Yes, and it's the perfect time of day. I'm usually completely alone out there. I run about an hour and a half. Then I come home and get the kids off to school, they leave around eight. Then I shower, get dressed, and work until dinner or if one of the kids has something going on, I'll do that instead of dinner. Most nights, I usually work in my home office after everyone's settled, and then I go to bed." Tristan listened closely, and at first, he thought Dylan's life sounded lonely until he realized he did about the same thing, minus the kids, every single day. That was an interesting thought. He'd thought Dylan's life was void of so many things, but maybe they were more alike than he realized.

"And golfing. You like that?" Tristan asked, when he caught Dylan staring back at him.

"Yes, that's usually Saturday mornings before going into the office. Every once in a while I can still get Chad to the range to hit a few after school and work." Dylan changed positions, turning to where he could better see Tristan. He liked having all of Dylan's attention focused on him. He bent forward and kissed his lips, just because they were a little upturned and slanting his way. "What's your day like? I bet it's full every day."

"I was sitting here listening, thinking we do about the same things. I really just work from the time I get up to the time I go to bed. I like sunset, but you know that, and I go to the gym at some point every day, but that's usually about nine in the morning or after nine at night because it's less crowded. But I do about the same as you."

"What about Julian? When does he come by?" Dylan asked and Tristan narrowed his eyes because the question sounded more like an accusation.

"Is that jealousy I'm hearing?" Tristan arched a brow, smiling big. Dylan remained quiet, and right then he knew if they were in a standoff, he would lose every single time, because after several moments of silence, Dylan's gaze went back to the television, ignoring him completely. He reached for the remote, probably to turn the volume back up, but Tristan stopped that move, grabbing Dylan's hand, pulling him back. "I haven't been seeing him or anyone else since I met you. I promise, you don't have to worry about that."

Dylan searched his eyes, again keeping quiet for longer than a simple pause. "I wouldn't ask that of you."

"You didn't. It's just hard to go back to adequate once you've had spectacular," Tristan said, hoping Dylan liked that statement. It was absolutely true, and Tristan smiled as Dylan's grin spread. Now he had all of Dylan's attention again.

"That's really a good answer," Dylan chuckled.

"Thank you and absolutely true." Tristan kissed his upturned, smiling lips.

"When are you leaving to go back home?" Dylan asked.

"As soon as you do, as long as that's in the morning. I flew in on the Wilder jet. They can be ready to go with a couple of hours' notice," Tristan said, trying to decide if he should formally ask Dylan to stay. He didn't want to push for more the first weekend he agreed to follow all the rules. He should be happy taking what Dylan was willing to give.

Except that wasn't really his nature. He bit the bullet and guarded his words.

"We can stay through tonight. I've already paid for the room, or you can leave. I'll be back in the next few weeks to announce the buyout. I can see you then or even before that if you need to come out to Wilder to meet some of the staff you'll be working with." Did that sound casual enough? He fought the urge to bite his lip as he waited for an answer.

"I should go home, but Teri said she's got tomorrow morning covered. I didn't want to assume you wanted me to stay. You have to be sick of hiding out in this room. You've only left to work out," Dylan said.

"Great! Then we can leave together in the morning. And you don't like this room?" Tristan looked around, throwing his arms out for dramatic effect. "I love this room. Every time I come to Dallas I'm asking for this very room. It's the room you told me you loved me in. I should buy the hotel just to keep this room exactly like it is."

"All right, that was a little over the top," Dylan said, reaching for the remote this time, turning the volume up.

"But still true and I win. We're leaving tomorrow, not tonight, so whatever. I can be cheesy if I want." Tristan kissed the top of Dylan's head as he turned back around to watch the last few minutes of the playoffs. Dylan was immediately absorbed back into the game after grabbing a water bottle from the small coffee table in front of them. Since Friday night, Dylan hadn't had anything else but water to drink. Tristan smiled, running his nose along the back of Dylan's head again, breathing him in. They were past the need for alcohol to be comfortable together. Although, he'd have been fine with plying Dylan with liquor for the rest of his life, this was far better. He was a happy, happy man.

CHAPTER.24

"Dad, I think I look stupid." Cate came through the kitchen where Dylan stood at the counter, taking his vitamins. He was in the middle of a long gulp of water when she entered in a huff. He tried to look over at her, lower the glass, and not choke to death in the process. Once the pills were down, he was pretty proud of himself for not spilling anything.

He ran a hand down his tie, making sure no water drops hit the satin. He'd picked one of the suits he'd bought for his first trip to California to wear today. From there, Teri had been a drill sergeant, fussing over their clothes for the day, and made sure he hadn't worn this suit during the trip. Once his clothes were defined, she had gone on a tedious, multi-day shopping spree, handpicking special clothing for her and the kids, trying to make them all match for the photos that were sure to be taken.

Satisfied he wasn't going to have to change ties and ruin Teri's whole color scheme, Dylan looked over at his indignant daughter. She wore a seafoam green dress that matched her eyes perfectly. To Dylan, she looked beautiful, but that was clearly not what she wanted in an answer from him. He tried for diplomacy.

"Caty-baby, it's what your mom wants you to wear. It's one day in your life," he said, hoping that wouldn't get him in trouble with Teri and appease his daughter at the same time.

"Look!" Cate put her hands down her sides. "We agreed to skirts that went to my fingertips. This goes all the way past my knees. I look like Granny Reeves."

That had Dylan barking out a laugh. Now, he completely understood her problem, and he hated that fingertip rule to begin with. She'd come to the wrong person in this argument. He'd have her dressing like this every single day. "You look beautiful and respectable and put a smile on your face and be happy. It's only one day out of your life."

"Dad! You aren't helping!" She stomped her foot and took off in a twirled huff, her dark hair flaring out as she stormed off.

"Dad, what's wrong with her?" Chad asked, coming through the kitchen toward the garage. "I can't find my wallet."

"Here, Son, you left it on the counter last night," Dylan said, going to the kitchen bar, reaching across the granite countertop to where he'd seen the wallet earlier.

"Thanks, Dad," Chad said, tucking his wallet in his suit jacket. "We're gonna look like a holiday Christmas card today."

That attitude had Dylan laughing again. "Yeah, I think that's what your mom wanted."

"I need everyone to stop whining and get in the car," Teri yelled out from somewhere in the living room. She had to have been heard throughout the entire house from that vantage point. "You have three minutes!"

Dylan could hear her high heels clicking on the hardwood floors as she headed in their direction. She came around the corner as frustrated as Cate had been a few minutes ago.

"We've raised terrible children," she announced and stuck her head back out into the open living room. "Two and a half minutes, and I'm not playing. There will be consequences, and there better be smiles on your faces!"

She turned back, eyeing Chad closely. "Do you have anything to say to me about your suit?"

"No, ma'am!" *Oh.* Dylan winced. He'd pulled out the ma'am.

"Good, then you're now my new official favorite child." She looked over at Dylan, her eyes blazing mad. She stopped him before he had a chance to tell her how pretty she looked today. "I'm going to my car. Chad, get in my car. We'll drive separately from you. Don't be nice to them when they come down. They've been wretched and ungrateful children." She was through the kitchen and out the back, the door to the garage slamming in her wake. Chad followed, raising his brows until something caught his attention and Chad turned.

"Oh my god, you look like twins!" Chad barked out on a laugh with wide eyes.

"Chad, get in the car and shut your mouth," Dylan warned, waiting to see the girls come around the corner. He couldn't help his smile when they did. They weren't exactly matching dresses, but most definitely not a color or style they would have picked for themselves.

"You look beautiful," Dylan started.

"No, don't even say it, Dad! And Mom's being terrible," Cate said, storming toward the back door.

"I bet she's on her period," Chloe mumbled, following behind.

"It's a big day for our family. Please put smiles on your faces and be nice," Dylan advised. The horn sounded off as Chloe gave him a big fake smile and Cate opened the back door.

"We're coming, Mom. Stop being so mad," Cate called out toward Teri.

"Can I ride with you?" Chad asked.

"Yeah, come on. I'll make the excuse to your mom." Dylan grabbed his suit jacket off the back of a chair, patting his son on the shoulder. Today was a monumental turning point in all their lives. Secret Networks was announcing its merger with Wilder, Inc. The whole day would be filled with parties, press announcements, meet-and-greet sessions. Just a very special day for the Reeves family.

He grabbed a duffel bag by the back door and slung the strap over his shoulder.

"Should I take a change of clothes?" Chad asked, stopping himself from walking out the door as he eyed Dylan's bag.

"No, I have to stay downtown tonight. Wilder has meetings into the night." Dylan never looked over at Chad after he told the lie. He went out the back door, hoping he sounded convincing. Teri was far better at lying to them.

Tristan was in town for the big companywide announcement. Dylan stayed with him last night and came home way before anyone woke this morning. He planned to do the same tonight. Two weeks had passed since the last time Tristan had been in town and nothing earth-shattering had happened, except that he missed Tristan. Over the last fourteen days, they'd stayed discreet, yet talked every single day, about a million times a day and even had some late-night, locked-in-the-bathroom Secret video sex chats. He really loved those nights.

The stark realization hit him—he'd become Teri. He had a romance outside of their family and the world hadn't broken apart into a million pieces. All things considered, even with a car full of angry women staring him down, it was an incredible day.

"He's riding with me," Dylan called out. Teri was behind the wheel of her SUV, the frown clearly in place as she began to back out of the garage. Both girls were in her backseat, looking sullen-faced and regretful. They must have gotten an earful in the last minute and a half they'd been in the car.

He smiled and waved at the girls. If he could gauge a look, he'd say they were begging him to come save them from the monster that had taken over their mother's body. Chad didn't carry any of that stress as he stood there looking at him over the hood of his car.

"You've been happy for a few weeks now. We should have sold Secret sooner." Chad's observation threw him off until he realized he was smiling right then. He'd been smiling a lot lately. Dylan didn't say a word, but hit the key fob to unlock the doors. Chad got inside as Dylan lifted the trunk and put his bag in the back. He guessed he should have done a lot of things sooner, but if he had, he wouldn't be here right now.

Honestly, he wouldn't change a thing. Tristan was well worth the wait.

Tristan paced the foyer of the executive offices of his newly purchased Secret Networks, nervous as hell. He adjusted his tie, bit at his bottom lip, all while walking a path in the carpet. He kept stealing glances at the clock on the back wall. With the hope of keeping this moment as private as possible, he relieved the executive assistant from the task of answering the phones today and had her down with everyone else, eating a breakfast hosted by Wilder, Inc. It was a huge day of celebration and Dylan had clearly spun this buyout well. Company morale remained high. Not the normal fear he usually walked into after acquiring a business. Everyone was excited about the future, including him, just not at this exact moment. Right now, he was nervous as hell, waiting for Dylan and his family to arrive.

"Smiles!" he heard a familiar female voice say. He quickly turned to the main doors as Teri, Chloe, Cate, Chad, and Dylan entered. They were as beautiful of a family as their pictures suggested. He forced himself to walk forward, his fake smile in place only because his nerves had heightened to all new levels.

"Teri?" Tristan asked, heading to her first. She was safe and on his side. Her face changed from one of frustration to one of happiness in the matter of a second. He reached out to shake her hand and she stretched up to hug him.

"Finally." Her arms wrapped tightly around him, and he did the same, looking over at Dylan who lifted his brow at their exchange. He'd never revealed how instrumental she had been in bringing them together. Apparently by the look on his face, she hadn't either.

"Tristan, I want you to meet our children," she said, keeping an arm wrapped around him as she turned toward their crew. She was a tall woman, and in her high heels, she was very close to his six foot two inch height. "This is Cate, our youngest, Chad's our middle, and Chloe's our oldest. Guys, this is Mr. Wilder."

Tristan took a deep breath. He'd never been good with children, but these three were so open and friendly, it didn't take much.

"I've heard so much about you guys," Tristan said, shaking each of their hands as he grinned at them all. "Cate, you and Chloe are beautiful. You look like your mom. I brought you guys some flowers." He extended an arm, motioning toward some wrapped bouquets sitting on a credenza behind him.

"Chad, I've heard a lot about you. You look exactly like your father. It's nice to meet you. I wanted to get you something too, but I wasn't sure what you liked, so I brought you an autographed Clippers poster," Tristan finished, taking a few steps backward to the gifts he'd brought.

For Dylan's sake, he kept his eyes on Teri and the kids. They had entered with tension but seemed happy now and he didn't want his new boyfriend to get skittish on this particular day.

"Dad, check this out. All the Clippers signed this!" Chad unrolled the poster, showing it off to Dylan.

"That's awesome, Son," Dylan said and offered out a hand to Tristan to initiate their greeting. That had Tristan looking at him for the first time since he'd walked into this room. Damn, his guy was hot and looked completely self-assured. His real smile spread as his cock plumped because Dylan smiled back at him, too, not creating the distance between them that Tristan had expected. Tristan shook Dylan's hand, caressing a bit before he pulled away.

"They're beautiful," Cate said, smiling big as she lifted the bouquet to her nose. She went to stand by her mom, beaming up at her. He remembered Chloe was the serious one, and she gave a slight nod, but had a big grin as well. He hoped he'd done okay.

"Dylan, everyone's ready downstairs for you." A young woman from the public relations department stuck her head inside the door to announce.

"Do they need all of us?"

"I think so. It would be good to show a united front. We've got CNN and ABC downstairs, plus every newspaper and the Associated Press. Just about everyone came," she said excitedly.

"Okay, good job! We'll be down in a minute," Dylan said, his tone turning more formal than before. A sure sign of his increasing nervousness.

"Tell Mr. Wilder thank you and let's go put these in the cooler." There was a three-way exclamation of *thanks* immediately given. He just smiled and nodded. "We'll take these to the break room and put them in water and meet you at the elevator in five minutes," Teri told Dylan directly. They exchanged something in that stare, something Tristan had no idea about. Then Teri said, "Chad, come with us."

"Dad, can you put this in your office?" Chad asked, thrusting the poster in his hands. He never questioned his mother as he left in a flash to catch up with her and the girls as she marched down the hallway.

"This was very nice of you. They loved it," Dylan said, heading toward his office. They were in the middle of renovating the conference room into a space for Tristan when he was in town, but right now, they were completely alone in this secluded area of the building.

Dylan stepped into his office, placed the poster on the desk, and used a large decorative mirror on one of the walls to straighten his tie and run a hand over his styled hair. He liked Dylan's hair back off his forehead this way. Tristan quietly shut the door and twisted the lock before he walked up and stood behind Dylan. He studied their reflection. He'd never paid attention to the image they presented standing side by side before, but by his estimation, they looked pretty good together.

Dylan's gaze shot to the door and then back up to Tristan's reflection.

"You look great. I thought the pinstripe was my favorite on you. Now, I think this one might be." Tristan pressed his chest against Dylan's back and continued watching his reflection in the mirror. "I want to kiss you."

"We agreed nothing at the office, that keeping the two independent of each other was best for now," Dylan stated, not turning around.

"Yes, I agreed. But I still want a little kiss." Dylan turned and took a step backward, eying him closely. Finally, he leaned in and gave him a quick peck.

"Okay, more than that. You left way too early this morning. Did you get your run in?" Tristan asked, taking a small step forward. Dylan started to answer, and Tristan reached out, grasped Dylan's face between his palms, holding his lover in place while he kissed him.

The kiss was intense, but swift. He kissed Dylan like a man in love, which was an accurate description. When he pulled away, a moment of shock registered on Dylan's handsome face. He loved that look, and he was growing to enjoy throwing the always steady Dylan Reeves off balance. Tristan retreated, taking another couple of steps backward so he wasn't tempted to reach out for his lover again. "Now you have something to fix when you look in the mirror."

"You promised." The uncertainty showed on Dylan's face as he spoke.

"Yes, I did, but I didn't bend you over the desk and hump you like I really wanted to do. It was a celebratory kiss on a very special day. I think Teri and the kids liked me. That was important to me." Tristan smiled, trying for nonchalant, hoping to banish that look from Dylan's eyes.

"Of course they would like you. Who doesn't like you, but I have an open-door policy for anyone to walk in," Dylan explained, turning back to the mirror and pushing the ends of his hair where Tristan's hands had been back in place.

"That's why I locked the door," Tristan rumbled and leaned suggestively against the neatly polished wooden desk, glancing at Dylan in the mirror. He inclined his head toward the locked door. "See, it's locked. I'm catching on to how things are done around here." He gave Dylan a wink and pushed off the desk. "So, are you ready for today? I've done these things many times before. Once you go down, it's non-stop until the end of the day."

"I think I'm ready. It's a great day for Secret." Dylan gave him a genuine smile and stepped closer. "I really love your tie…it brings out the color of your eyes," Dylan said as he adjusted Tristan's ice blue tie. After he finished, he turned without a word and headed toward the office door.

That made Tristan smile. Dylan should be proud, and he was glad he got to be here to enjoy the day with him. He'd managed to do something most people only dreamed of accomplishing.

"It's a hugely great day for Wilder. I hoped you would like it. Hey, before you go out there." Tristan took several steps forward and placed his palm on the door before Dylan could get it open. They were inches apart, and startled eyes met his as the scent of Dylan's cologne surrounded him. "Thank you for everything you've done for me. I'm not sure I've told you that."

Confusion replaced the startled look as Dylan absorbed those words. Tristan didn't give him time to ask any questions. He nodded his head toward the door and turned the knob. "Put your big smile on."

He placed a hand on Dylan's lower back, guiding him out.

"What have I done for you? I think it's more the other way around." They hadn't taken more than a step outside the main office doors before Dylan broke his self-imposed protocol, leaning over to ask that question. They were only a few feet from the bank of elevators where he knew Dylan's family stood, waiting on them.

"I'll tell you later," he whispered back. How did he explain everything to Dylan in the few seconds they had. How could he tell Dylan how much he'd changed his life, made everything better just by meeting him? Tristan experienced a wealth of emotion knowing Dylan waited for his call or visit. He couldn't put into words what Dylan's love had grown to mean to him. Tristan looked forward to every single day now that he woke up with this man in his life. There were so many things he needed to say. He didn't want to weigh Dylan down with all of that heavy stuff on his big day. As for Tristan, he'd attended several of these merger deals in the past. He was usually bored out of his mind at these functions, but it kept Wilder, Inc. in the media which was technically priceless for his organization. Since Secret was the hottest thing going right now, associating his two companies would help balance the budgets. And he got to spend the entire day close to Dylan. He angled his head, getting Dylan to move again.

"Are you guys ready?" Tristan asked as he rounded the corner to the bank of elevators.

"Yes, I think I have my job description down. I'm to stand there and smile," Cate said and did just that. She put on a giant toothy grin as Teri hit the down button for the elevators.

"She's funny," Tristan said, knocking Dylan in the arm with his elbow.

"Yeah, all I see is six thousand dollars' worth of orthodontics at its finest," Dylan responded, and Teri began nodding her head in agreement. Tristan's phone buzzed in his pocket. He didn't need to look at caller ID to know Landry was calling. He answered on the third ring.

"I'm going down now. Are you ready?" The overall companywide transition would take some time, and he suspected Landry of dragging his feet in the beginning, making everything a little harder than it had to be, but today served two purposes—the formal announcement of the merger as well as revealing the new WilderNation-Secret logo for the search engine. They were set to go live the moment he introduced the world to its existence.

"We are, just waiting for the word," Landry said.

"Good. Our people are in place. Get Amy to monitor the initial responses and message me. I know Market Research will, but they'll take some time."

"Already planned. Good luck today. Feels off not being there." He could hear the sulk still in his voice.

"Funny, I don't feel that way. I'm getting on the elevator," Tristan said, stepping on after everyone else. "I'll lose you soon. Hang up now. Stop whining."

"I should be there," Landry tossed out as Tristan disconnected the call. Landry was the kink in his otherwise perfect life. He still hadn't given in and adapted to these changes. Tristan forced those thoughts away. Now was not the time to dwell on his pain-in-the-ass COO. Instead he looked around and found Cate standing closest to him. He casually draped an arm over her shoulders.

"The staff can be difficult sometimes." He rolled his eyes for dramatic effect.

"My dad loves his staff. We're always giving or going to parties with them," Cate said.

"Hmm...I think I need to take lessons from him then. My operation's guy is a pain in my butt. Good thing I found your dad, maybe he can help me find the good in him again."

"Dad can do that, for sure. He sees the good in everyone except any guy we try to date, then there's nothing but bad," Cate said. That had him laughing as the elevator doors opened. The party was a few feet away with a stage directly across from them. The entire lobby was full of Secret employees.

"I was a teenage boy once, so I get that," Tristan said, giving her a wink. He walked out into the crowd with his arm still around Cate's shoulder. "Showtime."

CHAPTER.25

Damn, his feet were sore. Dylan stepped off the elevator, trying to decide if these new Italian loafers were headed for the trash can. With every passing minute, his feet hurt worse and worse and that said something for a man who ran miles every day. Ten or so hours after arriving at Secret's headquarters, he was finally able to come back upstairs to the peace and quiet of the executive office area and decide the fate of these stupidly expensive shoes.

"Great day, boss," Rob said, catching Dylan off guard. He instinctively lifted a hand, knowing a high five was inevitable. Rob grinned ear to ear, much like Dylan himself, even though his thoughts were focused on his feet. The exhausting day had finally come to an end with a dinner reception for the local media. His stomach let out a loud rumble, expressing its own anger that he hadn't been able to take even a small bite of food since this morning. "I'm heading out to dinner now. Wanna grab a bite?"

Dylan pretended to contemplate the offer. Under normal circumstances, he would have taken Rob up on the suggestion, but not tonight. Tristan was somewhere in this building with plans to head back home first thing in the morning. Their evening together had already been cut short with the dinner reception.

"Where is he?" Dylan asked.

"In your office. He complained about the lighting in the office he was using. I called maintenance. They'll get that worked out before he comes back. To be honest, I didn't see a difference, but he did." Rob shrugged.

Dylan just nodded. He looked over at his office and grinned. He couldn't wait to see Tristan. His heart sped up, and he had the familiar butterflies in his belly at the thought of Tristan sitting in there waiting for him. Lighting, huh? The brilliant business mogul, entrepreneur, and philanthropist couldn't come up with a better excuse than bad lighting?

"I should probably stick around, then," Dylan whispered when Rob began to lower his things, looking like he might wait on him. Dylan rushed on to say, "You go. I'll call you if I can break free, but I have a boss now. That's gonna be different."

"Yeah, you do!" Rob said, slapping Dylan on the back as he walked out. "I'll hold a spot for you down at the Mac."

Dylan waited until the elevator doors shut, taking Rob downstairs, and then checked David's office. The lights were turned out and he was gone. Dylan shut off the interior foyer light where his assistant sat and locked the suite's door from the inside. Only then did he make his way to his office. His breathing picked up when he opened that door and saw Tristan in the far corner sitting at his four-top table. The man was busily typing away on his laptop, his suit jacket neatly draped over the back of the chair next to him. He'd loosened his tie and undone a few buttons on his neatly pressed dress shirt. Tristan never looked away from his laptop, typing a few more strokes and hitting a final key before he glanced up at Dylan and extended his hand.

"Don't be mad. I stayed over here in the corner the whole time," Tristan said as Dylan shut the door and twisted the lock.

"I'm not mad. Is the lighting really bad?" Dylan asked, walking toward him.

"Of course not. It's all I could come up with, and for the record, Rob tried real hard to get the problem worked out for me. He stood on the table, working with the equipment. I seriously thought he might pull out a tool belt, but then he just gave up and opened this door to me." Dylan stared down at him. One of the most well-known pioneers in their industry could only come up with lighting problems as an excuse. For some reason, that just tickled Dylan to no end. Hell, Tristan now owned the entire company. He could have just come inside the office and shut the door.

"I know—stop looking at me like that. It's almost nine o'clock. I leave in the morning. I'm a man in love. I wanted to be around you. If not you, then your things." Ah, that was much better and Dylan smiled. He had to admit, he liked coming in to see Tristan waiting on him.

"It's fine." Dylan stepped closer and palmed Tristan's upturned face, then kissed him right on the lips. The kiss was no more than a soft brushing of lips, and it lasted only seconds before Dylan spoke. "What a seriously great day, but you bailed on the reception."

"It took me about five minutes to see those people didn't want to talk to me. It was all about you and your success. You were a hit today. I haven't seen you like this before. You're such a gentleman. I picked well." Tristan pushed the laptop to the center of the table and leaned back in his oversized chair, so Dylan propped himself against the table. Tristan ran his palm along Dylan's thigh, caressing and stroking him gently with that big smile still in place. The touch was one of encouragement, not sexually provoking like Dylan's body always tuned into.

"That's not true. They stayed glued to you during the press conference. Those were the same people at the dinner," Dylan said.

"I wanted to do some paperwork, check on our progress. Look, we're trending huge right now. Biggest hashtag of the day was Wilder-Loves-A-Secret." Tristan cocked his head to the side, looking past Dylan to his computer. Dylan followed his gaze and looked down at the screen. A grid sat open, tracking the trend minute by minute.

"That's great. Seems people like this idea. I always said Wilder was the best social network out there," Dylan said absently, staring at the screen. That had Tristan's hand moving in longer strokes across his leg. That switched Dylan's focus. He watched that hand move further up his thigh. All the while, Tristan's attention remained on the screen.

He had to give Wilder credit—this had been an incredible day. The whole community was excited about this merger. The mayor gave Tristan a key to the city for moving part of Wilder, Inc. to Dallas. Teri and the kids were perfect. The fight from earlier faded as they smiled and acted respectful and courteous. Although there was a small amount of whining behind the scenes about their cheeks hurting from all the grinning they had to do.

He heard about the hashtag earlier in the day. Chad was the first to catch the trend performing so well. The three of them followed the posts all day, giving him a regular whispered blow by blow when any big news agency or celebrity posted or retweeted about the merger. Cate was most excited that one of the guys from One Direction sent a shout out, commenting something about her and Chloe being the secret behind Secret. That was the only time they broke from the charming children they presented to the world. Cate squeaked out a yell and ran straight to him, interrupting an interview. But that was taken as normal, fun teenage conduct, making the whole company seem a little more down to earth and accessible.

The other huge success of the day, drawing his attention away from the festivities was the heightened usage both Secret and Wilder were experiencing. As a company, they prepared for the extra jolt, something a large team of technicians stayed out of the activities to handle and monitor closely for any problems.

He made a mental note to work on the Landry issue regardless of what Tristan said. He knew the guy wouldn't like the way this all played out. He prayed, for the time being, they could continue on this course and he didn't sabotage anything out of frustration. They needed the synergy both offices were building in order to make this thing a success.

The feel of Tristan's palm stroking his leg made it hard to think of anything other than what he truly needed at that moment—to see Tristan spread out on his office table, damn the consequences. The adrenaline coursing through him had him gripping Tristan's hand and guiding the palm to his dick. Tristan grinned up at him and squeezed through his pants. The look of lust that flashed across Tristan's eyes had his cock plumping even more. He already wanted Tristan so bad he hurt. Tristan didn't waste any time unfastening his belt and trousers. Tristan's strong hands stroked him lightly, almost reverently.

"I wanted to do this all day." Tristan growled and pushed Dylan's slacks and underwear down around his thighs, then leaned in and mouthed his shaft. Tristan's warm tongue licked and flicked at his sensitive tip before engulfing him in all that hot wet heat.

"Feels good." Dylan arched his hips forward and watched Tristan's blond head move back and forth on his dick. Yeah, he'd wanted Tristan's mouth on him all day too.

"Have I ever told you how much I love your mouth?" Dylan slid his hands into Tristan's hair and urged him on. His knees about buckled when Tristan did that swirly thing with his fist and tongue. He pumped his hips forward, pulling Tristan's head into his thrust, fucking his hot mouth with abandon. His need to possess this man was overpowering. Tristan gagged around him but he couldn't stop his movement; it felt too damn good, and hearing Tristan gag turned him on even more. He was being rougher than usual, but Tristan wasn't complaining. In fact, his lover's actions suggested he was into the moment as much as Dylan.

When his dick hit the back of Tristan's throat, Tristan moaned around him. The vibrations rushed through his body and settled in his balls. Dylan picked up his pace and thrust into Tristan's mouth. He loved how Tristan alternated between squeezing his balls while rubbing and pressing his fingers into the area behind them. The suction of that warm wet mouth was entirely too much. He was going to come before they even got started if he didn't do something now.

He pulled out of Tristan's mouth and used his fingers to tilt Tristan's head back. His lover's eyes lifted to meet his as he spoke. "I want you spread across this table or my desk. And we're both gonna come while I'm buried deep in your tight ass." Tristan groaned at his suggestion, and his own body tightened at the sound of Tristan's approval.

Tristan unfastened his pants and shoved them down his legs as he rushed to stand. He kicked his shoes off to the side and stepped out of his pants, leaving them in a bundle on the office floor.

Damn! The guy's gorgeous. Tristan's grin was back in place as he strolled over to Dylan's desk and shoved his papers and things to the side.

"So is that a yes?" Dylan smiled at the look Tristan gave him.

"Of course. You have all the best ideas." The guy unbuttoned his shirt and dropped it to the floor, but didn't bother to remove his tie, which was hot as hell. Dylan couldn't take his eyes off Tristan. He stood quietly as he took in the sight in front of him. Tristan had on a black jock strap that framed his perfect bubble butt. God, that man was going to be the death of him.

"This how you want me? Bent over your desk like this?" Tristan's voice drew his attention from the thoughts building in his head. Dylan watched as Tristan spread his legs, pushed his ass out, and looked over his shoulder at him. Dylan squeezed the base of his own dick. He could have come just from the sight of Tristan's tempting ass alone.

"Yes, I think we're on the same page." Wasting no time, he stepped up behind Tristan's wide-spread legs and ran his hand down and over his lover's full, round ass then back up again, smiling when Tristan's muscles quivered beneath his palm.

"So beautiful." He bent down and placed lingering kisses against Tristan's back, then bit playfully at his shoulder. Dylan sucked the skin between his lips, lightly marking Tristan as his. Dylan's dick left a trail of moisture along Tristan's crevice as his lover groaned and moved against him. His body was in overdrive. He wanted this man, needed this man. He wrapped his arms around Tristan, pulling him up and back against his chest. He slid one hand down his flat stomach, moving lower to push away the thin piece of material and lovingly stroke his cock. Using his other hand, he palmed Tristan's jaw, angling his head just right for a kiss.

Tristan responded by sucking greedily at his lips. He opened for Tristan's persistent tongue, meeting it with his own. He raked his fingers down Tristan's neck and gripped the ice blue tie still hanging there. Wrapping the silk material around his hand, he tugged his lover closer. Dylan let everything out in that kiss—his feelings of inadequacy, his need for Tristan, along with the hunger that had been building from years of denying himself. This was who he was, and Tristan was the man he wanted. The kiss turned intense as they probed and explored each other's mouth. He could kiss this man forever. Their tongues twisted and swirled in a heated dance that fueled his hunger. Dylan moaned into the kiss as they rocked hard against each other. He loosened his grip on the tie as Tristan broke from the kiss, dropped his head forward, and raised his hips.

"Please...I need you in me, Dylan."

"And I will be." Dylan licked and nibbled his way down Tristan's spine, lowering himself to his knees. He spread Tristan's ass cheeks wide, his dick twitched at the sight of this beautiful man in front of him. Dylan circled Tristan's hole with his finger and used his tongue to tease his lover's entrance. Tristan's essence burst across his senses, intoxicating him. Dylan pressed his face against Tristan's ass and worked him with his fingers and tongue. God, he loved the scent of his man, but his taste was even more incredible.

"That feels so fucking amazing." Tristan gasped and arched his back.

Dylan pointed his tongue, pressed inside, and began fucking Tristan with his mouth. His lover moaned and writhed wantonly against his oral assault. Dylan's own desire leaked against his skin, leaving the wetness cooling against overheated flesh. His need to be shrouded in his lover's body became too much to bear. He pressed a kiss against Tristan's butt cheek and sat back on his heels. "Please tell me you brought supplies."

"Always." Tristan dropped several packets on the desk before handing one to Dylan. "Good thing I brought these hoping I'd get lucky tonight." Dylan heard the teasing tone in his voice.

"Always one step ahead. I like that in a man." He stood, ripped opened the package, and spread the liquid across his fingers. "I believe we're both gonna get lucky tonight."

"Too much talking and not enough action, Reeves. Now, give me what I want and don't hold back. I'm a big boy." Tristan lowered his chest back to the desk and spread his ass cheeks. Dylan lost his breath at the sight. It took him a few seconds before words formed and he was able to speak.

"No holding back tonight, I promise." He pressed two fingers against Tristan's rim, circling them lightly across his opening before pushing them deep inside his lover in one swift motion. Tristan surged back on his fingers, the movement causing them both to moan. Dylan began driving his fingers in and out of Tristan, twisting and scissoring them as he opened his lover. Tristan kept pushing back on his digits, groaning and breathing hard. He curled his fingers and found that soft spongy knot and pressed. Tristan whimpered and widened his stance.

"Want your dick stretching me..." Tristan hissed, grinding his hips faster against Dylan's hand. Dylan added another finger and pumped them in time with Tristan's movements. "I'm ready."

Dylan withdrew his fingers and hurriedly tore open the package then rolled the condom on. He gripped the base of his dick and positioned himself at Tristan's opening. Dylan pressed the head of his erection into Tristan, slowly pushing past the tight ring of muscle before fully seating himself deep inside. Dylan froze for a moment, savoring the mind-numbing heat enveloping and drawing him in. After a few seconds, he began to move his hips.

"Oh damn, Tristan."

"Fuck me. I wanna feel you move faster," Tristan begged, driving himself back into Dylan.

Dylan did as his lover suggested. He held on to Tristan's hips and pulled out a fraction of an inch before pushing deeply inside Tristan. He repeated that movement over and over until he was almost pulling out completely and slamming back into his lover with powerful thrusts. Dylan took him hard and fast, driving deeper into Tristan with every snap of his hips. He canted his hips, changing his angle, and pounded into Tristan's prostate over and over.

"Yes, there...right there." Tristan moaned, his fingers turning white from the grip he had on the desk.

Dylan's hips pistoned uncontrollably in and out of his lover's body. The heat grew and spread through him till Dylan thought he'd combust. The fire breathed at the bottom of his spine, expanding to the base of his skull.

"I'm so close," Dylan said through clenched teeth. Hunger and need spiraled deep inside his belly.

Thrusting harder into Tristan, he reached around, shoved his hand in Tristan's jock strap, and found his stiff, leaking cock. He freed him from the damp material and began to stroke him with long, firm movements.

"Harder, fuck me harder," Tristan demanded.

Tristan cried out and came, hard tremors racking his body as his hot come spilled over Dylan's fingers. His lover's ass drew him in, constricting and clenching around him with every spasm, he couldn't hold off his release any longer. Dylan pushed in deep, thrusting twice more before coming unglued, and completely losing himself in Tristan's body.

"Oh fuck, Tristan." His balls tightened against his body, his muscles tensed, his dick started to pulse uncontrollably, emptying his load deep in his lover's still contracting channel. Dylan slid his free hand up Tristan's back, to the base of his neck and into his hair, pulling his head back. "You're mine," he growled possessively, forcefully plunging into Tristan a few more times, drawing out both of their orgasms.

"Yes, yours," Tristan answered as he gasped for air.

Dylan collapsed on top of Tristan, neither moved except for the last few post orgasmic shudders as they spiraled back down to earth. Dylan loved the feeling of Tristan beneath him, their sweat-covered bodies pressed tightly together. What he'd shared with Tristan was something he had thought he could never have with anyone. Never in his wildest dreams had he ever imagined he'd be in his office with Tristan Wilder bent over his desk. He was in love with this man. This man had found him and opened up a side of him that had been buried for so long. Dylan ran his nose up the back of Tristan's neck and into his hair. "I love you, Tristan Wilder."

Tristan used his arms to push up and lift his chest off the desk. Dylan groaned as his softening cock slipped from Tristan's body. He hated the loss of their connection. His lover turned in his arms and captured his mouth with a lingering kiss. "I love you too, Dylan Reeves," Tristan breathed against his lips. Tristan's mouth was on his, kissing him hard. He curled his hand in Tristan's tie and tugged him closer. Their flaccid cocks rubbed together as they lovingly feasted on each other's mouth.

"God, if you could see how sexy you are right now," Dylan growled into the kiss. Tristan pulled back and looked at him.

"Please say you'll come back to the hotel and stay with me tonight."

Dylan smiled. "I'll stay with you tonight."

"Good. Now that that's settled"—Tristan turned around, grabbed a tissue off Dylan's desk, and looked down at Dylan's free hand. His brow lifting as he spoke—"you're not touching me again, until you get that mess off your hand."

"No fair…it's yours!" Dylan started laughing and reached for the tissue to wipe the sticky wetness off his fingers. "I almost grabbed your tie with that hand. Good thing I caught myself, huh?"

"The tie is one thing, but accidently running that hand through my hair is another." Tristan winked at him and straightened the tie around his neck. "How about we go back to the hotel, and I'll let you grab my tie all you want."

"Deal." Dylan tossed the tissue into the trash then pulled him in for a playful kiss.

CHAPTER.26

"Mom, I promise I'll leave if it looks like there's gonna be any trouble. I got a primo parking spot in front of the rally. I can be back to the car in a few minutes," Chloe said with her hand on the lifted trunk, waiting for Allison to grab the poster boards they'd created after she got home from her father's big merger celebration.

"I gotta go, Mom, stop worrying! I'm smarter about everything now. I'll text you and keep you updated. Love you, bye," she said, ending the call right there before her mom could go on and on about the importance of keeping her record clean at this stage of her college career. That was the only thing either of her parents ever worried about. How her actions would affect her future. Like activism was a bad thing.

"She over-worries. So do my parents. They were like freaking out that I'm coming here tonight," Allison said, handing Chloe her sign. She gripped the poster board tight and slammed the trunk shut, clicking the key fob to make sure all the doors were locked.

"I know, right? My mom's like telling me all this stuff about police records and looking for a job someday," Chloe said, pushing her too long bangs out of her face. She abruptly came to a halt, stopping in the middle of the sidewalk, just north of city hall in downtown Dallas where tonight's equality rally had been planned. She bent over, placing her sign between her legs as she pulled her long hair into a ponytail with the rubber band at her wrist. The bangs immediately slipped free and fell right back in her eyes. Frustration ensued, drowning out all those lucky feelings she'd had at finding this perfect spot to park so close to the rally.

Sweat trickled down her back as she shoved the bangs aside. May in Texas wasn't good on the hair or the personal body odors all that sweat caused. She grabbed her designer sunglasses from her purse and slung the bag across her body.

"My parents don't care about that. They're so dumb. They're still saying gay marriage is against moral conduct. What about the weed my dad smokes all the time? Think most people consider that morally correct? No," Allison said, full of attitude. That was a family secret. Something Allison herself wasn't supposed to even know about.

"My parents aren't sanctimonious. They're actually the other end of the spectrum. They don't say anything about gay rights at all and that's wrong of them. I don't know when they became so status quo. The mayor of this city needs to take a stand and stop riding the fence!" Chloe demanded, building herself up for the march over the next few hours. She grabbed her sign right as a voice in a bullhorn started to speak.

"Come on! We're late!" She took off running for the rally where several hundred people had gathered. She declared her intention. Ready to stay and fight until the bitter end regardless of what her mom had to say. Bring on the brigade; she was ready and willing to go down for this cause.

Seven hours later, Chloe was still marching in a circle in front of Dallas city hall. The evening heat had done a number on her body. She was certain she was one of those hot smelly messes she'd worried about before. Her voice cracked, her throat raw as she yelled the all night chant, *'gay, straight, black, white, marriage is a civil right!'* Her arms ached at holding the sign high in the air and she swore the thin poster board felt like a million pounds weighing down on her tight shoulders.

Yet through it all, those police lining the street fueled her momentum. She stood ready to fight. Her spine was stiff with indignation. Everyone should have equal rights. As far as she was concerned, every person in Dallas should be out here demanding they all be treated equal.

"You've been here all night! What's your name?" A guy wearing an event badge came up beside her, stopping her chant as he motioned for her to step to the side of the large crowd. Only then did she lower her past-exhausted arms and dig the water bottle from her purse. The relief was audible as the moisture coated her aching throat.

"I'm Chloe Reeves." Her voice cracked again.

"I'm Jake. Can you be back here in the morning like by eight? We want to organize better for next week," he yelled loudly to be heard over the others still shouting the rallying cry.

"Yeah, I can be here. I go to OU, but I'm transferring up north because I'm sick of this Southern oppression. People should have rights!" she yelled back adamantly and that caused him to smile big. She'd found a kindred spirit in Jake.

"Good! We need people like you. Go home now and get some rest. We're about to call it a night. We shut the bars down and got more people here because of the news. It's what we wanted, but be back here in the morning," he called out, taking several steps back to his position on the front steps. "We're meeting right here so they can see us planning while they're all coming in to work!"

She smiled big, her inner energy filled with pride. She was already moving up to the planning committee. Somehow that validated everything she held dear in her world. This did make a difference tonight. They had given this community something to think about and tomorrow they'd start over again! With a fire burning deep inside her soul, she headed to the small grassy hill that Allison had crashed on hours ago. She'd burned out early and gone on a man hunt. Those didn't seem the right priorities in something this important to the future of their country. She might have to rethink bringing Allison to future events.

As Chloe scanned the crowd lying on the grass, she spotted Allison on a blanket, curled up next to some guy. She wasn't certain how she picked one of the only straight men there tonight, but Chloe had never seen the guy before.

"Hey, you!" Allison called out, patting the blanket beside her. Chloe eyed the guy closely because Allison would seriously just think anyone was okay to spend time with. Collapsing on the blanket took her mind off the guy that looked to be pretty normal, at least he styled the swoosh in the front part of his hair correctly.

All thought vanished as she stretched out her tired, aching legs in front of her. She dropped her arms to her sides and closed her eyes. Protesting was exhausting work.

It occurred to her that a gay rally was probably not the best place to pick up girls. She opened her eyes and turned her head toward Allison and the guy, wondering what he was doing here. Maybe he had a gay brother or sister and decided to support them. How cool was that? Man, she wished Chad would turn out gay.

"Chloe, meet Jacob. He has classes with me," Allison said.

"Hey," she said, and her voice cracked. "Where's some water?" Chloe asked, closing her eyes again, less worried about her friend since she knew the guy from school.

"Here you can have mine," Allison offered, handing hers over. Chloe opened her eyes and propped herself on one elbow to take a long drink.

"Hey, I want you to know your dad's a pretty cool guy. He's why I'm here tonight," Jacob explained, a big grin in place. He stared at Chloe as he said the words, but they made no sense. She looked over at her friend to find out why Allison's dad, Jack, had all of a sudden become a reason to attend tonight's rally.

"What did *he* do to make you come here?" Chloe asked, giggling a little at Allison's expense, the pain of her body now completely forgotten as they both turned toward Jacob. Allison looked as confused as she felt.

"He's just a good guy. Him and his boyfriend. They shouldn't have to hide—" Chloe cut him off in mid-sentence.

"Wait, what? Go back." Chloe snapped forward as Allison pulled back a little. They both stared at Jacob, but Chloe just knew they were about to get some good dirt on Allison's family.

"Where did you meet her dad?" Allison asked.

"I wait tables at Five Sixty and got an offsite gig. Your dad was pretty cool. It's not right they had to have dinner in their room and hide. When I saw them on the news today, I kind of got how wrong and unfair this all is."

"Why was your dad on the news today?" Chloe asked Allison.

"He wasn't," Allison answered very quietly. Jacob started working with his phone, lifting it between the two of them to show her a picture of her family, along with Tristan, Rob, and David on the front page of WilderNation.

"That's you, right? I recognized you right away tonight. I was going to come over and introduce myself and tell you to thank your dad for the big tip. But then I saw you with Allison and realized you were friends. It's a small world for sure."

Two things happened simultaneously. Jacob showed Allison another picture on his phone, and Chloe sat there completely dumbfounded, trying to make sense of Jacob's words. She watched Allison's face change as she looked down at his phone. Her eyes widened as she stared at the image.

"Is it Rob or David? I bet David!" Chloe grabbed for the phone as the screen turned dark. She did have a gay man in her life! She'd fight this cause for him. "Turn it back on! Which one is it?" Jacob reached over and tapped the side button. The screen lit up as she grinned from ear to ear and stared down at a picture of her father sitting at a table with Tristan. They were both in profile, talking to each other as Tristan held her dad's hand on top of the table.

Chloe stared at the screen, unbelieving, until it went dark again. Reality slowly crept in. She hit the screen button again, bringing the picture back up. "Is this your only picture?"

This didn't make sense at all. She looked up at Jacob who was taking the phone from her hand. He now carried the same bewildered look they all had.

"It doesn't make me gay that I have that. They were just cool guys and successful and great tippers," Jacob rambled, tucking his phone in his pocket, looking away from both girls. Which was a good thing because Chloe was having a complete out of body experience. She looked over to see Allison standing, panic on her face, and holding all of their belongings. She must have been down on this blanket for a while.

"Where are your keys? I'm driving," Allison said, holding out a hand to help her up. Everything centered into Chloe in that moment. She grabbed Allison's hand, using her as an anchor to the turbulent storm raining down on her overtaxed thought processes.

"That was my dad." In her mind, she thought she whispered those words to Allison, but by the look on her friend's face, she'd just made everything worse.

"Let's go. Where are your keys?" Allison asked, trying to tug Chloe along toward her car.

"She didn't know?" Jacob asked, immediately standing beside them. "Oh man, I ruined their secret?" Allison took hold of Chloe's arm, moving her swiftly to the car.

"Was he there all night?" Chloe asked.

"Tell your dad I'm sorry. Allison, tell him I'm sorry," Jacob said, following along behind them.

"Stop talking, Chloe. Just stop. You don't know anything," Allison hissed in her ear, dragging Chloe faster toward the car. "Jacob, go away."

"My dad's gay or at least bi, Allison. He was holding Mr. Wilder's hand like that wasn't the first time," she said, every aspect of that picture seared into her memory in vivid detail. Allison stopped them a few feet from the car. They were all alone, and she turned Chloe to face her. Allison, her very best friend in the world, looked worried as she moved the hair out of her face.

"Whatever happens, I promise we'll get through it. I'll always be there for you, no matter what," Allison said.

"Is that what you saw when you looked at that picture?" Chloe asked and stared at her friend, trying to gauge her reaction. She begged for anything that helped her deny what her eyes had seen so clearly. Except she and Allison were too close. They didn't need words said between them. "I need to call my mom."

"You need to think about this. Not react on every impulse like you always do, Chloe Reeves. This is a lot to process and it's big. It's life-changing big," Allison advised.

"I need my phone. I have to tell my mom. This is something she needs to know." Tears poured down Chloe's face as she realized the burden she was about to place on her mother. She dug for her phone through the things in Allison's arms only to remember she had it in the back pocket of her shorts.

"Are you sure you have to do this right now?" Allison begged her to stop by placing a hand over hers as she dialed. Both girls stared wide-eyed down at the phone in Chloe's hand as Teri's tired voice echoed on the other end of the line.

Chloe needed her mom more than anything right now. Tears slid down her face, and she lifted the phone to her ear.

"Mom, I have something to tell you," Chloe said, tears were in her voice as she looked directly at Allison who stood shaking her head at Chloe.

"Are you crying?" Teri asked.

"Yes, Mom. I have something to tell you. You need to listen to what I say, because I don't want to repeat this again." Allison stopped moving her head and stared at Chloe.

"Where are you?" Her mother's voice radiated concern. Chloe was about to rock her world. She had to be strong for her mom right now.

"Are you listening, Mom?" she asked, leveling out her tone.

"Chloe, what's wrong?"

"Mom, Dad has a boyfriend. It's Mr. Wilder. I think that means he's gay. I saw it with my own eyes," Chloe said and dropped down, clutching her knees with her arm as she gripped the phone tightly. "Oh god, I just betrayed Dad. I should have called him first." The tears were flowing in earnest now.

"Calm down, Chloe. Tell me where you are," Teri stated, the concern gone, her voice taking on a harder edge not near the meltdown she'd expected from a women who found out her husband was gay.

Denial. She'd read about this in her psychology course. Her mom was definitely in denial.

"Mom, I'm sorry. Allison said I shouldn't tell you. Maybe I shouldn't have, but it's true."

"Are you with Allison—hand her the phone," Teri instructed firmly. Chloe lifted her hand in the general direction she thought Allison was standing. Her mom probably needed the confirmation and Allison had seen that picture too. She rocked on her feet as she listened to them talk.

"Yes, ma'am," she heard Allison say. There were a couple more yeses before she felt Allison slipping an arm around her. "Come on, I need to take you straight home so your mom doesn't come down here to get you."

CHAPTER.27

Teri pushed herself up on the mattress. The lamp light was on and her e-reader lay on its side close to the edge of the bed where she'd fallen asleep reading. She looked at the clock on the nightstand beside her and lowered the phone to her lap. It was already three thirty in the morning.

This was enough. This lie needed to have ended a long time ago.

She never wanted her children to find out this way. Her dreams of a carefully planned vacation with a family meeting scheduled somewhere in the middle were finally dashed—the one dream she'd always looked forward to in ending this farce she and Dylan had created. She sighed deeply. If she were honest with herself, that dream had been destroyed four months ago.

The nausea started again, perhaps a little early this morning under all the stress, and she reached over to the nightstand to pull out a packet of crackers while gently rubbing her belly. She tried to soothe herself. To find comfort in the barely there bulge of the baby growing inside her. Her new little one was a surprise, and proof birth control wasn't a hundred percent effective. This was Mark's baby, and no one knew, not even him.

On instinct rather than steadfast certainty, she abandoned the crackers and called Dylan first. The phone rang four times before he answered in a groggy, exhausted voice. She cringed for him. He'd had a huge day, and he deserved to have that day without this coming down on top of him.

"Dylan, I need you to come home. Chloe knows. I'm getting the kids up now. We need to talk," she said, quickly and efficiently.

"What?" His voice was still gravelly with sleep, but clearing. "She knows?"

"Yes," she said, still keeping her resolve.

"I'm on my way." She could hear Tristan in the background questioning him until the phone disconnected. She sat there a minute more, staring at her cell before she called Mark. Based on the time, she had about twenty minutes to dress and get Chad and Cate downstairs before Dylan or Chloe could make it home. Mark answered on the first ring. It was just like him to do that.

"Hi, baby." He'd been asleep too, but always okay with whatever she had in mind.

"I'm sorry to wake you." Her voice cracked a little under the weight of this moment. Where Dylan was her best friend, Mark had become her rock. She wasn't certain she knew that until this very moment.

"What's happened?" he asked, sounding a bit cautious.

"I just want to really make sure I'm what you want. Chloe found out about Dylan tonight, and I'm not going to hide us anymore, but I want you to be certain before I say your name to them." Teri held her breath. At this point there would really be no turning back.

"I'm coming over." The sleepiness had dissipated from his voice. She could hear his movements from the other end of the phone.

"Mark, we need to tell them alone. I wanted you to be certain. It's one thing to talk about the future, but altogether different to have that future facing you."

"Baby, I want us. I can't wait until that day comes," Mark said firmly.

"Well, it looks like that day's here," Teri replied, her smile growing. She'd needed to hear those words. They made her strong. Helped her see a little bit more clearly.

"I'm coming over. I'll be out front. Don't stop me," Mark said.

"I don't know if I'll even be able to see you tonight. You're making a wasted trip. I'll call you when I'm done. I promise."

"Baby, it's not wasted. Dammit, Teri, I can't wait for the day that I don't have to sit back anymore. That I can be there beside you for the tough parts of life."

"I need to dress and wake up Chad and Cate. I'm glad they're home tonight. I love you, Mark," Teri said, rising from the bed. She rubbed at her belly again, the nausea completely gone.

"I'll be right out front if you need me," Mark stated, not backing down at all.

"Thank you." She smiled into her phone.

"I love you, don't thank me. I need to be beside you." Mark hung up first as she stepped inside her closet to change.

"What's wrong?" Tristan asked, holding Dylan tightly in his arms as he tried to pull away.

"I gotta go. Let me go." Dylan tugged free of Tristan's hold and rolled from bed. He stumbled around in the darkened hotel room, looking for his clothes, trying to remember where he'd been when they came off. A slow trickle of panic filled his gut. What did Chloe know?

"Dylan, what happened?" The room lit up. The bright light forced his eyes closed, needing to adjust, and that pissed him off as precious time slipped away from him. He turned his head, remembering they had been in the living room when they undressed. Enough light filtered from the bedroom to see they'd left the clothes in a pile by the sofa.

"I don't know. Teri just said she knows," he finally answered, tugging on his slacks, barely getting the zipper up before he reached down to grab his white undershirt. He didn't worry about the buttons on his pants or bother with putting on his socks.

"Teri knows what?" Tristan asked, valiantly trying to understand. He wasn't physically holding Dylan back, but all he wanted from Tristan at this moment was help out the door. He patted down his slacks to feel the weight of his wallet and keys inside the pockets.

"Chloe knows something and I have to go home right now," Dylan answered on the edge of frustration as he slid his loafers on his feet.

"Let me get dressed. I can drive you." Tristan had already been trailing along after him, following a few steps behind Dylan. He fished his clothes out of the pile, not hesitating to put them on.

"No, you can't go!" What was Tristan thinking? Of course he couldn't go to his house. This had to do with his family, his children. They were barely a month into whatever they were doing and Tristan was already trying to cross the boundaries Dylan had set.

"I should be there for you. You shouldn't have to do this alone," Tristan replied, searching for something in the back pocket of his slacks, not paying him any attention.

"Why? I handle my life—you don't. Besides, I don't even know what's going on." Dylan started walking straight toward the door and never looked back as the door slammed shut behind him. His entire focus rested on his children and what the hell was going on at his house. What did Chloe think she knew and how had she found out?

"Wait!" Tristan came running up behind him. "Dylan, please stop!"

"I'll call you later. It's not the time." Dylan punched the elevator button and the doors opened immediately. He didn't even hesitate. He rushed inside, hitting the button to the lobby. As Tristan followed, Dylan held out a hand, stopping him in his tracks.

"Not now. Back off, Tristan." He registered the emotions playing across Tristan's face as the guy took a step back. He saw pain flash in his eyes as the doors closed separating the two of them, but he steeled his heart. Teri would have never called him home in the middle of the night if things weren't seriously wrong. His obligations required he put them above everything, even Tristan knew that.

Ignoring the pain in his heart, he jogged across the lobby to the valet desk, fishing out his car's parking ticket. "I need to follow you to the car. I've got an emergency."

"No problem," the guy said, grabbing the keys from a side board.

"We need to hurry," Dylan said, antsy as hell, running his fingers through his hair.

"It's on the third floor," the guy said, heading to the front doors.

"Fastest way there." The guy took off out the front doors in a slow jog. Dylan came up right beside him. "Can you run faster?"

"Oh yeah." He took off like a dart and Dylan followed, down three flights of stairs to the bottom of the garage. As he spotted his car, he dug out his money clip, peeling off a twenty dollar bill. He grabbed the keys as the valet took the money. He was in the car and out of the garage in a matter of a minute. Luckily they lived in north Dallas, so he was fairly close to home.

Tristan stood there as those doors slid shut in his face. He couldn't ever remember being in a situation like this before. His heart was in that elevator, riding down without him. Pain filled him on an all-consuming level and the place his heart used to reside now ached. What should he do?

And another important question rained down on him. When exactly had Dylan become his reason for living?

He had no choice.

Tristan started back toward the hotel room as he dug inside his pockets. He had his phone and wallet. He kept going, patting himself down, until he lifted his wallet, looking inside for the cardkey. He stood in front of the locked door with no room key, completely dressed, all except for his shoes.

Fuck it! He pivoted on his bare feet, tucking everything back inside his pants. He ran his hands over his hair, hoping the bedhead might lie down on its own. He hit the elevator call button as he pulled up the Uber app on his phone. A car sat waiting out front, and he went through the steps to book the ride. The elevator doors opened. He ignored the stares as he ran for the front doors. The SUV pulled up as he rapidly took the steps down.

"I've got to find the exact address. I know it's Highland Park. Can you head that way?" he asked, sitting in the front seat.

"Most people sit in the back, man." The guy was more casual than most drivers, but he supposed that may have something to do with the late hour. Tristan just stared at him for a moment.

"Most drivers are already en route by now." Tristan had his phone in his face, digging through his contact information. He'd put Dylan's address inside there somewhere. "How much do you charge to wait?" Tristan asked.

"More than you can afford," the guy said, chuckling a little.

"I doubt that," Tristan responded. He might look like a scrub, but the tone he used had the guy's demeanor immediately changing. He found the address and spouted it off to the driver with urgency.

"I charge seventy-five an hour," he said, eyeing him closer.

"I need you to sit out front and wait. I don't know how long it'll last," Tristan added.

"You got the cash?" Tristan reached for his back pocket and opened his wallet, running a thumb over the bills inside. He pulled out two one hundred dollar bills and laid them on the console. They hit a red light and the guy looked at him, then at the wallet and down to the money. His eyes shot back up, and he palmed the cash, shoving the bills inside his pocket.

"I'm Darren. Need me to stop and get you some shoes, man?"

"No, I need to be in front of that house as soon as possible," Tristan said and rattled off the address again.

"Got it." Darren lifted his phone and entered the address.

"Want some music?" He didn't wait as the light turned green. By the time they hit the highway, a slow and steady rap song started. The guy knew every word. He sat there, singing quietly, driving a little faster than the speed limit, which was fine—even better in fact.

Tristan ignored everything and stared out the side window into the night. Why did this feel so much like he'd just been dumped? He took a deep breath to calm the thumping of his heart. Under no circumstance would he make this about him. Not right now. Besides, even if Dylan tried to end things between them, he had the security of having Dylan working directly for him. He could do everything in his power to win the guy back. But shit! Things had just gotten right between them. They were actually pretty perfect right now, and Tristan couldn't wait for the future. He was biding his time until they were together all day, every day.

Shit!

"Huh?" The driver looked his way.

"What's that?" Tristan looked over, completely lost in the deep worry of his thoughts.

"You just said something."

"Nothing, sorry." Tristan watched as they pulled off the highway and passed by Southern Methodist University. The houses got nicer as they drove the back way inside the town. As they pulled up to Dylan's place, Tristan stared at the house. The front windows were small and open. He could see lights on the inside, but the other houses in the neighborhood were dark. Tristan looked down at the time. It was a little past four in the morning.

"Man, we can't be sittin' here in a neighborhood like this in the middle of the night. The cops are gonna be called," Darren said as another car pulled in behind him on the street.

"Turn off the headlights," Tristan directed, trying to see who was behind him. The new car worried him. It wasn't Dylan's sports car, something bigger like a small SUV. "Can you see who's driving?"

Dylan told him to stay behind. There was no doubt Dylan didn't want him involved in any of this. What if he was already busted? The lights in the vehicle behind them dimmed, but it continued to idle.

"Nah, man, it's too dark. I can make out one guy in the driver's side, but I could be wrong," Darren said, looking between his rearview and outside mirror.

"Keep an eye on him. Let me know if he gets out of the car," Tristan responded, his focus immediately returning to the house.

CHAPTER.28

Dylan came through the garage door and followed the sounds until he reached the middle living room. The formal room. Teri sat quietly on a sofa, Chloe tucked into her side. Chad was in his pajamas, asleep on the other sofa. Cate sat between them, looking uncertain, her big eyes going straight to him as if he had the answers they needed. He tried for a small smile, but it didn't seem to ease her.

"Son, wake up, we need to talk." Dylan reached down and shook Chad awake. Right about then, Chloe caught sight of him and busted out with a fresh round of tears. She jumped up and ran to him, hugging him tightly. He'd had to steady himself to keep them both on their feet with the force she hit him with.

"Dad, I'm sorry." She gripped him tighter, crying openly onto his chest.

"Honey, it's okay. Nothing's this bad," he said, holding her tight, searching Teri's gaze. She gave nothing away. "Sit down with me. Let's talk this out."

"Chloe honey, let me handle this," Teri said from across the room before Chloe had a chance to say another word.

"Honey, here." Dylan handed her some tissue off the coffee table. The box was new. She never really let him go, so he guided them closer to Teri and took a seat. Chad now had the same look Cate carried. They both sat quietly, unsure as to what they were seeing, but Cate had moved over to sit closer to her brother. Chloe was clearly freaking them both out. Actually, he was on their side—he felt pretty freaked himself.

"Chloe, blow your nose and stop crying. We have to talk and you need to hear what I have to say," Teri said, handing her the bundle of tissues she held in her hands. To her credit, she did what was asked, but stayed molded to his side. He held her there, trying for comfort as he waited for Teri to begin.

"Guys, I called this family meeting tonight after Chloe saw something she was unsure of," Teri said. Her voice was different than he remembered before. She had compassion there, but resolve. Her tone strong and determined.

"Daddy, I'm sorry. I should have called you," Chloe added, looking up at him, but Teri held out a hand, stopping Dylan from responding.

"No, honey, it's not what you think," Teri said, reaching over to calm her back down. Those words took a second to sink in, but they did stop the latest round of tears before they had a chance to form. "Dry your eyes. Your dad and I have some things to explain to you all."

"Mom, what's going on?" Cate asked, coming over to climb in right next to Teri. Dylan cocked his head to Chad to bring him closer. He wouldn't come on his own because of his age, but he still carried that very big *you guys are freaking me out* look.

"Your dad and I have some things to tell you. We'd planned to wait until after Cate graduated, but regardless of Chloe's discovery tonight, we were already going to have to change our plans."

That confused Dylan even further, and he tucked Chloe in tighter as he felt her crying silently again. He patted Chad's leg and he whispered softly down to Chloe. "Shh, listen for me, okay?"

"I've practiced this talk so many times. Now that we're here, I don't know where to start. So let's go back to the beginning."

"Fuck it!" The time ticked by slower than Tristan ever remembered. He kept his eyes trained on the small, opened curtain inside the house, praying for some kind of movement. Anything that let him know that Dylan wasn't beating himself up for who he was as a man. Like any movement would help him identify what was going on inside that stubborn head of his.

Dylan's resolve could break the rock of Gibraltar, and he knew that would leave him completely cut loose and left behind. Dylan would most definitely sacrifice their relationship in a heartbeat. He wouldn't fight to keep them together, not yet. Not enough time had passed for Tristan to work his way inside Dylan's heart, like Dylan had done so completely to his.

"Dammit!" Tristan whispered.

"Dude, you keep scaring the shit out of me. I'm already in this uppity neighborhood, stalking a private residence with a guy with no shoes and a wad of cash, and then you bust out with a curse word every three or four minutes in nothing but all this silence you're making us sit in." A quick rap of knuckles sounded on Darren's side window.

"Shit! Goddammit!" Darren hissed, jerking his head toward the window as he frantically tried to get from his seat into Tristan's.

"Get off me and roll your window down," Tristan said, shoving him back toward the steering wheel.

"No fuckin' way," he hissed and scooted himself through the gap in the console, landing head first in the backseat. Tristan reached across the car to roll the window down. The driver gave a loud huff as he tried to correct his body's position. "My rate just increased to a hundred fucking dollars an hour. This is crazy. These high-class cops shoot first and ask questions later!"

The guy at the window stared into the car, not saying a word, and Tristan wasn't any more forthcoming. What did he need to say as to why he sat out front of this particular house? "It's dark. I can't see you real well, but you look like that Wilder dude."

Okay, he hadn't expected that. Hesitantly, he confirmed, "I am."

An arm reached in through the window and opened the door from the inside latch. He slid into the seat.

"Dude, you can't just let anyone get inside my car. Man, what's wrong with you people? Stalking rich folks in the middle of the night is a crime in about all fifty states," Darren said, clearly upset.

"I'm Mark, Teri's..." The silence ensued again. "Ummm...Yeah, well, she told me about you." He stuck his hand out toward Tristan who shook it, before Mark reached his hand toward the backseat.

"I'm not anyone you need to know," the guy said, completely indignant, refusing the handshake. "Wait a second, did he say Wilder? Did you say Wilder?" Darren asked, pulling himself back up toward the center of the car. "Are you that dude that's in town to buy somethin'?"

"Yes," Tristan said, lifting a hand to stop Darren from saying anything more. He was more interested in Mark. "What do you know?"

"Man, I should've asked for more money." Darren tossed himself against the backseat.

"I don't know a lot. I wondered what you knew," Mark asked, looking past Tristan. Tristan's eyes followed and they both stared out into the night at the house. Tristan's gaze focused back on that small open window.

"I don't know anything. Dylan didn't know anything when he left. Teri called and told him to come home," Tristan supplied.

"Did Dylan know that Chloe found out about him?" Mark asked and Tristan whipped his head around.

"How did she find out?"

"I don't know. We didn't get that far. Teri's whole plan was to bring the family home to have the talk now."

"She planned to tell the kids tonight?" Tristan asked.

"I guess, I don't know. It sounded big," Mark replied, and Tristan turned back to the house. Dread filled his soul. No way Dylan knew that when he walked into that house a little while ago.

Shit! This would traumatize Dylan.

He couldn't see Dylan wanting to continue their relationship right now. He'd blame himself for Chloe finding out. That *take-responsibility-for-everyone-around-him* attitude was one of the sexiest things about Dylan. Now, all of a sudden, it also seemed like the end to the short time they'd been together. But to Tristan, the time hadn't been short. It was a game changer. The last month had been the best of his entire life. He loved that man who had just walked into the collapse of everything he held dear in life.

Damn, he wanted to stick his head out of the car and throw up. Either that or storm through that house and grab

Dylan up, protecting him from everything falling down around him. Take him off someplace where he'd never be hurt again.

"How long will all this take?" Tristan asked quietly.

"I don't know. They aren't a beat it into the ground kind of family, but this might take longer," Mark said, equally quiet. "It seems like I've been waiting for her forever."

"I just found him." Tristan's breath made a small circle in the glass with those words and he lowered his forehead to the window on a sigh.

"You've eased Teri's heart. She was worried about what would happen to him," Mark spoke quietly.

"He eased me," Tristan whispered. "Do you worry she'll pick them and leave you?"

"All the time, but she's worth the risk," Mark said softly beside him. "At least that's what I tell myself."

"One twenty-five an hour," came from the backseat. Tristan sat there quietly, staring at the house, feeling his love slipping through his fingers with every passing minute.

Teri never minced words and Dylan respected that, but with as loudly as his heart hammered in his chest, he was surprised he even retained half of them. Chloe was still buried in the curve of his arm, feeling smaller than he ever remembered her seeming. He held tightly onto her. Chad sat beside him, and he kept a hand on his leg, holding him in place as he listened to Teri confess his most private secrets to their children. His eyes went between Cate and Chad, watching for their reaction. He saw shock more than the disgust he'd figured he might see. He couldn't see Chloe, because she had her face turned toward Teri, but her head lay on his shoulder.

"Wait, Mom," Cate said. She held Teri's hand now. "So you're saying Dad's been gay for his whole life?"

"Yes, honey, but there's more. Let me finish," Teri started, but Cate interrupted her again.

"Dad, you didn't leave us and go find someone better for you?" she asked him directly, and Chloe started crying again as her uncertain eyes searched his.

"There's no one better or more important to us than you three," Dylan said carefully. The hand he had on Chad's knee was clasped tightly by his son. Dylan gripped him back, appreciating that lifeline. "Just because your mom and I don't have a true marriage, you need to understand, I never considered I was sacrificing myself. Being your father's the most important role in my life."

"But that's so lonely for you and Mom," Cate added quietly, tears in her eyes now.

"Are you sure you're really gay?" Chad asked from behind him. Dylan had suspected the most resistance to come from his son. They were buddies. They played sports together, talked about the girls in Chad's life, and he'd even shared some secrets with Dylan. They were close, and he was afraid Chad would see this as a breach in that relationship.

He turned his attention back to his son. Both of Chad's hands were now clasped around his. The tables had suddenly turned; his boy needed him as a lifeline, and Dylan reached out, draping an arm around Chad's shoulders, drawing him closer against him. He took it as a good sign that Chad hadn't shrugged off the contact. The two of them would need to speak privately about this at the first opportunity he got.

"Please let me finish. I have something to say that your dad doesn't even know," Teri said, reaching for the tissues and handing some to Cate. Teri mimicked his move and pulled their youngest daughter in tight to her side. It didn't go unnoticed that they had this enormous house, with this huge living room, yet they were all cuddled together in the corner, holding on to each other for dear life. "I told you that we were waiting to have this conversation until after Cate graduated from high school. I haven't talked to your father, but I don't see any of our short term plans changing. Getting you graduated and off to college is still my number one focus."

Dylan nodded, immediately agreeing with Teri.

"Here are the additional facts you don't know—I met someone a few years ago. Your dad knows about him and I've been seeing him. I know it sounds like a lot to take in, but it's really not, because our base, this family right here, is so solid and our foundation and course are set."

"You have someone like Dad does?" Chloe asked, sitting up a little straighter in her seat. "And Dad met someone, too," Chloe added, trying to make Chad and Cate see the whole picture. He could tell they didn't.

"So you guys date?" Chad asked, a little confrontationally.

"Not date so much as there's one man for me and you've met him before at my office. When Cate graduates, I planned to introduce him into your lives with the ultimate goal of marrying him. It's Mark. Y'all know Mark, remember?"

That had all the kids quietly staring at her, and Dylan's heart broke a little in that moment. He could tell his children didn't understand any of this.

"So y'all have this whole secret life?" Chad asked. There wasn't so much disdain in his voice, just surprise with a bit of confusion.

"Let me finish. I'm almost done and then we can answer your questions," Teri said, silencing them when it looked like Cate would jump in right behind Chad. "In the spirit of laying everything out there all at once with no more secrets, you guys are the first to know that I'm four months pregnant," Teri announced, her voice growing quieter at the admission.

"You're pregnant?" Dylan asked, shocked.

"I am. It wasn't planned. I took precautions, and I honestly wasn't certain I was keeping the baby until about a month ago. Mark doesn't know yet." Her hand went to rest on her belly.

"Wow. The plan had changed then. We were going to have to say something soon," Dylan said to Teri.

"I wanted to wait until after Chad's graduation. Look, guys, I know we're dumping a lot on you all at once, but I honestly don't know a set of children more well-adjusted and accepting as you three. And I speak for both me and your father when I assure you nothing has changed in your base. We will continue to always be your parents. We'll always be there for you. We stand together—your dad is my best friend, and that will never change," Teri reassured, making eye contact with each of them as she spoke. Teri's nurturing voice was back, and she reached up to brush Cate's hair out of her face. "I have some counseling ready to start for you guys to help answer any questions you're uncomfortable asking us."

They both looked at their children who all just stared straight at Teri. Dylan knew they had a lot to absorb. Chad had finished his final exams and currently coasted, waiting until graduation. They were in the final six-month countdown to Cate's graduation, too. Would this jeopardize anything for her? Worse yet, would rebellion ensue?

"Nothing changes, guys. I'll be here every day for you. There's nothing we can't get through because we're a strong, committed family," Dylan added, trying for reassurance.

"I don't want you to be lonely," Cate said quietly, staring at him before she looked up at Teri. "So are you and Dad divorcing?"

"We can't until the baby's born. It's part of the state law, but we will after that. If I'm right on my calculations, the baby's due date will be a month or so before your graduation."

"So are you guys thinking of keeping things like they are? Or are you gonna move other people in our house?" Chad asked.

"Absolutely not, Chad. Things will stay the same for now. There won't be any more secrets from this point forward. When we know more, you three will be the first to know," Teri said. Chad was still tense in his arms, but hadn't moved away.

"What would you guys do if you were us?" Dylan asked, wanting them to feel part of the decision and curious as to their thoughts.

"I can't change schools right now. It'll mess with my applications," Cate said immediately.

"Honey, we would never ask you to do that. Our home base is secure until you all get settled in college—I promise, and even after that, you guys always have a place wherever your mom or I might be," Dylan stated. Chad shrugged out of Dylan's hold.

"What I think is that I'm graduating next week and leaving for college two months after that. Chloe's going off to school. She barely lives here anymore. Cate needs to graduate, but you guys have been living a huge lie," Chad stated very plainly.

"It's not really a lie, Son. We're a family. We love each other like a family does. That will never change," Teri started, but Chloe cut her off.

"No, I get what he's saying, Mom. Love is love. You should be with the people you love. Cate needs to finish school, but then she's gone too. You guys need to be happy in your lives," Chloe added to Chad's words. His son was shaking his head in her direction.

"Right. And I've taken a lot of finance classes. It's gonna take a long time to divide up Dad's assets. And yours, too, Mom," Chad tossed out when he realized his mistake.

"If y'all have to stay married until the baby comes, then maybe you can trade out and start to get a taste of what life's like without us since we're all you've been living for. And maybe you two need to be in counseling to learn to live without us every day," Cate added.

"Yeah!" Chad agreed, nodding his head. They were switching gears so fast it was getting hard to keep up. "I'm not sure a lot of our friends' parents are gonna understand this. We have to figure out the best thing to say."

"Allison was with me tonight, she knows. But I'll ask her to wait to tell people until Mom and Dad are ready," Chloe told Chad and Cate.

"Are y'all still paying for our college?" Chad asked.

"Of course we are," Teri answered. "That money's been set aside since you guys were little. Those are not worries you need to have." Out of all the ways he'd envisioned this conversation, never once had he expected that response. His gaze landed on Teri. They exchanged that look, and he knew she was on his page. Somehow in finding out their father was gay and their mother was pregnant by another man, their kids had made this all about themselves.

Chloe still hadn't weighed in on her final answer, but she also wasn't curled up against his side anymore. She sat more between him and Teri. "What're your thoughts, honey?"

"I think we're at a critical time in our lives and we need to make sure we stand by one another. Cate needs the most support right now out of all of us. I can stay at OU if I need to and come home on the weekends," Chloe offered.

"Absolutely not," Teri said before Dylan could manage to get the words out. In what world did Chloe put others before herself? Maybe his firstborn was truly growing up. He ran a hand down her hair with the pride her words had raised in him.

"I agree with what you guys are saying, though. You three are moving on and we need to find our new normal," Dylan said. All three of the kids nodded. Teri did too. "It's gonna take some time to sort this out, but under no circumstances are the three of you to take on any of your mom's or my burden. We don't want that. We'll figure out how best to handle the next six or seven months between us with as little disruption to you guys as possible."

"All right, so can I go to bed now?" Chad asked, letting out a loud yawn.

"We need to talk soon," Dylan said to Chad as he rose from the sofa.

"Wait. I wanna know who Dad's dating," Cate said. Chad rolled his eyes at her and started walking across the room.

"I knew I had some great kids, but I really expected some anger and shock when you found out about me," Dylan added, standing and stretching the tension out of his body. Again, never had he expected this conversation to go quite this way. He also let out his own yawn.

"Dad's seeing Mr. Wilder," Chloe whispered loudly toward Cate. That stopped Chad in his tracks and had Cate squealing.

"I like him, Dad! He's hot!" Cate said, jumping up and giving him a hug.

"Girls, I don't think your dad's ready to talk about things like this with you," Teri said, still sitting on the sofa, but smiling at their daughter's response. "This is all very new to him."

"I'm so not ready to talk about this. Not sure I'll ever be ready—" Dylan started, but Chad cut him off.

"Dad, there are cars parked out front," Chad said, pointing toward the front of the house. Dylan went to his side and looked out the small window, putting Chad behind him as he got closer. He did see the cars out front. There were two parked, one behind the other, right in front of their house. He reached for his phone and patted his pockets, but he didn't have it on him.

"It's probably Mark. I called him before we talked tonight. He wanted to come over. I need to talk to him. He doesn't know about this." She patted her belly.

"I can't believe you're having another baby." Chloe gave her own little squeal. Dylan ignored them, not completely convinced that was who sat in one of the two cars outside.

"Maybe you can get pregnant, Chloe, and y'all's kids could play together," Chad teased, like an annoying brother would do.

"That's not funny at all," Dylan said, nudging Chad to the side with his elbow. "I'm going out there to make sure it's him. I don't understand two cars and they crowded each other. Something's not right."

"No, let me go. He's got to be worried," Teri said, pushing herself up out of her seat.

"No. You're not going out to some unknown cars in the middle of the night." Now, they were both standing in the living room, staring out the two front windows of their home. Dylan went for the door.

"You stay back. If it's anyone other than Mark, lock this door and call the police, hear me?" Dylan didn't wait for their answer and opened the front door then shut it behind him. He kept the lights off and fully stepped out on the front porch. As he got to the steps, someone inside decided to turn the porch lights on. He was momentarily blinded as two people got out of the first car. Then he heard a third door shut. Three people made absolutely no sense. He took the porch steps down, trying to get a better look and move the distraction away from the house. He hoped they were in there calling the police right now.

"Are you guys all right?" Mark asked. Why had Mark brought two people with him?

"Yeah, who's with you?" Dylan asked from about the middle of the front yard. Mark was stalking forward, but bypassed him with a quick pat on the shoulder as he went straight to the porch. Teri had come outside after he'd told her to stay in and protect herself. His kids were standing in the doorway, watching. Dylan turned back to the car to see Tristan standing several feet away.

Neither of them seemed to know what to do or say, and he looked back at the porch to see the kids watching him as Teri hugged Mark.

"I shouldn't have come. I was just concerned," Tristan said, still standing several feet away.

"You've been here the whole time?"

"Pretty much." That touched his heart, and Dylan took a couple of steps toward him. "I didn't expect them to see me."

"It's okay, I guess. I mean, I don't know, but they know about you. You should come inside," Dylan said, now a step or two away from Tristan. His eyes were better adjusted and Tristan looked so unsure. "How did you get here?"

"A driver." Tristan didn't move a muscle. He'd never seen him like this before. Tristan was always so self-assured and strong-willed that he never doubted himself in anything. "You're too important to me. I don't know what to do here," Tristan confessed softly.

"I needed to hear that right now," Dylan said and that had Tristan taking a step toward him. "They seem okay with it all. Teri did the talking. She's good at giving just enough information."

"I can attest to that," Tristan agreed. They rarely stood this far apart without Tristan touching him in some way.

"Come in. They should meet you again. It looks like Mark's already inside." Dylan looked back through the front door, seeing them all standing in the foyer.

"Hang on. I need to pay this guy." Tristan went to the car, pulled out his wallet and shelled out a stack of bills. Before he stepped away from the curb, the car had started and was already pulling away.

"Where're your shoes?" Dylan asked.

"I followed you out of the room without the key. I didn't want to take the time to get a new one and go back upstairs. I felt strongly about being here in case you needed me."

"You've just been sitting out here, waiting?" Dylan asked. By his estimation, Tristan should already be halfway to California by now after how rude he'd been at the hotel.

"I was worried. How do we stand?" Tristan asked. It seemed an unexpected question even for him, and Dylan furrowed his brow, slowing his step. Maybe he wasn't out of the woods like he'd thought.

"How do you want to stand?" Dylan asked. He came to a stop in the middle of his walkway, dropping his hands inside his slacks pockets. He didn't want his kids to hear this exchange, and he didn't want to lead Tristan up to the house if things were coming to an end. Panic raced through him for the second time that night. Except this time, the worry coursing through his veins was worse than earlier. He'd sat inside that living room, listening to Teri confess his secrets, feeling stronger because Tristan would be beside him in the end. Now he wasn't sure how Tristan felt and his heart was being torn from his chest at the thought of losing him.

"I want a long-term commitment between us and for you to move in with me—whenever that's possible," Tristan said, sending his world spinning again. The highs and lows of today were beginning to catch up with him, and his heart pounded violently in his chest. He ducked his head, let out a deep sigh, and absently ran a palm over his heart. He hoped he'd heard right.

"I thought you were backing out," Dylan confessed, his eyes not meeting Tristan's as he stared at the ground. He ran his hand up to rub the stiff muscles in his neck.

"I thought you were giving up on us. Is it okay if I touch you?" Tristan questioned. Dylan looked up and then over to the front door where Chloe now stood in the doorway, staring out at them.

"Can we wait on that?" Dylan asked as he watched Chloe.

"Yes. If you say yes to a future with me," Tristan countered, drawing Dylan's attention away from his daughter and back to them.

"I would've thought that was a given." Dylan looked Tristan straight in the eyes. God yes, he wanted a future with this man. He was so thankful he had a boyfriend who hadn't left him tonight and kids that hadn't turned their backs on him. Everything was turning out so much better than he'd ever imagined. Who would have thought?

"Say it anyway."

"Yes," Dylan whispered, his eyes locked onto Tristan's beautiful gray stare.

"I want to kiss you more than ever before," Tristan whispered, his eyes dropping down to Dylan's lips. Dylan could see the passion etched on his face. Tristan's lips parted slightly. As hot as that was to witness, that meant the kiss was coming, he knew that much already about Tristan. Damn the consequences.

"Wait!" He pivoted on his heel and went to the front door, hoping Tristan followed. He had to get out of that moment; it was too much. Telling his kids he was gay and kissing men in front of them were two different things. Baby steps, he reminded himself. Chloe came out on the porch, meeting him on the first step.

"I'm sorry, Dad. I should have called you first." Chloe threw herself into his arms, and she was crying again. He took her easily in, hugging her tight and kissing the top of her head.

"You did the right thing, honey. I'm proud of you. I promise." He lifted her face with his finger. "You did the right thing. Just keep doing the right thing for me and help keep an eye on your sister and brother. Let me know if anything isn't right for them."

"I will, I promise," Chloe said, giving a huge ugly sniffle in his face. That had him smiling.

"Can you say hello to Tristan for me?" She nodded and quickly wiped at her nose and her eyes, running her hands on her shorts before she looked past him. Tristan had stayed on the bottom step, giving them a moment.

"Hi, Mr. Wilder, I need to apologize to you, too. I started this tonight." Lord, his children were so well-adjusted. He'd have never acted like this at her age. His pride increased ten-fold as he watched her extend a hand toward Tristan.

"Please call me Tristan, none of this Mr. Wilder stuff anymore, and you don't need to apologize to me. I'm not even sure what happened," Tristan said, taking her hand, but drawing her in for a quick hug.

"I met a waiter tonight at the equality rally who had a picture of you and Dad holding hands. Oh no! Dad, I gotta go to sleep. I have to be downtown at eight in the morning. I have a position on the planning committee." Chloe kissed his cheek and hugged Tristan quickly again before she was off, heading toward her bedroom. "Goodnight, Mom, I have to go to bed. I have a meeting in the morning!"

"You'll get used to things like that; they happen all the time." Dylan gestured with his hand, letting Tristan walk in before him, but he just shook his head at him.

"I'm not walking in there first," Tristan said. That might have given Dylan his first smile of the night. He walked inside, Tristan followed, and Cate, Chad, Teri, and Mark were standing in the foyer talking. The quiet surrounded them as they stared at one another. Every adult in the room kept their distance from one another, respecting boundaries. These kinds of things gave him hope that they could get through this with as few scars as possible.

"You guys remember Tristan?" He missed Chloe's lack of decorum, where she would introduce herself to anyone, anytime.

"Hi," Cate said and let out a yawn. Chad was a little bit standoffish, but he got that. They'd probably need to talk, maybe hit a round of golf or something this weekend. Let him know things were still the same between them.

"Hi, Mr. Wilder." Chad turned to Cate. "Mom said we could go to school late tomorrow. But we should probably hit the hay." Chad looked at him and finally smiled. "Will you be here in the morning, Dad?"

"Depends on what time you get up. I have a full day tomorrow at the office, but call me, we can talk then."

"All right, goodnight," Chad said and did the absolutely right thing—he stuck his hand out to Tristan who stood there quietly through the exchange.

"Goodnight," Tristan said, shaking his hand. Cate popped up to kiss Tristan's cheek unexpectedly. Tristan bent in and smiled down at her.

"Goodnight," Cate sing-songed. She trailed behind Chad up the center staircase until all that was left was Teri, Mark, Tristan, and Dylan.

"That wasn't so terrible," Teri said quietly.

"You're pregnant and didn't tell me?" Dylan narrowed his eyes in her direction. Her gaze shot straight over to Mark.

"You're pregnant?" Mark gasped.

"Shit, I thought you would've told him!" Dylan panicked again.

"Dylan, no! When was I supposed to tell him? With the kids right here? Just go! Mark, I was waiting to tell you when we were alone. I'm sorry."

"You're pregnant? Teri, are you kidding me? How wonderful!" Mark exclaimed.

Dylan rolled his eyes at his blunder. "Follow me," he said to Tristan. He wound his way through the kitchen toward the garage, grabbing his keys off the counter as he passed by.

"She's pregnant?" Tristan whispered as they stepped out into the garage.

"Yeah, four months. I thought she would have told him the second he made it onto the porch. I don't know how the kids kept it quiet," Dylan replied, hitting the garage door opener. He clicked the remote to unlock the car and Tristan slid inside the passenger seat beside him.

"Are you okay?" Tristan asked once they were shut inside the car. Dylan stopped before he started the ignition. He weighed that question carefully. It took some self-reflection to answer properly.

"I think so, yeah." He stared at the keys in his hand as he finished. "I spent most of my adult life in fear of that moment. I thought they'd feel betrayed and disgusted. I was so afraid of losing them. They took it way better than I ever hoped for."

"What was the general reaction?" Tristan asked, and Dylan smiled when he looked over to see Tristan sitting on his hands. His guy was a toucher and was obviously trying hard to follow his rules tonight.

"I was a little shell-shocked so I'm not entirely certain. I think Cate or one of them said something about living a lonely life." He looked up at Tristan. "Teri was the one with the bombshell. I never saw that coming."

"Your kids are incredible."

"Yep, they sure surprised me tonight," Dylan agreed as he started the car.

"Not me; I know their father." Tristan smiled broadly at him. "Now take me to the hotel so I can kiss you."

Dylan laughed and put the car in reverse. "Thank you for understanding."

"When you left me at that elevator... God, my heart was crushed. I had to come after you. I was so afraid you'd be pissed, but I couldn't do anything else. I wanted to be with you," Tristan said, dropping his head back on the head rest.

"You've made this much easier, you know."

Tristan sighed, swiveling his head toward Dylan. "This is all new territory for me. I don't know what to say or do. I needed to hear those words."

"I'm glad you pushed for us. In a million years, I'd have never thought tonight would turn out like this. They were just fine with everything. My kids were really great." Dylan idled at the end of the driveway. "They really had no reaction to the gay thing at all. Their concern was more of me being alone and shocked about the baby. I admit *I* was shocked about the baby."

"I told you, they're good kids," Tristan said quietly and patted his thigh. The touch comforted him. Dylan looked over at him and smiled. It warmed his heart to see Tristan so compassionate and patient as he sat beside him. Honestly, if he were really looking at things clearly, he'd been very hard on Tristan since day one. Anytime things got difficult, he pushed him away and that wasn't right.

For whatever reason, this brilliant, charming man wanted him. And he wanted Tristan. From this moment forward, he needed to set things right between them and do whatever it took to keep things good.

"Really they were only concerned about themselves. Those two points were the only highlights they hit that didn't include them flying the nest. They're ready to start their lives," Dylan said, putting the car in park and taking Tristan's hand in his.

"I didn't say they weren't normal." Tristan smiled, intertwining their fingers.

"I'm sorry for the pain I've caused you." Dylan turned in his seat, facing Tristan. "Don't shake your head. I've seen it in your face. I was just worried about that moment in there. I was afraid to fully let you in."

"If you haven't always been out, it's hard finding your way. I knew you needed room and support," Tristan said.

Dylan watched him a minute more before tugging at his arm, pulling Tristan in to meet him halfway.

"I'm sure it's not over. I'm certain of that, but thank you for being here tonight." Dylan leaned across the console and pressed his lips to Tristan's. He was in complete control of this moment. For the first time in their relationship, Tristan didn't push and let him take the lead. Dylan reached up and trailed his hand along Tristan's jaw, sliding his fingers into his messy hair.

"Thank you for loving me." Tristan's breath danced along his lips as he uttered those simple words that eased every burden he carried. Dylan angled Tristan's head, smiling as he licked at the seam of his lips. Tristan's lips parted, and he seized the opportunity to push his tongue forward, holding nothing back in the kiss.

ꝺEPILOGUE

Dylan sat with Tristan in the downstairs section of his Laguna Beach home, working on a prototype of the robotic arm he'd designed. They were both at the desk. Tristan was entering the variances of coding Dylan suggested after many long minutes of silence between the both of them. Tristan studied the changes, getting lost in the code until a voice broke through, interrupting his train of thought. After spending all of his adult life alone, he still hadn't gotten used to the randomness of other people being around. He scribbled his thoughts on the notepad in front of him so as not to forget and looked back over to Dylan who continued to study the prototype.

"Dad." The voice a little stronger this time. Tristan sat back in his seat, stretching his tired muscles. Dylan shared this project with him now. It had become their secret hobby from almost the minute he'd shown him what he had been working on. They were so in sync with every part of their lives. Every day, Dylan proved yet again how right Tristan had been in pushing for a relationship between them.

The only things they didn't do together were running and weightlifting. Except, thanks to the downstairs renovations, he squeezed three new bedrooms in and a small gym. When they spent time in California, they were able to work out together, meaning Tristan never had to run again in his life.

"Dad!" That one startled Dylan, proving Tristan's theory the guy had been oblivious to her before then. That must have been the selective parent hearing he'd heard about. Tristan had to get better at ignoring the noise. Ever since Chloe and Chad had arrived a few days ago from school, his house had been overrun with noise and a somewhat controlled chaos. Chloe circled the door and stopped in her tracks.

"What? Chloe, you have to stop yelling. We're working, honey," Dylan said, clearly frustrated.

"Hi, Tristan."

"Hey," he said, giving her a small smile.

"It's time to pick up Mom and Cate," she replied, not really paying attention to her dad's outburst. Tristan figured she'd probably heard those words from her father before.

Tristan looked down at the time on the computer. They'd lost hours again inside this room.

"I should change clothes and shave." Dylan immediately stood. The sourness of a few minutes ago was now completely gone, along with the concern over the project. Where Tristan made notes at these critical points, Dylan would just retain where they were and pick up where they left off, no matter how much time had passed since they'd been here.

"I like you unshaven. Keep it through the holidays?" Tristan stopped him with a hand on his thigh, before he went and altered that sexy five o'clock shadow. Dylan would occasionally lean in to tell him something and his stubble would rub along his neck as he spoke, purely on accident, but, man, did that turn him on when the scruff was there.

"All right." Dylan bent to kiss him lightly on the lips.

"You and Mom never kissed each other. I don't know how I didn't figure everything out sooner than I did." Chloe rolled her eyes and pivoted around the doorframe as she left the room. Technically, this was the first time Dylan's children would see them sharing a bedroom. As Tristan had grown to learn, they were well past the point of caring about the small details. All three were well-adjusted young adults that were fully vested in their own futures, really only calling when they had a problem or needed money—that was especially true with the oldest two in college.

"Are you coming with us?" Dylan asked.

"If you want me to," he responded.

"Of course I do," he said, not even questioning the thought. He left the room, not glancing back.

He still tried hard to give Dylan space. Teri had had the baby, a little boy, less than two months ago. She and Mark were planning to marry. Cate had just graduated from high school and planned to leave for college right after the holidays. Surprisingly, he'd been included in both events as well as the cross-country U-Haul trip Dylan planned to get Cate moved in and settled into her dorm room.

Dylan and Teri's divorce would be final soon, and Tristan had even managed to talk Dylan into moving the Secret Network's headquarters to Irvine and take up residence with him. By all measures, he and Dylan were a committed couple. They weren't showy about their relationship. The people Dylan truly cared about were on board with all these changes. So, although he and Dylan worked a lot of hours, they found a way to spend every free moment together. His jet racked up a lot of air miles to Dallas and back, but they would soon be living under the same roof every single day.

Tristan swiveled in his chair toward the door, listening to Dylan bark out some instruction he was certain Chloe and Chad were ignoring. He had dressed for the day, even if Dylan hadn't. He still liked to be at his best when the kids were around. His phone vibrated in his pocket, and he fished the device out as he reached over to save their work and shut everything down.

"Hey," he answered after seeing Landry's number on the phone.

"It's not Christmas. Where the hell are you? We have work to do."

"Still taking the next two weeks off. Like I told you this morning, and last night, and yesterday." Landry used to be better at the jokes, but this one was growing old.

"Vacationing with the boyfriend?" Landry asked, but it didn't come with the usual snicker. Tristan closed the door with his foot.

"I know you want the details because you're a perv, but I'm not sharing him with you or anyone else for that matter," Tristan shot back.

"Huh. Well, I got nothing to say to that. I'm calling for a reason. I'm sure your boyfriend told you. The usage numbers for Secret are skyrocketing. We're already turning a profit in WilderNation this quarter," Landry said and Tristan lifted his brows. He and Dylan only talked business while working, never when they were off. He hadn't heard this bit of great news, but he was certain Dylan knew. "So you were right. Is that what you're waiting on?"

"No, but it's nice to hear." Tristan left the office to go back upstairs and find Dylan to congratulate him on a job very well done.

"Right, and I'll reflect on my behavior. You've been keeping him away from here. I won't bite anymore. Maybe we can have dinner sometime before he heads back," Landry offered, and Tristan tripped on the step going up.

"Is this a joke?" he asked, catching himself before the trip became a solid fall.

"No, not at all. I have ground to make up. I'm eating crow. Besides, his team didn't seem to bat an eye when he came out to them. I can't have them showing me up," Landry replied.

Tristan had never shared with anyone the tense few weeks his Dallas office had once their relationship became public knowledge. There had been some turnover in the ranks, but David and Rob stood firm with them, making the whole outing pretty much a non-event and guaranteeing a substantial increase in their annual Christmas bonuses.

"I'll talk to him and get back with you." Tristan stood at the top of the stairs to the main portion of the house. The noise grew louder on the other side of the door.

"You've got a house full, which is weird. Call me and we'll set it up," Landry said.

"Thanks for this. It'll make life easier."

"Yeah. I'll give you this one. Bye." Landry disconnected the call.

Tristan opened the door to find Dylan standing right there in front of him, which startled him. Actually scared the shit out of him, and he wobbled on the step. "Are you ready?" Dylan asked, not paying a lick of attention to him as he called out for Chloe and Chad to get in the car.

"Hey, I got something to tell you," Tristan said, following behind him.

"Can you tell me in the car? We're a little late," Dylan responded, heading for the garage. He'd rented an oversize SUV for the next few weeks to carry them all wherever they needed to go. Several times, he had caught Chad eyeing the Ferrari but still wasn't ready to hand over the keys no matter how many cool points that would earn him.

"Do I turn off the Christmas tree?" Chad asked. Tristan looked back at his normally pristine home and saw a large, real decorated tree in the corner. Presents overflowing from where Teri, Mark, Dylan, and he had gifts sent for everyone. As far as he could remember, he'd never had any sort of a Christmas tree as an adult. It was nice and his planned backdrop for the marriage proposal he intended to surprise Dylan with in front of his whole family. That thought gave him the jitters, but Dylan was the kind of guy you put a ring on as quickly as you possibly could before someone else snatched him up.

"Don't you normally turn them off when you leave? Or should we leave it on for Cate?" Tristan asked.

"Off." Chad unplugged the lights and headed over to him. "Listen, I got a deal for you. You let me drive the Ferrari, and I'll tell you what Dad's been eyeing for Christmas."

"Really? Wait, do you even know how to drive a stick?" Tristan questioned, following along behind him.

"Of course I do, and if it helps in your decision-making process, I think you're way cooler than Mark. But don't tell him. I don't want Christmas to be awkward since we're bunking together under your roof." Chad reached back to give him a fist bump before descending the steps into the garage. Man, the kid was a natural-born salesman. Dylan stood at the vehicle's back door, listening to Chloe explain something to him.

"We didn't put this base in right. Apparently these hooks lock inside the car's seat," Dylan said, watching Chloe work the baby seat properly.

"You had three kids. You'd think you'd know," Chad teased, sliding in his spot in the SUV.

"Dad's old. This is new technology," Chloe said, sitting back in her seat when she was done.

"Hey now, none of that talk. I'm not that old. I had you when I was young." Dylan chuckled and shut the door in Chloe's face.

"You'll be forty soon enough. That's pretty much middle-age," Chloe announced proudly. Dylan started the SUV and backed out. Tristan pressed the remote and closed the garage before they'd hit the street.

"Teri always said we had really bad kids and I think she was *right*!" Dylan teased back. "What did you want to tell me?"

When they started this banter between the four of them, Tristan barely got a word in. He wasn't fast enough or comfortable enough to tease them back, but Dylan gave them hell.

"Landry told me about the Secret numbers. They're incredible."

"Yeah?" Dylan asked. That confused him. Did he not know?

"You're up, we're up. It's a first in that division," Tristan said.

"Yeah, I know. And that's what you pay me to do. I'm just doing my job," Dylan added, pulling through the streets of his neighborhood without any help from him. They'd spent a lot of time here together, and he'd learned his way.

"Dad, when are you and Tristan gonna have a baby?" Chad asked. He found the question incredibly funny, laughing before he could even get the words out. Dylan looked in the rearview mirror and then slammed on his brakes. Tristan felt Chad ram against his seat seconds before Dylan and Chloe started laughing. Probably not the first time that had happened.

"You're so funny. Put on your seatbelt, wise guy." Dylan laughed, smiling big into the backseat. It took a second for Chad to get off the floor and they were all giggling at that.

Tristan reached over and took Dylan's hand in his. Work, the numbers, none of it mattered to Dylan while he was with his family. Tristan looked up suddenly. Maybe that was why they never spoke of work when they were off the clock. Dylan considered him part of his family. The emotion of that thought had him smiling like the Cheshire cat.

"What?" Dylan asked him.

"I'm happy. I love you."

"I love you, too," Dylan replied and was immediately back to questioning him with that look he knew so well.

"Chloe, we're making a pact right now. We're never acting like that when we fall in love." Chad held out his hand for a shake, but Chloe refused to participate.

"Whatever. I want it to be *just* like that."

Tristan turned back and gave her a wink. He planned to stay like this forever.

The End

Books by Kindle Alexander

What did you think of Secret? Email us at kindle@kindlealexander.com. We would love to hear from you.

If you enjoyed Secret, then you won't want to miss Kindle Alexander's bestselling novels:

Full Disclosure
Always
Double Full
The Current Between Us
Texas Pride
Up in Arms

* * * *

Coming Soon:
Full Circle
A Nice Guys Novel
Fall 2015

Closet Confession Novella
Summer 2015

Meet Mitch Knox in <u>Full Disclosure</u>

In the end... OMG the end.... let's just say Mitch and Cody have their happy, one that touched my heart.
— Denise, *Shh Mom's Reading*

I definitely recommend this book. I will continue the series, no doubt. And I give this story five+ perfectly delivered stars.
— *Toni FGMAMTC*

Do not miss this wonderful story. Kindle, I love you! ***6 Hearts***
— Kara Hildebrand, *Two Book Pushers*

I find my reading pattern changes with Kindle Alexander's books, I slow down my reading hoping and praying that the story will never end. Mitch and Cody, are perfect and so bloody hot, it made my IPAD melt.
— *Jules Swoon Worthy*

Experience the life and love of Avery and Kane
in <u>Always</u>

Awards
Book of the Year 2014 Member Choice Awards
  Goodreads MM Romance
Book of the Year 2014 Sinfully Sexy Book Reviews
LGBT Book of the Year 2014 eLit Awards

Beautiful. Heart Wrenching Love Story!!!!
If you love a good, heart pounding love story than ALWAYS is the
book for you!
— *Gay Media Reviews*

Be assured there is nothing cheesy or too saccharine about *Always*,
it's just the **perfect love story**!
— *Sinfully Sexy Book Reviews*

The word is out on *Double Full*

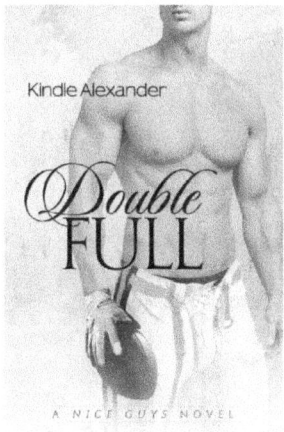

"Kindle Alexander knows the rules of romance and she applies them good."
— *Elisa My Reviews and Rambling*

"These two hunky men had me in tears, their love for one another is magically."
— Jennifer Robbins, *Twinsie Talk Book Review*

"*Double Full* is a compelling and fabulous read!"
— Monique, *Sinfully Sexy Book Reviews*

"Double Full will be in my heart for some time to come."
— Paul Berry, *Gay Media Reviews*

"Kindle Alexander sure can write a red hot sex scene like nobody else."
— Vickie Leaf, *Book Freak*

"Without a doubt one of the **BEST** m/m romances I have ever read."
— Mandie, **Foxylutely* Blog*

Everyone's talking about *The Current Between Us*

"Ms. Alexander has become one of my favorite M/M authors; check that one of my favorite authors. Her characters are mature, well rounded and seem to find a place in my heart."
—Denise, *Shh Mom's Reading*

"I loved this book! Everything about it was just perfection...great characters, suprises, and the story...seriously, it was so sweet and romantic and just really good reading."
—Christi Snow, *Author*

"Kindle Alexander has given us another great book. The characters Trent and Gage grabbed my heart and haven't let go. This isn't just a love story, it has a mystery going on that keeps you hooked."
—Teri, *The Bitches of Eastwick Book Reviews*

"This book is an excellent love story, where even the most hardened heart and disillusioned soul can find the romantic streak hidden deep within and see it blossom into something neither thought possible. I fell in love with the author, her writing and the characters... just go read it!!!"
—Monique, *Sinfully Sexy Book Reviews*

Rave Reviews for _Texas Pride_

"I would DEFINITELY like this to be a series…hint hint to Kindle Alexander!!!"
— Brenda, _Twinsie Talk Book Review_

"I have a severe case of book hangover. Seriously readers – you need to read this book. Ten stars for me!"
— _*Foxylutely* Blog_

"The end of this book was so well done!"
— _Shh Mom's Reading_

"Definitely a great read...I didn't want this sweet story to end."
— Christi Snow, _Author_

"Recommend this to those who love cowboys and movie stars …and a very happy ending."
— _Mmgoodbookreviews_

"I highly recommend it."
— Samantha, _Passionate Books_

What readers are saying about *Up in Arms*

"*Up in Arms* is a compelling, fascinating drama that honestly explores the conflict of love in the military without taking away from an enchanting romance." —*Joyfully Reviewed*

"This story not only follows these men's love affair, which is sweet and sexy, but we also see the aftermath of how they deal with tragedy. I love these boys, how they interact, how they overcome, how one of them blushes *sigh*." —*The Bitches of Eastwick*

"This is a tender love story.... She taps all the sensory elements that binds a romance reader to the narrative, characters, conflicts and resolutions." —*Blackraven Reviews*

Have you discovered these authors?

The Men of Halfway House Series
by Jaime Reese

Texas Soul Series
by Sara York

Finally Found by Aria Grace
(June 13, 2015!)